# THE
# LAST
# HEIRESS

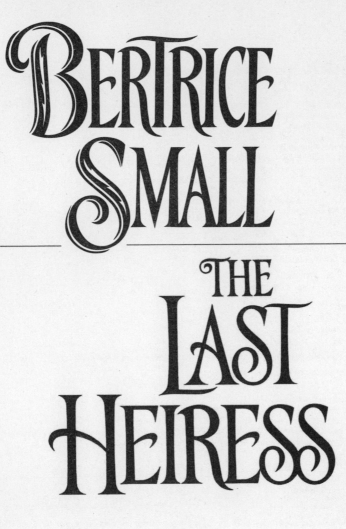

# BERTRICE SMALL

# THE LAST HEIRESS

NAL NEW AMERICAN LIBRARY

New American Library
Published by New American Library, a division of
Penguin Group (USA) Inc., 375 Hudson Street,
New York, New York 10014, USA
Penguin Group (Canada), 90 Eglinton Avenue East, Suite 700, Toronto, Ontario, Canada M4P 2Y3 (a division
of Pearson Penguin Canada Inc.)
Penguin Books Ltd., 80 Strand, London WC2R 0RL, England
Penguin Ireland, 25 St. Stephen's Green, Dublin 2,
Ireland (a division of Penguin Books Ltd.)
Penguin Group (Australia), 250 Camberwell Road, Camberwell, Victoria 3124,
Australia (a division of Pearson Australia Group Pty. Ltd.)
Penguin Books India Pvt. Ltd., 11 Community Centre, Panchsheel Park,
New Delhi - 110 017, India
Penguin Group (NZ), cnr Airborne and Rosedale Roads, Albany,
Auckland 1310, New Zealand (a division of Pearson New Zealand Ltd.)
Penguin Books (South Africa) (Pty.) Ltd., 24 Sturdee Avenue,
Rosebank, Johannesburg 2196, South Africa

Penguin Books Ltd., Registered Offices:
80 Strand, London WC2R 0RL, England

First published by New American Library,
a division of Penguin Group (USA) Inc.

First Printing, October 2005
10 9 8 7 6 5 4 3 2 1

NEW AMERICAN LIBRARY and logo are trademarks of Penguin Group (USA) Inc.

LIBRARY OF CONGRESS CATALOGING-IN-PUBLICATION DATA:

Small, Bertrice.
   The last heiress / Bertrice Small.
      p. cm.
   ISBN 0-451-21692-X
   1. Great Britain—History—Henry VIII, 1509–1547—Fiction. 2. Inheritance and succession—Fiction.
   3. Administration of estates—Fiction. 4. Courts and courtiers—Fiction. I. Title.
   PS3569.M28L37 2005
   813'.54—dc22        2005013031

Set in Goudy
Designed by Leonard Telesca

Printed in the United States of America

FOR MY LIVELY LADIES

*Prologue*

FRIARSGATE

*Winter 1530*

"*Y*ou are going to court," Rosamund Bolton Hepburn said firmly to her daughter, Elizabeth Meredith, in a tone that ordinarily no one challenged.

"I am not!" Elizabeth answered back in a tone that all listening knew boded ill for the conversation.

"You have to have a husband, Elizabeth," Rosamund replied, an edge to her voice. This was a conversation they had both been avoiding for some time now.

"Why?" Elizabeth demanded. "Have I not shown that I am capable of managing Friarsgate, Mother? A husband would want to take my authority for himself, and I will not allow it. Friarsgate is mine, and it has been since the day I turned fourteen."

"That was almost eight years ago," Rosamund countered. "You will be twenty-two in a few months, Elizabeth. We have to find you a husband before it is too late, if it is not already too late."

"Why?" Elizabeth said again, and this time her hazel-green eyes grew angry.

"You are a perfectly competent mistress of Friarsgate," Rosamund began. "Indeed, you are doing a better job than even I did. But one day you will not be here, and who is to take over the Friarsgate inheritance then if you have no heirs or heiresses to follow you? Be reasonable, Elizabeth. You need a husband to sire children upon you."

"Banon and her Neville have children. Philippa and her earl have children. I will leave it to whomever of them I feel is the right heir or heiress," Elizabeth said.

"Banon has only one son, and he will one day inherit Otterly. He will not want—nor does he need—Friarsgate. Philippa's sons would never suit. The eldest will be the earl one day. The second is a page in Norfolk's household. The third is intended for a place in Princess Mary's household. As for the baby, he will make a great match for Mary Rose one day. Like their parents, my St. Clair grandchildren are creatures of the court. You have no choice, Elizabeth. You must marry."

Elizabeth Meredith sighed deeply.

"Is there any young man hereabouts who pleases you?" Rosamund gently asked. "If there is, speak up so that we may arrange the match between you. I do not want you unhappy, daughter. Both your sisters have married for love. I would give you the same privilege if it is possible." Reaching out, she took her daughter's hand in hers in a gesture of comfort. Of her three Meredith daughters Elizabeth was the one who looked like her father, with her soft blond hair and her hazel-green eyes. Rosamund could always see Owein in Elizabeth eyes, and while Owein had not been considered particularly handsome, his daughter was indeed a beauty. At least she was when her face was clean.

"Who would I know, Mother?" Elizabeth said. "Friarsgate is large, and it is isolated. I have no time for the niceties of society. I am too busy with my lands."

"Then you must go to court to seek a husband," Rosamund replied. "You have no other choice. You are too old to be a maid of honor, and I cannot ask the queen to take you on as one of her ladies. You have no skills for such a position. You will have to stay with Philippa and Crispin. They go to court for the month of May, and can introduce you into society there. May is a wonderful time at court. I remember it well."

"God's wounds!" Elizabeth swore softly. "You would have me stay with Philippa? You know we do not get along, Mother. She is so high-flown you would think she sprang from a duke's loins, and not those of a simple Welsh knight. And she always brings out the worst in me. I try not to let her aggravate me, but it takes less than a few moments, and I am ready to throttle her. It is hard to believe we are sisters with the same sire and mam," Elizabeth said with a shake of her head.

"I have no choice but to send you to Philippa," Rosamund responded.

"Yes, you do! Don't make me go!" Elizabeth said with a grin.

Rosamund laughed. "Bessie"—she chuckled—"what am I to do with you?"

Bessie. Her childhood name. Elizabeth allowed few to address her by it these days. It was infantile, and not a proper name for the heiress of Friarsgate. She was Elizabeth Julia Anne Meredith now. Not Bessie. "If you would make me go, could not Uncle Thomas take me the way he did Philippa and Banon? He still retains his London house, and the house at Greenwich. He and Will were speaking of a foray south at Twelfth Night. It seems that Banon's noisy household is beginning to grate on his nerves. And it is at least three years since his last visit to court."

"He swore he would never go again," Rosamund noted to her daughter.

"Uncle Thomas always says that when he returns home. But then several years go by, and he begins to long for the color, the excitement, and the delicious gossip that only the court can offer him. And let us not forget his London tailor," Elizabeth said dryly. "He always comes back with the most magnificent wardrobes that he may both dazzle and shock the local gentry around Otterly."

"I don't know," Rosamund said slowly.

"Please, Mother! As it is, spring is a dreadful time for you to send me away, but I will go quietly if Uncle Thomas can take me. But I shall not go to Philippa's. I won't!"

"You will if I say you will," Rosamund answered her daughter. The conversation, pleasant for a few moments, was beginning to degenerate again into a battle of wills.

"How will you make me?" Elizabeth challenged her mother. "Will you have me trussed up like one of my lambs and delivered to Brierewode? And after that what? And if Philippa drags eligibles into my presence I shall belch, fart, speak with a broad North Country accent, and make myself generally undesirable. I doubt she could last a month with me, and will send me packing back home as quickly as she can. Besides, she gave up Friarsgate because no court gentleman would have an heiress with a Cumbrian estate. What makes you think I can do any better? And I shall not give up Friarsgate, Mother."

Rosemund glared at her daughter. She had absolutely no doubt that Elizabeth would behave exactly as she threatened if sent to Philippa's unwillingly. But if Lord Cambridge escorted his young relative then perhaps, just perhaps, there might be the chance of Elizabeth snagging a husband with whom they could all live. Philippa and Crispin would be their entrée into the court, but Thomas Bolton would be Elizabeth's guardian, adviser, and protector. Even as he had been for her those many years ago, and then her two oldest daughters, Rosamund considered. "I will ask Tom then," she conceded, "but swear to me, Elizabeth, that you will follow his advice, and obey him. He is hardly a young man now, and if he agrees to do this for you, you cannot embarrass or defy him."

"Uncle Thomas and I have always gotten on well, Mother," Elizabeth said, "even if Banon is his favorite. I was Glenkirk's favorite. I still remember him, you know."

"Do you?" Rosamund said, and pulled herself up from her seat. "I must get back to Logan, and my laddies," she said. "I'll write Tom now before I go, and Edmund will see it delivered to Otterly." She bent and kissed Elizabeth's cheek. "We will see whomever you wed must defer to your authority here, Bessie. I promise you that. You are a good mistress for Friarsgate."

"Godspeed, Mother," Elizabeth said, escorting her mother from the hall. "Tell Logan I send him my love."

Rosamund hurried to the small room that served as the estate's place of authority. Seating herself at the oak table, she drew a sheet of parchment from the basket and picked up the quill. She considered her words carefully as she wrote. She was asking a great deal of her beloved cousin Tom, but Rosamund knew that Bessie would not cooperate in this endeavor unless he would agree to help her. Her youngest daughter was a clever young woman. Polite society, however, was not her forte. She would need to go into this adventure with a strong advantage. But Tom Bolton was no longer a young man. He had just turned sixty at the beginning of the month. Elizabeth was a great responsibility with which to saddle him. Still, her cousin's secretary and companion, William Smythe, was a much younger man. He would go with them. Perhaps together the two men could manage the very independent and stubborn heiress of Friarsgate. Perhaps together they could find a husband suitable for Elizabeth, and suitable for the great estate she possessed. It wasn't that she didn't have enough grandchildren, Rosamund thought wryly. It was just that none of them belonged to Friarsgate.

# Chapter 1

Thomas Bolton, Lord Cambridge, read over the letter his cousin Rosamund had sent him from Friarsgate prior to her departure back to her own home along the Scots border. He pursed his lips, and his brow wrinkled in thought. "Hmmmm," he said.

"What is it?" William Smythe asked. "Is all well with your cousin?"

"Do you recall our discussing a little visit to court just a few weeks ago?" Lord Cambridge said. "My darling Rosamund has just offered me the perfect excuse. We shall go in the spring, dear boy! And while we are gone the workmen can complete the new wing of the house. While I adore Banon and her brood, I do not think I can live much longer in such close proximity to them."

"Her daughters are lively lasses," William noted dryly.

"Lively? They are five veritable little demons!" Lord Cambridge cried. "While each is prettier than a summer's morn, not one is blessed with more than a flea's wit. I shudder to consider poor wee Robert Thomas's fate with such sisters dancing about him."

"He will either learn to defend himself early, or become one of those poor lads who is fearful of his own shadow, and ruled by his womenfolk," William said. "Now, tell me what Rosamund has written, and how is it to take us to court?"

"The Friarsgate heiress needs a husband," Lord Cambridge said, his amber eyes dancing with glee. "She does not want to go to court. God's foot, Will! How that reminds me of Rosamund in her youth. But she has consented to go only if I will take her. Rosamund apologizes for imposing what she refers to as an onerous duty upon me. She wanted to send Elizabeth to Philippa."

"The Countess of Witton?" Will shook his head. "Oh, no, my lord, that would never do, I fear. The two sisters do not get on at all."

"Precisely what Elizabeth told her mother, and then said she would go only if I escorted her. We shall be at court in May, dear boy! Greenwich! There will be masques, for I hear the king's little friend, Mistress Boleyn, has introduced such elegant entertainments into the court. It will be heavenly, dear boy! And we must pay a visit to Master Althorp in London, for my poor wardrobe is surely aeons out of fashion. Ahh, Will! What would I do without my darling cousin Rosamund?"

"One wonders indeed, my lord," William Smythe said with a small smile. Eight years ago Thomas Bolton had lifted him from obscurity, taking him into his service. Being in Lord Cambridge's service meant being taken into his family as well, and that family had welcomed and accepted him. In his entire lifetime William Smythe had never felt so secure, or so content. "When shall I plan our departure, my lord?" he asked.

"We must leave April first," Lord Cambridge said. "If we are to be down to Greenwich in time for the May Day celebrations we must go then. Dear Will, there is so much to do, and so little time in which to do it. We must write to Philippa, for she will be our entrée into court for this visit. And you must contact Master Althorp. I will want him at Bolton House in London with my new clothing as soon as we arrive. He will have all the latest gossip for us." Thomas Bolton chuckled. "But first we will have to pay a visit to Friarsgate. If I know our heiress she will have not a garment suitable for travel, let alone the court. You will have to get her measurements, dear boy, so we may have some decent clothing made for her. So much to do! And barely time in which to do it, Will."

"We will proceed as we usually do, my lord, in a calm and an orderly manner," William Smyth assured his master. "I will begin today. Now let me bring you some wine, my lord. You will need all your strength and wits about you, for Elizabeth Meredith will not be an easy girl for whom to find a husband. Her manners, my lord, if you will forgive my mentioning—and she is already considered an old maid by many."

"Fiddle-faddle!" Lord Cambridge replied. "The king's little friend is even older, and she is yet unwed. And Mistress Boleyn has not the dower portion that Mistress Elizabeth Meredith has. Who will ever marry her, I wonder?" He sniffed.

"When shall we plan our visit to Friarsgate, my lord?"

"As soon as possible, dear boy," Thomas Bolton replied. "I have always liked Friarsgate, but more so now than ever. The hall is a peaceful one there these days. And Elizabeth is an excellent hostess. Her table is always well served, and her guests well fed. Go and ask old Ben in the stables what the weather is to be for the next few days. He is always correct in his predictions about such phenomena."

"At once, my lord!" William Smythe replied, placing a small goblet of wine in his master's hand. Then, bowing, he hurried from the chamber.

"The weather," old Ben pronounced, "will be fair for the next few days, particular considering it were January, but February were a terrible month, and not likely to be any different this year, sir." William Smythe reported back to his master.

"See we are packed for a long stay, my dear Will," Lord Cambridge said with a wicked chuckle. "If I am to be snowed in then I prefer Friarsgate this year to my own dear Otterly, though I should have never imagined the day I would admit to such. My dear heiress and her mate can handle any emergencies that might arise. After all, Otterly will one day belong to Banon. When I tell her why I must away to Friarsgate she will understand better than any. Of all of Rosamund's children she is the most reasonable, which is fortunate, for her husband, while still a pretty fellow, is not a man of intellectual strengths. So many of these old northern families interbreed too much, and barely educate their children. They still believe we live in a time when their name alone is all that matters. I chose well when I made Banon my heiress. She is wise beyond her years."

"Indeed she is, my lord," the secretary agreed. "Except perhaps where her husband and offspring are concerned. She is most indulgent with them all."

"She has a kind heart, Will," Thomas Bolton said with a small smile. When he had purchased Otterly all those years ago he had determined to make Banon, his cousin's second child, his heiress.

Philippa, the eldest of Rosamund's daughters, was to inherit Friarsgate, and to Elizabeth he had promised a large dower. But Philippa had gone to court at twelve to serve the queen, and had quickly found that no suitable young man wanted a girl, even a great heiress, with a northern estate. So Lord Cambridge had purchased a small estate in Oxfordshire for her, and then found the perfect husband for Philippa. It had elevated her into the ranks of the nobility, and was in the eyes of the court a spectacular match for a girl of Philippa's background. As Countess of Witton, Philippa had filled her husband's nursery with three sturdy sons and an infant daughter.

But Philippa had renounced any claim she had on Friarsgate, and her husband had surprisingly agreed with her decision. Most men would have been delighted to gain the great lands of Friarsgate, but Crispin St. Clair believed a man should live on his lands, the better to oversee his own wealth. His estate of Brierewode, along with the matching lands his marriage to Philippa had brought him, were more than enough for him.

And when his cousin Rosamund had despaired of what would become of her beloved Friarsgate, it was her youngest daughter, Elizabeth Meredith, who had spoken up and declared she would have it, for of the three sisters it was Elizabeth who loved Friarsgate the best. So it had been agreed that upon her fourteenth birthday Friarsgate would be turned over to Elizabeth, and it had been. Rosamund, who had spent much of her life caring for, loving, defending, and making Friarsgate prosper, retired to her Scots husband's home at Claven's Carn to raise Logan Hepburn's five sons, four of whom were theirs.

Elizabeth Meredith, like her mother before her, had been born to manage the Friarsgate inheritance. She loved the land. The raising of sheep fascinated her. She tried breeding different kinds of the creatures to see whether the wool they grew was different, or better. She spent two days each week in a chamber set aside for estate business, where she oversaw the export trade her mother and uncle had set up. No one had yet to match the Friarsgate blue wool cloth they sold through their factors in the Netherlands, and Elizabeth had been working for several years now to develop a new and unique color. So far, nothing had satisfied her.

She was a great chatelaine of her lands, and therein lay the problem. Nothing meant more to her than Friarsgate. It was her raison d'être. Elizabeth did not acknowledge the passing of time, or bother to consider a future in which she would play no part. Like all great estates, Friarsgate needed to be assured of a new generation.

Thomas Bolton sighed to himself. Elizabeth Meredith was by far the loveliest of Rosamund's daughters. But her social skills were practically nonexistent. She had been taught them, but had no use for fine table manners, or the playing of an instrument, which she had once done quite well. Her clothing was that of a country farmer's wife, and not a young heiress. She spoke directly, and sometimes roughly. All the niceties she had been bred and born to were forgotten in her passion to oversee Friarsgate.

And that in part, along with his desire for a quieter household, was his reason for going to Friarsgate for the rest of the winter months. Before he might introduce Elizabeth into court he would have to reeducate her in the ways of her station. They were going to need Philippa's aid once they were at Greenwich, and Philippa was unlikely to give it, blood kin or no, if Elizabeth was going to prove an embarrassment to her oldest sister. That would be one of the first things he must work on with Elizabeth, Thomas Bolton decided. He had to convince her before they departed Friarsgate not to deliberately irritate Philippa. Finding a husband for Elizabeth Meredith was going to prove a far greater challenge to him than finding a husband for her two sisters had.

William Smythe was an invaluable servant and companion. By the following morning he had his master prepared to depart Otterly. The cart carrying their baggage had left at first light for Friarsgate. Six Otterly men-at-arms were waiting to escort Lord Cambridge and his secretary. It was a long ride, but if they rode out early enough they would reach Friarsgate shortly after dusk.

"Oh, Uncle, must you leave us?" Banon Meredith Neville asked him as they broke their fast in the hall. "When will you return? Jemima, stop teasing your sister!"

"My dearest girl, you know how your mother relies upon me in such matters. Elizabeth must have a husband, and seems not of a mind to find one for herself. I must drag her off to court and seek a miracle, Banon, my angel. I hope you will pray for our success." He spooned some egg into his mouth, smiling as he tasted a hint of both chive and cheese. Then he took a swallow of his morning wine. "Your youngest sister is not an easy creature, as you well know."

"Will you ask for Philippa's help?" Banon queried him, her pretty face curious. "Katherine, Thomasina, Jemima, and Elizabeth, it is time for your lessons. Run along to your tutor now, and take Margaret with you. I know she is but three, but perhaps an early start will help." Banon sighed.

"I fear I have no choice," he answered her. "Philippa's connections at court are impeccable, as you know." He waved to the little girls leaving the hall, for he did love them all despite their high spirits, and his heart warmed as they blew him kisses.

"Perhaps no longer," Banon noted. "Even here, Uncle, we get the gossip. Later than most, but eventually it comes. You know the queen is no longer in favor with the king. And he pays most public court to the younger Boleyn girl. I doubt my eldest sister approves, for like our mother her devotion to Queen Katherine is deep."

"Indeed it is," Lord Cambridge agreed, "but I suspect now her loyalty to her sons will be even stronger. She must look to their future, and the king will decide their fate, not the queen. Philippa may love the queen, but it is the king who wields the power, Banon. Your sister will not embrace Mistress Boleyn, but neither will she offend her."

"Well, Uncle, you shall soon see," Banon replied. "How long will you remain at Friarsgate, and when will you depart for court?"

"There is so much to do." He sighed, taking a piece of fresh, warm cottage loaf and buttering it lavishly. The butter ran down his fingers as he popped it into his mouth. "Elizabeth must be reminded of her heritage and her breeding. She must begin to practice her social skills again. The court is not filled with sheep. At least not those with woolly coats," Lord Cambridge amended. "And she will need clothing." He licked his fingers clean of the butter. "Maybel and Edmund have little authority over her, I fear."

"They are old, Uncle. Edmund will be seventy-one in the spring, but he is still strong enough to steward Friarsgate for Elizabeth." Her blue eyes grew thoughtful, and her plump fingers drummed upon the tabletop. "But what will she do when Edmund cannot aid her? I do not know if my sister has even considered such a possibility. Elizabeth seems to think that nothing changes, but of course it does."

"First things first, my angel girl. And the first thing is to recivilize your little sister, and then take her to court to show to her best advantage. There has to be one younger son of some sense who could find it in himself to live in the north. I shall track him down and get Mistress Elizabeth married properly before year's end." He stood up. "I must go now, Banon, if I am to reach Friarsgate by nightfall. I shall send word when I plan to return. In the meantime Otterly is yours to care for and watch over." He kissed her cheek and gave Banon's husband, Robert Neville, a friendly wave as he turned and departed the hall.

"Well," Banon said, turning to her husband, "what do you think of all of this?"

"Tom knows well what he is doing," Robert Neville said. He was a man of few words, which was fortunate, since everyone else around him had a great deal to say. And he had quickly accepted the fact that his wife ruled Otterly. It suited him, as he far preferred hunting and other gentlemanly pursuits. Leaning over he gave her a kiss on the cheek, knowing it was expected of him. Then, grinning lecherously at Banon, he remarked, "We shall have Otterly to ourselves all winter, my sweet. Only the children to consider, and the nights are yet long."

Lord Cambridge's party rode hard the day long, and as he had anticipated it was dusk as they came down the hills to Friarsgate. The fields about them lay fallow, the plow ruts frozen and touched with white frost. The lake had a skim of ice upon it, and already a moon was rising in the half-light to reflect itself in the frozen waters. William Smythe rode ahead to alert the house to their arrival. The cook would need to be informed, and places must be made in the stables for the horses and their riders. But stable lads were there to take Thomas Bolton's horse and lead his men-at-arms to the stable.

The front door was flung open, and light poured forth through its opening as Elizabeth Meredith came forth to greet her uncle. "You did not wait very long after receiving my mother's plea," she teased him. "Or have you come to tell me you are too old to go to court? That is what Mama said." She kissed his cheek, and then, linking her arm in his, brought him into the house and through into her hall. She was wearing a long blue wool skirt, a wide leather belt about her narrow waist, and a long-sleeved white linen shirt.

It suited her, Lord Cambridge thought. "I shall never be too old to go to court," he replied a trifle indignantly. So Rosamund thought because he had begun his sixth decade he was not the man he had always been. Well, she would see soon enough. He would turn Elizabeth into a little princess in spite of herself. "Nor will I ever grow too old to fail Rosamund's daughters, my pet," he said, smiling with pleasure as she kissed his cold cheek in welcome. He plunked himself into a tapestry-backed chair by the fire and, pulling off his gloves, held his hands to the fire. "God's wounds, 'tis cold!" he exclaimed.

"Wine for my lord!" Elizabeth shouted to her servants.

Lord Cambridge winced. "Dear child," he pleaded, "do not call out as if you were in the taproom of a crowded inn. A lady's voice should be gentle but firm in tone when instructing her servants."

"Oh, lord!" Elizabeth said almost wearily. "Are my lessons to start at once?"

"Aye, they are," he said, taking the goblet of wine from a hovering servant. "You are obviously in sore need, Elizabeth Meredith, of civilizing. And I shall not be driven off. Your mother is correct: You must have a husband. Friarsgate needs to be assured of another generation of those who love it and will care for it. I am going to turn you back into the lady you were born to be, and then, dear girl, we shall go hunt for a nice young man who will not be frightened of you, and who shall wed you and give you the sons and daughters this estate nurtures so well." He put the goblet to his lips and drank half of the contents down. "Now what is for dinner? I have not eaten since we left Otterly, except for a wedge of hard cheese and a bit of bread. I must have a good meal if I am to take on this incredible task, dear girl."

Elizabeth laughed aloud. "Uncle, you have not changed, and if anyone can make me presentable long enough to snag a healthy young ram to mate with, 'tis you!"

He raised a sandy-gray eyebrow. "You will have to learn to temper your speech no matter your thoughts, my pet," he advised, and drank down the rest of his wine. This would be a herculean task indeed.

Elizabeth grinned back at him. "Well, isn't that what we're going to do, Uncle? Find me a mate for the purpose of getting heirs for Friarsgate?"

"You might put it a bit more delicately, dear girl, and there is always the possibility that you might fall in love," he suggested dryly.

Elizabeth made a rude noise. "Love? No, thank you! Love weakens a body. Philippa gave up Friarsgate for love. Even Mama gave up Friarsgate for love. I shall never give up Friarsgate."

"Ahh," Lord Cambridge responded, "but the right man will never ask such a sacrifice of you. Your own father, who had lived all his life at court, was more than willing to come to Friarsgate, for love of your mother. And he quickly grew to love this land. And Philippa made her own decision in the matter. She did not want Friarsgate, for her passion is for the court. And your mother would have never left to live at Claven's Carn had not you been here to accept her responsibilities as she has always accepted them. Even now she raises her sons in their father's house as she should. You would not have had Friarsgate so soon otherwise, Elizabeth. Remember that."

"Oh, Uncle, I doubt I will find a man who can love Friarsgate as I do! Philippa threw away her inheritance because no young man at court would have it," Elizabeth said. She pushed a lock of her long, straight blond hair from her face. "I shall never do such a thing, I assure you."

"Philippa was a creature of the court from the moment she first visited it when she was ten, Elizabeth. For her, Friarsgate paled in comparison after that first visit. I saw it, but your mother would not until she could no longer avoid it," Thomas Bolton said.

"What if I find the court fascinating, and do not want to return?" she asked him.

"I doubt that will happen, my dear child," he reassured her. "Your heart is here, and wherever your heart is, is home. Somewhere out there, Elizabeth, is a man who will make Friarsgate his home because you are here." He patted her arm. "Now, where is my supper? I am about to swoon with hunger. And where is Will?"

"I am here, my lord," William Smythe said, entering the hall. "I was seeing to your things. Good evening, Mistress Elizabeth." He bowed politely.

"Welcome back, Will," Elizabeth greeted him. "Are you hungry too?" She chuckled at him. She signaled a servant to bring William Smythe some wine.

"Indeed I am, Mistress Elizabeth, and your board is always a most excellent and tasty one, if I remember correctly." He took the proffered goblet from the servant.

"Ah, but tonight I fear it will be a very simple meal, as I had not enough notice of your arrival. Now, Uncle, that is not at all like you. Were you so eager to depart Otterly that you could not send to me?" Elizabeth teased Thomas Bolton. "How are Banon's little girls? Still as full of fun as always?"

"They are, it seems to me, overly lively," Lord Cambridge said. "How simple a supper?" His look was anxious.

"Broiled trout, venison stew, a roasted duck, a potage of winter vegetables, bread, butter, cheese, and baked apples with cream," Elizabeth told him.

"No beef?" Lord Cambridge looked disappointed.

"Tomorrow, I promise," Elizabeth said with a small smile, and she patted his arm.

"Well, I suppose it will have to do, dear girl," Thomas Bolton said with a sigh.

"It is your own fault," she repeated, "for not giving me more notice. But I did have Cook make that sauce you like so for the trout."

"With the dill?" He looked hopeful.

Elizabeth nodded. "With the dill," she answered him. "And the apples have been baked with cinnamon," she continued.

He smiled. "I shall survive then until morning, but you must have Cook do those poached eggs with marsala, cream, and nutmeg for me, my pet," Lord Cambridge told her.

Elizabeth Meredith laughed. "I well know your tastes, Uncle. The order has already been given. And you will have ham too," she promised him.

"You are a perfect hostess, my dear Elizabeth. Now if I can just re-

mind you of your other duties as a lady we shall be quite successful at
court."

Elizabeth's hazel-green eyes twinkled with mischief. "We can but
hope, dear sir," she said, and then she grinned at him.

She was the most charming girl when she chose to be, Thomas
Bolton thought. But there was no denying she was a country woman.
She was not particularly anxious to emulate her two elder sisters. Her
mother had probably been like her before she was whisked off to court
an early age and learned how a lady behaved. Her eldest sister was delighted to gain the court, and absorbed its manners and ways like a sea
sponge. Banon, his own heiress, Elizabeth's middle sister, stood between Elizabeth and Philippa. She saw no disadvantage in good manners and womanly ways, although she was not nearly as high-flown
about it as was Philippa.

But Elizabeth must be properly wed, and to do so meant that she
must regain her ladylike ways. But had she ever really had them?
Thomas Bolton wondered. After Owein Meredith's unfortunate
death, Rosamund spent much time away from Friarsgate and her
daughters. She traveled to the king's court at the invitation of Queen
Katherine. She visited the court of the late King James IV, and his
queen, Margaret Tudor, who had been Rosamund's girlhood friend.
She disappeared off to San Lorenzo with Patrick Leslie, the Earl of
Glenkirk. She returned to both courts, taking Philippa with her. Her
younger daughters were almost forgotten, particularly Elizabeth, who
was known as Bessie in those distant days.

Elizabeth Meredith had grown up at Friarsgate, and she had never
lived anywhere else except for brief visits to her stepfather's home at
Claven's Carn before her mother turned Friarsgate over to her. She
had lived among the simple folk of her holding, meeting few outsiders.
She had met Philippa's husband once, when he had come north to
meet his in-laws. Elizabeth vaguely recalled the Earl of Glenkirk, who
had been so taken with her when she was a little girl. And he, Lord
Cambridge thought, had been taken from the start with Banon. No
one had a great deal of time for Elizabeth Meredith, it seemed. Because
she had been healthy and well fed she had managed to grow up. If her
mother had not been there, her mother's old nursemaid, Maybel, had

been there for her. Elizabeth had never been neglected, but neither had she been nurtured. She had grown up independent, outspoken, and completely capable of running her own life. She was a girl for whom sentiment had little meaning.

Lord Cambridge sighed and shook his head. How was he to find a husband worthy of Elizabeth? A man whom she could respect? A man who would respect her. He doubted any man at court would serve his family's purpose. Finding Philippa's noble husband had been a stroke of pure luck. Banon's husband, also found at court, was the younger son of a northern family delighted by their good fortune, and convinced that they had wasted their coin to send John to court when they might have found Banon for themselves nearby. Yet they had never looked.

It would be a very special man who could live in the north; who could accept the fact that his wife was an excellent chatelaine of her lands, and that she was heavily involved in a cloth trade her family had set up themselves. What son of a family used to being surrounded by the kingdom's high and mighty could understand a girl like Elizabeth Meredith? She would be welcomed at court because the king would accept her as Rosamund Bolton's daughter; because her sister was the Countess of Witton; because her father was the late Sir Owein Meredith, a man respected and well thought of by those few who would remember him. Who one knew at court, to whom one was related among the aristocracy, was important, and so Elizabeth would be welcomed. But she would not be accepted as Philippa had. And her age was against her. An unmarried woman of twenty-two. An unproven breeder. She would be considered little more than a glorified farmer once she began speaking of Friarsgate and her sheep.

But Elizabeth Meredith was what she was, and Lord Cambridge knew there was very little he could do to change that. Nor was he certain he wanted to change her. She was not Rosamund. She was not her sisters. She was unique. Beautiful, witty, intelligent, and charming when she chose to be. There had to be a man out there who would appreciate those qualities. A man who could live with a young woman who took her duties as the heiress of Friarsgate far more seriously than had those before her. And by the Christ's blessed body, Thomas Bolton was going to find him!

The next few weeks were difficult. Lord Cambridge had brought one of Banon's old court gowns with him. He himself had been at court just three years prior. The ladies' fashions had changed only slightly. Philippa, who wrote him several times a year, was always full of news of all kinds. She had not mentioned any great difference in styles, and she most certainly would have had they happened, for she knew how much Lord Cambridge appreciated such details. If enough gowns were made now, any small alterations needed could be made once they reached London. With this in mind he had had Will pack several bolts of fine materials, trimmings, and other stuffs from his own storehouse. There was an excellent seamstress here at Friarsgate, and she would, under Lord Cambridge's direction, fashion the gowns and other garments needed for Elizabeth's visit to King Henry's court.

Elizabeth, however, had very little patience when it came to standing still and being fitted for those gowns. She grumbled, and she fidgeted until even Thomas Bolton was close to losing his usually even temper. But strange to say Elizabeth had an unerring eye for the colors and the cloth that suited her best.

"I like fabrics," she told her uncle. "One day I shall learn how these fine silks, brocades, and velvets are dyed and made. I wonder if the threads that are woven to make them could be combined with our finest and softest wool? Do you think there is a merchant in London who could sell me silk threads in large enough quantity, Uncle? London would have a better source and vaster variety than our friends in Carlisle. But would our cotter's looms be right, or would we need new and specialized looms?"

Her acumen surprised him, and again he realized there would be no noble name for Elizabeth Meredith. He wondered if they would not be wiser to seek a husband for her among the merchant class, but he had no entrée into that society. No. He would keep to his original plans. Not all the young men at court these days came from families of rank, and the times were changing. King Henry was more interested in intelligence and ambition than he was in the old names. Advancement based on one's father was no longer the norm.

"Do you like this green, Uncle?" Elizabeth broke into his thoughts. "It is quite bright, isn't it? Would you call it Tudor green?"

"Grass green," he replied. "The Tudor green is a bit darker, but I must say it is a color that well suits you, Elizabeth. While you are delicately made, dear girl, it is the delicacy of Toledo steel. I would do both the skirt and bodice in it. We'll use a green-and-gold embroidered edging about the neckline, and the slashed grass-green silk sleeves will show a gold-and-white silk fabric. What think you?"

"That I shall look like a farmer's prize pig all done up for judging at the Michaelmas fair," Elizabeth said with a giggle. "Uncle, I have never had such fine garments, and I shall have no use for them when I return from court. It seems such a waste to make me so many beautiful gowns under such circumstances."

"Going to court and finding a husband, my dear girl, is a game. The prize must be the richest, the most perfect, the most beautiful if we are to lure the proper players," he told her. He turned to William Smythe. "Is that not so, Will?"

"Indeed, Mistress Elizabeth, your uncle speaks the truth. In my few years at court, even in my humble position as one of the king's undersecretaries, I saw many a match successfully concluded by just such means as Lord Cambridge now employs for you. You told your mother that you would go to court only if my master escorted you. Now you must trust him, as did your older sisters, to find the right husband for you," William Smythe said. "He will not fail you."

So Elizabeth Meredith fidgeted less at her fittings, and eventually she had a dozen beautiful gowns to take to court. And a boxful of contrasting bodices and sleeves so she might appear to have even more garments. And there were undergarments and underskirts, ribbons, embroidered girdles for her gowns, a cordeliere, a particularly fine marten skin, and other accessories necessary for a lady of the court. There were caps and headdresses and veils, as well as gloves of both silk and leather, and beautiful shoes.

While Thomas Bolton had given much jewelry to his cousin Rosamund and her two elder daughters, he had kept some back for

Elizabeth. "For you, dear girl," he said, handing her an ebony box edged in silver.

"What is this?" she asked, opening the box. "I do not wear jewelry, Uncle."

"A lady of the court always wears jewelry, dear girl." He lifted a strand of pale pink pearls from the box. "These belonged to my sister," he said. "Now they are yours." Then he showed her pear-shaped matching pearl earrings.

Much to her surprise, Elizabeth began to cry. "Uncle," she sobbed, "I shall never forget this kindness. To think you would have saved these for me." Her fingers lifted two more strands of pearls together. One was black and the other a creamy shade of white. They had matching earrings. There were two fine gold chains: one with a gold enameled cross, and the other of gold squares studded with blue stones he told her were called sapphires. She found a cream-colored ribbon Lord Cambridge told her was to be worn about her forehead. In the center of the ribbon was another large oval-shaped stone of pale blue. An aquamarine, he explained. There were two brooches. One was of diamonds and pearls set in gold filigree. The other of sapphires and diamonds set in Irish red gold. There were several rings for her fingers, which would be refitted if necessary.

Elizabeth closed the box finally. "I am really going to court," she said softly.

He nodded with a small smile. "You are, dear girl," he replied.

She sighed. "It is so difficult to watch my tongue, Uncle. If they are all like Philippa, I shall have such a hard time of it."

"The fun of the game, dear girl," he told her, "is in being able to outwit your opponent. Philippa will be expecting the outspoken little girl she hasn't seen in eight years. But you are no longer that little girl. You will be a beautifully dressed and coiffed young lady. An heiress of respectable, if not grand, lineage."

"But alas, Uncle, I am still quite outspoken, and Philippa can irritate me so."

"I will tell you a secret, Elizabeth. She can irritate me too," Lord Cambridge said. "But you will fool her by not giving in to your temper when she is annoying. Philippa likes her world to be an orderly one.

You will surprise her greatly if you remain calm in her presence, and we can use her help in this delicate matter. Now, you cannot travel without a tiring woman, dear girl. Do you have someone here who is suitable?"

"I will ask Maybel, Uncle. She will know."

And indeed Maybel did have a serving woman in mind. "No young and flighty lass for you, Mistress Elizabeth. Nancy is who I have in mind. A sensible woman is Nancy. And she knows how to do hair nice. You know her, my lord."

"The creature is terrifying," Thomas Bolton said. "She has a face like a hawk. Will she appreciated being uprooted and dragged to London, and Greenwich, and probably Windsor? She doesn't have an adventurous look to me. I want no one accompanying Elizabeth who will grumble and grouse at every turn."

"Not old Nancy, my lord. Young Nancy, her daughter," Maybel said, chuckling. "Her face is more like a ewe sheep's. She's just two years older than Mistress Elizabeth."

"And not married?" Lord Cambridge was surprised. Country girls married young as a rule, and had a houseful of children aging them long before their time.

"Left at the altar, she was, by a shepherd lad who run off with a Gypsy girl," Maybel said disapprovingly. "She needs to get away from Friarsgate, if only for a short time, my lord. Like Mistress Elizabeth she knows nothing of the world outside of Friarsgate. If she did it might help ease her sorrow. And when she comes home there is a fine widower with but one little boy who would gladly have her to wife. He does not think now is the time to ask her. He's a better match for her, I can tell you."

"It's Ned, the blacksmith, isn't it?" Elizabeth said, grinning.

"Now you just mind your beeswax, Mistress Elizabeth," Maybel said sternly.

"It's Ned," Elizabeth replied, turning to her uncle and Will Smythe. "He lost his wife almost a year ago in childbirth. One of his married sisters is nursing his son along with her child. So he likes young Nancy, does he? Does she know?"

"Of course she knows, but she's so set on bemoaning her loss of the shepherd she can't be bothered. I've trained her myself to be a lady's maid for the day when you should need one, Mistress Elizabeth. As I said, she's good with hair, and she is clever with her needle."

"Is she pleasant?" Lord Cambridge asked.

"Sweet as honey is Nancy, but not as wise as she ought to be," Maybel answered him frankly. "She's just what Mistress Elizabeth needs, and is looking forward to serving her. Now shall I tell her it's time to begin her service?"

Elizabeth turned to her uncle. "What think you?"

"It is still some weeks before we must leave," Thomas Bolton said. "It is probably wise for the girl to begin serving you now so you may both get used to each other. You must have a woman servant, dear girl. All fine ladies do."

Elizabeth looked to Maybel. "Tell Nancy I'll have her then," she said to the older woman. "But she must have her own chamber. I will have no one sleeping in my room, and particularly not at the foot of my bed on a trundle."

" 'Tis no problem here, although it may be on the road, my child," Maybel said.

"There are more fine inns now, Maybel, than in the days you went to court with Rosamund," Lord Cambridge said. "I shall send ahead before we depart, and book our accommodations. There may be a time, Elizabeth, when you and Nancy will share a bed, but I shall try to avoid it for your sake, dear girl. And, of course, in my houses there will be no difficulty." He smiled broadly. "Just a few more weeks and we shall begin our adventure, my pet. Your wardrobe is almost finished, and you will take the court by storm with your fair beauty."

"I am not beautiful, Uncle," Elizabeth replied.

Lord Cambridge looked startled by her words. "Not beautiful?" he cried, his hand going to his heart. "My darling Elizabeth Julia Anne Meredith! Why, you are the loveliest of Rosamund's three daughters with your pale golden hair and hazel-green eyes. Such coloring is quite unique at the court. My hope for you is that your beauty will overcome any prejudice toward your northern estates. Your features are even, your teeth are white, and your breath sweet. You will be very sought after, for you are indeed beautiful, Elizabeth."

"Beauty fades, Uncle. What is in one's heart is more important," she told him.

He nodded. "Aye," he agreed. "But before any may know your heart, dear girl, they will be ravished first by your beauty."

Elizabeth laughed. "And then they will be very surprised, won't they, when I don't simper and blush?"

"Simpering is for ninnies," he told her. "You are not a ninny."

"Nay, I am not," Elizabeth replied.

In late February a great snowstorm came down from the far north, lasting several long days and nights. The evening before it began there came a hammering on the door of the manor house. The little maidservant opening the portal jumped back with a small scream, for standing in the open doorway was a tall, muffled figure who pushed inside, stamping his boots free of dirt and shaking his cape out with a grunt.

"I've a message for the lady of Friarsgate," he finally managed to say.

"Come into the hall, sir," the little servant said, ushering him inside. When they entered the hall the young girl called out, "A messenger for Mistress Elizabeth."

The tall man stepped forward, and they saw he was a Scot.

"Are you from Claven's Carn?" Elizabeth asked, but the clan badge he wore was unfamiliar to her.

"Are you the lady of Friarsgate?" the messenger asked in return.

"I am," Elizabeth replied. Lord, the man was tall, and big-boned as well.

The Scot held out a packet to her. "I am Baen MacColl, lady. I've come from Grayhaven, in the Highlands above Edinburgh."

"I do not know it," Elizabeth said, looking very puzzled.

"But you surely know Glenkirk, lady. My father spoke with Lord Adam, and 'tis he who sent me here." The tall man shifted uncomfortably.

"Please sit down, sir, by the fire, for from the look of you, you are nigh frozen. The weather is particularly bitter this night, and the air smells of snow," Elizabeth said to her visitor. She glared at a nearby servant and snapped out one word. "Wine!"

The servant dashed to comply, knowing he would later be reprimanded for his dereliction to duty, but he had been so amazed by the great size of the Scot.

"Aye," Elizabeth said to the messenger. "My family is acquainted with the Leslies of Glenkirk." She turned the packet in her hand over, and then said, "This is addressed to my mother, sir. My mother does not reside at Friarsgate. She lives at Claven's Carn with her Hepburn husband. You have ridden too far. I will give you directions to my mother's home, and you will go in the morning. Have you eaten?"

"Nay, lady, not since the last of my oatcakes at dawn," the Scot said.

"A big fellow like yourself can't live on oatcakes," Maybel told him. "Come to the kitchens with me, and I will see you well fed. Then there will be a nice bed space for you in the hall next to the fire," she promised.

Baen MacColl arose and bowed politely to Elizabeth. "Thank you for your hospitality, mistress," he said. Then, turning, he followed after Maybel.

"What a handsome young fellow," Thomas Bolton said.

"If you like the type," William Smythe responded.

"What type, Will?" Elizabeth asked.

"Rough-hewn and half-savage," came the answer. "These Scots are very different from our English gentlemen. Your stepfather, for instance, is not at all like Lord Cambridge."

"I didn't think the messenger like Logan," Elizabeth replied. "Logan seems civilized to me now. This Scot is more rugged in appearance, but perhaps it is just his Highland dress that makes it look so. And his face was chapped with the cold, poor man."

"I wonder what the master of Grayhaven has to write to your mother about," Thomas Bolton said thoughtfully. "I suppose we can ask her the next time we see her."

Maybel returned to the hall. "Gracious, that young man has an appetite on him! Why, he wolfed down two game pies and was gnawing on a leg of mutton when I left him. Cook is fussing over him, for he loves to see a man enjoy his food. He was holding out the promise of an apple tartlet. The laddie is most respectful, and mannerly. And handsome too." She cackled. "Why, if I were a young lass I'd have my eye on him, I would!"

"Why, Maybel, you know nothing about the fellow," Elizabeth said.

"I know what I like, my lass, old though I may be," Maybel retorted.

"What would Edmund say?" Elizabeth teased her.

"I think he would tell you that for an old woman I still have good eyes in my head." Maybel laughed. "And do not think he doesn't appreciate a pretty lass, for he does, Mistress Elizabeth."

"You will see to his sleeping arrangements," Elizabeth said.

"Aye, I shall make up the bed space nearest the fire for him," Maybel responded.

"Then I think I shall seek my own bed," Elizabeth decided. "Cold winter nights are for sleeping. Tell our guest I bid him a good night, Maybel." She arose from her place by the fire and, crossing the hall, went upstairs.

In the morning when she returned to the hall Elizabeth was just slightly disappointed to discover the Scotsman had already departed for Claven's Carn. After eating she fetched her cloak and hurried out-of-doors to speak with her shepherds. She knew that a storm was coming, and she wanted her flocks safely gathered in, for even now the ewes were dropping their lambs. Caught in the snow they could lose many of the young ones if their mams were not properly sheltered. Riding her horse from flock to flock, she supervised the gathering of the sheep, helping to drive some of the groups of animals towards the barns. Wolves were also a danger at this time of year. They seemed to sense the birthing process, and came skulking about seeking to catch a hapless lamb, and perhaps even its defensive mother.

By midevening they had completed the task, aided by the light of a weak but full moon. The sheep in the farthest pastures were enclosed in barns built in scattered meadows for just such a purpose, as well as for storing hay. Their shepherds and their dogs would remain with them in sheds connected to the barns. Each little accessory structure had been built with a small stone fireplace. They contained supplies of wood, food, and water. Elizabeth Meredith was a woman who thought ahead and considered all possibilities.

As she entered her house, tired but invigorated by her long day out-of-doors, the clouds were beginning to obscure the watery moon, scudding across the face of it as the winds began to rise, keening eerily in advance of the storm. Thomas Bolton and William Smythe had eaten earlier, and were both gone from the hall. Elizabeth sat alone at her board while her servants brought her a supper of mutton stew thick with chunks of meat, carrot, and onion; a small fresh cottage loaf; butter; and cheese. They filled her goblet with her own October ale, and she ate hungrily, mopping the gravy from her plate with the last of the bread, reaching for an apple as she swallowed down the rest of her ale.

Then, leaning back in her chair, Elizabeth contemplated her hall with pleasure. The dogs lay sleeping before the hot fire. The oak furniture glowed with a combination of age and good care. Outside the snow was falling, and the world was sweetly silent. She had worked hard this day, and she was content. She didn't want to go to court or wear the beautiful but constricting gowns that had been made for her. She didn't want to have to remember her manners, or be careful of each word she uttered. She wanted to remain here at Friarsgate. She wanted to enjoy the spring and the annual counting of her flocks, but instead she would be on the road to London. To a court she didn't want to join, and a sister who would find fault with her because she wasn't a real lady. Elizabeth Meredith sighed deeply, then jumped as there came a thunderous knocking on the manor door.

# Chapter 2

Elizabeth heard a servant going to answer the knocking, and moments later the Scot stumbled into her hall, shaking the snow from his cloak as he pulled it off. "Come to the fire, sir," she beckoned him. "What brings you back to Friarsgate, and in such dangerous weather?" Tonight she did not have to ask. A servant was at the Scotman's side with a large goblet of wine. "Drink," Elizabeth said, "then sit and tell me. Albert, fetch a plate of stew for Master MacColl. He will be hungry."

Baen MacColl had accepted the goblet gratefully. His hand was shaking with the cold, and he wondered if he would ever be warm again. He drank half the goblet in a single gulp, and began to feel a faint warmth spreading up from his belly. Perhaps he would live after all. "Thank you, lady," he said.

"Sit down, sir. You can eat by the fire, for I suspect it will take both food and the heat of the flames before you are truly warm again."

He nodded. "Aye," he said, briefly attempting to be polite, but just wanting to bask in the warmth of the hearth until he could feel his extremities again.

Elizabeth understood, and so she quietly directed her servants to bring a small table for their guest. She took the large bowl of stew from Albert and set it before the Scot, putting a spoon into his hand as the serving man placed a loaf of bread and a large wedge of cheese before the guest. "Eat first, and we will talk afterwards," Elizabeth said.

Baen MacColl nodded gratefully and, crossing himself, quickly began to spoon the hot stew into his mouth as rapidly as he could. It was obvious he had not eaten in many hours. Did her mother not offer the messenger hospitality? Elizabeth wondered. How unlike Rosamund. Or perhaps the Scot had not reached Claven's Carn at all. It was a very long ride. She watched, almost amused, as he tore off pieces of the bread, mopping up the gravy even as she had earlier. He took a knife from his belt and sliced himself several wedges of cheese, which he ate both separately and in combination with the bread. Finally, when every morsel had been eaten, Baen MacColl sat back with a gusty sigh.

"You have a good cook, lady. I thank you for the supper," he said.

"Have you had enough?" she asked him. "It seems to me that it would take a great amount of food to fill up such a large man. I would not offer you poor hospitality."

He looked at her and smiled a slow smile. "You have no need to apologize for your board, lady. I am well fed." And then the smile turned into a little grin as he said, "For now."

Elizabeth laughed. "Very well then, Master MacColl. Now tell me why you have returned to Friarsgate. Did you not reach Claven's Carn?"

"Nay, but I did meet your mother, lady. She was out hunting with her lord. She opened the packet, and then said that while it was addressed to her, the message was not for her, as she was no longer the lady of Friarsgate. You are. So I turned about and came back, but the snow caught me. There was no place where I might shelter with my horse, and so I just kept riding until we reached your house."

"You were fortunate!" Elizabeth exclaimed. "The snow and the dark surely compromised your trail."

"I have a knack for tracking, lady. If I've been to a place once I can always find my way back no matter the circumstances," he told her.

"I'll make up your bed space, sir," Elizabeth said. "I hope you are not needed elsewhere, for you are going to be with us at least a week, if my weather sense is correct, and it usually is. This storm will last several days."

"What of your sheep?" he asked her.

"Safe in their barns," Elizabeth said. "I'll not lose my new lambs to the wolves or the weather." She stood up. "Continue to warm yourself. I've suffered that chill now gripping you. It goes right to the bone.

When I have arranged your sleeping space I will bring you something that will remove the cold." Then she hurried off.

*A fair and most competent lass*, Baen MacColl thought as he watched her. He wondered where her husband was. He was a lucky man to have such a wife. She was a good manager, and a country man needed that kind of a helpmeet. He moved his chair closer to the fire and leaned forward, stretching his hands out to warm them. He was beginning to feel his toes again, and the stiffness was leaving his fingers. Well, if he must be stuck somewhere for a week this was not a bad place to be. The company was pleasant, the food good, and the bed space cozy.

"Here. Drink this," Elizabeth Meredith said, handing him a small pewter dram cup.

The Scot took it from her hand, eyes widening as the aroma of whiskey touched his nostrils. He swallowed it down, and immediately was suffused with swift warmth that rose up from the pit of his stomach. He looked at her questioningly.

"My stepfather is the Hepburn of Claven's Carn. He thinks no house civilized without a barrel of whiskey," Elizabeth explained. "I prefer my ale, or even wine, but whiskey does have its uses, doesn't it?" Then she laughed. "More?"

"Aye, please," he answered her, looking up as she poured the whiskey from a decanter. Her hand was delicate, and he thought her skin very fair.

His eyes were gray, Elizabeth noted. Gray beneath the thickest eyelashes and bushiest black brows she had ever seen. "I'll leave the decanter," she said, setting it down on the little table. Your bed space is ready, and the fire will burn all night." Looking even briefly into those gray eyes had made her nervous, and she was surprised by her reaction. "Good night, sir." She curtsied to him and then departed the hall.

He watched her go, her nut-brown wool skirts swaying gracefully as she walked. When her glance had met his he had found himself startled, and his heart had jumped. Her eyes were hazel-green. The eyes, he had heard, were a mirror to the soul, and hers were certainly beautiful. But she was not for him, Baen MacColl knew. She was a lady with her own lands. He was the bastard of the master of Grayhaven. He didn't even bear his father's surname. MacColl meant son of Colin.

His mother, Tora, had been fifteen when she had met the twenty-year-old Colin Hay, the master of Grayhaven. She was to marry an older cousin, a widower with two half-grown daughters. It was a good match for a cotter's daughter, but Tora knew her cousin wanted a housekeeper, a cook, and someone to mother his children. She was foolish enough to want love. She was angry to have her life planned, and over before it had really begun. And then she had met Colin Hay while herding her father's two cows out on the moor. He had looked down on her from his horse and smiled a slow smile.

Colin Hay, a man whose charm was already legend in the region. Tora was easily seduced at that single meeting. But he had been tender and passionate, and afterwards she was ready to accept her fate because now she knew what love was. Then she had found herself with child from the brief encounter. Her father had beaten her severely, and her mother had wept with shame. But strangely Parlan Gunn, her blacksmith betrothed, had said he would have her anyway, but now there was a condition. Relieved, her family would have agreed to anything. Parlan Gunn was a hard man. He dictated that the child Tora carried must bear its father's name, and its mother's shame. He might have only daughters, but he would not give a stranger's bastard his name. Tora, who well knew her seducer, would say only that her lover's name was Colin. And so her son when born was called Baen MacColl. Baen meant fair. MacColl, son of Colin.

It had not been an easy childhood. His mother had never conceived another bairn, and Parlan Gunn grew to hate her for it. He had wanted his own son. And he hated the handsome, healthy Baen. And the more he did, the more Tora protected and lavished all her love upon her lad. Baen's stepsisters, taking their cue from their father, were mean and spiteful to the boy. He learned to evade them in order to avoid their vicious words—words he at first did not understand—and to elude their slaps and pinches. And then when he was twelve his mother grew very ill and was unable to leave her bed.

Calling him to her side, she told him, "I hae ne'er told any who yer da is, my fair laddie, but now I must tell ye. Dinna remain here. When

I am buried go to Grayhaven. Colin Hay, its master, is yer da, and ye look just like him but for yer eyes. Tell him my dying request was that he acknowledge ye and take ye in. He is a guid man, laddie. He never knew what his passion wi' me bore." And several hours later she had died.

They had buried Tora Gunn on a hillside near their village. And early the next morning before any in the village were awake, Baen MacColl had slipped from away from the only home he had ever known and made his way to Grayhaven. Seeking out Colin Hay, he told him exactly what his mother had told him to say. The master of Grayhaven had looked at the boy and shook his head wonderingly. Then he smiled.

"Aye, ye're my get, and there is no denying it. Why did yer mam nae tell me she hae given me such a fine son? And she is dead now? Poor lass!" He turned to his third wife, Ellen. " 'Twas before ye," he explained.

"Aye," Ellen Hay said. "Ye're a man for the lasses, and I knew it before I wed ye."

Baen MacColl had two younger half brothers, and an older half sister. While his stepmother was surprised by his sudden appearance, she had welcomed him warmly and treated him with kindness. He was given his own small chamber within his father's house. His gentle half sister, Margaret, and Ellen Hay taught him manners. Meg had entered her convent the year after he came to Grayhaven. While she loved her father, Margaret Hay did not approve of his earthiness. She did not, however, hold Baen responsible for the behavior that had led to his birth.

"But ye're nae a cotter's lad anymore, Baen," she said in her quiet voice. "Ye must learn to eat and to behave like a man of good breeding."

And he had. He had learned how to read, and to write, and to do sums. He had learned how to use a sword, a dagger, and a staff. And when he had shown a good intellect, and that he was no simpleton, the master of Grayhaven began to consider what was to happen with this third son he had suddenly inherited. Would he do for the church? But Baen would not do for the church. He soon demonstrated that he had his father's instincts for and charm with women. Colin Hay tried not to be too proud, and his stepmother just shook her head and laughed. She loved her man. And she loved his son.

Baen liked the outdoors. When his eldest son had turned twenty, the master of Grayhaven gave him his own cottage and put him in charge of his flocks and his shepherds. And Baen was content with his father's generosity. He considered himself fortunate and worked very hard. While he was the eldest he felt no jealousy toward his father's heir, his half brother James. Baen was the bastard, and he understood the way of the world, for hadn't Parlan Gunn and his daughters taught him his place? Colin Hay had wanted him to bear his surname, but Baen refused. He was proud to be the MacColl.

His relations with his brothers had been easy from the start. As they grew older they rode and drank and wenched together. They gambled and won. Gambled and lost, but they always took care of one another. Colin Hay watched with satisfaction as his two legitimate sons and his bastard grew as close as if they had come from the same womb. The master of Grayhaven was relieved that there was no jealousy between his sons. Each had a place in his heart, and each knew his place in his father's life.

And his third wife, Ellen, mother to James and Gilbert, had taken Baen into her heart with her usual generosity and calm manner. Unable to have any more children after her two sons were born, she enjoyed this third boy and grew to love him, for he was so like his father. "Are there any more out there like him?" she teased her husband.

"Not to my knowledge," he had replied with a small grin.

Ellen Hay had died just two years ago, and she was missed by all of her menfolk.

And of his three lads Baen was the most like Colin Hay, but for Tora's stormy gray eyes. It was in those eyes the master of Grayhaven saw the cotter's daughter with whom he had once lain in the heather that summer so long ago. She had been a virgin that afternoon, and his eldest son had come from their passionate couplings on that single day. He thought it strange that after birthing such a strong lad that she had never had another child. Baen had told him that his mother's marriage was an unhappy one, and that his stepfather had been cruel to her, that his daughters had neither respected nor loved her.

"She was good to them," Baen told his father, "yet they followed their da's lead. In the end it was to their detriment, for none would have them to wife. They are sour lasses. Now they have no choice but to remain in their father's house, but when he dies one day I know not what will happen to them, for there is no man to look after them."

The fire in the hearth crackled noisily, bringing Baen MacColl back to the present. Reaching for the whiskey, he filled the dram cup a third time, drinking it immediately down. Then, getting up, he walked to his bed space, pulled off his boots, loosened his garments, relieved himself in the bucket supplied for such activity, and climbed into his bed, yanking the coverlet up over his shoulders. He was such a big man he barely fit into the space.

He lay quietly for a time, listening to the wind howling outside the house as the storm intensified. He had been on the road forever, it seemed, and he was weary, and he ached. Gradually the whiskey which had brought the warmth back into his big frame eased him into a dreamless sleep. When he finally awakened it was to the sounds of morning activity common to a household's hall. He was silent for a time, knowing he must get up, but strangely reluctant to leave the cozy nest in which he lay. Finally, throwing off the coverlet, he climbed out of the bed space.

"Good morning," Elizabeth Meredith said from her place at the high board. "I wondered when you intended getting up. Half the morning is gone. Come and eat."

Baen straightened his clothing and pulled on his boots. He walked to where she sat waiting. "Half the morning gone?" he said.

"Aye." She smiled at him. "You were obviously very tired, sir. Sit next to me."

He joined her. "Has everyone eaten?" He was embarrassed.

"Nay. My uncle and his secretary do not arise early as a rule, and then are served in their apartment," she said. "He will be surprised to see you back."

"And your husband?" He had to ask.

"Husband? I have no husband. I have never had a husband. Friarsgate is mine by right of inheritance, sir. I am the lady of Friarsgate," Elizabeth explained.

"Then why did you send me off to Claven's Carn?" he asked her.

"The packet you carried was addressed to Rosamund, the lady of

Friarsgate, who is my mother," Elizabeth explained. "Friarsgate was her inheritance, and my eldest sister, Philippa, was to be her heiress. But Philippa is a creature of the court, and married into the aristocracy. She did not want Friarsgate. Nor did my second sister, Banon, who is our uncle's heiress to his estates at Otterly. But I did want Friarsgate, and so when I was fourteen my mother conferred these lands upon me and my descendants. I am Elizabeth Meredith, the lady of Friarsgate. When I saw my mother's name on the packet I assumed it must be for her, although she is no longer the lady. But it had come from those strange to us in Scotland. They could not know of the changes here, and I am not Rosamund."

"Have you read the message yet?" he asked her. "Can you read?"

"Of course I can read!" Elizabeth said indignantly. "Can you?"

"Aye." He began to spoon the oat stirabout in his trencher of bread into his mouth. The hunger was beginning to gnaw at his belly again.

She poured him a goblet of ale. "It was too late last night to be bothered with reading your message," Elizabeth said. "Do you know what is in the packet?"

"Aye." He reached for the cottage loaf and the butter. "Is that jam?" He pointed to a bowl near the butter.

"Aye," Elizabeth replied. "Strawberry."

He pulled the bowl over and, dipping his spoon in it, smeared the buttered bread with the jam, a smile of pure bliss lighting his features as he ate it.

"Well?" she demanded of him.

"Well, what?" He had finished his porridge, and was now filling the bread trencher with jam and devouring it.

"What does the letter to the lady of Friarsgate say?" Elizabeth wanted to know.

"I thought you could read," he said, popping the last bit into his mouth.

"I can! But if you know you can satisfy my curiosity before I read it in detail," Elizabeth almost shouted. "I cannot believe you are that much of a dunce, sir."

He burst out laughing, and his laugher echoed through the hall, startling the servants who were busily cleaning. "My father wants to buy some of your Shropshires, if you are of a mind to sell any," he said.

"They are not for eating," Elizabeth replied stiffly. "You Scots are much for eating sheep, I am told. I raise Shropshires for their wool."

He chuckled. "My father sells his wool."

"We weave ours into cloth here at Friarsgate," Elizabeth told him.

"You do not send the wool to the Netherlands?" He was surprised.

"We send cloth to the Netherlands," she told him. "Our Friarsgate blue cloth is much sought after. We regulate how much we will sell each year in order to keep the price high. The Hollanders have tried to copy it, but they have not succeeded. It is shipped in our own vessel, so we are able to control the export completely."

"This is very interesting," he said seriously. "Who does the weaving?"

"My cotters, during the winter months when there is no other work for them," Elizabeth explained. "By keeping them busy they earn a bit of coin, and do not grow lazy. Come the spring they are ready to go into the fields again. In the old days there was nothing for the cotters to do in the dark days and long nights. They drank too much, grew irritable, and beat their wives or children. They often fought with other men, causing serious injuries to the otherwise able-bodied. Now everyone is busy the winter through."

"Whose idea was this?" he asked her.

"My mother's, and then my uncle decided that we should have our own vessel, so he had one built," Elizabeth said.

"How long have the duties of Friarsgate been yours?" he wondered.

"Since I was fourteen. I will be twenty-two at the end of May," Elizabeth said.

"My dearest girl, a lady never reveals her age," Thomas Bolton said, coming into the hall. "I was told the Scot was back." His amber eyes swept over Baen MacColl, and he sighed most audibly.

"You have broken your fast, of course," Elizabeth said. "If you have not there is no jam left, I fear. It has all been eaten up."

"Will and I have been up for at least two hours, dear girl," he told her. "We have been discussing your hair and the state of your hands, Elizabeth."

"What is wrong with my hair?" she wanted to know.

"It hangs," he told her. "We need to decide upon an elegant style for you, and then Nancy must learn how to do it. And from now on you must sleep every night with your hands wrapped in cotton cloth after they have been properly creamed."

"Why?" Elizabeth demanded of him.

"Dear girl, only yesterday Will noted that you have hands like a milkmaid. A lady should have smooth and soft hands. The cream and the wrapping will accomplish just that effect. And you must cease all manner of manual labor, my pet," he told her.

"Uncle, I am what I am," Elizabeth said, exasperated.

"She can be so difficult," Thomas Bolton said, turning to Baen MacColl. "She is going to court in a few weeks. Her sisters were delighted at the prospect and looked forward to it, but alas, my darling Elizabeth does not." He turned back to Elizabeth. "And you must practice walking, dear girl."

"I have been walking since I was a year old, Uncle," she said. "What is wrong with the way I walk?"

"You clump, dear girl. Ladies do not clump; they glide like swans on the surface of the water," Lord Cambridge said.

"Uncle!" Elizabeth's tone was exasperated.

"Well, we must at least rid you of the clump," Tom Bolton said, undeterred.

Baen MacColl snickered, and Elizabeth shot him a black look.

"Those gowns of yours will not take to clumping, dear girl," Lord Cambridge said. "And you look so beautiful in those fine feathers, my pet." He turned again to Baen MacColl. "She is the fairest of Rosamund's daughters, dear boy. Now tell me what brings you back to Friarsgate. I thought you bound for Claven's Carn."

Baen explained, and then Elizabeth told her uncle what was in the missive from the master of Grayhaven.

"You are his son?" Thomas Bolton asked.

"Aye, the eldest, but I am the bastard," Baen said candidly. "I have lived in my father's house for almost twenty years. I was raised with my legitimate half brothers and my half sister, Margaret, who is now a nun," Baen said candidly.

"I have always considered that as long as a man is responsible for his appetites there is no harm done," Lord Cambridge replied. "Two of the Bolton sons belonging to Friarsgate were born on the wrong side of the blanket: Edmund, the manor's steward, and Richard, who is the prior of St. Cuthbert's. Guy was the heir, and Henry the youngest. Both the legitimate sons are now dead and buried."

"And where do you fit in the family tree?" Baen inquired boldly.

"There were twin sons several generations back. The second-born twin was sent to London to wed a merchant's daughter and make his fortune there. His wife, however, lay with King Edward, and then in a fit of remorse killed herself. The king felt guilty, as her family were most generous supporters of his in the war. So he gifted my grandfather with a peerage," Thomas Bolton explained.

"Yet you live nearby, if I am to understand Mistress Elizabeth," Baen said.

"Aye, I sold my estates in the south but for two houses, and returned to the north so I might be near my family. It is a decision I have never regretted. Every few years I go to court for a few months, and then eagerly return home."

"Vowing to never go again"—Elizabeth laughed—"but he always does."

"Only to get the latest gossip and procure a new wardrobe," Thomas Bolton assured his companions. "My Otterly folk would be most disappointed if I did not continue to appear at my most fashionable best."

"And you never disappoint, Uncle," Elizabeth assured him mischievously.

"Wretched girl!" he said. "And do not think I have forgotten your lessons in proper court etiquette, for I have not. Come out from behind the board now, and walk across the hall for me."

Elizabeth groaned, but she complied with his request. Outside, the snow was falling heavily, and there was no escape for her, she knew. She stepped down from the high board and stamped across the chamber. The pained look on Lord Cambridge's visage caused Baen Mac-Coll's handsome face to break into a grin, but he kept silent. He was rather enjoying this quite unexpected entertainment, and it was about to get even better, he discovered.

Thomas Bolton sighed deeply. "No, no, dear girl!" the older man said. "What are you wearing on your feet? Perhaps that is the difficulty."

Elizabeth stuck out a foot from beneath her skirts. She was wearing a very well worn square-toed boot of brown leather.

"Hmmmm. That may be it," Lord Cambridge said. "One can hardly glide in such footwear, dear girl, can one? Albert!" he called to the manservant. "Go to Mistress Elizabeth's chamber and have Nancy bring a pair of court slippers to the hall."

The manservant ran off to do Lord Cambridge's bidding.

"At court, dear girl, you will not wear your boots, although they will do nicely for the days that we travel," Thomas Bolton explained. "You cannot be expected to walk properly unless you wear the shoes you will wear at court."

"They hurt my feet," Elizabeth said.

"A lady bears such torment for the sake of fashion," he told her gently.

"I wonder if swans' feet hurt," Elizabeth muttered darkly.

Thomas Bolton chuckled. "Your mother left this endeavor too long, I fear," he said. "But go to court you will, darling girl, and you will be a sensation if it is the last thing I ever do for this family!"

The shoes were brought, and Nancy fitted them onto her mistress's feet.

Elizabeth stood up. "They are too small, and much too tight," she said.

"Show me!" her uncle barked, and she held out her foot. Thomas Bolton looked up at Nancy. "Fetch your mistress a pair of silk stockings at once, girl! No wonder these shoes do not fit. She is wearing her heavy wool boot stockings. Such elegant footwear is not made for wool stockings." He sighed. "I must speak with Maybel."

Nancy ran off again, and returned quickly with a pair of silk stockings and garters to hold them up. She rolled her mistress's wool leg coverings off and replaced them with the fine silk stockings. Then she fitted Elizabeth's feet into her slippers. Elizabeth stood up, swayed just slightly, and looked to her uncle.

"Try walking across the room again," he said.

Elizabeth complied, but this time she moved more carefully, slowly, and seemingly without any purpose other than to get from one side of the hall to the other. The shoes were not as comfortable as her boots, but neither were they as uncomfortable as they had previously been. She turned and looked to Lord Cambridge again.

"That was better, my angel girl, but we still have a lot of hard work ahead of us," he told her.

And for the next hour Elizabeth walked her hall in her silk stockings and court shoes until at last Thomas Bolton was satisfied with what he saw and allowed her to sit down. She collapsed into a chair by the fire, kicking off the shoes. "I don't want to go to court, Uncle," she said. "I don't care if I ever marry!"

*And what a pity that would be,* Baen MacColl thought. No one as lovely as Elizabeth Meredith should die a virgin. Why was it this beautiful girl was not yet married, and a mother? Was there something wrong with her that he did not know about?

Why had her family not seen properly to her future?

Elizabeth called to Nancy. "Give me my boots and wool stockings, and take these others back to my chamber. I have work to do."

"Today? In the midst of a blizzard?" Lord Cambridge said.

"It is the day of the month I set aside for going over the accounts. There have been many lambs born, and I must enter them in my ledger, Uncle. I collected the numbers as I was out yesterday seeing to my flock's safety," she said, standing up, her feet reshod. She turned to Baen MacColl. "I am sorry there is naught for you to do, sir, but sit by my fire. As you can see the storm outside these walls is only just beginning to roar." Then she was gone from the hall.

"Do you play chess, dear boy?" Lord Cambridge asked hopefully.

"I do, my lord. My father taught me when I first came to live with him," the Scotsman replied. "Tell me where the board is, and I will set it up for us."

When William Smythe entered the hall shortly afterwards, he found his master and Baen MacColl engaged in a very lively game. He watched, and then he smiled. His master was beginning to become alive with his court personality once more. It was a side of Thomas Bolton he did not see often any longer. He came and stood by his side, saying, "He is beating you, my lord. I am quite surprised."

"We have only been playing for a short while, Will. Like most young men this one is in a hurry, and when one is in a hurry one makes mistakes." He took Baen's knight in a smooth motion, and set it on the side of the board with a small grin.

The Scot laughed. "Well played, my lord," he said with a bow of his head.

*Why, the clever young fellow,* William Smythe thought as he continued to view the game. *He is going to let my lord win this contest when he is really the better player. How diplomatic of him, considering he is little more than a rough Highlander.* He moved off. He had his duties to complete despite the bad weather, and he would complete them far more quickly if his lordship was being amused.

In the little chamber she used for estate business, Elizabeth read the missive sent her by Colin Hay, the master of Grayhaven. He had, he wrote, two nice-size flocks of black-faced Highlands, but while the wool sheared from his sheep was good, it was ordinary, and hardly worth the bother of shipping to the Netherlands. His friend, Adam Leslie, had said Friarsgate raised several kinds of sheep, and the wool sheared was excellent. The master of Grayhaven wanted to improve his flocks. Would the lady of Friarsgate be interested in selling him some of her sheep?

Elizabeth sat back in her chair and considered his request. Her Shropshires, Hampshires, and cheviots all produced an excellent and high grade of wool. But there were two secrets to the Friarsgate blue wool: the secret of how its color was obtained, and the fact that the wool came from merino sheep. Her mother had learned of this breed from Queen Katherine, and with the queen's aid had imported several ewes and a young ram. The flock had grown over the years, and now a quarter of the Friarsgate sheep were merinos. Their fleece was heavy and snow white. They were self-lubricating, so that their inner wool was incredibly soft.

*There are enough lambs being born now,* Elizabeth thought, *that I could sell some of my sheep off and be none the poorer for it. Shropshires, Hampshires, or cheviots, but not the merinos. There are few estates in England with sheep like mine. I cannot be certain the Scots won't eat them anyway, and use their lungs to make that disgusting dish they call haggis. So they shall not have my merinos.*

She laid the parchment aside. It would be weeks before any sheep could be taken north. Certainly not until they were well into spring. And she would want her own shepherds and dogs to escort them. There was nothing for it but that Baen MacColl would have to remain at Friarsgate until he could return with his sheep. She would discuss it with him this evening in the hall. *Damnation!* She did not want to go to court. How was Friarsgate to manage without her? Edmund was over seventy now, and she had chosen no one to follow him. Not that he would allowed it anyway. But when she came home they were going to have to discuss it.

It snowed for almost three days. And then the sun came out, and Baen MacColl insisted on helping the men shovel paths from the house to the barns and the sheepfolds. He could not, it seemed, remain idle, and he was certainly not afraid of hard work. He had listened to Elizabeth's suggestion that he remain at Friarsgate until he could return north with the sheep she would sell him.

"Your father can send the price of the sheep back with my shepherds," she told him, and he agreed.

"You're not afraid we'll steal the sheep and slay your men?" he teased her.

"The Leslies have sent you to me," Elizabeth said seriously. "I trust them. Besides, my stepfather is the Hepburn of Claven's Carn. If you attempted to cheat me Logan would gather his clansmen up and go north to seek you out, sir."

He chuckled, the corners of his gray eyes crinkling. "I suspect you would ride with them, Mistress Elizabeth," he said.

"Aye." She nodded. "I would. Friarsgate is my responsibility, sir."

"Do you think you might call me Baen?" he asked her.

"I could," she agreed. " 'Tis an odd name. Doesn't bane meet woe or ruin?"

"*Baen* means fair in the Scots tongue," he told her. "*MacColl* is son of Colin."

"Was your mother in love with your father?" Elizabeth asked him, curious.

"They met but once," he replied.

"Once?" Elizabeth blushed, shocked by his revelation. If they had met but once, then his mother had lain with the master of Grayhaven without even knowing him. It was difficult enough for her to contemplate a man in her bed.

"Once," he repeated, the gray eyes twinkling. "I never knew who my father was until my mother was on her deathbed. She told me then, and said I was to go to him as soon as she was gone. My stepfather was not the kindest man."

"How old were you?"

"Twelve," he answered her.

"Since you're here," Elizabeth said, "I assume your father took you in and cared for you." Twelve. He had been so young. She thought of herself at twelve: all legs and arms, and constantly baiting Philippa when she was home. She hadn't had a care in the world at twelve, while he was almost an orphan. How odd life was.

"The master of Grayhaven is a good father," Baen answered her.

"And you have siblings? Did they mind when you came to live with them?"

"Nay. Within a few days it was as if we had always been together. I am ten years older than Jamie, and Gilbert is even younger. My stepmother was kept very busy with the three of us. Meg, of course, was a good lass. She was our father's only daughter, born to his first wife. Ellen, our stepmother, was his third, and my brothers were her lads."

"What happened to the second wife?" Elizabeth asked, curious.

"He strangled her when he caught her with another man," Baen said matter-of-factly.

"He was jealous," Elizabeth said.

"Nay, but he was dishonored. Killing her restored that honor," Baen replied.

"Gracious!" Lord Cambridge, who had been listening, exclaimed. "How deliciously savage, dear boy! Are you much like your sire?" His eyes were twinkling.

"I am his image but for the eyes. His are green. Mine the gray of my dam's. But I too possess a strong sense of honor, my lord."

"You must keep your wife close," Elizabeth noted.

"I have no wife, mistress. I owe my father my allegiance for his kindness and care of me since that day I arrived so unexpectedly upon his doorstep. How can I ever repay him? He did not have to take me in, and yet he did. And when he did, I gained a family. But for my mother, God assoil her good soul, I have almost forgotten those early years when I was so sadly mistreated."

"Why does your father want more sheep?" Elizabeth asked him.

"It was my suggestion that we improve our flocks," Baen explained to her. "I thought a better grade of wool would bring in a decent profit. The more prosperous Grayhaven is, the better matches my younger brothers can make. Jamie, of course, will inherit one day, but Gilly needs a bit more of an advantage."

Elizabeth nodded. She understood, of course, but she had never before considered the obtaining of a match from a man's point of view. It was interesting to think that men had a similar problem to women. "Tomorrow," she said, "we will visit some of the folds, and you can see the sheep. Mine are very different from your black-faced Highland breed. Their wool is finer. You would do well with any of the three."

"I want to know as much about how you manage your sheep as you can teach me," Baen said earnestly.

"Very well," she agreed. "I will put you with some of my best shepherds. And you must have your own dog, who will answer to your calls alone. There are some half-grown pups from one of my shelties in one of the barns. I doubt they're all spoken for yet. When the weather gets better you will work with the dog and the sheep that will be yours," Elizabeth told him.

"I am grateful, lady," he thanked her.

"If you are Baen, then I am Elizabeth," she said.

"Have you always been called so formally?" he asked.

Elizabeth smiled. "As a child I was called Bessie, but it is not a name for the lady of Friarsgate."

"Nay," he agreed, "I can see you are no longer a Bessie." And then he smiled at her, and for a brief moment Elizabeth felt dazzled. "Your name suits you," he told her.

"Aye, I think it does," she agreed, and then she gave him a small smile in return.

Thomas Bolton watched this exchange silently. Too bad Baen MacColl was a bastard. A landless young man with not even his sire's name to distinguish him. It was a pity, but there it was. Despite the fact that Elizabeth seemed to like him, and he her; despite the fact that they had much in common; he was not the man for her. Surely at court there would be one young man for whom Friarsgate was a golden opportunity, as it had been for Elizabeth's late father, Sir Owein Meredith. The times were different, it was true, Lord Cambridge thought. Tradesmen's sons were now serving within the hallowed precincts of the court. But did that not make the chance of finding a husband for Elizabeth even better?

Elizabeth Meredith was a plainspoken girl. She was not interested in a great name or in serving the court. Her passion was for Friarsgate, even more so than her mother's had been. For Rosamund there had been no choice. Elizabeth, however, had chosen to take on the manor's many responsibilities. There had to be one man at court to whom a girl like Elizabeth Meredith would seem a great blessing. She was beautiful. She was wealthy. She was intelligent.

And there was the ant in the jam pot. Elizabeth was clever and intuitive. She knew everything there was to know about Friarsgate. She was not going to easily share her autonomy with anyone. Rosamund had been that way, but Owein had understood, and she had gradually shared her rule with him. Elizabeth was a creature of a different stripe. Lord Cambridge sighed. He feared that they had waited too long to find Elizabeth a husband. And if they had, what was to happen to Friarsgate?

The storm was the last one of the winter season. The days were growing longer, and the sun warmer. It melted the snow that had so recently fallen, and the snows beneath it. Sheets of white slid from the roofs, sometimes catching a passerby unawares. The meltoff ran in little runnels off the edges and corners of the barns. The lambs shyly ventured out into the bright day, hiding within the shadows of their mams, but then growing bolder with each passing hour.

"Which breed do you like best?" Elizabeth asked Baen as they walked across the muddy enclosure one afternoon.

"I think the cheviots, although the Shropshires are handsome enough beasts," he told her.

"I will sell you some of each," she said. "It cannot hurt your endeavor to have several different breeds to go with your black-faced Highlands." The mud squished beneath her boots, and Elizabeth sighed.

"Why do they insist you go to court?" he asked suddenly.

"Because it is the place my mother found my father, and my sisters their husbands," Elizabeth answered him. "My mother was a child when she went, and her match was arranged with my father because it was good for the king. Fortunately my parents adored each other. She had been wed twice previously: at three to a cousin who died of a childhood complaint, and then at six to an elderly knight who taught her how to control her own destiny before he succumbed."

"Why was she Friarsgate's heiress?" he inquired.

"Her family perished and she alone was left," Elizabeth explained.

"And your sisters?"

"Philippa visited the court at ten. She was invited to return at twelve to serve the queen. After that it was all she wanted. Uncle Thomas found her a husband when the boy she thought to wed preferred a churchly life instead. And Banon found her Neville at court. His family had dragged him there to hopefully gain a place in the royal household. Instead he saw Banon, and was lost. She is Uncle Thomas's heiress, and rules over Otterly like a queen bee. That is why he had been so delighted to winter with me. Banon's brood of daughters drive him mad." Elizabeth laughed. "They say I must be wed so that Friarsgate may have another generation of heirs or heiresses. I have no time for a husband, let alone children. But to court I will be dragged, and they will find a husband for me, I fear. My sister, the countess, will already be looking for just the right man," Elizabeth finished with a grimace.

He laughed, but then he said, "They are right, you know. This is a fine manor that you possess, Elizabeth Meredith, and you love it dearly. But like each generation that lives upon this earth, ours will one day pass away. Then who will care for Friarsgate?"

"I know," she admitted, "but the thought of having some perfumed fool for a husband does not please me."

"Are either of your brothers-in-law perfumed fools?" he asked her.

"Nay, but then Crispin manages his own estates, and Philippa is happy to let him do it, for it allows her time at court to see to the future of their children. And Robert Neville is more than content to allow Banon to control Otterly. He prefers hunting and fishing; and Banon makes his life such an easy one I think he has no idea she is wearing his breeks."

"Is that the kind of man you want?" he said quietly.

"I think I could share Friarsgate with a husband, but he would have to love it as much as I do," Elizabeth noted thoughtfully. "And he would have to understand that I know my lands, and I know how to buy and sell at no loss to Friarsgate. I do not believe that there is a man like that out there in the world, but I will go to court because it will please my family that I am being cooperative and doing what they want of me. But I will marry no man who cannot share my burden with me, or who wants that burden all for himself," she said firmly.

"What of love?" he wondered.

"Love?" Elizabeth looked surprised at his query.

"Do you not want to love the man you wed, Elizabeth Meredith?" Baen MacColl asked her. He was leaning against the fence of the sheepfold as he spoke, his gray eyes perusing her face carefully.

"I suppose it would be nice to love the man I wed. My sisters certainly love their husbands, but neither has the responsibilities I do. I must choose the man who will be best for Friarsgate, if indeed there is such a man," Elizabeth said.

Baen MacColl reached out and took her heart-shaped face in his two big hands. Then, leaning forward, he kissed her lips slowly and tenderly.

Elizabeth's eyes widened with surprise, and she pulled back. "Why did you do that?" she demanded to know.

"You've never been kissed before," he replied by way of an answer.

"Nay, I haven't. But you still haven't answered my question, Baen."

"It seemed to me at that moment that you needed to be kissed," he told her. "You are very serious in your devotion to your duty, Elizabeth Meredith. Have you ever in all of your life had fun?"

"Fun is for children," she answered him.

"You had better learn how to kiss if you are going into society," he advised.

"And you are volunteering to be my instructor," she snapped.

"I am told I kiss well, and you obviously have a great deal to learn about kissing," he said with a grin.

"What's wrong with the way I kiss?" she insisted upon knowing.

"When I kissed you your lips were just there," he said. "They did not kiss back or offer me anything other than flesh."

"Perhaps I didn't want to be kissed," she said, blushing to her annoyance.

"All girls want to be kissed." He chuckled. "Shall we try again?"

"No!"

"You're afraid," he taunted her.

"Nay, I'm not!" she insisted. "I simply don't wish to be seen kissing a virtual stranger in the middle of my sheepfold. What would my shepherds say, Baen MacColl?"

"Of course," he agreed, to her surprise. "We'll continue our lessons this evening in the hall, when your uncle has gone to his bed."

"We will not!" Elizabeth told him. "Like all Scots you are far too bold."

"If you don't learn how to kiss properly before you go to court the gentlemen will make fun of you," he said to her.

"A respectable maid is not experienced in matters of the flesh," Elizabeth told him primly.

"A lass of your age should know how to kiss," he said. "If you don't kiss me in the hall tonight I shall know you are a coward, Elizabeth Meredith." His gray eyes were serious as they gazed on her.

"Oh, very well!" Elizabeth said impatiently. "But only one more kiss to prove my courage, and then no more," she told him, turning and hurrying back to the house.

# Chapter 3

*B*ut after the evening meal had been served, Elizabeth slipped quietly from the hall and went to her bedchamber. She was certainly not going to engage in kissing games with her Scots visitor. He was a bold fellow. Too bold! And his lips on hers, even briefly, had been disturbing. Kissing, it would seem, was an intimate thing, and Elizabeth Meredith was not certain she was ready to share herself with a man. *Well, you had better get used to the idea,* the voice in her head said impatiently. *No man is going to want a wife who doesn't kiss and cuddle.* She debated returning to the hall, but did not.

Rising earlier than usual the next morning, Elizabeth dressed and hurried down to the hall. But for a few sleepy servants it was empty, but seeing their mistress the servants brought a trencher of hot oat cereal, placing it before her. A goblet of cider was poured. Elizabeth ate slowly, her mind busy with all she had to do today. She sliced cheese from the half-wheel on the table before her, placing it atop a thick, warm slice of bread that she had already buttered. The butter was melting and running down her fingers. She licked them. Finished, she went to sit by the fire for a few minutes before beginning her rounds.

"Coward!"

She jumped at the word whispered in her ear and, turning, found herself looking up at Baen MacColl. Then, before she might react, he kissed her lips, and she gasped with surprise. "Rogue!" she managed to say.

"Soften your mouth, lass, and then kiss me back," he replied, drawing her up and into the circle of his embrace. "You have lips that were made for kissing, Elizabeth Meredith, and I never could resist sweet lips."

His mouth descended on hers now with obvious and serious intent. The arms about her tightened. She felt herself relaxing against him, her mouth working against his.

"That's it, lass," he encouraged her.

What was she doing? She felt weak and drained of all energy. The pressure of lips on lips was intoxicating. She sighed, and then to her surprise he released her, gently settling her back into her chair again. "How dare you!" Elizabeth managed to say, and she felt a flush coloring her cheeks.

Baen MacColl laughed softly, and knelt before her so he might look into her face. "Did you really hate it?" he asked her, taking her small hand in his big one.

Looking into his gray eyes made her almost giddy. "Well, no, but . . ." Elizabeth began, desperately attempting to gain some measure of control over herself, for she had obviously lost all sense of proportion. The hand holding hers pulsed with warmth.

"Then you enjoyed it," he replied. The gray eyes twinkled wickedly.

"You had no right to kiss me!" Elizabeth said indignantly. What else was there to say in defense of herself? To her mortification she had kissed him back.

"No, I didn't," he answered calmly, "but I did."

"Do you always do just what you want?" she demanded. Her lips were tingling with the memory of his mouth on hers.

"Nay, I don't, but I found myself unable to resist you," he said with absolute and ingenuous charm. "You are very beautiful, Elizabeth Meredith," Baen told her, reaching up to caress the line of her jaw with the knuckle of his forefinger.

"Was I better this time?" she queried him.

"Much better," he told her with a grin.

"Good! Then we don't have to kiss again," she said in a firm tone. "Now I know how to kiss should the spirit move me to kiss, sir."

Standing up, he burst out laughing. "Do you think that is all there is to it?"

"What more could there possibly be, sir?"

"There is cuddling," he murmured seductively.

"Sit down at the board, and the servants will bring you your breakfast, Baen MacColl," Elizabeth instructed him. "We have much to do this day. As for cuddling, put it from your mind. The kissing was bold enough, and I am no fool. More kissing leads to cuddling, and cuddling leads to coupling. I will not permit my virtue to be tampered with by any man, let alone a villainous Scots Highlander. Send Albert for me when you are ready to ride," she said, and then, rising from her chair, she left the hall.

Baen MacColl grinned after her, and then sat down at the high board to break his fast. What the hell was the matter with him? Why was he behaving like such a fool? The girl was an heiress, and not for the likes of him. Still, he had wanted to touch her blond hair. It would be soft, and it was clean. *She* was clean, smelling of clover and freshly scythed grass. He had grown dizzy those few moments he had held her. He dug his spoon into the trencher of hot oats. He had to control himself, he thought grimly.

From his place in the shadows, Thomas Bolton had watched the scene between Elizabeth and Baen play out. He had considered at one point that he might have to intervene, but Elizabeth had obviously been quite capable of managing the randy young Scot without his help. The knowledge pleased Lord Cambridge greatly, for she would undoubtedly be forced to defuse similar situations at court in defense of her honor. He was delighted to find she was not easily flustered by a gentleman's attention. Not that Baen MacColl was a gentleman. Elizabeth had been right: He was a bold man.

"Good morning, dear boy!" Thomas Bolton pretended to have just entered the hall. "You slept well? I find these quiet winter nights quite conducive to slumber, don't you?" He waved away a servant. "No! No! I have already eaten." Then, turning back to the Scot, he asked, "And what plans has my adorable girl for you today, sir?"

"I believe we are to ride out to inspect some flocks in the far meadows," Baen answered the older man. "Would you ride with us, my lord?"

"God's boots, dear boy, nay! I know these late-winter days as the spring approaches. The sun may shine warm on one's back, but the damp cuts into your very bones. Riding in such weather is not for a man of my years," Lord Cambridge declared vehemently.

"Yet you will ride south in the rain," Baen MacColl said.

"Do not remind me, dear boy," Thomas Bolton replied with a shudder. "Only for Rosamund or her daughters would I make what is sure to be a most uncomfortable journey. However, at journey's end we shall arrive at court for the month of May, which is always delightful. May is the king's favorite month. Every day is a celebration filled with games and amusements and feasting. We will be at Greenwich, which is beautiful. You have never been south, have you, dear boy?"

"Friarsgate is as far south as I have ever been," Baen MacColl answered.

"Master MacColl, the mistress has said you are to meet her at the kennels immediately," Albert said as he came upon the two men.

"The kennels?" Lord Cambridge looked curious.

"Elizabeth has said I am to have one of the Shetland pups. I suppose she wants me to see it," Baen replied. He arose from the board, bowing to Lord Cambridge. "You will excuse me, my lord." Then he hurried from the hall.

He found Elizabeth surrounded by several dogs of various lineages, all of whom obviously adored her. She was holding a rather large puppy. It had silky black and white fur. "Do you like him?" she said. "He's the biggest of Flora's litter. She's Tam's dog, and he has already begun to work with this youngster. What will you name him?"

"I never had a dog of my own," Baen said slowly. "I think I shall call him Friar, for Friarsgate. The way his head is marked he reminds me of one of those traveling religious, don't you think?" He reached out and let the pup sniff his hand. Then he patted the dog. "We're going to be good friends, Friar," he said.

"We'll take him with us today," Elizabeth said. "Come on! The horses should be waiting by now. I gave instructions before I came to the kennels."

"He's too little to run with the horses," Baen protested.

"I know," Elizabeth said. "You can lay him across your saddle. He has to get used to you, your scent, and the sound of your voice. Tam will continue his training, and when Friar has learned the basics you will join them. He's going to be your dog, and should obey you first and foremost."

They rode out, and he again thought how perfectly in tune with her lands and her animals she was. The horses picked their way carefully through the thawing meadows where the ground could be muddy and soft or hard and icy, depending on the angle of the sun. The sheepfolds near the outlying barns were filled with bleating, woolly creatures. Baen decided that he did indeed like the Shropshires and the cheviots best. They were hardy beasts who could easily survive a Highland winter.

The puppy lying across his saddle before him had at first protested being removed from his mother and his siblings. But he quickly quieted down, and after a few miles closed his warm brown eyes and fell asleep, snoring softly, to Baen's amusement. In one meadow a small herd of sheep had been allowed to roam free. He and Elizabeth stopped, dismounted, and went to inspect the animals. Friar romped noisily, yapping at their feet, and then suddenly he began to nip at the heels of a ewe, instinctively herding the creature.

"Oh," Elizabeth said, "he's going to be very good. He has hardly begun his lessons yet, and look at him." She laughed as the ewe protested noisily at being forced to move along by the young pup. Kneeling next to the sheep, Elizabeth pushed her fingers into the wool. "See," she invited him, "how thick her coat is, Baen. When she is sheared, you will gain a nice harvest of wool from a sheep like this."

He knelt by her side and inspected the sheep's wool. Their hands touched briefly, and then Elizabeth stood up. "Aye," he said softly, "I can see she's a fine beastie." Then he stood again and, reaching out, picked up the noisy puppy, cradling it in his arms. "Hush, laddie, I can see you will do your duty, and do it well." He stroked Friar's head.

Elizabeth turned away, walking to her horse. Her hand seemed to burn where his had touched it. She felt almost faint, and shook her head to clear it as she pulled herself into the saddle again. "It's growing late, Baen. We have a long ride back to the house," she told him.

Together they rode back, and when they reached the stables Elizabeth dismounted, and immediately crossed the stable yard towards the house. Baen took the puppy back to the kennels and settled it in with its mother for a good supper. Then he followed after her, but she was already inside and nowhere to be seen when he came into the hall. He found that he was disappointed.

"Dear boy!" Lord Cambridge waved at him. William Smythe was by his side. "How did the sheep viewing go? And have you a dog of your own now?"

"Aye, a fine young fellow I've named Friar. Elizabeth says Tam will teach him the basics, and then we will learn to work together, Friar and I." He smiled at the older man, and at his gesturing hand joined him. "And was your day productive, my lord?"

"It was long, and it was dull," Thomas Bolton complained. "Elizabeth's wardrobe is finished. She has jewelry and shoes. We but await the month of April to depart."

"You will not return to your own holding before?" Baen asked.

"Nay. I am having another wing added to Otterly. It will not be completed until sometime this summer. My heiress's brood is both large and noisy. Friarsgate may not offer me the amenities that Otterly has, but its hall is delightfully peaceful. I shall not see Otterly until I return. Dear William, however, will have to come back ahead of us in order to see to the transfer of my furniture and other belongings from my apartments to the new wing, which has no direct access to the main sections of the house." He grinned wickedly. "I have no intention of being overrun again, dear boy. I shall make my final stand in the new west wing of my home."

Baen chuckled. "I understand," he told the older man. "My father's house is not very large, and when I arrived so suddenly it seemed, my stepmother said, to grow smaller. My brothers and I are all big men. 'Tis fortunate none of us is wed yet."

Young Nancy came into the hall to say her mistress had a headache, and would not be joining them for supper.

"I am not surprised, out all day in that dampness," Lord Cambridge said. "And Elizabeth always refuses to wear a head covering. One day she will catch her death, I fear, but she will not listen to reason. A most stubborn girl." Then he brightened. "But we shall have a lovely supper together, and then I shall beat you once more in chess, dear boy. You seem to get worse with each game we play," Thomas Bolton noted.

"I shall endeavor to give your lordship a better game tonight," Baen

MacColl replied with a quick grin. Then he saw William Smythe's faint smile, and knew that Lord Cambridge's secretary was aware of his deception, yet he kept silent. *Well,* Baen considered, *Thomas Bolton is an odd fellow, but he is amusing, and has a good heart. It would break that heart if I made him lose. He does so enjoy the game.* He nodded imperceptibly to William Smythe, acknowledging his part in the deception.

The month of March was quickly coming to an end. It was decided that Baen MacColl would go north back into Scotland in mid-April, for by then the snows should be gone. Elizabeth and Lord Cambridge, however, would depart for court on the first day of April. Several days before that departure the Hepburn of Claven's Carn arrived with his wife and four of his five sons.

"You did not think I was going to let you go to court without saying good-bye," Rosamund said to her daughter. She was still a handsome woman, approaching her forty-first birthday. She hugged Elizabeth. "I am so pleased you are going. And I want to see all the beautiful gowns that have been made for you. You must wear one into the hall tonight so Logan and your brothers may see what a fine lady you have become."

Elizabeth hugged her mother back, and said, "Where is Johnnie?"

"At Claven's Carn, taking on a bit of the responsibility that will one day be his," Logan Hepburn answered his stepdaughter. Then he turned on his heel, pierced Baen MacColl with a hard look, and said, "Who are you? A Highlander, from the look of you."

"This is Baen MacColl, Logan," Elizabeth said quickly. "He has been with us for some weeks now, waiting for better weather to return home. His father, the master of Grayhaven, is purchasing a small flock from me. He wishes to improve his stock. He was sent to us by the Leslies of Glenkirk, whose neighbor he is."

Logan Hepburn held out his hand, and Baen took it, looking directly at the older man as he shook the proffered hand. "My lord," he said.

"Och, man, Logan will do," the Hepburn said with a grin. He liked the look of the Highlander. "Your clan?"

"My father is Colin Hay," Baen answered.

"Well, he spawns big lads," Logan noted. "Are there any more at home like you?" The man had been introduced as MacColl, which meant he was a bastard, Logan realized. Still, he was obviously well thought of by his sire.

"Two. My half brothers, Jamie and Gilbert Hay," Logan answered, knowing the Hepburn had already figured out his heritage. Well, he wasn't ashamed of it.

"Has Elizabeth allowed you a wee dram of my whiskey?" Logan wanted to know. "Lass, have it brought forth at once! You have half a dozen Scotsmen in the hall."

"Tavis and Edmund are not drinking whiskey!" Rosamund said firmly. "They are far too young. Why, that stuff you brew will stunt their growth, Logan."

"Awww, mam," Rosamund's youngest sons, twins, protested in unison.

"Your mother's right," Logan said, and his sons grew quiet.

James Hepburn, who was fourteen, remained very quiet. He watched as four small dram cups were poured and brought forward. The first went to his half sister's guest. The next to his father. His brother, Alexander, who was seventeen, was served. Then the servant offered him the last dram, and no one protested. Jamie Hepburn took the pewter cup and, following his father's lead, raised the little vessel up in toast. Then he drank it all down in a single gulp, gasping audibly as the whiskey hit the bottom of his belly like a hot coal. His eyes watered, but he gamely said nothing.

Logan Hepburn grinned, well pleased. These sons he had sired on Rosamund were braw lads. They were strong and filled with the joy of life, unlike his eldest son, who desperately sought to leave Claven's Carn and enter a religious order. He had fought with John before they had departed Claven's Carn, for he wanted his heir to remain behind to oversee his lands. John had wanted to go to a nearby abbey on a retreat. He was glad his first wife, Jeannie, wasn't alive to suffer the disappointment that John had become. She had been so proud to give Logan Hepburn his first son.

Rosamund, however, had scolded Logan for his intransigence, as she put it. It was important to love one's lands. John Hepburn loved

God more and, having experienced a similar disappointment with her eldest daughter in the matter of Friarsgate, Rosamund understood both her husband's side of the matter and her stepson's. He had four other sons, she reminded him, and their eldest, Alexander, was like his father in every way, right down to his sense of responsibility regarding Claven's Carn.

"It tastes terrible, doesn't it?" Elizabeth remarked to her brother, Jamie, about the whiskey he had just consumed.

"Nah," James Hepburn said stoutly. " 'Tis grand!"

"Liar!" She laughed, and the others laughed too.

"Your face got all red," Edmund Hepburn said.

"And your eyes watered," Tavis, his twin, noted.

"At least I'm man enough to be offered whiskey," Jamie taunted them. "You two runts have a ways to go."

"At least our faces are not full of pimples like yours," Tavis, the bolder of the two twins, replied. Then he took a defensive stance. "Aye, Jamie, come on! Try and hit me if you dare!" He danced mockingly before his brother.

"That is enough!" Rosamund snapped. Then she turned to her daughter. "Sons are more difficult than little girls," she said. "Remember that."

"Uncle Thomas does not think a great deal of little girls," Elizabeth teased her relation mischievously. "He has endured the lack of amenities in my hall all winter rather than remain in his own comfortable house with Banon's brood of little darlings—or demons, as I have heard them referred to by a certain gentleman."

"Oh, poor Tom," Rosamund said sympathetically. "Are they really that bad?"

"Perhaps it is that there are so many of them," Lord Cambridge said.

"I had three, and you found no fault with them," Rosamund reminded him. "Indeed, you have spoiled all my girls most shamelessly, dear cousin."

"Banon's lasses run constantly. They shriek and quarrel among one another. If Katherine Rose receives a blue ribbon and Thomasina Marie a pink, Katherine Rose wants the pink. But Thomasina Marie wants it too. Then Jemima Anne, Elizabeth Susanne, and Margaret

Mary, the littlest girl, all cry because they did not get ribbons at all. Because their charming dunce of a father has forgotten to purchase ribbons all of one color at the fair, and has remembered only the eldest two, who want to argue over colors, while the others weep. It is like that at all times. Banon's children are never silent, and she seems not to notice it at all. I built myself a private wing when Otterly was reconstructed, but the builder made the error of putting a door between the wings. Neither Banon nor her family has any respect for my privacy," he grumbled.

"So Uncle Thomas is building an entire new wing at Otterly with no access to the main wings," Elizabeth said. "He has threatened his builder with murder and mayhem if he returns and finds another door." She laughed.

"Well enough for you to find it amusing," Lord Cambridge said, aggrieved. "Your house is quiet. Mine has not been. Still, I adore Banon, and I even adore her brood in moderation. As for Robert Neville, he is most likable, for he is a mild-mannered gentleman. We ride and we play chess together. A most companionable fellow."

"Will you stop at Otterly on your way south?" Rosamund asked her cousin.

"Nay," he replied. "We must travel quickly in order to reach London in time for my tailor to make any alterations on the new wardrobe he is bringing me. And we must see if anything must be done to improve Elizabeth's wardrobe. We will stop at Brierewode, however, for it is on our way."

"Will you carry some messages to Philippa for me?" Rosamund asked him. Despite the fact that Philippa's renunciation of Friarsgate had hurt her deeply, Rosamund still loved her eldest daughter. It did not matter that Elizabeth was the perfect Friarsgate heiress. Rosamund had always wanted Owein's eldest child to have the estate. Especially after she had lost their son.

"Of course," Thomas Bolton replied. "And I shall bring you back all the latest gossip from not only the court, but from Philippa's family as well," he promised her.

The manor priest, Father Mata, having arrived to join them, said the blessing before the meal was served. Afterwards Elizabeth was sent to her chamber to be dressed in one of her beautiful court gowns. She chose a dress with a rose-colored silk bodice decorated with small sparkling crystals, and a skirt in a slightly deeper shade of the color. The neckline was squared and edged with the crystals, and the full sleeves had a deep cuff, turned back to display more of the sparkling crystals. The French hood on Elizabeth's head had a crystal-decorated edging, and the pale pink veil attached to it was made of sheer silk shot through with bits of silver.

"Oh, my!" Rosamund exclaimed. She had never seen Elizabeth in such finery. Then she said, "Let me see the shoes, daughter."

Elizabeth stuck a foot from beneath her skirts to reveal a square-toed shoe covered in pink silk and decorated with crystals.

"How beautiful!" her mother breathed. She turned to Lord Cambridge. "I remember when you and I went to court, Tom, and you insisted on having a wonderful new wardrobe made for me. And then Philippa, and Banon. Now Elizabeth. How good you have been to us, cousin." Her eyes grew misty with her remembrances.

"Such shoes hurt my feet," Elizabeth complained, breaking the mood, "but Uncle Thomas says I cannot wear my boots, even though they would hardly show beneath all these skirts. He says my feet will be displayed when I dance. But I don't dance."

Thomas Bolton paled. "God's nightshirt!" he cried, his hand going to his heart in a dramatic gesture. "I knew there was something I had forgotten. I have not taught her to dance, and she must know how to dance. The king always expects the ladies at court to dance. Why he danced with you, dear Rosamund! And he danced with Philippa too. How could I have forgotten such an important element of Elizabeth's education?"

"Oh, Uncle," Elizabeth attempted to soothe him. "The king will not notice me. It does not matter if I dance or I do not dance."

"My dear girl," Lord Cambridge replied, "the king will most certainly notice you. You are young and slender and fair, which he has always liked best in a woman. And you are Rosamund Bolton's daughter. Remember that your mother's friendship with the king goes back to their shared youth at his father's court. I will have to introduce you to his majesty. If I did not I should be in grave breach of etiquette, and though many things have been said of me, it has never been suggested that I lacked the most exquisite of manners," Thomas Bolton said. "You must learn to dance! And as your mother is here it is the perfect time. She and I will demonstrate some of the court dances for you. Then we will try together, for I am an excellent dancer, dear girl, as you will see."

"We need music," Rosamund reminded her cousin.

"I will fetch some of the lads who are skilled in such an art," Maybel said, getting slowly to her feet. "They cannot play as finely as those at court, but they will do." She moved off on her errand.

Alexander Hepburn grinned at his half sister. "So you're to learn to dance, Elizabeth? 'Twill be vastly entertaining, I've nae a doubt."

Elizabeth smiled sweetly at him, and then said to their mother, "Do you not think Alex should learn to dance, Mama? While Uncle Thomas partners me, you should partner your son. Certainly you do not want him deficient in the social graces, for he might go to his own king's court one day, as you and Logan did."

"That is a fine idea, Elizabeth," Rosamund replied, knowing very well what her daughter was up to, but pleased at her ability to defend herself in such a skilled manner. She would need such instincts and abilities at court if she was to succeed.

Jamie, Tavis, and Edmund Hepburn snickered as Baen MacColl grinned openly at Alexander Hepburn's discomfort. The lad would learn from this experience how better to pick his battles, and when to hold his tongue. He was foolish to believe his older sister could not fight back. She was a braw lassie, was Elizabeth Meredith.

"When would I ever go to King Jamie's court?" Alexander protested. "Da! Tell my mother I do not need to know how to dance such fancy steps. I'll not mince and prance like some weak fop."

"Nay, lad," his father answered. "I think you should learn such dancing. You do not know where fate will take you one day. And when you have learned well you will teach your brothers, for one of them might need to go to court one day to make his fortune." The laird of Claven's Carn was almost laughing as he spoke, and he gave his stepdaughter a broad wink of approval for her cleverness.

The musicians entered the hall in Maybel's company. She settled them by the fire and told them to play until they were instructed to cease. Two held reed pipes, one a drum, and another cymbals. It was a most countrified grouping, but it was the best the manor could provide. The quartet began their music, and Lord Cambridge led his cousin Rosamund from the high board. They danced beautifully together, and Rosamund was amazed to find she remembered the steps of the more intricate court dances after all these years. Soon her face was flushed from her endeavors, and she was laughing. After a time Lord Cambridge signaled to the musicians to stop.

"Now it is your turn to learn, Elizabeth. Alexander, partner your mother," he called to them.

Reluctantly brother and sister made their way from the board, and Lord Cambridge signed to the players to begin anew. To her surprise Elizabeth discovered that mimicking the steps she had watched her mother dance was easy. Soon, in spite of herself, she was dancing with her uncle as if she had been doing it since early childhood. Her half brother, however, stumbled over his feet; tripped their mother, almost causing her to fall; and finally returned to his place, swearing under his breath that dancing such dances was a complete and utter waste of a man's time. It did not help that his younger brothers all took to the floor, dancing with each other in a mockery of his efforts. Soon the entire hall was laughing uproariously at their antics.

"With your permission, my lord," Baen MacColl said, asking Rosamund to dance.

"Aye," the laird replied, smiling as the Highlander led his wife to the floor.

"You dance?" Rosamund said, surprised.

"My stepmother taught me the basics," he replied. "I may be a bit clumsy with these more intricate steps, but I am of a mind to try if you are of a mind to be patient."

Rosamund nodded. "I admire your spirit of adventure, Baen Mac-Coll," she told him, leading him as they danced.

After a while Lord Cambridge cried out, "Let us exchange partners, my dears, and we shall see how well Elizabeth has learned dancing with a less skilled partner, for she will surely have a few at court." And he handed the girl off to Baen MacColl, taking Rosamund's hand in his once again. "You were always the most divine dancer, dear girl," he said. "I remember how well you did at court those many years back."

"Surely not that many years?" she teased.

"Aye, I fear it was," he replied with a smile. "I am getting old, dear girl, but I will admit to you that I have never been happier in my life. I think, however, that this may be my last visit to King Henry. Once we have obtained a suitable mate for Elizabeth I will be content to retire from the social scene and remain home."

"I do not believe that for a moment," Rosamund told him. "You cannot resist going to London at least every few years for a new wardrobe."

"Alas, dear girl, I fear I may, for my years are now beginning to tell on me, and my girth is widening so that my figure is not as fashionable as it might be," he answered her.

Baen MacColl smiled, listening to them banter back and forth. The warmth and love this family felt for one another was obviously genuine. He was almost envious.

"You are not paying attention to the steps," Elizabeth's voice broke into his thoughts. "What are you thinking about, Baen?"

"How much you all love one another," he answered her candidly.

"Aye, we do," Elizabeth agreed with a small smile.

"Which is why you will be obedient to your mother and your uncle's wishes," he noted softly.

She nodded.

"Perhaps you will find a husband at King Henry's court," he said, and saying it he felt both anger and regret.

"I doubt it, but they will not be satisfied until I am perceived to have made an effort," Elizabeth responded as softly. "The problem is that none of my sisters' offspring are suitable as an heir for me, and Mama will not give Friarsgate to one of her Scots sons. She is most adamant that Friarsgate remain an English holding, and as you know, here in the borders the lines between England and Scotland are often blurred and can change."

"Do you not want love?" he asked her. "Or children of your own?"

"I have never really considered it," Elizabeth answered candidly. "I was born at Friarsgate, the youngest of my father's surviving children. No one paid a great deal of attention to me as I grew up. Mama was called back to court. Then she visited her friend Queen Margaret at the Scots court. Then she fell in love and went away with her lover for several months. They were to wed, but he fell ill, and that was the end of it. Then it was back to King Henry's court with Philippa, who so impressed the queen that she was invited back as a maid of honor when she reached the age of twelve. Then Mama married Logan, who had long pursued her. And always there was Friarsgate to be watched over. I got into the habit of pretending it was my holding when Mama was away, or involved with my sisters, or Logan and my brothers." She laughed.

"And then at last my opportunity came, for Philippa, who was Mama's heiress, would not have Friarsgate. But I did want it, and I said so.

"If I marry, Baen, my husband will want to take my authority. I am not of a mind to give it. How could a stranger understand Friarsgate? How could another know what I know? It is not just the sheep; it is the cloth trade as well. A husband would want me to have bairns and keep the house. I have Maybel to oversee all that. It holds no interest for me. Friarsgate would be ruined in a short time. I should rather remain unwed than see all that I love destroyed."

"Perhaps you will find someone who can love Friarsgate as you do, and learn from you," he said. "Did not your father come from court? And I have heard it said that he loved Friarsgate dearly."

"My father was unique. He fell in love with my mother long before it was even considered that he be the one to wed her and protect these lands from invasion. It was a different time when my father came to Friarsgate, Baen. He was a knight who had begun his service in the household of the last king's uncle as a small child. He understood service and rendered it loyally. Now I am told by my uncle that the court is not only filled with young noblemen seeking to ingratiate themselves with the king, but the wealthy sons of tradesmen as well. A girl with a northern holding would not interest them, and if she did they would not want to come north to husband either me or my lands. And I will live nowhere but Friarsgate, and my mother would not accept any match unless the man agreed to remain here. Nor would I accept a husband who wouldn't."

"A man like that might be the perfect mate for you," Baen said, and he led Elizabeth from the floor, as the music had now ceased. "You would remain here looking after Friarsgate, and he would remain at court seeking advancement."

"He would return to court thinking himself a rich man to borrow on my lands, and even lose them," Elizabeth said. "Nay. Whatever fate may have in store for me, it is not to be found at King Henry's court."

"But you will go anyway," he remarked.

"Aye," Elizabeth said with a great sigh.

"To please your family," he continued.

"Aye, and to make them stop attempting to force me into a marriage that I neither want nor would be happy with. So I will go, and then I will return, hopefully in time for midsummer," she finished with a little smile. "I do love our summers!"

"I think you will find a husband," he told her. "You are very beautiful in this gown, Elizabeth Meredith, and you sparkle when you dance."

"If you think flattering me will gain you a better price for my sheep, you are mistaken," she teased him in an effort to cover her discomfort. No one had ever said she was beautiful, or looked into her eyes with such admiration as did Baen MacColl. It was an odd feeling that sent a shiver down her spine.

"Those pink pearls are lovely, daughter," Rosamund's voice interrupted them. "I suspect they are a gift from your uncle, are they not?" She came to stand next to them.

"Aye," Elizabeth said. "Uncle has presented me with lovely jewels for my court visit. Will you come now, Mother, and see them?"

"Indeed," Rosamund replied, and linking arms with her daughter she led her from the hall. She had been uncomfortable with the way the young Scot was looking at Elizabeth. Surely he had no pretensions in her direction. He certainly knew his place in the world. He was a bastard son. Well loved, that was obvious. But not the sort of man who was suitable for the heiress of Friarsgate. And Elizabeth, unused to suitors, would not understand whether his intentions towards her were honorable or dishonorable. Tom would have to keep a very close watch on her when they were at court. And she would advise Philippa as well of the situation. Philippa had a strong sense of propriety that had increased greatly since her elevation to the peerage. *I shall remain here at Friarsgate until Elizabeth leaves for court,* Rosamund decided. *In my desire to be a good wife to Logan, I have overlooked this youngest daughter of my beloved Owein. She has been such a good chatelaine I have not considered her ignorance where men are concerned. It is a very dangerous gap in her education.*

Baen watched them go, and silently chided himself again for speaking to Elizabeth as he very well knew he should not have. And she was too innocent in the ways of men to understand it. But she had been wondrously fair in that pink gown. She was like a perfect rose. An English rose. And he was a Scot, and entirely unsuitable in so many ways for a girl like Elizabeth Meredith. He had seen a look in her mother's eye that told him she suspected his regard for her daughter, and did not approve. Of course she would not approve. The bastard of the master of Grayhaven was not a proper match for the heiress of Friarsgate. And for the first time in his life, Baen MacColl was ashamed of his birth. And he silently despaired, for he knew he was falling in love with Elizabeth, and it could come to nothing. Nothing at all. He walked back to join the other men.

"Which of the breeds will you purchase?" the laird of Claven's Carn asked the younger man.

"The Shropshires and the cheviots," Baen replied.

"You didn't like the merinos? Their wool is the finest if you are seeking to improve your father's flocks," Logan Hepburn said.

"I have not seen the merinos," Baen answered him. "Until this moment I have never even heard of such a breed."

"That is because the merinos are not for sale," Lord Cambridge quickly said. "The first of the flock were imported from Spain several years ago at the behest of the queen. She and my cousin are old friends. It is a small flock, and we have none to spare." He smiled pleasantly at Baen. "I suspect dear Elizabeth did not bother to show them to you because she could not sell them."

"Of course," Baen answered him. "If the sheep are few, but valuable to her, it would be imprudent to sell any. Perhaps in the future when the flock is larger, and she can spare some."

"Of course," Thomas Bolton replied, smiling.

"I did not realize I was speaking out of turn," Logan Hepburn said.

"Not at all, dear boy," Lord Cambridge assured him.

There was an awkward silence, and then Alexander Hepburn said, "When are we going home, Da? Tomorrow, I hope."

"Aye, tomorrow will do, lad." He turned again to Tom Bolton. "Johnnie is watching over the holding. He cannot do a great deal of damage in the short time we have been here. I am hoping I can get that foolishness over the church out of his head, if he will understand his responsibilities for once."

"You have five sons, dear boy. If John seeks God, why do you attempt to stop him? I suspect Jeannie would have approved. She was a gentle girl herself," Thomas Bolton recalled. "Cousin Richard would gladly take him into St. Cuthbert's."

"God's foot, Tom, he's my firstborn!" Logan exploded.

"And entirely unsuitable to be the next laird of Claven's Carn," Lord Cambridge shot back. "Alexander is a far better choice, and you know it. You are just being difficult, dear boy. Having an eldest son who seeks to be a priest is not a slight to your vaunted manhood. What say you, Mata?"

Father Mata, Logan Hepburn's bastard brother, had been sitting quietly listening to the others. Now he looked at his half brother and said, "Let Johnnie go, Logan. If he seeks the priesthood, let him have it."

"I don't want people to say that I pushed my firstborn aside for Rosamund's sons," the laird of Claven's Carn said quietly.

"Those who know us will rejoice in your generosity towards Johnnie. Those who do not will say what they will say," the priest responded. "You endanger your own immortal soul by keeping from the priesthood a son who seeks it."

"Will you speak with Prior Richard?" Logan Hepburn finally said.

Father Mata nodded. "As soon as Elizabeth had departed for London, I will go to the abbey and intercede for my nephew. Tell him when you return to Claven's Carn, Logan, and heal the breach between you as quickly as possible," he advised.

The laird nodded. "I will," he said.

The men sat talking for a while longer, and then with Thomas Bolton going first they began to depart the hall for their beds.

In the morning the laird and his sons rode out for their home, while Rosamund remained behind that she might see her daughter off on her own journey. She involved Elizabeth in the packing of her trunks so that her time with Baen MacColl was reduced to almost nothing. She recruited Maybel, and together the two instructed young Nancy in the many aspects of her duties. Nancy had a way with hair, and showed Rosamund the different styles she could do, using Elizabeth as her paradigm.

Only in the evening was Baen MacColl in evidence, and Rosamund was pleased to see he kept his distance while remaining most polite. Obviously the lad did know his place, and she was relieved. Elizabeth could not be allowed to fall in love with an unsuitable man. And the young Scot should not fall in love with her, lest he be driven to foolish actions. Bride stealing was not a thing of the past in the borders between England and Scotland.

And finally the morning of April first dawned. And the day was bright with sun. Elizabeth had hardly been able to sleep the previous night. It was not that she was excited about her impending journey. Indeed, if anything she was fearful, and fear was not an emotion that came readily to her. It made her irritable that her stomach was in an uproar, and that her bowels had emptied three times after she had risen. Her mother was chattering. Maybel and young Nancy were chattering. They sounded like nothing more than the sparrows in the ivy that covered the outside of the house. Elizabeth wanted to scream with her aggravation.

"You are certain the little trunk has everything your mistress will need on the journey?" Rosamund asked Nancy for the tenth time.

"Yes, my lady," Nancy responded patiently.

"The boar's-bristle brush for her teeth?"

"Yes, my lady."

"The woolen stockings?"

"Yes, my lady."

"An extra flannel petticoat?"

"Yes, my lady."

"Mama, Nancy has proved most capable. Do not worry," Elizabeth said. "We have both checked everything several times now. I think we can do no more."

"Your jewel case?" Rosamund demanded. "Where is your jewel case?"

"In the trunk with my bodices and sleeves," Elizabeth said. "Mama, you will make me sick if you do not stop. I make this journey to please you and for no other reason. Surely you understand that?"

"You must come back with the hope of a good match, Elizabeth," her mother said.

"Yes, Mama," was the response.

"You are just nervous," Rosamund soothed her daughter.

"I must go out and walk in the meadow," Elizabeth said suddenly.

"The sun is not even up yet!" Rosamund cried.

"It will be, and I would see it rise today. It will be weeks before I see the sunrise from my own fields again," Elizabeth answered her, and, turning on her heel, she ran from the chamber. Outside, the air was cool and fresh. The sky above her was clear and light, the hint of the sunrise showing just over the hills. In the meadows surrounding the house the sheep were browsing. Looking at it, Elizabeth began to weep softly. She didn't want to leave. She wouldn't leave! She didn't care if it upset her mother or not. She would not go. Friarsgate was her strength. She needed to be here.

"Get your greeting over and done with, lass," Baen MacColl's voice advised her quietly. "Then gather your strength and go forth as you must. You are no coward, Elizabeth Meredith."

Turning about, Elizabeth threw herself at him, and his arms closed about her. He held her tightly while she sobbed and sobbed. Then, as his big hand smoothed down her blond head in a gesture of comfort, her weeping slowly abated. He said nothing, allowing her the time to regain her dignity and her courage. When she stirred against him he released his embrace. Elizabeth looked up at him, her eyelashes, dark in contrast to her hair, in clumps.

"Thank you," she said softly. And then, turning, she walked back to the house.

# Chapter 4

Lord Cambridge had quite forgotten how long and tedious the trip from Friarsgate south could be. But then Elizabeth's ingenuousness over so many new sights began to infect him with his old enthusiasm. He remembered the first time he had traveled the route with Elizabeth's mother, Rosamund, in his charge, and then later her two older daughters. The days began to pass quickly. Suddenly, one afternoon they found themselves riding up the drive to Thomas Bolton's London house where an elegant female figure was waiting to greet them.

"Well," Philippa, Countess of Witton, said, looking at her youngest sister, "you certainly look respectable enough, Bessie."

"You will remember, Philippa, that I am Elizabeth, not Bessie. Not even our mother calls me that any longer." She shook the dust from her burgundy velvet riding skirts. "Are we to go in? Or do you wish to remain outside so all may partake of our tender reunion? How long has it been now since we have seen each other?"

"Eight years," Philippa snapped.

"And you are as beautiful as ever, dear girl," Lord Cambridge said, attempting to ease the tension already building between the sisters. "How do you do it, and yet have those fine children of yours?" He kissed her on both cheeks.

"Uncle, you are ever the scamp," Philippa replied, but she was smiling. Thomas Bolton was responsible for her happiness, and she could never forget it. She adored him, and she always had. Hopefully he could do something for her youngest sister. It was obvious that Bessie—or Elizabeth, as she now preferred to be called—was still a difficult creature.

71

"Thank you so much," Lord Cambridge said as they entered Bolton House, "for meeting us in London, dear girl. I know you meant to entertain us at Brierewode, but I so feared not arriving in time to get down to Greenwich for the May celebrations. Did you bring your little daughter, my pet? Another little girl for me to spoil." He chuckled.

"Nay, Uncle, you will have to come to Brierewode if you wish to meet this new relation of yours. I did not wish to travel with an infant and her wet nurse," Philippa replied. "There is so much involved when one travels with children. I am going to Greenwich to enjoy May as well. Hugh Edmund was left at home too. Next year he is to go into Princess Mary's household as a page," she said proudly.

"And will we see the others?" Thomas Bolton asked.

"Oh, yes! We have been so fortunate in obtaining positions for Henry and Owein, Uncle. You know how important these things are if one is to advance within the court. And there is the matter of marriages to be made too. Henry, of course, will succeed his father one day, but it cannot hurt him to be well-known and respected within court circles. His brothers, of course, have not the advantage of his inheritance, which is why it is even more important that they succeed," Philippa said. "My eldest sons are already perfect little courtiers, Uncle."

Elizabeth, in a great show of restraint, swallowed her observation of her sister's ambitions. Children, she believed, belonged at home with their parents. Instead she looked about her. They had been brought into a long hall with windows overlooking the river Thames. It was very beautiful. While she had not wanted to leave Friarsgate, she had to admit that she had enjoyed the trip so far. She had never been any farther than Carlisle, and then only once. The countryside and the towns they had passed through on their way south were a revelation to her. And now London. She had already decided that she didn't like London.

"My sister is very quiet," Philippa noted. "I hope this is not her usual manner, for the court prefers lively girls, Uncle, as you well know."

"I think you will find I am very lively, sister, perhaps even too lively for your tastes," Elizabeth spoke up, "but I am tired now, and wish to rest. I have also learned that it is better to observe new surroundings and get one's bearings before leaping into the fray. I am a careful and practical creature, I fear. Do you think I shall find such a man at court to love and wed?" She was baiting Philippa, and Philippa knew it.

"You will not be an easy girl to match, Elizabeth, but we will do our very best, I promise you," the Countess of Witton answered her sister. "But when I was the Friarsgate heiress there were none who would accept me or my northern estates. Why is it that you have not found a suitable young man near you?"

"Society in Cumbria is scant at best, as you well know, sister," Elizabeth answered. "And when one has my responsibilities there is little time for merriment."

"Was there not a Neville you might wed? Certainly Robert has cousins aplenty," Philippa remarked. She had changed little over the past few years. Perhaps her waistline had thickened a trifle with her four children, but the auburn hair was as thick and rich as it had always been, and her hazel eyes were as bright with interest as they had ever been.

"I will admit that Rob dragged several of his cousins before me, but I did not find them suitable. All of them were most obvious in their desire to gain control of Friarsgate. None of them could have managed the estate or the cloth trade. And most of them had debts of one kind or another that I was not of a mind to pay to gain a husband," Elizabeth replied. "One of them even attempted to seduce me in order to have his way."

"You did not ever tell me that, dear girl!" Thomas Bolton exclaimed. "Dare I ask what happened to him?"

Elizabeth grinned wickedly. "Let us say it was necessary to carry the fellow from my presence. I understand he kept to his bed for several days afterwards, and then said the most unkind things about me. I was not troubled with any more Nevilles after that."

Philippa was forced to smile at this revelation. "I am glad you are wise enough to know how to deal with a seducer, sister. You will, I fear, meet many at court interested in your wealth, but not in Friarsgate."

William Smythe entered the hall of Bolton House in the company of another man and a boy. "Master Althorp is here, and he has brought your new wardrobe, my lord." He stood waiting for Lord Cambridge to give his instructions.

"Take the tailor and his lad to my apartments, dear Will. I will join you shortly," Thomas Bolton said. "And tell Nancy to unpack her mistress's gowns. Althorp must look at them and correct any deficiencies in the fashion for us. We will be leaving for Greenwich in a few days."

"So Uncle," Philippa teased him as William Smythe and his companions left the hall, "you cannot resist a new wardrobe, eh?"

"My dear girl," Thomas Bolton said, "can you imagine me appearing at court in anything less than the latest fashions? It would be absolutely unthinkable." He chuckled. He then looked across to hall to where Elizabeth had settled herself in a window seat overlooking the river. Her blond head was nodding towards her shoulder. "Be kind, Philippa," he said to the Countess of Witton. "It is all really a great deal for Elizabeth to take in, for she had never before left the north. You were still half-grown when you first set eyes on Londontown, dear girl. Your sister will be twenty-two next month. She is not a child, but neither is she a woman."

"She is beautiful," Philippa said. "The fairest of us all, I must admit. And she wears her clothing well, but I sense a deep reluctance in her to even be here, Uncle. And how will she behave at the court? She was an impetuous girl, as I recall, and one apt to say the first thing that came into her head. Things are not now as they once were."

"Tell me," he said quietly. "I want to hear it from you before Master Althorp begins his litany of gossip. What is happening with the king and the queen?"

"My poor lady," Philippa began. "We all know that the king has had his little friends, but until now he has behaved in a most discreet manner. He wants his marriage declared invalid so he may wed a younger woman who will give him a son. The cardinal was his ally in this, but when he failed the king he fell from power. Everyone knew that Wolsey would eventually be destroyed. He had few friends, I fear. As much as I love Queen Katherine even I am beginning to feel she is being very stubborn in regard to this matter."

"I understand her desire to want to protect Princess Mary's position. To have the princess declared a bastard would ruin any chances of her making a good marriage. And the princess is an innocent party in all of this," Lord Cambridge acknowledged. "What says Rome about the matter?"

"The pope has agreed to say that the previous pope was in error when he gave the king and the princess of Aragon, his brother's widow, a dispensation to wed. He is willing to grant a divorce to the king which at the same time would preserve Princess Mary's status as the king's legitimately born daughter, and also as his heir until a male child is born."

" 'Tis quite a reasonable solution," Lord Cambridge said. "But what arrangements will be made for the queen?"

"Under such an arrangement the queen would enter a convent to live out the remainder of her days," Philippa explained. "But she would live out that time in the utmost comfort, for the king has said he will be most generous in the matter of her support. And she may choose her own place of refuge, either here or in Spain."

Lord Cambridge nodded. "There is precedent for such an arrangement, and there would be no shame in her agreeing to it."

"But Queen Katherine will not countenance this arrangement. And the king will persist in his efforts to remove her from his life."

"Perhaps if the queen were to be replaced by the French Princess Renee she could be convinced. The French girl is the cardinal's choice," Tom Bolton noted.

"But the king is besotted by the younger Boleyn girl. I have never seen him behave in such a manner as he now does," Philippa almost wailed. "While the queen still appears at public functions like May Day, Easter, and the Christmas courts, her presence is embarrassing, for she is virtually ignored. It is Mistress Anne who presides over the court now, and the king will have it no other way, Uncle. My family and I are put into a most difficult position, for you know our ties with and our devotion to the queen. My two older sons have coveted places within the court, Henry as a page in the king's household, Owein in Norfolk's household. If we incur the royal disfavor my sons' careers could be ruined. But how can I desert Queen Katherine now, when she has been so good to me, Uncle?"

"This is a far more serious situation than I had been led to believe, dear girl," Thomas Bolton said gravely. He sighed. "I see no other course for you than to continue to serve the queen while avoiding the wrath of both the king and Mistress Anne. This means you must remain silent no matter your outrage. Can you do that, Philippa?"

"I have to, for my lads' sake," she answered him. "Now I am beginning to understand my mother better, Uncle, which would amuse her, I am certain, if she but knew how I feel. She protected us and worked for our happiness even as I do for my sons'."

"And what is Crispin's position in all of this?" Lord Cambridge inquired.

Philippa laughed. "Brierewode is his domain, and the court is mine. He has said that as long as I do not endanger the family he trusts in my judgment. He is a model mate for me, isn't he?"

Thomas Bolton chortled. "Aye, you are fortunate in each other, dear girl. Well, you have given me much to consider. Does the king know we shall be coming to Greenwich, and are we welcome at court?"

"Aye. Henry told him of your impending visit, and that you would bring the last of Rosamund's daughters to present to him. My son said the king was delighted, and says you are always welcome in his presence, and that he looks forward to meeting Elizabeth."

"Good! Good! Then that is settled, and all that remains is for our garments to be approved and improved by Master Althorp before our trip down to Greenwich. We will go by barge, of course. When does the court leave? The thirtieth, as usual?"

"Aye, Uncle," Philippa answered him.

"I will go now and greet my tailor. I have kept him waiting long enough," Thomas Bolton said. "See to your sister. I think you must take her to her chamber. If she will not wake up have one of the footmen carry her."

"There is no one in the north for her, Uncle?" the young countess asked again.

He shook his head. "None, and Friarsgate must have an heir for the next generation. Your mother is most upset about it." Then, turning, he left the hall and hurried up to his apartments, where William Smythe, Master Althorp, and his assistant awaited him. "Althorp!" he greeted the tailor effusively, shaking his hand. "What wonders have you fashioned for me this trip, my good fellow?"

"We have laid everything out here in the dayroom and your bed-chamber, my lord," the tailor said. "The newest trend is much slashings on full sleeves this year, the sleeves with circular shoulders, and high necklines. Both doublets and jerkins are being wrapped over in the front. Wine and black are the colors favored for a gentleman. And, of course, silk and velvet trimmings on the breeches," Master Althorp concluded.

"Thank God I have you, Althorp. None of this has filtered into the north. My tailor there is adequate, but not the genius that you are with fashion and fabric," Lord Cambridge said. "I can always rely on you to keep me looking perfect."

"I note that your lordship has perhaps gained a bit of girth since our last meeting three years ago," the tailor said.

"Do you think so?" Lord Cambridge sounded genuinely surprised.

"I do, my lord, and we both know the key to a perfect appearance is a well-tailored and well-fitting garment," Master Althorp replied. "If you will allow my helper to assist your lordship in disrobing we will have a fitting. These minor adjustments should not take long, and I am assuming you are leaving London with the court on the thirtieth."

"Indeed we are," Thomas Bolton said. Then, "Will, see that young Nancy has her mistress's gowns out and displayed so Master Althorp may see them when we are finished. Put everything in the dayroom. I believe my dear Elizabeth is already asleep."

"Yes, my lord," William Smythe said, and hurried out.

"So, Althorp," Lord Cambridge said, "I understand his majesty would rid himself of an old queen to take a young one. Tell me all, and spare nothing of the most intimate details, for I know you know them all." He stood quietly as the young tailor's assistant helped him from his outer garments and into his new ones.

"Well, my lord," Master Althorp said as he began to note the adjustments he must make, "it is all true, and while the cardinal wanted a French princess for the king, I can tell you that the king would have none of it. His heart is set on Mistress Boleyn. And now that the cardinal is disgraced and dying, I have heard, none can keep the king in check, and the Howards are an ambitious family, though you did not hear me say it."

"And what is she like? Mistress Anne?" Lord Cambridge wanted to know. "As round, soft, and fair as was her sister, Mary?"

"Nay, my lord. She is nothing like Mistress Mary at all. She is tall, slender, and very elegant in a most French way. I have never seen a more fashionable woman at the court. All the young girls are copying her manner of dress. She has the most beautiful long and thick dark hair. Her eyes are almond shaped, and dark too. Her skin is perhaps a bit sallow for certain colors like apple green and saffron, which have been popular. She favors bright, clear colors that flatter her best. I would not call her beautiful, but rather intriguing and exotic. And the king is besotted by her, there is no doubt. It is said she will not go to his bed, for she will not be compared with her sister, who whored for little advantage to herself or her family. Her Howard relations expect more of Mistress Anne, and they may well get it. It is said the old duke himself directs her behavior."

"Interesting," Thomas Bolton noted. He looked at the sleeves on the doublet he was now wearing. "My dear Althorp, so many slashings?" He turned to look questioningly at Will Smythe who had just hurried back into the room.

" 'Tis fashion, my lord," the tailor replied.

"It seems a bit excessive even for me," Lord Cambridge noted, "but I do like the silk beneath the velvet. And the bright blue with the black is pure genius!"

"Thank you, my lord."

"What do they say of Mistress Boleyn?" Lord Cambridge inquired casually. "Is she charming, or quiet like the more recent mistress I heard of in my northern eyrie? What was her name now? Something quite outrageous, as I recall."

" 'Twas the Countess of Langford, Blaze Wyndham," the tailor answered. "A lovely woman. Not only discreet, although everyone knew the king was swiving her, but very deferential and polite to the queen. She never used her position for personal gain, I am told. Quite unusual in a royal mistress. Nay, Mistress Boleyn is nothing like Blaze Wyndham. She is very lively, and clever, and has a quick tongue. She has attracted quite an amusing coterie of young courtiers to her side. It is said of her that she is quite high-strung, my lord, and has a bad temper; but there are always those ready to speak badly of any, especially women like Mistress Boleyn. She makes enemies as easily as she makes friends. The cardinal never approved of her. 'Tis said she vowed to overcome Wolsey and have her revenge on him for taking Northumberland's heir away from her. They had planned to marry, but the king wanted her, and Wolsey was ever his loyal servant. He got the duke to claim his son was precontracted to another girl, and saw them married so the king might be free to pursue Mistress Boleyn. Disgrace was how the cardinal's loyal service was rewarded, and Mistress Boleyn has indeed had her revenge upon him."

"She sounds like a most complex young woman," Lord Cambridge noted.

"Indeed, my lord, a fair assessment," the tailor said. "We are finished now. If you will approve the garments I shall return them to my shop and have the alterations done. We will bring them back to you in two days, which is in time for your valet to see to the packing, my lord. I trust that will be satisfactory."

"Most, Althorp. Now if you will go with Will and view my dear Elizabeth's garments to be certain they are every bit as fashionable as they should be, I would appreciate it. If she is sleeping, as I suspect, you will not see her. The colors have been chosen to flatter her, for she is blond and fair."

"Of course, my lord," the tailor said. Then he followed William Smythe from the chamber and down the hallway.

When Will returned he told Lord Cambridge that Elizabeth's gowns passed the tailor's muster, but for some minor alterations that could be easily managed without removing any of the garments. "Standing collars are the fashion for the ladies, my lord. Master Althorp will have several made to match the gowns, along with the rebatos necessary to hold them up. Other than that everything is in order, thanks to Lady Philippa. Her fashion sense was, as always, perfect."

"Excellent!" Lord Cambridge said, and then, "If you will look in your room, dear boy, you will find several new suits that Althorp has made for you. You need no alterations, as you never change. And you will find a new gold chain I will expect you to wear, as well as a pearl-drop earring that is particularly fine. I cannot treat myself, dear Will, without treating you. I do not know what I would do without you. Now go and tell Garr that I am ready to be dressed for the evening."

"Thank you, my lord! At once!" William Smythe said.

Thomas Bolton smiled and, reaching out, patted his secretary's hand. "Dear Will," was all he said, and then he waved him off. He was already looking forward to joining the court. Perhaps tomorrow he would venture to Richmond, where he knew the king was now in residence, and announce his arrival. He would not remain long, and one of his old suits would do for that brief visit. But he did not intend introducing his lovely charge until they were at Greenwich. Let the king's appetite be whetted to meet Mistress Meredith, the last of Rosamund's daughters. He would be quite surprised, for of the three sisters it was said that Elizabeth was the most like her father, with her fair hair and hazel-green eyes. She was quite different from her auburn-haired mother and sisters.

But in the matter of the queen Lord Cambridge was not quite certain how to proceed. He could not ignore Katherine, but neither did he consider it wise to involve Elizabeth with her under the circumstances. He would have to introduce Elizabeth to her, for Rosamund, not realizing the scope of the breach between Henry and Katherine, would be distressed if he did not. And whatever the difficulties between the royal couple, Katherine was still England's queen. But he would attempt to see that there was no other contact between the out-of-favor queen and his charge. He needed the right husband for Elizabeth, and to accomplish that impossible task he needed the king's favor. Yes, he thought to himself. It would be a difficult balancing act, given Rosamund's long association with the queen, but he knew his cousin would understand his reasoning when he wrote her, which he intended doing this very night.

Their journey had been a pleasant one, but for the April rains that had begun three days after they had departed Friarsgate. Still, they had ridden hard those first three days, and it had allowed them to reach London in plenty of time for their business here. He was surprised that

Elizabeth had become so tired when they arrived, for she was an active young woman. But perhaps the excitement of it all had overcome her. He ate with Philippa that evening, having sent a tray up to Elizabeth's chambers. She sent back her thanks with young Nancy.

In late morning the following day Lord Cambridge, clad in a suit of Tudor green, a flat cap decorated with ostrich tips on his head, a jeweled codpiece and matching pouch hanging from his girdle, departed Bolton House in the smaller of his two barges for Richmond Palace, where he knew the king would be in residence these few days before he left for Greenwich. Giving his name as he stepped from his little transport, he was surprised to find young Henry St. Clair waiting for him.

"Greetings, my lord," the royal page said. "The king expected you might come today, as my mother told him of your arrival. I was sent to wait for you and escort you to him when you came." He bowed neatly.

"How old are you, young St. Clair?" Lord Cambridge asked.

"I shall be nine on the first of May, my lord," was the reply.

"Astounding! How long have you been in the king's service?" Thomas Bolton followed along with the boy.

"Like my maternal grandfather, my lord, I have served the Tudors since I was six," was the proud answer. "It is an honor to continue in my family's tradition. I hope someday to have a son who will follow in our footsteps."

"God's nightshirt!" Thomas Bolton murmured. "You are a serious lad, I see."

"I am fortunate to have obtained such an honored position in my sovereign's household, my lord," came the reply.

"Which your dear mother has undoubtedly told you over and over again, I am quite certain," Lord Cambridge said.

"Yes, my lord," the boy answered, and there was a humorous lilt to his voice.

"Thank God you have some of your father about you, lad! I feared you were all your mother," the older man told Henry Thomas St. Clair, and the boy flashed him a grin.

The king was in his privy chamber, to Lord Cambridge's delight. He recognized several of his majesty's more constant companions, Charles Brandon among them.

"My lord." Thomas Bolton bowed low.

"Thomas! It is good to see you once again. What brings you to court?"

"Did not the Countess of Witton tell your majesty? I have brought her youngest sister to meet you. We plan to join the May revels, my liege. Elizabeth Meredith has never been out of the north. She has scarce been off her estates," Lord Cambridge explained to the king. "I have the tedious task of seeking a husband for her."

"How old is she?" the king demanded to know.

"She is facing her twenty-second birthday, my liege," Lord Cambridge replied.

"And not wed yet?" The king was surprised. "Rosamund's two older daughters have long been wed. What is the matter with this one?"

"Nothing, my lord, except her passion is for Friarsgate, even more so than was her mother's. I believe she would die a maid before allowing it to fall into the wrong hands," Thomas Bolton explained. "There is no one in the north who suits her, or who would be suitable. So at Rosamund's behest I have brought Elizabeth Meredith south to join the court and see if there is a young man who would suit her."

"We will think on it," the king said. "Where is the girl now?"

"Recovering from our long journey, my liege. I thought not to bring her to court until we reached Greenwich," Lord Cambridge said.

The king nodded. "She will be welcome, and I shall look forward to meeting her. Is she like her sisters and her mother, Thomas?"

"Nay, my lord. She is like her father, Owein Meredith, God assoil his good soul," said Lord Cambridge as he crossed himself. "She is fair and blond."

"I have a taste for dark hair these days, Thomas," the king remarked.

"So I have heard it said, my lord," was the reply.

The king burst out laughing. "You have been talking to Althorp, I have not a doubt. If he were not the best tailor in England I should have lopped his head off long ago, but no one can fashion a doublet like he can, eh, Thomas?" And King Henry VIII laughed harder. "Perhaps I should cut his tongue out, for he needs it not to sew, but then I should not learn half the things I learn of those who people my court. He is valuable to me in many ways, I must admit."

"He speaks kindly of you, my liege," Lord Cambridge assured the king.

"He dare not speak otherwise"—the king chuckled—"eh, Will Somers?" He looked to his fool, who sat by his knee.

"I shall have to consult with Margot," the king's fool said, looking at the small monkey on his shoulder. "She knows far more than I do, Hal." The king's favorite fool, Somers had certain privileges that others close to the king did not.

"Does she still bite?" Lord Cambridge inquired of the fool.

"Indeed, my lord, she does, but she is most particular of the fingers she nips." The fool chuckled, and he tickled the little monkey beneath her chin as it chattered its approval, and then nestled closer to Will Somers's neck.

The interview was over, and Lord Cambridge bowed to the king, saying, "I shall look forward to seeing your majesty again at Greenwich." He backed from the privy chamber as the king waved an acknowledgment of his departure. It had gone well, Thomas Bolton thought. It was almost as if the years between his last visit and this one did not exist. But they did. And much had changed at court with Wolsey gone. He debated whether he should pay his respects to the queen, and decided against it. He needed to know the lay of the land better. He could not involve himself or Elizabeth in the politics of whatever was happening between the king and the queen, and Mistress Anne Boleyn.

But he decided to remain at Richmond for a few hours. He greeted old friends, listened to gossip, and just before he left he finally saw the lady at the center of the scandal. She was a tall, slender girl with sharp features, but she was indeed, as all the talk he had heard that day, the most elegant creature he had ever seen. Beautiful as Elizabeth was? Nay. Anne Boleyn could not be called beautiful, but there was an aura about her that was absolutely mesmerizing. Unable to help himself, he stared.

And as if she sensed the admiration directed at her, Mistress Anne turned and met his glance, her dark, almond-shaped eyes taking him in slowly and carefully. She leaned her head to speak to one of her companions. Then, fixing him with her gaze again, she said, "You are Lord Cambridge, I am told."

Thomas Bolton bowed. "I am," he said.

"I had heard it said that there was no one who visited the court who dressed so fashionably, my lord," Anne Boleyn remarked. "How is it you live in the north, yet your garments are so à la mode?"

"I would consider it a deficiency, madame, to appear at court otherwise," he told her with a small smile. "If the truth be told, this garment is not quite up to my standards, but Master Althorp is not yet finished with my new wardrobe. I had not meant to come to court until it had arrived at Greenwich, but I could not resist presenting myself before the king today. I have brought my cousin's youngest daughter, an heiress, for her first visit."

"Ah, you are shopping for a husband for the girl," Anne said boldly. "Well, there are plenty here who will be happy to take a rich wife."

"But Elizabeth seeks not a man like that, madame, but rather one who will husband not only her, but her estates of Friarsgate," Lord Cambridge explained. "Any man who wants her must live in the north."

"Well, that should narrow the field," Sir Thomas Wyatt, who was Anne's relation, said. "What think you, coz? Do we know such a fellow?" He was among Mistress Boleyn's boon companions, as was her brother, George.

Anne ignored him. "I hope Mistress Elizabeth will enjoy her stay, my lord," she said. "The court is a most fascinating place."

"Made more so by your presence," Thomas Bolton heard himself say, to his surprise. Then, bowing, he moved away. What on earth had prompted him to voice such a thought? Was it some instinct that this slight girl would be a power to be reckoned with one day? He shook his head and hurried to reach his barge. He needed to go home and consider everything he had seen and heard today.

He found Elizabeth walking about in his riverside garden as he came up the stone steps from the barge quay. "Dear girl," he exclaimed with a smile, "are you well rested? And where is your sister? I have just come from Richmond, where I paid my respects to his majesty, and I have even spoken with Mistress Boleyn. I must tell you, dear girl, she is a most interesting lady. I did not, however, visit the queen. I do not yet understand the full measure of what is happening, but from all I have heard the poor woman is indeed out of favor, and being virtually ignored except by a few old and loyal friends."

"Then your day has been a productive one, Uncle. I am glad. The sooner we conclude this visit and return home, the happier I will be," Elizabeth said.

"Have you and Philippa quarreled, dear girl?" he asked her.

Elizabeth sighed deeply. "I have held my tongue, Uncle, though she tries me sorely. I understand that my sister loves the court, and being here makes her happy. But I love Friarsgate, and being there makes me happy. Why can she not understand it? All day I have listened to her cry the glories of the society she inhabits while carping on how backwards our upbringing was in that cold northern clime, as she persists in calling it."

"You are wise to say naught, dear girl," he told her. "She would only argue her point harder. I understand that you love your home, and we are here but for one purpose: to attempt to find you a suitable mate who will love Friarsgate as well as he loves you. If after a reasonable period of time that man is not available to us, then we shall return north. But if we do, dear girl, then we must actively seek a mate for you there, which I suspect we might have done with more vigor previously. But 'tis water beneath London Bridge now. We are here, and you should enjoy the revelries we will encounter. There is no better month than May, except perhaps December, in which to visit court, dear girl."

"I must take your word for it, Uncle," Elizabeth said dispiritedly.

"I found the Boleyn girl rather interesting," he continued in an attempt to intrigue her, for Elizabeth enjoyed a puzzle.

"Why?" He had piqued her interest. "Philippa says she is no better than her older sister, and that Mary Boleyn is a whore who had the king's child."

"I think Philippa's words stem from her deep loyalty to Queen Katherine," Lord Cambridge said. "And now she must avoid any show of that loyalty lest she endanger her sons' careers. She wants everything back the way it was. But time does not stand still for any of us, Elizabeth. Philippa will have to come to terms with what is happening, and her first loyalty must be to the sovereign. And her son does serve the lady's uncle. Now, as for Mistress Anne, I found her intelligent and, while the most fashionable woman I have ever seen, a lady I would hardly consider a coquette or a wanton."

"But the king has a wife," Elizabeth said.

"And no male heir," Thomas Bolton reminded her. "And that wife is old and dried-up now, dear girl."

"What is so wrong with a woman ruling England, Uncle?" Elizabeth demanded to know. "Is not England just a larger version of my estates? And I rule Friarsgate quite well, do I not?"

"The last woman to claim England put the country into civil war for years," Lord Cambridge said. "A queen must have a king. Princess Mary's husband will come from either France or Spain, and more likely Spain, if Queen Katherine has anything to say about it, which she will. Even if a female inherits, dear girl, her husband will take precedence over the land. Would you have a foreigner ruling England? Better the princess be queen of France or Spain, with a brother ruling England. But Queen Katherine cannot give the king a living son. She is incapable of giving him any child now. I do not know if you heard your sister yesterday, for it appeared you were falling asleep, but there is a reasonable solution to the problem. Unfortunately Queen Katherine will not take it. I am afraid I find that most unreasonable of her, dear girl."

"I heard," Elizabeth said. "It was just before I nodded off. It cannot be easy for the queen, Uncle. She loves her husband, Philippa says. She prays for him daily."

"A most devout woman, to be sure," Lord Cambridge agreed, "but if she did indeed love Henry Tudor she would want what is best for him. He needs a son. She cannot provide one. She should step aside. But she will not, I think, for Katherine of Aragon is a very proud lady. And for all her Christian piety she cannot help but be angry at her husband, and want to punish him for his neglect of her. What better way than to refuse his petition to dissolve their marriage so her daughter may one day inherit, and not some other woman's son?"

"I never knew that love could be so cruel," Elizabeth said. Then, changing the subject, she remarked, "Uncle, your garden is already filled with flowers, while at home the plants were just beginning to show faint signs of life. And your statuary is certainly quite unique." Her hazel-green eyes twinkled.

"Italian marble," he replied. "I had them imported years ago. In the garden at Greenwich, however, you will find both male and female figures represented."

"When will we go to Greenwich, Uncle?" Elizabeth asked.

"In two days, dear girl. We shall go by the river with the rest of the court. I mean to send my dear Will down tomorrow to see to the opening of the house. He must take some of the servants with him to see to the cleaning and airing. You will adore Greenwich, dear girl, and my house is next to the palace. I cannot tell you how many have offered for it over the years, but I have refused. I am perfectly happy to rent it out when I do not need it, but I will keep it and one day give it to Philippa, as I will this house. Banon and I have discussed it. She does not want it, but to have a home in London and at Greenwich will mean much to the Countess of Witton and her clan."

They walked together arm in arm in the spring sunshine as they returned to the house. The breeze off the river had a damp warmth to it.

"You are so generous to us all, Uncle," Elizabeth said.

"I would be generous to you as well, dear girl, but there seems to be nothing I have been able to do for you. A few trinkets and escorting you to court is no more than I did for your older sisters. Yet they will inherit my properties one day, for these are things that they want. You, it would seem, want for nothing as long as you possess your beloved Friarsgate," Lord Cambridge noted. "I find I am distraught by this knowledge."

"Then give me something I do want, uncle," Elizabeth said.

"What?" he asked her, curious, for of all of Rosamund's daughters, Elizabeth was the least acquisitive.

"A favor," she said. "There could come a time when I want something that perhaps seems wrong to everyone around me. If that time ever came then I would want your support no matter your own feelings in the matter. Please do not ask me what I want for I do not know, Uncle. But if that time ever comes, will you promise me you will stand with me?"

He thought it an odd request. What could the sensible Elizabeth

Meredith ever seek to have that might gain everyone else's disapproval? But he nodded to her. "You have my word on it, Elizabeth," he promised her. "If the day comes that you need my support, I will give it to you no matter my own sentiments."

"Then I am content, Uncle," she told him.

Two days later, on the thirtieth of April, the court departed Richmond for Greenwich. Lord Cambridge's barge came down from Bolton House on the edge of the city to join the royal party. Philippa was in her element, waving to all of her friends as they went. She was garbed in lime green, one of the new fashionable colors this year. If their barge drew next to someone she knew, she would point at Elizabeth and say, "My younger sister has come to court." Heads would nod, and Elizabeth would acknowledge it with a nod of her own head.

The king had Mistress Boleyn with him in the royal barge. The queen had been forbidden to come to Greenwich this May. She had been sent to her favorite house at Woodstock with the few ladies she was still allowed. Without her presence the entire atmosphere of the court was lightened. Even Philippa was relieved, for it meant she would not have to choose sides this time. It was becoming more difficult to keep out of the terrible divide between the royal couple. Secretly the Countess of Witton agreed with her uncle. The queen had been offered a perfect and graceful exit with no harm to her child. Philippa didn't understand why she would not take it. But Katherine of Aragon had been her mother's friend, and Philippa had been in her service at one time. There was love and loyalty between her family and the queen.

"Is that the palace?" Elizabeth's voice broke her older sister's reverie. She gazed, impressed, at the fine brick buildings along the river.

"Aye," Philippa said. "Lovely, isn't it? And there is Uncle Thomas's house nearby. There is a gate from his garden into the royal gardens. You will find it most convenient. Tomorrow is May Day, and it is the king's favorite holiday. We will celebrate the day long, and it is just the beginning of this holiday month. We must retire early if we are to be there at the beginning of it all," she said enthusiastically.

Their barge turned towards the shore and the stone quay that belonged to Lord Cambridge's house. It bumped against the dock, where servants were already waiting to tie it fast. They were all helped out and began to move towards the house. Elizabeth stopped to view a statue in the garden of a young girl and a creature that seemed to be half-boy and half-goat. The creature had clasped the girl tightly to him, obviously catching her in flight. One hand clasped a round stone breast. And the creature's male member was quite visible as it probed between the flowing draperies of the maiden's gown from the rear. The face of the creature was avid with his lust. The girl's mouth was open wide in a shriek.

Elizabeth raised an eyebrow, turning to her uncle. "Aye, these statues are quite different from the garden in London, Uncle," she said.

"Uncle's statuary is quite disgraceful," Philippa said primly.

"How so, dear girl?" Thomas Bolton asked, knowing Elizabeth would have a clever answer, and enjoying the gasp of outrage from Philippa.

"The statues in your city garden are passive, while the statues here seem to be most active," Elizabeth replied with a small smile. Then she turned to her sister. "I am not shocked, Philippa, for while I am yet a maid, I am a farmer. I have seen all of this activity in the animal kingdom, and have stumbled upon several of my people in similar situations. I think it is better to know what to expect of marriage before the fact rather than after it." And she patted her oldest sister's hand.

"Elizabeth! Do not say you are a farmer! You are the heiress to Friarsgate, a great northern manor, not some milkmaid!" Philippa cried.

Thomas Bolton swallowed his laughter, and only chuckled.

"I apologize, sister, for speaking the truth. I shall attempt to be more circumspect in the future. But I would have no prospective husband believing that I shall sit in my hall and weave at my loom while the bairns play about my feet," Elizabeth said.

"Uncle! Reason with her!" Philippa said, distraught.

"Is Crispin planning on joining us, dear girl?" Thomas Bolton said instead.

"I do not know," came the answer. "The responsibilities of Brierewode weigh heavily upon him. If everything he needs to do and to oversee is done in time, perhaps he will come to join us towards the middle of the month. A marriage is a partnership, Elizabeth. Crispin does his part, and that is why I come to court when I can to keep up our connections for the sake of our children. Being the Countess of Witton is not all frivolity and fetes, as you well know, Uncle. But Elizabeth should understand that God created husband and wife to serve their common good," Philippa concluded.

"I find your instruction most interesting, sister," Elizabeth said sweetly.

*Amazing!* Lord Cambridge thought. *So she can be devious as well as direct. It would seem Elizabeth is a more complex girl than I had anticipated.*

"I only want your happiness!" Philippa said, throwing her arms about her younger sibling and hugging her. "I am so happy with my husband, and I know Banon is happy with her Neville. I just want you to know that same happiness too."

"You are most kind, sister, to come to court to help me," Elizabeth said, "and were it not for the need of another generation for Friarsgate I believe I could be happy without a husband."

"You are a most unnatural girl to say such a thing!" Philippa said indignantly. "It is only because you fear to lose your power over Friarsgate that you say it."

"I shall not lose my autonomy," Elizabeth replied quietly. "Any man who weds me must know that I am the heiress to Friarsgate, and while I will welcome his help, I will not be overruled."

"We are never going to find a husband for her!" Philippa wailed as they entered the house. "What man of breeding and honor could put up with a wife like that, Uncle?"

"I do not know," Lord Cambridge said, giving Elizabeth a wink of encouragement. "But tomorrow we shall go to court and begin to find out. Magical things happen on May Day, my dear girls."

"Perhaps I am like you, Uncle," Elizabeth said. "Perhaps I am not destined to find a mate at all."

Philippa looked as if she were going to faint away with shock.

"Nay, my darling girl," Thomas Bolton replied. "I do not think you will be like me. Somewhere in this world is a man who will love you, and put up with your pride, and be content to let you rule over your little kingdom. If we cannot find him here at court, we will eventually find him elsewhere. Philippa, dear girl, do not despair. All will be well. Am I not the uncle who makes magic for Rosamund and all her daughters?" He put his arms about the two young women, hugging them close. "Come now, my darlings, we must decide what it is we will wear tomorrow, that we may dazzle all around us."

# Chapter 5

lynn Stewart looked across the lawns at Greenwich Palace. It was May Day, and the weather was perfect. The bright sun reflected on the silken swath of the river beyond the greens. A maypole had been set up, and a bevy of pretty young women were now dancing about it as a group of gaily clad musicians played a sprightly tune. Some of the dancers he recognized. Others he did not. The king was walking about greeting his guests. He was clad in his favorite Tudor green, and the cat-faced Mistress Boleyn was by his side. She too wore green, and her thick black hair flowed down her back. There was a wreath of flowers atop her shining dark head. Henry Tudor was in a jovial mood on his favorite of all holidays.

While not a diplomat, Flynn Stewart was at the English court at the behest of his half brother, King James V of Scotland. Officially his job was to carry any messages between King Henry and his nephew in Scotland. Unofficially he was his king's eyes and ears. James Stewart did not trust any of the Tudors, including his own mother, now married to her third husband, Henry Stewart, Lord Methven. Yet he trusted Flynn Stewart, for not only were they half brothers, but Flynn had long since proven his loyalty to his late father's house, though some thought it odd. While everyone knew that Flynn was the late king's son, James IV had never officially acknowledged him, although he had insisted the boy bear his name.

"Flynn, lad, look there," his friend Rees Jones murmured, and he pointed.

"Aye, a beauty," Flynn agreed. "Who is she?"

"I don't know. She's new. But that is the Countess of Witton with her. I know her. Shall we go and be introduced?"

"How do you know the Countess of Witton?" Flynn asked his companion.

"We're distantly related," Rees said. "Her father was Welsh. His brother was my maternal grandfather. She's a delightful woman, if a bit restrained."

"In other words, you have considered seduction," the Scot said.

"Philippa St. Clair is not the sort of woman you seduce," Rees Jones replied. "She is one of the queen's adherents. No. I like her sense of honesty and her wit, Flynn. Now, if we are to meet the exquisite creature in her company, we had best hurry, for new blood always attracts the gentlemen of the court."

The two men strolled casually through the gardens until they had reached the place where Philippa stood with Thomas Bolton and Elizabeth.

"Cousin!" Rees greeted the Countess of Witton. "How are you, and who is this lovely lass by your side?" He smiled broadly, showing all his unusually fine white teeth.

Philippa held out her hand to be kissed as she replied, "Rees, how nice that you are here. This is my youngest sister, Mistress Elizabeth Meredith, come to court with our uncle, Lord Cambridge, of whom I have spoken. She is your relation too." Philippa gave her sister a little poke to remind her to offer her hand to the gentlemen.

Elizabeth quickly picked up on the signal, holding out her hand to be saluted. Lord Cambridge was relieved to note the weeks of creaming had had their effect. It was an elegant hand. "And how are we related, sir?" Elizabeth asked Rees Jones.

"We share a great-grandfather," he said, and then explained further, adding, "It was your father's success at court that paved the way for me," he concluded.

"I do not really remember my father," Elizabeth said. "I was very young when he died. But I am told he was a good and honorable man. I am said to resemble him."

"He died young then?" Rees Jones said.

"In a fall from an apple tree," Elizabeth replied.

"Elizabeth!" Philippa looked mortified.

"My sister considers the manner of our father's death an embarrassment, I fear. Perhaps if he had perished in battle, or in his bed of a wasting sickness, she would find it more acceptable," Elizabeth murmured.

"What was he doing in an apple tree?" Rees asked her, ignoring Philippa.

"Helping our people harvest the crop. None at Friarsgate had ever thought to go to the top of the tree and shake the fruit down. They picked what they could reach, and left the rest to fall and rot. My father considered that a great waste, I am told. So each autumn he would go into the orchards with the peasants and help them. One year, sadly, he lost his balance and fell to his death," she explained.

"He was a good Welshman to the end then, Mistress Elizabeth," Rees Jones told her with a chuckle, "for waste is an anathema to the Welsh race." Then, turning, he drew Flynn Stewart forward. "Cousins, my lord, may I introduce my friend Flynn Stewart."

Flynn stepped forward to kiss first the Countess of Witton's hand, and then Elizabeth's. He bowed politely to Thomas Bolton.

"Flynn is King James's personal messenger to King Henry's court," Rees explained.

"Ah," Lord Cambridge said, eyeing the young man. "Then you are the spy."

The Scotsman burst out laughing. "Nay, nothing so glamorous, I fear, my lord, although I can understand you might assume that. Some do." His amber eyes twinkled. He stood just over six feet, and had a thick head of red hair.

"You look like your father," Lord Cambridge remarked. "The resemblance is quite remarkable, dear boy. Did you know him well?"

"I had that privilege, my lord," Flynn Stewart replied quietly. The Englishman had surprised him, for he had taken the man, given his most fashionable garb, for nothing more than a foppish courtier. Stewart's parentage was known, but rarely spoken about.

"I spent many a delightful hour at his court in Edinburgh, and in his company. He was a rare and unique gentleman," Lord Cambridge said.

"Uncle!" Philippa looked truly uncomfortable.

"My dear girl, the fellow is dead, and King Henry triumphs. There

can be no harm in my speaking of Jamie Stewart, the fourth of his ilk."
He patted her shoulder.

"Thank you, my lord," Flynn Stewart answered Thomas Bolton.

Elizabeth had listened, fascinated. She had quickly realized, given
the references, that Flynn Stewart was one of James IV's bastards. The
royal Stewarts did have a predilection for spreading their descendants
around the countryside.

"Madame," the Scot said, "may I have your permission to walk with
your sister?"

"Of course," Philippa replied. The Scot was not the sort of party
that Elizabeth should be involved with, but she could honestly think
of no reason to refuse him. "You will remain within my sight, of
course," she added.

"Of course." He bowed politely, and then offered Elizabeth his arm.

Well, at least he had good manners, and he was their cousin's
friend, Philippa considered. And Elizabeth had to start somewhere.

Elizabeth took the Scotsman's arm and they moved off. "You are
every bit as much an outsider here as I am," she remarked softly as they
walked.

"You do not look like an outsider in that gown," he replied. "Pale
blue suits you."

"So my uncle says," she responded.

"You do not look like your sister," he continued.

"Nay, I do not. My two older sisters look like our mother. I favor
the father I cannot remember."

"Why are you here?" he wondered.

"I am the heiress to a rather large holding," Elizabeth told him. "I
have not married yet, and I have been brought to court with an eye to
finding a husband."

"I would have thought a beautiful girl like yourself would have been
wed long since," Flynn Stewart said.

Elizabeth laughed. "Why?" she asked him mischievously, looking
up into his face. "Just because I am considered beautiful and rich,
though my sister would shudder to hear me express such sentiments?
My mother believes in allowing her daughters to make their own
choices in the matter of marriage. It is unusual, I know, but there it is."

"And there is no one you would wed, so you have been sent to court in an effort to broaden your search," he remarked. "Well, you will find plenty of young men here—and not so young men—more than willing to have a beautiful heiress to wife."

"I will find no one," Elizabeth said. "The man I marry must be willing to live at Friarsgate and help me manage the manor. I have had the responsibility of it since the day I turned fourteen, and I will not allow anyone to take that autonomy from me. I will share it with the right man, but I shall never relinquish it. Look about you, sir. Do you think any of these perfumed fellows will suit me?"

"Then why are you here if you think it is a waste of time?" he asked her.

"I have come to please my family, my mother in particular," Elizabeth said.

"What will happen when you return without a mate then?"

"My mother will fret and be angry, I suspect. My stepfather, the laird of Claven's Carn, will attempt to drag out a younger son of one of his friends. But eventually they will all calm themselves," Elizabeth said. Then she sighed. "I know I must wed if I am to have an heir one day, but none of this seems right to me." Then she looked up at him. "You ask many questions, sir, and I find myself answering when I really should not. We are strangers to each other."

"No longer, Elizabeth Meredith," he told her. "Now, would you like to meet some other young people? Your sister may not consider them entirely suitable, but if your stay at court is to be a short one, then you should have some fun."

"Will we be out of Philippa's sight if I say yes?" she asked him.

He nodded with a grin.

"Then lead on, sir," she told him.

"You are not an easy girl, are you?" he teased her.

She laughed, and then to her surprise he led her to where Mistress Anne Boleyn sat surrounded by a group of gentlemen.

"Mistress Boleyn, may I present the Countess of Witton's sister, newly come to court," Flynn Stewart said.

Anne Boleyn looked at Elizabeth sharply. She was beautiful, and very fashionably attired in pale blue silk, the bodice of her gown and the turned-back cuffs of her sleeves embroidered in silver threads and pearls. Her underskirt was brocade. She wore a French cap on her head that was edged in pearls. She was just the sort of perfect English beauty that the king could be attracted to, and Anne was uneasy. She nodded slightly to Elizabeth in answer to the introduction, and the blond girl curtseyed to her.

"You are a Meredith then," Sir Thomas Wyatt said.

"I am, my lord."

"Was Sir Owein Meredith your father then?" Sir Thomas probed.

"He was, God assoil his soul," Elizabeth replied.

"Are you husband hunting then, Mistress Meredith?" he questioned boldly.

"My family is, but I am not, my lord," she answered him pertly.

Anne Boleyn laughed, as did the others about her. She could not help it. The girl was not the least intimidated by the high and mighty surrounding her. There was a freshness about her, but she was still too beautiful.

"Are you rich?" George Boleyn, Anne's brother, demanded to know.

"I am," Elizabeth said. "Are you interested in offering for my hand, sir, and coming north to Cumbria to wed me?" She was mocking him, and they all knew it.

"Cumbria?" George Boleyn looked horrified. "Is not that where all the sheep are raised, Mistress Meredith?"

"Indeed, sir. I raise Cheviots, Shropshires, Hampshires, and Merinos," Elizabeth replied.

"Sheep have names?" he said, curious in spite of himself.

"They are breeds, sir," Elizabeth responded.

"And you are able to recognize them?"

"I can recognize all sorts of beasts, sir, even a jackass," Elizabeth told George Boleyn with a mischievous twinkle in her eye.

"God's blood, George! You have been launched on your own petard," Sir Thomas Wyatt said, and the group of courtiers surrounding Mistress Boleyn burst out laughing.

"What is all this merriment?" The king had come to join them, slipping his hand into Mistress Boleyn's hand. Then he stared at Elizabeth Meredith. "Why, you are the last of Rosamund's daughters," he said. "And you look like your father, God assoil him. Your sister said you were here, as did Lord Cambridge. Welcome, Elizabeth Meredith!" And he held out his big beringed hand to her.

Elizabeth quickly took the hand and kissed it, curtseying low as she did. "Thank you, your majesty." She rose from her curtsey.

"And how is your dear mother?" the king wanted to know. "Still shackled to that Scots border bandit she would insist on wedding?"

"Aye, your majesty," Elizabeth replied, laughter in her voice.

"And how many children did he sire on her?" the king demanded.

"Four sons, your majesty," Elizabeth said.

"He is a fortunate man, that Scot," the king remarked. "You are having a good time, Elizabeth Meredith? Your mother, despite her protests, always enjoyed her visits."

"It is my first day at court, your majesty, but I have been made to feel most welcome, and especially by Mistress Boleyn and her companions," Elizabeth said.

"Indeed?" The king turned to the girl at his side. "That is good of you, sweetheart, and nothing could make me happier. Mistress Meredith's father was a most loyal servant of the Tudors, and her mother spent part of her girlhood first in my mother's household, and then in my grandmother's house. Rosamund Bolton and my sister, Margaret, were close friends. Do they still correspond, Mistress Elizabeth?"

"Now and again, your majesty, they do. I bring you greetings from my mother, your majesty. She said I was to remind you that she is always your loyal servant."

The king laughed. "When you write her, you will tell her that the king said if she were as loyal as she claims she would not have wed that Scot of hers, and then gone over the border to live."

"I will quote your majesty precisely," Elizabeth promised with a smile.

Flynn Stewart watched and listened to this exchange. So Elizabeth Meredith's mother was a friend of his half brother's mam. And she was wed to a Scotsman. It was indeed a small world, he thought.

The king was now laughing, for Mistress Boleyn had repeated Elizabeth Meredith's jest on George Boleyn. "Be careful, George," the king warned the young man. "If Mistress Meredith is anything like her mother, you will never get the best of her." And he chuckled.

"Did you never get the best of her?" Anne Boleyn asked him.

"Nay, sweetheart, I did not," the king said. He knew how jealous his Annie could be, and he did not want her transferring her jealousy from his long-ago relationship with Rosamund Bolton to her daughter. It had been the most discreet of all his dalliances, and never been public knowledge.

Anne Boleyn smiled. "Mistress Meredith is a beautiful girl, Hal. You have always favored fair women." She was probing.

"Aye," the king agreed. "She is like her father. But I prefer a dark girl with sparkling eyes and a quick wit. Do not fret, Annie, love. I could never be attracted to Mistress Meredith, having been her parents' friend. It would be like incest, I fear."

Anne Boleyn sighed happily at the king's admission. She was always fearful of losing the king to another woman. A less chaste woman. She had led him a merry dance for several years now, but while she had allowed him many privileges of her body, she had never allowed him in her bed, and she remained a virgin. Anne Boleyn would not be one of Henry Tudor's whores like her foolish sister, Mary. Anne Boleyn meant to be the king's wife. But now she could be friends with Mistress Meredith, for the girl obviously posed no threat to her ambitions. Anne had no real women friends, though some pretended to like her.

Her Howard relations were almost wild with fury over her actions. They wanted her to yield to Henry Tudor and get what she could from him for them. The Duke of Norfolk, the head of the family, thought her mad, but he did not desert her. Eventually Anne would yield to Henry, and they would all profit from her lost virtue. But queen?

She would never be queen. In the end the king would marry a princess as he should, and Anne would be given a husband, and that would be the end of it. That was what they told her. But Anne would not give over. "I will be queen," she insisted to her uncle, the duke.

"I remember your mother saying that you were musical," the king said to Elizabeth.

Actually Elizabeth played several instruments, but she knew the instrument of choice at court now was the lute. "I play the lute, your majesty, and I sing," she answered with a small smile.

"I am composing a special song for a certain lady right now," the king said to Elizabeth. "You will learn it, and sing it for us when it is finished."

"I would be honored, your majesty," Elizabeth said with a curtsey.

"Let us go boating!" Mistress Boleyn suddenly cried. "The river is sweetly still, and the day so fair, my lords." She drew away from the king and began dancing towards the Thames, singing as she went. "Now is the month of May, when merry lads do play! Fa-la-la-la-la-la-la-la-la! Fa-la-la-la-la-la-la!"

The king looked amused. He turned away. He had other guests to greet. He well knew his beloved. She had grown impatient with him. He had given Mistress Meredith too much attention, and she was jealous. But Anne was no fool, and she knew she had no reason to be jealous, so she was embarrassed by her emotions. When she turned to look back at him, Henry Tudor winked at her. The relief in her smile touched him. *Sweet Annie,* he thought.

Flynn Stewart led Elizabeth by the hand as they followed Mistress Boleyn down to the riverbank, where several small punts were pulled up on the mud. "Have you ever been in a punt?" he asked her as he helped her into it.

"No, but I can swim should you tilt us into the water," Elizabeth assured him as she sat down on a cushion in the flat bottom of the boat.

He grinned. " 'Tis good to know, for I am not particularly skilled with a punt pole."

"Then why are we doing this?" she wanted to know.

"I don't know," he admitted, and his amber eyes were dancing with amusement.

Elizabeth began to laugh, and Flynn Stewart began to laugh.

"What is the jest?" Mistress Boleyn asked. She had not entered a punt but was standing on the shore surrounded by her gentlemen friends.

"Why are we here? On the riverbank?" Elizabeth asked Anne Boleyn. "Are you really going boating?"

Anne thought a minute, and then she shook her head. "Nay," she said. "These little punts are too inclined to be tipsy. I cannot swim."

"Then please tell me why you suggested it?" Elizabeth wanted to know.

"I thought it might be fun," Anne replied, "but on reflection I do not. Get out of the punt, Elizabeth Meredith! We will play cards instead. You do have monies to bet?"

"I do, but I warn you I am an excellent player of card games," Elizabeth responded. "Flynn, help me out of this dangerous little craft."

He stepped forward to give her his hand, but his foot slipped in the mud of the riverbank. The Scotsman began to fall forward, and in doing so reached to steady himself on the punt's prow. Instead he accidentally shoved it out into the river. Anne Boleyn cried out with alarm. The gentlemen about her stood openmouthed, staring as the little boat began to drift. One had the presence of mind to try to help Flynn Stewart up. He looked horrified at Elizabeth's plight.

*How tiresome,* Elizabeth thought, *but if I do not do something right away, I shall surely be caught by the current.* The Scotsman was facedown in the mud, and none of the other finely dressed dandies seemed inclined to come to her aid. Quickly she undid the tapes holding her skirts to her bodice. She undid her sleeves and pulled them off, along with her French cap and veil. She kicked her shoes from her feet. Then, standing gingerly in the little punt, she dove into the river, leaving much of her clothing behind. Surfacing, she stroked the few feet to the riverbank to be pulled out by Flynn Stewart, now on his feet and covered in mud.

"Are you all right?" he wanted to know.

"Except for a want of clothing, sir, aye." She stood in the sleeveless bodice, now ruined, her silk chemise clinging to her legs, her feet bare.

"Surround Mistress Meredith," Anne Boleyn's voice suddenly spoke sharply. "Put your backs to her so she may be protected and not embarrassed by your gawking. George, go and find her a long cloak! I don't care if it's May; she'll catch her death of cold." She squeezed into the circle now obscuring any view of Elizabeth to join her. "You are very brave, and it was so quick-witted of you to do what you did. I am so sorry you have lost your gown. I will have the king send you a new one, for 'tis all my fault." She smiled her small cat's smile at Elizabeth. "You will forgive me, won't you?"

Elizabeth nodded, her lips twitching with her amusement. "You all looked so astounded to see me suddenly out in the river." She began to giggle.

Anne found the sound infectious, and she too began to giggle.

"My sister will be furious," Elizabeth said. "I suspect when she learns of this incident she will wish I had floated out to sea fully clothed rather than take my gown off and swim to shore." She began to laugh. She couldn't help herself.

Anne Boleyn laughed with her. "But I was so afraid for you," she admitted.

"And none of your fine friends would move a muscle to save me." Elizabeth cackled. "I could see them thinking they could not damage their own garments. It never occurred to them to take them off as I did."

"Ohhh, what a fine show that would have made." Anne howled with laughter. "My brother has legs like a stork!"

Suddenly the king was there, and Philippa and Lord Cambridge.

"What has happened?" Henry Tudor demanded to know.

Anne explained between the laughter that she and Elizabeth could not seem to control now. She finished by saying, "You must give her a new gown, Henry, for it was my fault she had to swim back to the shore and lost her own."

"My sister is not properly garbed?" Philippa pushed into the widening circle of gentlemen, and gasped. "Elizabeth! What has happened to your skirts? To your beautiful sleeves and cap?"

"Were you not listening, Philippa? They are in the punt, floating down to the sea," Elizabeth replied. "I am sorry, but it was an accident."

"You will never live down this unfortunate incident!" Philippa cried. "Could you not have waited for someone to rescue you? If word of such behavior is spread about, we shall have no luck at all in what is a difficult task to begin with. What respectable man wants a woman who removes her garments in public?"

If was fortunate that Philippa did not see the gentlemen with their backs to her, who were all smiling broadly at her distressed query.

"I think your sister showed great bravery and intelligence, Countess," the king said quietly. "It would have been difficult to rescue Elizabeth. By the time a barge could have been dispatched the pole-less punt would have been in the current with no means of guiding it to safety. The river is busy, and all the main shipping channels come up from the sea to the London pool here. She could have been hit by a larger vessel, thrown into the Thames in her heavy skirts, and drowned. We are fortunate indeed she is safe."

George Boleyn dashed up now with an all-enveloping cape. Elizabeth was wrapped in it, and Flynn Stewart picked her up.

"Where shall I carry her, my lord?" he asked Lord Cambridge.

"We shall go back to my house," Thomas Bolton said. He was somewhat astounded by what had taken place. "Follow me, sir."

"I am perfectly capable of walking," Elizabeth protested.

"Shut up!" Philippa spat furiously, and totally out of character. "You have already caused enough of a scene. Let us at least attempt to repair the damage. Can you not behave like a lady just once in your life, Elizabeth?"

Elizabeth looked to Anne Boleyn and rolled her eyes. Mistress Boleyn winked back at her with perfect understanding.

Flynn Stewart followed Lord Cambridge, who hurried through the royal gardens and into a light wood. On the other side of the trees he came to a tall brick wall. Tom Bolton opened a small door in the barrier. Ducking his head, the Scot stepped through the door into the gardens of Lord Cambridge's dwelling. "So you are the owner of this charming jewel box," he said. "I have admired it often on our visits to Greenwich."

"It suits me, as do all my dwellings," Thomas Bolton said.

They entered the house, and the older man led his guest up two flights of stairs, Philippa following behind them, still spitting her outrage angrily.

"Ah, here is Elizabeth's apartment." He opened the door, calling, "Nancy, come quickly. Your mistress has had a slight mishap."

Nancy came hurrying as Flynn Stewart set his burden on her feet.

"Mishap? You call this a mishap, Uncle?" Philippa exploded. "I call it social ruination of the worst kind! When in the history of the court did a respectable young woman take off her garments and jump into the river? Not in my lifetime, or yours!"

"Thank you, sister, I am quite all right," Elizabeth said wickedly.

Flynn Stewart thought it wise to withdraw. He did so with a bow to the chamber's inhabitants, feeling sympathy with them as he made his hasty escape.

The women did not notice him. Lord Cambridge nodded, and mouthed his thanks.

"It was an accident, Philippa," Elizabeth tried to palliate her older sister. "We were going to go punting, then changed our minds. Master Stewart fell attempting to aid me in disembarking from the punt. The little boat got pushed into the river, and they all stood there staring, not knowing what to do next. I had no choice. And I certainly couldn't have swum back to shore in all those heavy skirts. I would have drowned with the weight of them pulling me down. I'm sorry, but it is rather amusing in retrospect."

Philippa drew a long, deep breath to calm herself. Why was it that Elizabeth could make her so angry? "If you had not been consorting with that creature and her minions, this would have never happened. And how was it that you were, I should like to know?"

"A bath, Nancy," Elizabeth said quietly, and, nodding, the young servant hurried off to prepare the bath for her mistress.

"Well?" Philippa demanded.

"Master Stewart introduced me to Mistress Boleyn," Elizabeth said.

"I knew I should not let you go off with that royal by-blow," Philippa said. "I watched you until he broke his word and took you from my sight. Was it then he involved you with that creature? You cannot speak to her again, Elizabeth. Mother would be most distressed. The queen is our friend."

"The queen is not here. Nor is she likely to be again," Elizabeth snapped. She was wet, and she was chilled. She could smell the river on her skin, and it was not a pleasant scent at all. She stank of garbage, offal, and brackish salt water. "I like Anne Boleyn, Philippa. But more important, the king likes her."

" 'Tis a passing fancy, and that is all there is to it," Philippa replied weakly.

"It has not passed in eight years," Elizabeth shot back, "nor is it likely to, sister. The queen is finished unless a miracle occurs and she produces a healthy son for the king. Do you see that happening,

Philippa? He does not even live with her any longer, which means he does not bed her either. I am mindful of Queen Katherine's kindnesses to our family, but she is not here, and she is no longer in favor."

"How can I possibly find you a good husband," Philippa said, "if you will not behave properly? I know the queen is out of favor, but her favor was of value to us once. Without it, I am at a disadvantage, Elizabeth, yet it is my duty to help you make a proper match with the right man."

"There is no man here at court who would suit me, Philippa. I could not keep Friarsgate as well as I do had I not learned to judge men's character quickly. When I went into the river today the men with Mistress Boleyn just stood there gaping. Not one of them would soil his fine garments, and not one of them had the wit to remove them so they might enter the river and aid me. I saw that at once, which is why I saved myself. The Scot might have come to my rescue had he not been facedown in the muck, but he was. How could I entrust Friarsgate to men like that, sister?"

"If you will not cooperate with me," Philippa said as if Elizabeth had not spoken, "I shall wash my hands of you for good and all." She was near tears, for failure was not a part of her nature, and her younger sister was being so stubborn.

But Elizabeth would not give way to Philippa's bullying. "You must do what you think best," she said softly, "but there is no man here worth my time."

"Then why did you come to court if you did not mean to take a husband?" Philippa demanded, now angry.

"I came to please our mother, and to please Uncle Thomas, who really did need an excuse to come south this spring. Did you not, Uncle?"

"I think I shall avoid quarreling with either of you, my darlings," Lord Cambridge said. "We are here. It is May. Let us enjoy the good times."

"Philippa"—Elizabeth attempted to placate her elder sibling—"it is just the first day of May. My mishap will be quickly replaced by someone else's faux pas by the morrow. Let us not war with each other, I beg you."

"If you do not want a husband, then what good am I to you? To Mother? You asked for the responsibility of Friarsgate, and you have done a fine job of caring for it, if our mother is to be believed, and she is. But I feel a certain obligation to Friarsgate, as it was to have been mine once. You have a duty to supply Friarsgate with the next heir, Elizabeth, and refusing to do so because you do not wish to give up your own authority is both selfish and childish!"

"Ho! Is the pot calling the kettle black, sister? You did precisely what you chose to do to live your own life as you wished to live it. You renounced Friarsgate. How dare you tell me what to do!" Elizabeth cried. "I took up the burden you cast aside."

"Aye, I did not want Friarsgate, but I do know how to accept my duty and do it well," Philippa shot back. "Do you think you will be young forever? You will be twenty-two on the twenty-third of this month. You are an old maid, sister. Mother had birthed all of us by the time she reached that age. You are growing long in the tooth, and you must wed soon if you are to have a child of your body to inherit in the next generation. What will happen if you do not? It will go to one of Logan's lads for want of another. Is that what you want? Mother will have no other choice."

"The choice of the next heir is not Mother's," Elizabeth said quietly. "It is mine." Aye! She needed a husband, but from what she had seen today there was little hope of finding one among the king's court. Still, she did not want to quarrel with Philippa, who really was trying to help. She sighed. "I am sorry you were embarrassed by my accident today, sister. I shall endeavor to have no more mishaps while I am here, but know that I shall begin my journey home in June."

"It is not enough time," Philippa complained.

"If there is a man I can consider, and who will consider coming north with me, he will be found in that time. But if, as I believe, there is no one here who will suit me, there is no use in my remaining. I will have been gone almost three months by the time I return. Edmund is old now, Philippa. He is no longer used to shouldering the entire burden of Friarsgate, as he did when our mother was away. No one else can but me."

"Which makes it even more important for us to find you a husband," Philippa said eagerly. "You need a helpmeet. A woman should not be managing such an estate as yours, Elizabeth. A husband would be more suited to the task, I am certain."

Lord Cambridge waited for the explosion certain to follow Philippa's words, but to his surprise it did not come. He actually believed he saw Elizabeth bite her tongue.

The footmen had been lugging pail after pail of steaming water through the dayroom and into the bedchamber. Now Nancy came out to announce to her mistress that her bath was ready, and likely to get cold if Elizabeth did not come quickly.

"I appreciate your kindness, Philippa, but you will understand my adventure has left me chilled and stinking. I must bathe. Go back to your friends. You also, Uncle. I believe it best that I spend the rest of my day in bed recovering from my ordeal." She smiled sweetly at them both.

Lord Cambridge wasn't in the least fooled, but he bowed, saying, "I believe, dear girl, that you are absolutely right. By tomorrow all will have blown over. Will is here should you need him. Come, Philippa, my angel. 'Tis May Day, and the celebrations have only just begun."

"You will be all right?" Philippa's tone had softened, and she evinced concern for her younger sibling. "Uncle is correct, of course. Few if any will remember your mishap by the morrow. Ohh, I hope Crispin comes soon!" She kissed Elizabeth's cheek, and then, taking Lord Cambridge's arm, they departed the dayroom.

Elizabeth sighed gustily with her relief. "What a pother Philippa makes over naught," she said to Nancy. "Did you hear?"

"Enough," Nancy said. "Gawd! I hope they can find that punt. Them sleeves was beautiful, mistress." She was a tall, lanky girl with a plain but pretty face. Her braids were nut brown, and her eyes a light blue. Like Elizabeth, she had never before been away from Friarsgate, but she had to admit she was enjoying her adventure. She helped Elizabeth out of the remainder of her sodden garments and into the hot tub. "I'll take these to the laundress," she said. "I think they're salvageable. Are you really going to spend the rest of the day in bed?"

Elizabeth laughed. "Nay, but at least I won't have to spend it gliding up and down the palace lawns being inspected by snobs and parvenus, being gossiped about and having my wealth speculated upon. I shall rid myself of the river's stink, re-dress, and sit in Uncle's gardens listening to the music from the palace."

Nancy hurried out, and Elizabeth washed first herself, and then her long blond hair, which had been soaked in the river. Climbing from the oak tub, she dried herself off with one of the towels on the warming rack by her fire, then wrapped her head in another towel. Nancy had laid out a clean chemise on the bed, and Elizabeth donned it. Then, sitting by the fire, she unwrapped her hair from the towel and began to rub it dry before the heat of the hearth.

Returning, Nancy came to stand behind her mistress and began to brush the long hair. " 'Tis like thistledown," she noted. "Golden thistledown, and straight as a poker. Now Lady Philippa has all them fine curls, and Mistress Neville's hair has a bit of a curl to it too, but not yours." She plied the brush vigorously now as the damp hair dried, becoming thicker with each stroke of her brush.

"It suits my nature," Elizabeth said, "as curls suit Philippa. She is all fussy and intent on being the perfect courtier."

"And you are happiest being a wild child," Nancy teased her mistress.

Elizabeth laughed. "I suppose I am, but I am not irresponsible, nor unmindful of my duties. And before I had to jump into the river to save myself I met two gentlemen, the king, and Mistress Boleyn, Nancy."

"Ohh," Nancy said, "was the gentlemen handsome?"

"One is related to me. His name is Rees Jones, and we share a great-grandfather. The other is a Scot. He is King James's personal messenger, and sent to live at court so that should King Henry need to send to his nephew he has a messenger to do it. Uncle Thomas says he is a spy, though he denied it." Elizabeth chuckled.

"What was the king like?" Nancy wanted to know.

"Very handsome. Quite tall, with wonderful red-gold hair and a beard. His eyes are small, but they're quite a brilliant blue. He's a big man too. And Mistress Boleyn is not at all beautiful, but she is so elegant, and her wit is swift. I quite liked her, but I also felt sorry for her, Nancy. She hides it well, but she is afraid. I sense it."

"Probably fears for her immortal soul, stealing the queen's husband away from her," Nancy said with a country woman's practicality.

"The queen's plight is of her own making," Elizabeth said. "The king needs a son, and she cannot give him one. There must be a new queen."

"But the old one ain't dead," Nancy said, and then she put the hairbrush aside.

"Find me something simple to wear," Elizabeth said, "if indeed I have something like that anymore."

Nancy found a long, deep-green silk skirt with a plain square-necked bodice that had long, fitted sleeves. Elizabeth donned it and, sliding a pair of house slippers on her feet, she went out into the garden. She had left her hair loose but for a green silk ribbon with a small oval crystal she wore about her forehead. In the garden the first of the early roses were coming into bloom, and the statuary, while as flamboyant as the London garden's, was of both men and women in various poses of an erotic nature. Sitting on a bench by the water, she watched the river traffic.

Suddenly a small punt appeared around a little bend in the river, and it was headed directly for Lord Cambridge's quay. Looking closely, Elizabeth saw it was poled by Flynn Stewart. He waved at her and, reaching the dockage, jumped from the little boat, making it fast. He carried in his arms the skirts and petticoats she had left behind earlier, and atop the pile of silk and fine lawn were her sleeves. "Mistress." He bowed and laid the pile on the bench next to her. Then, reaching into an interior pocket of his doublet, he drew forth her two shoes, setting them in her lap.

"How did you find them?" she asked him, truly surprised. "And thank you, sir! My sister was most put out by my loss of the sleeves."

"It was my fault," Flynn said. "In my efforts to help you from the punt I fell, and in reaching for the damned little boat set you adrift instead. And I could not rescue you because I was facedown in the riverbank. Then those bloody fools who accompany Mistress Boleyn everywhere and haven't the sense to come in from the rain stood there gaping while you were in danger. If you hadn't had the presence of mind to do what you did, you'd be halfway to the Wash by now. I took a barge, and we rowed after the punt. When we reached it, we took it in tow back to the palace, and then I rowed it from there."

"I am most grateful, sir," Elizabeth said. "It was a kind thing to do, and I doubt anyone else would have done it."

"You were right earlier. Neither of us belongs here," he said.

"Sit down," Elizabeth said, and he sat in the grass next to her. "Are you really nothing more than King James's messenger?"

He grinned engagingly at her. "Nothing more," he said.

"They say your father was a very loving man, and it angered his queen. I heard that she once discovered his large family living in the same palace she inhabited, and sent them elsewhere. Were you among those unfortunate children, Flynn Stewart?"

"Nay," he said. "I am the only one of my father's known bastards who was never officially recognized, although my father knew I was his, and saw to my well-being, and visited with me regularly. It was because of the way in which I was conceived." He chuckled. "Would you like to hear the tale, or would it shock you?"

"I breed sheep," Elizabeth said dryly, "although I suspect my older sister would swoon at such an admission from my lips. Respectable virgins are not supposed to admit to knowing such things."

"And are you a respectable virgin, Elizabeth Meredith?" he teased her.

"I am a virgin, sir, but as to the other that is a matter for debate," she answered. "Now tell me your shocking tale, and of how you were bred."

He grinned. He liked Elizabeth Meredith. She was exactly what you saw. Plainspoken with no foolishness about her. No. She didn't belong at court. "It was at my mother's wedding to Robert Gray, the laird of Athdar, who is my stepfather. Rob was a friend of the king, and he had invited him to the wedding. It was a grand affair, my mother recalls, and there was much drinking involved. The king was mourning his separation from his great love, Meg Drummond. My stepfather knew it, and sought to comfort his friend. As my mother tells it, he said, 'Jamie, my Nara looks much like yer Meg. Would ye accept the droit du seigneur of her this night, and let her comfort ye?'"

"He didn't!" Elizabeth gasped. She knew what the droit du seigneur was. It allowed the bridegroom to offer his bride's virtue to his overlord.

"Ah, but my stepfather did. Both he and the king were very drunk. My mother was fair with dark hair and eyes, like Meg Drummond. She says she was just drunk enough herself to feel sorry for Jamie Stewart. She decided if it was all right with Rob then it was fine with her. So the king bedded her, and afterwards the bridegroom bedded her. Nine months later I was born. There was no doubt whose son I was, and I was named Flynn, which means 'son of the red-haired man.' The king was embarrassed at the manner in which I was conceived. My mother says he apologized to her half a dozen times. He insisted I bear his surname, but he would never formally recognize me because of his shame. But he visited me when he was in the area, and never forgot my natal day.

My stepfather was a good man, and loved me every bit as much as the children he sired on my mother. But Rob Gray died at Flodden with the king. My twelve-year-old half brother, Ian, became the new laird of Athdar, and I his watchdog.

"A year later Robert Gray's only male relation appeared at Athdar. His name was Muir Gray, and he claimed to have survived Flodden, but been gravely wounded. He had not come sooner, he told our mother, because he had been recovering. I never believed he was at Flodden. Muir Gray was by nature a coward. But my mother welcomed him. Several months later my brother, who had always been healthy and strong, began to sicken. And all the while my mother was being slowly seduced by Muir Gray. He asked her to marry him, and despite our warnings that he was not a good man, our mother wed Muir Gray. Her belly was already swelling with his spawn on their wedding day. My brother died shortly thereafter. I am certain Muir murdered him, but I could never prove it. Then my mother died, and her stillborn son with her.

"Muir Gray was now the undisputed laird of Athdar. He barely mourned my mother before he was sending my younger half sister, Janet, into a convent, and bedding the older of my half sisters, Mary. As soon as she was with child, he married her. I protested both these acts, and was told as my mother's bastard I could have a place in the stables, but I could no longer live in the house. When I suggested his blood relationship to my sister was close enough to forbid the bonds of marriage between them, he said he would kill me if I ever questioned the legitimacy of his children. He had offered me a home and work only at the behest of my sister. I tried to speak with Mary, but she would not listen to me. She loved him, she said. I packed my few possessions, and left Athdar that day."

"I am sorry that you lost your home," Elizabeth said.

"Athdar was never mine," he said quietly. "Wherever I can serve my king is where my home is, Elizabeth."

"How did you come to serve the king?" she asked him.

"I went to Edinburgh, and discovered that my face can open a great many doors. You see, not only did I have James IV's red hair, I had his face as well. I wangled an introduction to the Duke of Lennox, who was the regent for the little king, and asked to enter his service. He welcomed me as a kinsman, and put me into the little king's household. It was my duty to teach James V how to ride, and to sit by his side as his companion at all times. Actually the duke wanted my eyes and ears to prevent the mayhem that always surrounds Stewart kings. When he was gone my first loyalty went to my half brother. As he grew we had some grand adventures." Flynn chuckled. "When he was eighteen my royal half brother seized his power from those attempting to rule for him. He sent me to England so that should his uncle, King Henry, ever need to communicate with Scotland quickly I am here for him."

"And to be his eyes and ears, I am quite certain," Elizabeth teased him.

"But you'll not tell anyone that," Flynn said seriously, and she was not certain whether he was teasing her back or it was the truth.

"Nay," she agreed. "I will not tell. 'Twill be our secret, Flynn Stewart."

He grinned. "I think I shall like sharing secrets with you, Elizabeth Meredith. May it be the first of many between us."

Elizabeth blushed, but then she giggled. "I can only imagine what my sister would think if she came upon us now. She would complain that I was not behaving like a proper lady should behave."

"Oh, you are a lady, Elizabeth," he told her, "but I will agree with

Lady Philippa. You are not in the least proper. But I far prefer a woman who is honest, and you are that. There is no deceit in you."

"I am a country woman," Elizabeth said quietly.

"Beware the seducers," he warned her. "They will be the most highly thought of and respectable men."

"Why would they bother to seduce me if they could wed me?" she asked him candidly.

"They want your wealth, sweetheart, but not the responsibilities entailed. If they can seduce you, and brut it about, then they have you for no other will," he explained.

"It's like being one of my own lambs in a pasture of wolves, wild dogs, and bears," Elizabeth complained. "I do not see what Philippa sees in this court of hers."

"I will guard your back, Elizabeth," he told her. "Stay in Mistress Boleyn's company, and do not wander off alone with any. You should be safe."

"Do you like her?" she asked him.

"Aye, I do," he replied, knowing exactly whom she meant. "But she has dangerous relations. They will be the death of her, I fear. And the ambitious crowd about her. She can really trust none, but God's wounds, she needs a friend!"

"I will be her friend," Elizabeth said, realizing as she did that she meant it.

# Chapter 6

Flynn Stewart departed back to the palace, and, gathering up her garments, Elizabeth returned to the house to bring them to Nancy.

"He likes you," her tiring woman said.

"We met only this morning," Elizabeth responded.

"Well, he likes what he saw then, for why else would a man go chasing after a runaway punt down the Thames to bring back your clothing?" Nancy asked in practical tones. "You've made a friend, mistress. 'Tis not a bad end to your first day at court. Now I'll just take these things back upstairs and see if I can sort them out and repair any damage. Then we'll decide what you are to wear tomorrow. Come along and take a nice nap. If Maybel is to be believed you'll get precious little rest once you become involved in court life." She bustled up the stairs, Elizabeth following.

In late afternoon Lord Cambridge returned to his house, and together they sat in the hall of the Greenwich house, which also overlooked the river, having a meal together. William Smythe joined them, and Elizabeth told them of Flynn Stewart's visit.

"I could not imagine someone being so kind here," she said. "Philippa will be pleased to learn I have those beautiful sleeves back. Why did she not return with you, Uncle Thomas? Is she still angry with me?"

"She is like one possessed," Lord Cambridge said as he helped himself to a thick slice of ham. "She is determined to find you a husband, dear girl. She is prowling the court like a veritable tigress in search of the right man. But you were astute in your observations today. There is no one here for you. However, let us enjoy the month of May, and then we will return north. I know your mother will be disappointed, but it is obvious fate has something else in store for you." He turned to his secretary. "And you, dear boy, was your day successful?"

"I have made an arrangement with the French merchant in London for the silk thread we want," Will answered. "He likes doing business with us because we do not cheat him like so many others do. The thread will be sent directly to Friarsgate."

"How soon?" Elizabeth wanted to know. "In time for the winter weaving?"

"Yes, mistress," Will responded.

"I have been thinking of a new color," Elizabeth said.

Lord Cambridge laughed. "Dear girl, no business at court, I pray you."

Elizabeth smiled. "Very well, Uncle," she said mischievously, "but what would you think of a new green?"

"Wicked creature! It would depend on the particular shade of green," he murmured. "Now, tell me more about this handsome royal by-blow. Do you have a weakness for Scots like your mother, dear girl?" His brown eyes twinkled at her.

"Is he not unsuitable, Uncle?" she said seriously.

"Aye," Thomas Bolton said, "and yet perhaps not. He has no lands of his own, or title. Do you think he would make a good helpmeet?"

"I think his loyalty to his king might interfere," Elizabeth replied. "We spoke at length this afternoon, for he is indeed a pleasant conversationalist, but he owes this king his place, his honor. I do not see him as a man ready to settle down. I wonder if he will ever be, Uncle. He is that sort of a gentleman."

"Still, we might consider him. Perhaps he is tired of being away from home all the time," Lord Cambridge suggested.

"He told me that home was wherever he might serve his king," Elizabeth noted.

"That does not bode well," William Smythe noted. "Perhaps, my lord, he is not the man for Mistress Elizabeth."

"I so dislike returning north only to admit defeat," Lord Cambridge said.

"Perhaps," Will soothed, "Lady Philippa will find some suitable gentlemen. If anyone can, she is the lady for the task."

But Philippa was having no more success finding eligible gentlemen willing to go north for Elizabeth than she had been able to find one for herself those years ago. Yet she understood. King Henry's court was the center of the universe. One came here because one wanted to be here. Not in the north of England forever. And Elizabeth was not helping herself at all. She had taken up with Anne Boleyn and her coterie of young people. Of all the people she might have involved herself at court, Elizabeth had aligned herself with the king's whore, even knowing how much Philippa disapproved.

But Elizabeth had taken Lord Cambridge's advice, and decided to enjoy herself. It was not often she had or even made time for herself. While many who knew her said her burden was heavy, Elizabeth never considered it in that manner. She was the lady of Friarsgate, and she had responsibilities. Now, however, she was at court, and an entire new world had been opened up to her. She found she was actually enjoying being frivolous, if only for this month. She did not grow weary with all the excitement. It was actually quite refreshing for her.

"You are the only lady I have found able to keep up with me," Anne Boleyn said a week later as they sat together in the gardens of the palace. "How is it so, I wonder?"

"I am used to hard work, unlike most of the ladies of the court," Elizabeth said. "I do wonder, though, if you ever sleep, dear Anne." They were now on a first-name basis.

"Sleep is a waste of time, Bess." Anne Boleyn had christened Elizabeth with this appellation, and Elizabeth had not forbidden it. "I have so much to do, to see, to be!"

"You have a lifetime, Anne," was the reply.

"I am to be twenty-five in November," Anne said. "That is practically old, and I am not yet a wife." She sighed. "I might have been, you know. I was courted by Harry Percy, Northumberland's scion, but Wolsey, damn his eyes, stopped it."

"Why?" Elizabeth wanted to know.

"Because the king wanted me," Anne said candidly. "But he has not had all he desires," she confided. "I told him I should never be his mistress, and while the queen was in the picture I could not be his wife. I follow the example of King Edward's wife." She smiled grimly. "But I have had my own back on Thomas Wolsey. I said I would when he forced Harry Percy into marriage with another. And everyone laughed at me, but they are not laughing now. Wolsey has been brought down, and is gone from court."

"Where has he gone?" Elizabeth wanted to know.

"He has been sent to York, for it is his archbishopric, but he cannot seem to get any farther than Cawood," Anne replied. "No matter. He'll never have the king's ear again. A man of the church, Bess, and he pimped for the king! If he had just let me have Harry I should be a wife and mother now. But no one ever allows me my way. I must do this, and I must do that! The king commands. My uncle, the duke, commands." She sighed. "And everyone hates me. They but wait for the king to stray again."

"I do not hate you, Anne," Elizabeth said.

"You know little of me but what you have heard," Anne said forlornly.

"Aye, I have heard the gossip," Elizabeth admitted, "but I know you now, Anne, and there is little truth to rumor, I have learned."

"You always say exactly what you are thinking, don't you?" Anne said. "How I envy you that ability. I must couch every word that I utter carefully so that that which I mean is understood perfectly, and cannot be confused or used against me."

"I have not been brought up as you were, Anne. When you were nine, you were off to France in Princess Mary's wedding train. I was running barefoot through my mother's meadows chasing the sheep. When you were twelve, you were in the household of Queen Claude of France. I was learning the business of how my estates are managed. When you were seventeen, you joined this court. When I was fourteen, the responsibility for Friarsgate became mine. I am a country woman by inclination and breeding. You are a noblewoman, a courtier. I should not be understood in my world if I spoke as a courtier speaks," Elizabeth said with a small smile. "My family has attempted to smooth what they consider my rough edges, but they have not, I fear, been as successful as they would wish. If my forthrightness does not offend you, then I am glad. I cannot be that which I am not."

"Nay, you do not offend me," Anne replied. "You are the only person whom I can believe or trust, Bess Meredith. My uncle, the duke, asked what it was I saw in you. He would not approve our friendship but that your nephew is one of his pages, and the son of the Earl of Witton. I said your honesty pleased me."

"And that I am here for but a short while," Elizabeth said with a twinkle in her eye. "I have seen the duke. He is a formidable-looking gentleman."

"Aye, he is formidable," Anne agreed. "He is the head of our family, and I must do what he tells me to do." She shivered. "Sometimes I say no because I know now I can go to the king, and he will protect me. My uncle does not like that, but he must acquiesce, for he has no other choice. The king will be obeyed above all."

"He is kind to you, and yet you are not lovers," Elizabeth noted.

Anne Boleyn looked startled. "Why would you say that?" she asked.

"You said it first," Elizabeth replied.

"Everyone thinks I am," Anne responded, "but I'll not be like my sister, Mary, poor creature. The king married her off. He has recognized one of her children, although she says the other is his too. Her husband uses her to his own advantage, and cares not that the king kept her as a mistress even after their marriage. I will not let my children be born with the stain of doubt upon them."

"I think that you follow the correct course. The king will get his divorce eventually, Anne. And he loves you. I have been here but a short time, and I can see it in his eyes when he looks at you," Elizabeth said.

"But when we are wed," Anne said, and there was a hint of fear in her voice, "I must give him a healthy son. What if I cannot? What if I fail as Katherine of Aragon has failed? What will happen to me?" Then she caught herself up sharply. "I will not think on it. Of course I will give the king a son when we are wed one day."

"You will be queen," Elizabeth said softly.

"Aye, I will," Anne Boleyn answered her, and a tiny smile touched the corners of her thin mouth. "And I shall do what I want, and no one, not even my uncle, the duke, will gainsay me, Bess. And everyone who has been unkind to me will suffer for it! What good is it to be queen if you cannot even the scores?" And she laughed wickedly.

"You must be a good queen," Elizabeth said.

"I suppose I must. The mother of a king should be above reproach," Anne Boleyn murmured, but her dark eyes were dancing with mischief as she spoke. Then suddenly she changed the subject. "I have told you I will be twenty-five in November. I was born beneath the sign of the Scorpion. You have not told me your age or natal day."

"I will be twenty-two on the twenty-third day of this month," Elizabeth answered.

"Your birthday is in May?" Anne cried. "Then we must have a celebration, dear Bess! I shall tell the king, and we shall have a masque! A theme. I must have a theme! Ohh, I know! It shall be a country fair, and the guests must come as animals! We shall have wonderful masques made. How wonderful to be born in the month of May!" She jumped up from the bench where they had been seated. "Come along now! It's just two weeks until your natal day, and we have a great deal to do." Catching Elizabeth's hand, she hurried her back into the palace.

The king was with his council, but it meant nothing to Mistress Anne. She brushed by the guards at the door to the council chamber and burst in, dragging Elizabeth Meredith behind her. The younger girl's eyes swept the room, and she saw the deep disapproval in the eyes and on the faces of those present, including the Duke of Norfolk.

But the king smiled and held out his hands to Anne. "Why, sweetheart, what is it?" he asked her.

"Bess Meredith has a natal day before the month ends, my lord. I should like your permission to hold a masque."

"His purse," Elizabeth heard a voice murmur, and low laughter.

Anne Boleyn released her companion's hand and drew herself up. She had heard too, but she gave no indication of it. "I though that since Bess is a country girl we would hold a country fair and all wear animal masques. We shall dance, and there will be an archery contest for both the ladies and the gentlemen, my lord. What say you?" She looked up at him, her dark eyes meeting his blue ones, and she smiled her little cat's smile.

"I think it is a wonderful idea, sweetheart," the king enthused. Then he turned to Elizabeth. "And how old will you be, Elizabeth Meredith, or should I not ask?"

"Your majesty may well ask," Elizabeth told him with a smile and a deep curtsey, "but I shall not necessarily answer. But if pressed I would admit to being as old as my nose, but much older than my teeth," she said.

Laughter erupted among the council, and the king grinned broadly. "Aye, you are your mother's daughter, mistress, and you may tell her I said so." He chuckled. His glance went again to Anne Boleyn. "Now, sweetheart, you must leave, for the council and I still have unfinished business to complete. If we are to spend the summer at Windsor and on progress I must finish the tasks a king has."

The two girls departed the council chamber.

"So you are to be feted," Flynn Stewart said to Elizabeth later that day as they met before the meal. "It is all over the court that Mistress Boleyn is to give you a masque. Usually such entertainments are reserved for visiting royalty, but then you are an heiress from the north," he teased her. "What does your family think? For I am certain your sister has an opinion on the matter." He grinned at her.

Elizabeth smacked him with her hand upon the arm. "Philippa is furious," she replied. "Uncle Thomas, however, is already working very hard with Will designing our costumes and masques. I am excited, but embarrassed, I will admit. All I did was mention that my natal day was at the end of the month, and suddenly she was crowing about a masque and dancing and archery."

"And what shall you come as?" he asked her with a grin.

"Uncle Thomas's masque will be that of a ram sheep, and mine that of a ewe sheep. Philippa says she will not go, but she will in the end, for she would rather die than miss such an affair," Elizabeth explained. "She will have a peacock masque, and her gown is to be an iridescent blue-green silk. When she stops sulking, Uncle Thomas will surprise her with it. He loves surprising people, and Philippa loves surprises."

"Can you shoot a bow?" he asked her.

Elizabeth shook her head. "I never learned, although my sisters can."

"Then I must teach you," he said. "You cannot go to your own fete and not take part in the archery contest that will be held for the ladies. It does not matter if you are good or not, for in order for you to be polite, someone else should win. There are some butts set up by the river. Come, and I will teach you."

Servants brought them bows, and Elizabeth's was a smaller version of the longbow they handed to Flynn. A large quiver of arrows was set on the wooden bench near them.

"It is really quite simple," Flynn said to her. "Watch me, and then you will try." He picked up the longbow, took an arrow from the quiver, and notched it carefully. Standing sideways, he slowly drew the bowstring back, and then suddenly he let the arrow fly. It struck the target neatly. "Now it is your turn," he said. "I will help you." He handed her the bow and, standing next to her, first showed her how to hold it. "Now take an arrow, and we will notch it," he said. His arms were around her as he helped her.

Elizabeth selected the arrow and fitted it neatly, as she had seen him do it, in the bowstring. She could feel his breath on her skin, and wondered if he should be standing with his arms about her, his long, lean body pressed against her in so intimate a fashion. She could sense her heart beating faster than it ever had.

"Draw the string back slowly," he said in her ear. "That's it. Now release!"

"Ouch!" Elizabeth cried as the arrow flew, and the bowstring scored her arm with a small burn.

"You should really have gloves on," he said, turning her wrist over to inspect the damage. It was not great, but he knew it probably stung. Boldly, he placed a kiss on her injury. "To make it better," he told her.

"Did I hit the target?" Elizabeth wanted to know. She pretended to ignore the little kiss, but her cheeks were burning, and her pulse had raced when his lips touched the sensitive skin of her wrist.

"I think your arrow went into the river," he said, laughing. "We are going to have to make a better archer of you if you are not to be teased."

"Give me another," she demanded. "If I must play this game at Anne's masque, I will not disgrace myself. I must simply learn to hit the target."

He handed her the requested arrow, and she notched it into her bow. "Now draw it back slowly, slowly," he instructed. "Move your hand just a bit or your wrist will be burned again by the bowstring. That's it. Now release!"

This time the arrow flew straight, burying itself into the butt.

"I did it!" Elizabeth shrieked excitedly. "I hit the target, Flynn!"

"Indeed you did, Elizabeth Meredith! Can you do it again?" he challenged her.

She took a third arrow, affixing it properly, and released it. Again it buried itself in the straw butt. "I can do it!" Elizabeth crowed. She whirled about to face him. "Am I not a good student, Flynn Stewart?" She laid the bow aside.

"Am I not an excellent instructor?" he replied, and then his arm tightened about her, and he pulled her deeper into his embrace, his lips finding hers in a searing kiss. A single hand cradled her head.

Elizabeth drew away. Her hazel-green eyes were wide with surprise. "Why did you do that?" she wanted to know. Her hands moved to straighten her cap and veil.

"Because I wanted to," he answered her honestly.

"Do you always do just what you want?" she said, recalling the same words spoken to her by another Scot of her acquaintance.

"Usually," he admitted.

"You are, sir, I fear, much too bold. I did not give you permission to kiss me," Elizabeth said. Her heart was racing again, and she even felt a bit dizzy.

"If I had asked, would you have?" he replied softly, and a single finger caressed her jawline with a slow, seductive motion.

"Of course not!" Elizabeth said much too quickly.

"Which is precisely why I did just what I wanted, Elizabeth Meredith. You have a sweet little mouth, my adorable lambkin." The amber eyes twinkled. "It was meant to be kissed, and despite your righteous indignation you enjoyed every moment of our kiss."

She was taken slightly aback by his words, but then she said, "I have not had the time yet to consider it, but you are probably right, and I did enjoy your kiss, Flynn Stewart. You are only the second man to kiss me, and by coincidence the first was a Scot too." Then she smiled sweetly at him, enjoying the look of surprise upon his handsome face at her rather bold admission. He look positively stunned.

"Who was he?" Flynn said, attempting to recover the advantage which she had so cleverly snatched away from him.

"Who he was is not your concern," Elizabeth replied, very much enjoying herself now. "He has no hold over me, nor do you. Now, I should like to see if I can hit the target without your arms about me, or if those arms are the magic that gives me skill with the longbow." She picked up the bow again, notched her arrow, took her stance, and let the arrow wing away. It struck the target neatly. "Either I have a talent for this," she remarked, "or you are indeed a good instructor." She chuckled mischievously. She laid the bow aside. "I think I have learned all I can today, sir." Then she turned and left him standing, making her way across the lawns, waving to Sir Thomas Wyatt as she went.

He laughed softly to himself. Elizabeth Meredith might be a little country lamb come to court, but he did not believe that she would ever be eaten by wolves or wild dogs. She was a clever little lambkin, but he was clever too. He wondered if he would get into difficulties with the king or her relations should he seduce her. But he was very tempted to throw caution to the winds where Elizabeth was concerned. And she was such a challenge. She was not coy or simple, like so many maidens come for husbands. She was outspoken and intelligent. And so beautiful.

Elizabeth could feel him watching her as she made her way over the green. His eyes seemed to bore into her back. She moved towards the small woodland that separated her uncle's house from the palace. She needed to be alone. Flynn Stewart's advances had been very pleasant, but also very disturbing. He was a fascinating man, but was he the man for Friarsgate? Her instinct told her nay, for his loyalty to his half brother was paramount in his life. A man like Flynn was unlikely to give up that loyalty, that kinship, and settle in England. But there was nothing wrong with a little flirtation, was there? How was a maiden to know the right man if she did not dally with the wrong man? Reaching the brick wall dividing the king's wood from her uncle's house she drew the key from her pocket, fitted it into the lock, opened the little door, and stepped through into the garden. At once she felt more at ease.

She was going to miss the evening meal at the palace, but she could not sit through another interminable banquet with Philippa and her friends. Seated below the high board, they would carp in low tones about Anne Boleyn, seated at the high board in the queen's place next to King Henry. It was the same every evening. They would bemoan Queen Katherine's exile to Woodstock, and decry the king's behavior. He who had been the most princely and noble gentleman in all of Europe was behaving like a man bewitched. And there were rumors, they would murmur in dark tones, that Mistress Boleyn was indeed a witch.

Elizabeth was tempted each time she heard this silly accusation to ask them why, if they knew Anne was a witch, they did not denounce her to the church. But she knew very well that if she dared to utter such a sentiment Philippa would be furious and mortified. And Philippa was already upset because Crispin had sent word that he could not join the court this month. It had something to do with his cattle, Elizabeth remembered. Philippa had cried a little, complaining that Brierewode always seemed to take precedence with Crispin. And Uncle Thomas had remarked dryly that she was fortunate that it did, and Philippa had grown silent.

Elizabeth entered the house and went to the hall. It was quiet and peaceful. She sighed with relief. The month was but half-over. It seemed as if she had been here forever, and in the end the whole purpose of their coming was for naught. She wished she were back at Friarsgate. Then to her surprise she realized she was not alone.

"Will! I did not see you there in your chair," she said.

"I wish we were back at Otterly," he replied. "When your uncle comes to court he is like a gadfly, flitting here and flitting there. I rarely see him. But back at Otterly we spend our days together on matters concerning the estate and the wool trade."

"Why do you not go with him to court?" Elizabeth asked.

"It would not be proper for me to accompany your uncle into the court, especially as the king was my last employer," William Smythe said. "Sometimes your uncle does not come in until half the night is over," he complained.

"He is very social," Elizabeth said, "but Philippa says he is not as active as he once was. That he hardly dances at all, and spends most of his time at the card tables."

"He has great fortune with the cards, but then he has great luck with everything that he takes on," William Smythe noted.

"Well, I want to go home too," Elizabeth said, "but we must remain until May is over. And now with Mistress Boleyn holding her masque to celebrate my birthday, I have no excuses to depart early. I am sorry, Will."

"It is quite an honor," Will said. "It is strange that with your family's connection to the queen you should become friends with Mistress Boleyn. And I can tell you like her. They say she is very clever and quick-witted, which the king likes."

"She is," Elizabeth said, "but she is also afraid, Will. Her uncle manipulates her fate like some wicked wizard. I wonder if the king will marry her. She does not make friends easily, Will. Those who surround her do so for their own benefit. Indeed, she has more enemies than she has friends. It is very sad. I am just as glad to be the Friarsgate heiress, and live in the north."

"But still," Will said, "you cannot help but be excited by having a fete planned for your natal day, Mistress Elizabeth. My master has been telling me all about the masques that are being made for you. And the costumes."

"Costumes?" She was surprised. "I thought I was to wear a gown with the masque." But then she laughed aloud, for knowing Thomas Bolton, she should have known better. Of course he would costume them. "What has he done?" she asked Will. "I know the masques are sheep, but what will we wear?"

"It is quite amazing, Mistress Elizabeth," William Smythe said excitedly, "but I think you must ask your uncle. I do not want to spoil his surprise."

"Then I will wait up for him to come home," Elizabeth said.

William Smythe felt better. Mistress Elizabeth always cheered him up just by her presence. "Shall I tell Cook you will be expecting an evening meal?" he asked her.

She nodded. "We'll eat together, Will," Elizabeth told him.

He chuckled. "You'll get nothing more out of me, Mistress Elizabeth," he told her, giving her one of his rare smiles.

When Thomas Bolton arrived home just before midnight he found his secretary and his niece engaged in an exciting game of Hare and Hounds. And William was actually laughing. "So this is where you have gotten to, dear girl," he said by way of greeting. "You were missed this evening, and had Flynn Stewart not been in plain sight the entire time I fear your reputation could have suffered damage. 'Twas said he was seen with his arms about you, and kissing you this afternoon by the river. Is it so?" He tossed his gloves aside and, going to the sideboard, poured himself a goblet of wine before joining them. "Who is winning?"

"I am," William Smythe said. "You know how proficient I am at Hare and Hounds, my lord. Although Mistress Elizabeth is a far better player than you are."

Lord Cambridge looked just slightly aggrieved, and then he realized that Elizabeth had not answered his query. "Dear girl?" he pressed her.

"Flynn Stewart was teaching me how to use a longbow. There is to be an archery contest for the ladies the day of my fete. I have never learned, and to be polite I thought I should be able to join in with the other women, Uncle. His arms were about me so he might guide my first few efforts. Does nothing, even the most innocent of pastimes, escape the vigilant eye of the gossips?" She was annoyed.

"And was there a kiss, dear girl?" he queried her further.

Elizabeth's irritation was answer in itself. "Yes, when I succeeded in hitting the target several times instead of sending my arrows into the river," she admitted. "But it was hardly earth-shattering, or even worthy of mention, Uncle."

"The gentleman flushed when teased about it, dear girl," Lord Cambridge said. "And he would neither deny nor confirm the accusation."

"Because it was not important, Uncle. A congratulatory buss between friends was all it was, although there are others who would wish it otherwise for gossip's sake," Elizabeth replied.

"Yet you departed the court afterwards," Thomas Bolton said.

"Because I was bored, Uncle. The king is charming. Mistress Boleyn is delightful, the intrigue is fascinating, but I have no real part in it, nor do I want any. People wonder at Mistress Boleyn's giving a fete in honor of my birthday. I do not. She is as bored as I am, Uncle. If I had stayed I should have been forced to listen to Philippa and her friends. I chose not to spend another moment doing that. So I came home and had a well-cooked meal and good wine and good company in your Will. But I have remained up awaiting you, Uncle, because I understand that you are having costumes made for us, and not just masques. Tell me!"

Lord Cambridge chortled. "Dear girl, we shall be the talk of the court for months to come. Upon reflection I decided that the sheep masques were simply not enough. You are aware that there are many here who mock your background. Not before the king, mind you, but among themselves. Small-minded, mean-spirited creatures with noble names, and not a penny to those names. Still, they consider themselves better than most others. How they mocked Wolsey for his humble roots, though they feared him for his power. And they are threatened by those wealthy newcomers at court who can offer the king their intellect to be used to his benefit, and not just a family tree to be admired by a king whose family they consider upstarts.

"So I considered, dear girl, that it might be amusing to rub the noses of these noble ladies and fellows in with the truth of what you are, and your pride in it. The king and Mistress Anne will understand the jest, and be diverted by it. Our costumes will be almost identical. We shall wear sleeveless jerkins made from sheepskin with the curly wool side out to be seen. Our doublets shall be fashioned from silk, with tufts of wool showing through the slashings." He chuckled. "Yours shall be creamy white. But mine shall be black, for I am to be a black sheep." And he laughed aloud. "Our breeches will also be slashed, with wool tufts showing through. Our stockings shall be silk, and our shoes shining black leather simulated to appear like sheep's hooves. Our masques, yours of gold, and mine of silver, shall have sheep faces. I shall sport marvelous curved horns on mine, but you, dear girl, shall wear bows in your hair."

"Uncle! This is outrageously clever of you! We shall indeed be the talk of the court for months to come. But you must not tell Philippa.

In the end she will relent and join us in her beautiful peacock's garb. But she is also astute enough to understand the jest. And she will not be pleased that I am showing my legs. 'Tis quite daring of you to suggest it, but then you knew I would do it."

"Dear girl, it will be your last hurrah, and I wanted you to have some fun out of this little adventure. I do not know why I agreed with your mother that coming to court was right for you. For Philippa and Banon, aye, but not for you, Elizabeth. I frankly do not know what we will do about finding you a husband, but this is not the place for such a venture, and I apologize to you." He took her two hands in his and kissed them.

"Uncle, you need not come to me on bended knee. I should have refused my mother's demand. Still and all it has been interesting, and I am happy to have met King Henry and poor Mistress Boleyn."

"And Flynn Stewart?" he inquired slyly.

Elizabeth laughed. "Was I ever a naive maiden, Uncle?" she asked him.

"Never," he agreed, "and yet, dear girl, he is very handsome."

"Aye," she agreed. "It does not hurt my eyes to look upon him, but he is far too bold to suit me." She would never admit that Flynn had caught a bit of her fancy.

"Bold men are more interesting, dear girl," Thomas Bolton remarked.

"I have learned what I waited to learn, Uncle," Elizabeth said. "Now I shall go to bed and dream of Friarsgate and my sheep." She arose from the game table. "I must concede to you, Will. You were going to beat me anyway." Then she kissed her uncle and departed the hall.

"You have truly given up the hunt?" William Smythe wanted to know.

Lord Cambridge nodded. "I had hoped that I could perhaps snag the son of one of these nouveau riche; that there would be a father more willing to lose a lad to the north than to let him take his chances at court. But they come to the court because they see opportunity, and they are ambitious. There are the younger daughters of the nobility for them to wed, for the nobility is usually poorer than they are, and willing to sell their lasses. Each family profits by the arrangement. Three years ago when I was last here I did not notice these changes, but I see them clearly now. Elizabeth may have a large estate, and she may be wealthy, but no one wants to leave the court to live in Cumbria. If she were happy to let a husband remain here, and he were happy to allow her to continue to manage Friarsgate, perhaps. But that is not a marriage, and Elizabeth would never settle for such an arrangement, nor would her mother. Alas, Will, I reached my peak with Philippa. Marrying her into the ranks of the nobility was an incredible achievement. I cannot do it again. There must be a man for Elizabeth, but he is not here."

"The Scot will not do?" William Smythe asked.

"He is too much a Scot, I fear," Thomas Bolton answered. "He could not be content at Friarsgate. But I must watch him to see he does not seduce my darling girl, for the man has a look in his eye that is positively dangerous, dear boy. I shall let Elizabeth play with him a bit, but I shall be observing him carefully."

"It is late, my lord," William Smythe said.

"Aye," Lord Cambridge agreed, "and I find to my surprise that I am indeed not as young as I once was. Let us away to our beds, dear boy. The morning is almost here!"

At court the next day Sir Thomas Wyatt attempted to kiss Elizabeth, and was smacked for his trouble. "But you let Flynn kiss you," he complained.

"Did he say it?" Elizabeth demanded, her tone angry.

"Well, no," Sir Thomas Wyatt admitted, "but I have the evidence of my own eyes, Mistress Elizabeth. I saw you together."

"Yet if I do not say it, and he did not say it, how can it be so, my lord?" Elizabeth wanted to know.

Anne Boleyn laughed. "She has you, cousin!" She linked her arm with Elizabeth's. "Come, Bess, we shall be gone, and leave these randy gentlemen to their own devices." She led her friend off, and when they were far enough away not to be heard she asked, "Did he kiss you?"

"Aye, and I was mightily surprised, I can tell you," Elizabeth admitted.

"What was it like?" Anne wanted to know.

"You have been kissed," Elizabeth said, surprised by the question.

Anne lowered her voice. "When the king kisses me he kisses me as if he would devour me whole," she whispered. "Does Flynn Stewart kiss like that?"

Elizabeth thought for a long moment, and then she answered, "Nay. It was a powerful kiss, I will admit, but I did not feel consumed by it except in the nicest possible way. The manner he touched my face was, I believe, tender. I quite liked it. I shall let him kiss me again, Anne."

"Do you love him?" Anne wanted to know.

"Nay," Elizabeth said. "We do not know each other well enough for such a relationship to develop. But it is exciting to be pursued by such a man."

"Would you wed him?"

Elizabeth shook her head. "Even I know he is unsuitable."

"But is your mother not married to a Scot?" Anne wanted to know.

"Aye, but she is no longer the lady of Friarsgate. I am," Elizabeth replied.

"Then who will you wed?" Anne wondered. "I so want to be married and have a son for the king. The princess of Aragon is being so difficult! I do not know what she thinks she will gain by it. Her wretched daughter will never be her father's heir. Mary hates me, you know. The king sent the brat from court for insulting me. And do you know what she said to him? That she would pray for his immortal soul! The presumption of her!"

"My mother says she is her father's darling," Elizabeth offered.

"No longer!" Mistress Boleyn snapped.

"Then you surely understand her pique, for it is you who have taken her father's interest away from her. She is jealous, Anne. You must not be angry with her for it."

"My child will take precedence over hers when it is born one day," Anne said.

"But you have no child now," Elizabeth reminded her.

"But I will one day," Anne assured her friend, "and so will you."

"If I can find a husband," Elizabeth said with a grimace.

"My uncle says I must stop holding the king at bay," Anne confided. "I am afraid. He is so big, and I am so slight. I have held his manroot in my hand."

"You haven't!" Elizabeth didn't know whether to be shocked. And this wasn't just a man they were talking about. It was the king.

"I have," Anne said. "It throbs and is sometimes warm and sometimes cold. Often it lies flaccid in my hand like a small bird. And other times it swells and lengthens, growing hard as stone. Have you ever seen a manroot?"

Elizabeth shook her head. "Not really, but I have seen animals when they mate. The male mounts the female and pumps her full of his seed. Rams, horses, dogs, and cats, I have seen it all. I have even seen the rooster mount the hen in the barnyard."

"Humankind does not mate quite that way," Anne said. "We lie upon our backs and are mounted that way, my mother says. Humankind mates face-to-face. But I have not let the king mount me yet. They say I must give in to him soon or I will lose him. Yet I have held him at bay for all these years, and I fear if I give him his pleasure now he will leave me then. He could not do that if I were his wife. If I were queen."

Elizabeth drew a deep breath. She had just been allowed intimacies that she should not know. *Poor Anne*, she thought. *Is there no one in whom she may confide but a country woman from Cumbria?* But then, Anne Boleyn was no fool. She had relieved herself of a burden, and she knew that Elizabeth Meredith would not be long at court. "A king may do what he pleases," she reminded her companion softly.

"Am I wise or foolish, Bess?" Anne wanted to know. "What say you?"

"The court is a place in which I am a stranger, Anne," Elizabeth began. "There is much intrigue, much gossip, much plotting of plots, all of which come to naught. The king is wed to Queen Katherine, though she be out of favor and unlikely to ever again gain it unless she gives him his way. That much is fact. He needs a legitimate son, which means he needs a new wife. Since she will not agree to an annulment or to a divorce, he must continue to pursue a means of dissolving his marriage. Or the queen must die a natural death, which seems unlikely in the near future. Until then any child born to him of any but his lawful wife will not be eligible to inherit the throne. You have often said you are not your sister, Mary, nor would you be. What if you gave in to the king's blandishments and yielded your virtue to him? And you bore him a son. And perhaps another. Both would be deemed bastardborn. And then finally the king would be free to remarry. Would he marry you? Or would his advisers convince him that he was perfectly capable of having sons, given the example of your sister, you, and Mistress Blount? And he would allow them to arrange his next marriage with a proper princess. The king is usually most considerate of his reputation. Would you be content to accept such a situation?"

"Never!" Anne Boleyn spat angrily.

"Then do not listen to your uncle, Anne. Or to anyone else who tells you to give yourself to the king. They do so in hopes he will tire of you and marry the princess they will choose for him one day when this matter with Queen Katherine is settled. And he who makes a successful marriage for the king will have great power. But he who fails the king will suffer as the cardinal has suffered. They say his heart is broken."

"He was a horrid little man," Anne said darkly. "He hated me, but then I hated him. Had he not interfered I should be Harry Percy's wife, and happy."

"You have the heart of a king in your keeping, Anne. Are you not happy knowing that? The king loves you."

"I wonder if he does," was the candid reply. "Or if it is that he just wants what he cannot have." She tossed her dark head impatiently. "I am so unhappy," she admitted.

"Did you love Harry Percy?" Elizabeth probed. At this point there was little point in being politic. "Do you love the king?"

"I did love Harry," Anne replied. "And strangely I find that I love the king. He can be the most wonderful man to be with when we are alone. But oddly I believe he is no happier than I am right now. The matter with the queen troubles him greatly. His need for a legitimate son worries him. I comfort him as best I can, but you are correct, Bess, when you tell me to keep myself as chaste as I can until I can be his wife." She laughed weakly. "There are those who say I have bewitched the king, you know."

"I know," Elizabeth responded, "but the court is populated by fools, as you well know. If the king is bewitched it is by your wit, your beauty, your charm."

Anne took Elizabeth's hands in hers. "I have never had a friend before," she said sadly. "Must you return to your Friarsgate, Bess?"

"I don't belong here, Anne. I am able to survive because I know I will be leaving shortly. Friarsgate is where I gain my strength. I must go home!"

"I could make you stay," Anne said. "If I asked the king he would order it."

"Aye, you could," Elizabeth agreed. "But if you are really my friend you will not. You will let me go. You will not lose my friendship by my going. My mother has always continued her friendship with Queen Katherine and with Margaret Tudor, despite the distance between them. I will always be your friend, Anne Boleyn. And when you are queen one day, I will still proudly proclaim our friendship. But I must go home."

Anne sighed. "I envy you, Bess Meredith. You have a home and a purpose in life. My home is, of necessity, wherever I am. My purpose is to help my family in any way in which I can. That is the Howard law. Advance oneself."

"My family motto is *Tracez votre chemin*," Elizabeth offered with a small grin.

"Trace your own path," Anne smiled. "It is a good motto, Bess, and it suits you, for despite what others think or say, you are most determined to do just that."

"I am," Elizabeth agreed.

"But you have to have a husband, Bess. All girls do. What will happen now that your trip to court has proven unsuccessful?"

"I don't know," Elizabeth replied. "I do not believe my family will force me into a union that I do not want. It is not their way. I suppose I must leave my fate in God's hands. I see no other way."

Anne nodded. "I think both of our fates are in God's hands," she said. "I hope he will be merciful to his humble handmaidens, Anne Boleyn and Elizabeth Meredith."

# Chapter 7

❦

*E*lizabeth kept her conversations with Anne Boleyn to herself. She did not even discuss them with Lord Cambridge, and certainly not with her older sister Philippa. She was flattered to be the confidante of a girl who was obviously destined for great things. But at the same time she was uncomfortable with the situation. Yet she was wise enough to understand that Mistress Boleyn had needed to unburden herself to someone she knew she might trust. Someone who would shortly be gone from court. *I shall never again be able to look the king in the eye*, Elizabeth thought, blushing at the word pictures that Anne Boleyn painted of her faux lover.

Henry Tudor, however, was delighted that the object of his desire had apparently become companionable with the daughter of Rosamund Bolton. Rosamund's daughters were models of discretion, as their mother had been. Still, the knowledge that two of Rosamund's daughters were wed, and the third seeking a husband—the fact that someone he had known as a boy was now a grandmother—made him even more aware of the passing of time. Of his need for a legitimate son. He watched, amused, as Anne and her friends played Blindman's Buff on the lawns of Greenwich. The air was delightfully warm, and the days growing longer. For the moment he was content.

Elizabeth Meredith could not see from behind the blindfold. She could hear the scuffling of shoes and boots, the swish of fabric, the giggles around her as she moved carefully forward, hands outstretched seeking a target of opportunity, listening for someone to make a mistake. There was someone behind her. She was certain of it. Whirling, she felt her quick fingers catch at the velvet of a doublet. "Aha!" she cried, and lifted her blindfold, blinking at the sunlight as she did so. "Flynn Stewart, you were careless, I fear. I heard you."

"Bah, mistress!" he replied. "I merely took pity on you."

"Liar!" She fastened the blindfold securely about his eyes and twirled him about, moving out of his way as she did. Eventually there would be a pretty girl to take pity on him, deliberately standing in his way to be caught. And sure enough, two giggling lasses were quickly vying for the honor.

Flynn caught one easily, and exchanged his blindfold for sight again while the girl stumbled off, seeking to find herself a willing victim. The Scotsman moved quickly out of her reach to join Elizabeth. "Walk with me," he said. "I've had enough of games for the nonce."

"I know. It seems such a waste of time," she said. "It is all these courtiers seem to do. When you are not your king's messenger, what do you do in Scotland, Flynn?"

"I am generally with the king. I hunt, fish, dice, and golf with him. I sit by his side in the council, and listen to the bickering of his earls. I listen for information that might be of use to him. My life is full. I am much older, of course, than the king. I taught him to ride when he was just a wee laddie."

"Was she ever there? His mother, I mean," Elizabeth asked curiously.

"Sometimes, but she was never really accepted by the Scots. On one hand I believe she loved her husband, yet her loyalties were often divided, for she loved her brother in England too. Finally, after King James IV's death, I think she realized there was no one to really protect her, and her loyalties were fixed of necessity on herself. She married Angus first, but he wanted her for the power, and when she realized it she divorced him. Now she is wed to a husband much her junior, but she is a fascinating woman, I have to admit, and this Stewart adores her."

"You are most astute," Elizabeth noted.

"A spy should be," he teased her.

"But you told me you were not a spy," she remarked.

He chuckled. "Every foreign national here at the Tudor court spies for one reason or another, my lambkin, but of course none of us will admit to it."

"I do not find what is happening here particularly fascinating or worthy of repeating," Elizabeth said seriously.

"It isn't," Flynn agreed. "At least not now. But now and again something occurs that is worth passing on to my king."

"So you are not interested in the mundane details of the court," she said.

"Nay. Reporting on how many times the king visited his privy is not of great interest, unless, of course, he were aged and dying," Flynn said. Then, changing the subject, he asked her, "Are you ready to partake in the archery contest in two days' time?"

"I am," she said. "You are a most worthy instructor."

"Perhaps we need to practice again," he suggested.

"If you want to kiss me, Flynn Stewart," Elizabeth replied mischievously, "I suggest we forgo the longbows, and simply find a private place where we may cuddle."

"Are you attempting to seduce me, lambkin? If that be your intent I am more than happy to oblige," he told her boldly. To his delight she blushed with his words.

"Nay! Nay! Nor do I wish to be seduced, sir, but I did enjoy kissing you, and you have not attempted it since that day you taught me to use a longbow," Elizabeth explained. "Do you not find me worthy of your attentions?"

"Oh, lambkin, I find you more than worthy," he said, and taking her hand he led her towards the small woodland that separated the palace from her uncle's house.

"If we go into my uncle's garden, Flynn Stewart, we will have all the privacy we need," Elizabeth told him boldly. Her other hand dug into the hidden pocket on her rose-colored gown for the key to the little door.

He stopped at her words and pushed her up against an old tree. "You are, lambkin, a bold baggage, I have begun to consider." He brushed a lock of her long blond hair from her cheek. "You should not play such games unless you are prepared to pay the price," he advised her.

"I have been told that both lovers can win in the game of love," she answered him low. He was pressed against her, and she could smell his very male scent. It almost made her dizzy with a temptation she had never before felt.

His laughter was insinuating. "Who told you that?" he asked her, and his lips brushed her forehead.

"My mother," Elizabeth answered him.

"A wise woman," he told her. Then he tipped her face up to his, and his mouth closed over hers in a passionate kiss.

His lips were warm. Dry. Firm. She had closed her eyes when those lips had met hers. She reveled in their touch even as his lips worked hers gently, forcing her mouth to open that he might plunge his tongue into it. Elizabeth started, but he held her firmly as he sought out her own tongue. She retreated. He advanced. And finally the two tongues touched. He caressed hers tenderly. She shuddered, and it was as if liquid fire had been released in her veins. She was hot and weak at the same time. She didn't know how she was managing to remain upright, and then she realized he was holding her tightly. She sighed and drew her head away from his. "That was nice," she murmured to him.

He laughed. "You appear to have an aptitude for kissing, lambkin."

"I am pleased to learn it," she said. "Until recently I had never been kissed."

"Ah, your other Scotsman," he replied. "Should I be jealous?"

Now it was Elizabeth who laughed. "Neither of you should be jealous of the other," she told him. "I kiss you, allow you to kiss me, because it pleases me."

"You must be careful of such speech, Elizabeth," he warned her. "I know your words are direct and truthful. Another man might misunderstand and think you a wanton. I know you are not, but then I am an honest man, and there are few at court who are. You must beware of appearing to be what you are not. Especially given your friendship with Mistress Anne Boleyn, the king's little friend."

"Why are you not married?" she asked him, changing the subject entirely. "Do you have a mistress? I understand most Stewarts do."

"I am not married because I have nothing to offer a wife. I am bastard-born for all my father was a king, but I have little to call my own. A name, aye, but no land. No house. Few possessions. I serve my half brother with both love and loyalty. I am not a man for marriage, Elizabeth. And as I cannot afford a wife, I can scarce afford a mistress. Mistresses are far more expensive to keep than a wife would be."

"You would think your brother would reward your service," she answered him. "You are in the same position my father once was, but at least he was rewarded with my mother's hand in marriage, and in those days it was my mother who was the heiress to Friarsgate. You need a propertied wife." What on earth was she saying? Certainly she wasn't offering herself to this man because he had kissed her? But nay! She found his company pleasant and his kisses heady. It was, she thought, as good a foundation for a marriage as any, and they kept telling her she had to marry. A poor man of good breeding, Flynn Stewart would never presume to pursue her, so she must pursue him.

"A propertied Scots wife," he corrected her gently, his emphasis on the word *Scots*. "I will always serve my king, lambkin. My loyalty extends beyond our bond of blood. My birth was an accident, yet my father gave me his name and treated me with loving kindness. And when my mother died and I was forced from the only home I had ever known, my half brother's guardian recognized me for who I was, and took me in. I was given a purpose in life, and trusted. I am a Scot, lambkin, and I can never be anything else but a Scot."

"I think I should like to be kissed again," she announced, and slipped her arms about his neck. "Would you like to be kissed again, Flynn Stewart?" He was rejecting any suggestion, direct or indirect, that he might take his place by her side as her husband, but perhaps she could convince him otherwise. After all, her stepfather was a Scot, and it didn't seem to bother anyone except perhaps the king. Looking up into his handsome face she gave him a seductive smile.

And he laughed, to her mortification, shaking his head and saying, "You are a proper minx, Elizabeth Meredith, and you are learning court ways. I am not certain I like them on you. Yet I would be a fool to not accept what you are so freely offering me." And then he kissed her.

But this time his kiss was neither sweet nor innocent. It was hard, demanding, and burningly passionate. Elizabeth almost swooned with the fierce pleasure it gave her. She kissed him back, matching him kiss for kiss. His mouth left her mouth, and he kissed her closed eyelids, traveling down the curve of her throat, brushing across the tops of her young breasts, which seemed to be struggling to break forth from her bodice. And then he suddenly ceased, groaning as he released his hold on her.

Elizabeth pressed herself against the trunk of the tree to prevent herself from falling. She could scarcely draw a breath, and when she did the first few she drew hurt her chest. "What is the matter?" she finally managed to ask him, for he looked both pale and pained.

"I cannot play lovers' games with you, Elizabeth," he finally managed to say.

"Why not?" she demanded.

"Because you are a virgin of means and breeding with powerful friends, and I want more from you than kisses. I cannot have you, lambkin. Your king and my king maintain the barest of cordial relations. There is always the chance that war will ensue between them based on the slightest pretext."

"There are many mixed marriages in the borders," she told him.

"But there is only one heiress to Friarsgate, Elizabeth," he said softly. "You are not nobility, but your lands, your flocks, your cloth trade give you a power you do not even understand. You are a prize to be had. The king's father gave your mother to one of his most loyal knights. It was done to keep the part of the border you inhabit safe for England. When you came to court the old story made its rounds, lambkin."

"My father loved my mother!" Elizabeth cried.

"Aye, that is what they say of him. That he loved her the moment he saw her. But how rare is that? I am surprised that this king has not rewarded one of his minions with you, but should you even consider taking a Scot for a husband, he would forbid it. As he should, Elizabeth Meredith. His duty is to England, as yours must be as well."

"The king would not dare arrange my marriage, for he knows my mother too well. She would never allow me to be parceled off to anyone who would not come north to Friarsgate and help me care for the land," Elizabeth said angrily. "And no one can ever make me marry someone I don't want to marry!"

"I have not a farmer's nature," Flynn told her brutally. "I am a man of the court as your sister, the Countess of Witton, is a lady of the court. I thrive on the very air that surrounds the mighty, their intrigues and schemes. I should be bored if I had to live in the country, lambkin, even as you are bored here at court."

"Then why did you kiss me, Flynn Stewart?" she wanted to know.

"Because you are pretty, and tempting, and oh, so ripe for seduction," he told her.

"But you did not seduce me," she countered. "In fact at no time did you not act the gentleman."

"A proper seduction takes time, Elizabeth. First the wolf must gain the trust of the little lambkin. And when the foolish creature is thoroughly beguiled by the wolf, he strikes!" Flynn said, yanking her back into his arms and looking down into her face. "Do you want me to ruin you? Do you think if I do, and you tell Mistress Anne, I would be forced to wed you? Nay, lambkin. I should be thrown in the Tower, and perhaps, depending on his mood, my brother might intercede for me. Then I should be sent home in disgrace. Or my brother might wash his hands of me, and I would languish forever. As for you, lambkin, you would be sent home with your uncle. And he would carry a list of suitable northern eligibles from which your family would choose a husband for you. Provided, of course, my seed had not taken root in you. Stewart seed is most potent, you know, and you could bear a bastard."

"Whom I would recognize and raise to be a good Englishman. Then I should have an heir. It is a more pleasant outlook than being forced to the altar with a man I couldn't love, and should probably have to kill in the end when he attempted to usurp my authority," she told him defiantly.

He laughed again, and when he did his eyes crinkled endearingly. "I will not act as your breeding ram, lambkin. Nor in the time you remain at court will I allow you to do anything foolish. There is no one here for you, but perhaps when you return to Friarsgate you may look upon some of your neighbors more kindly." He caressed her face. "I should never be a docile mate, lambkin," he told her, "and I would keep you on your back so that you would have no time for anything else other than me." Then he kissed her, a slow, sweet kiss that left her breathless.

Finally she pulled away from him, and, drawing the key from her pocket, she went to the little door in the wall, and, opening it, stepped through. "You are a fool, Flynn Stewart," she said, slamming the door shut, and to her fury she heard his boisterous laughter from the other side of the garden wall. With a sputter of outrage Elizabeth hurried up to the house. He was an impossible man, and she had made a perfect fool of herself with him. But, oh, his kisses were so delicious!

She needed to think, and so Elizabeth took to her bed. Was she ill? Philippa fussed about her. Her birthday fete was in just two days. She had to be well for it, her sister insisted. "I thought you didn't approve of Mistress Boleyn," Elizabeth said wickedly to her older sister.

"I do not," Philippa replied loftily, "but the king does approve of her, and she has planned a birthday fete in your honor, which is, as of the moment, considered an honor. If you are not well enough to attend it will cast a pall over the whole thing."

"I do not think I can go unless you are at my side, sister," Elizabeth said in a weak voice. "I rely upon you and your knowledge of court customs."

"You are a little liar," Philippa said, "and I suspect there is nothing wrong with you at all." But she smiled and smoothed her sister's hair from her forehead. "What has happened, Bessie? And do not say nothing, for I am older and wiser than you."

"I threw myself at a man, and was quite firmly rejected," Elizabeth said. "And do not call me Bessie!" Why she was telling Philippa she did not know, but she simply couldn't keep it to herself.

"Ah," Philippa replied, "so you can be tempted. I was fearful that only your sheep could appeal to your heart, sister. Who is the gentleman? Is it possible he would make you a good husband? And why would he reject you? Unless, of course, his heart was engaged by another, but surely you would know that, and not be foolish enough to throw yourself at someone already taken."

"He is not taken. He doesn't even have a mistress. I asked," Elizabeth responded.

Philippa closed her eyes momentarily to swallow back the admonishment that sprang to her lips. Her sister was really quite unskilled in the ways of polite society. "Will you tell me his name, Elizabeth?" she said quietly.

"He says he is unsuitable, and a marriage between us would not be allowed," the younger woman replied.

"Does he?" Philippa was intrigued. How unusual for a gentleman to understand such a refinement. Now she was very curious. She cocked her auburn head questioningly at her youngest sister.

"It is the Scotsman, Flynn Stewart," Elizabeth said, and then braced for the explosion sure to come at her revelation.

"He is handsome, I will admit," Philippa said calmly, surprising her sibling. "But, of course, he is absolutely correct. He is not suitable at all. He is more a gentleman than I would have given him credit for, Elizabeth, that he would be so candid with you."

"We have kissed," Elizabeth told Philippa.

"But no more than kiss?" Philippa queried.

"Nay, no more." Elizabeth sounded so sad that her sister almost hugged her.

"You are fortunate that the object of your unrequited affections has been so honest," the Countess of Witton said. "There are many here who might have taken advantage of you. Why the Scot?" She was curious.

"I suppose because he is from the north, as I am. Because he is an outsider, as I am. Because he is charming, and does not make me feel so damned gauche," Elizabeth said. "He has escorted me about and introduced me to Anne, who seems to be the only friend I have made. He has been kind, Philippa. Even you must admit there is no one here for me, as there was no one here for you once. Had you not realized that your heart and your fate were here at court, had not Uncle purchased the lands adjoining Brierewode, you would not have found your true love here. You did not want Friarsgate. But like our mother, I love it. That is where my heart lies. I thought Flynn might want to share my fate with me, but his loyalty is entirely to his brother."

"Do you love him?" Philippa wanted to know.

"I don't think so, but I like him, and I believe I could live together with him as man and wife. Passion can die, sister. A good friendship cannot," Elizabeth said.

"Friendship is a strong basis for a lasting love," Philippa said quietly. "But if his loyalty is to Scotland first he is not the man for you, or for Friarsgate."

"There are plenty of mixed matches in the borders," Elizabeth reminded her sister. "Our mother's, for example."

"But none of those involved are people of importance, or have great estates. Mother turned Friarsgate over to you because she saw how deeply you loved it. As much as, if not more than, she did. It allowed her to finally live at Claven's Carn with Logan and raise our wild Scots brothers in their father's house, where they belong. Our brothers will have no divided loyalties, Elizabeth. Nor should the man you marry one day. Friarsgate is English. You are English."

"I am an old maid," came the dour reply.

Philippa couldn't help but laugh. "I thought you wanted no man so you could rule over your kingdom unencumbered," she teased.

"I did," Elizabeth said, "but I am now realizing the importance of having an heir, and the necessity of having a husband to obtain one. I want to go home! I was not so confused at home. Everything is just as I like it at home."

Philippa put her arms about her sister. "First you rest, and then you attend the birthday fete planned for you, and then you can pack for home," she said, hugging Elizabeth. "Now go to sleep. You have dark circles beneath your eyes, and that will not do on your birthday. I will go with you to the fete, and wear that magnificent peacock costume that Uncle Thomas has had made for me, because he knew in the end I could not resist missing such an event. And then I shall go home to Brierewode, because I find the court not really to my liking these days, yet I do not wish to lose favor with the king lest it reflect upon my sons and their careers."

"Life is simpler at Friarsgate," Elizabeth said.

"Life is never simple." Philippa smiled.

"It is when you are a country farmer," Elizabeth replied.

"But not when you are a courtier," Philippa countered.

They laughed with each other. They were so different that sometimes it seemed to Elizabeth it was hard to imagine that they were sisters. But they were. Philippa left her younger sibling, and Elizabeth closed her eyes to sleep. On reflection she had been very foolish with Flynn Stewart. She hoped it had not spoiled their friendship. She still thought he would make a fine husband. Her situation was not unlike Philippa's had been all those years back, when the boy she thought to marry jilted her for a life in Holy Mother Church. Philippa had gone to pieces and behaved badly. But then, she had been dreaming of her lad for five years. *I have just met Flynn Stewart, and my heart is not broken*, she decided.

While she pondered all that had happened between them, Flynn Stewart had a momentary crisis of faith in the life he had chosen. Elizabeth's words had pricked him. Why hadn't his brother rewarded him with something other than a posting in England? Was he not worth a cottage somewhere? A house in Edinburgh? A wife with a goodly dower portion? A Scotswoman who would understand his loyalties, and concur with them? He knew he would hardly be in his royal half brother's daily thoughts, but surely his service and loyalty all these years was worth something to King James V.

But James V was a cold and ruthless young man, although he had incredible charm when he chose to exercise it. And his smile could be most winning. He had learned to be hard in the years he had been in the wardship of his stepfather, his mother's second husband, the Earl of Angus. When the Duke of Lennox, who had been James IV's nearest kinsman, had returned to France, Angus had stepped in to oversee the boy king. He had had him declared of age when James V had turned fourteen, but it had been an excuse to rule in his stepson's name. He kept the boy relatively uneducated, unlike his predecessors, who had all been highly educated men. He saw to his sexual initiation in hopes the boy would be kept so busy with his mistresses that Angus could manage the government. And Flynn watched as the earl attempted to ruin his half brother.

In secret he had forced James to practice his writing so that his hand would be legible when he signed papers. When Angus wasn't there to observe he made him read the documents put on his writing table. "You're the king," he told his half brother. "You should always read everything before you sign it."

"Why?" James demanded, their father's eyes looking directly at him.

"Because I would not like you to sign my execution order unknowingly," Flynn Stewart had said with a grin, and he gently cuffed his half brother. "You'd feel dreadful about it afterwards, Jamie."

But the two areas where the young king excelled were in music and in warlike pursuits. How odd, Flynn thought, that both he and his uncle of England had such wonderful musical ability. Were they any two other men they would be friends, drawn together by their musical passion. But they were not. They did not know each other, but they distrusted each other, for unlike other men they were England and Scotland.

And then when James V was in his sixteenth year, he escaped from the Earl of Angus's clutches, exacted his revenge on Angus and his kin, and began to rule on his own. One of the first things he had done was send Flynn to his uncle in England. Flynn would be the personal messenger for his royal half brother. He would bring any messages Henry wanted to send to James with all possible speed, and return with answers. Flynn had not wanted to go.

"You need me here as I have always been. I am your eyes and your ears, my lord," he had said to his brother.

"Which is why I need you at my uncle's court, Flynn," King James had told him. "You are the one person in all the world whom I can trust. I know that you cannot be bribed away from your loyalty to me. There is no one else among my retainers for whom I can claim that virtue. My ambassadors will couch everything in the language of diplomacy. It seems that they are unable to speak plainly. They will curry favor with my uncle. But you, brother, will tell me the truth of whatever is happening in my uncle's court. You will be discreet, and none will consider you a threat."

"I am loath to leave you, my lord. I have been by your side since you were a small lad," Flynn said. "I would give my life for you."

"I know that," the young king had said. "I will not keep you away forever, Flynn, but you must do this for me. I am yet young, and my uncle of England would snatch my kingdom from me, given the opportunity. And he would choose a wife for me if he could. I have already chosen to wed with King Francois's daughter, Madelaine, but it will be several years before she is ready to be a wife. In the meantime I must fend off Uncle Henry's efforts on my behalf."

"I will go, my lord," Flynn had said. His life was his service to his half brother. Yet Elizabeth Meredith was correct. His king had taken his loyalty for granted. He was out of James's sight, and therefore out of his thoughts. Yet he knew if he asked James for a wealthy wife or a bit of land it would eventually be forthcoming. His brother had never been mean or closefisted. Then Flynn sighed. What a pity Friarsgate wasn't on the other side of the border. Elizabeth had made most plain her interest in him, and the hurt in her eyes when he had been forced to reject her advances had saddened him. But the English lambkin was not for him. Sooner or later England and Scotland would find themselves at war with each other again. And he had no doubt that Elizabeth Meredith would defend her beloved Friarsgate from all comers, as her mother before her had undoubtedly done. He had never thought to really care for a woman, but he knew that he could easily love the lovely heiress of Friarsgate. Ah, well! She would be gone in just over a week, and he was unlikely to see her again.

Elizabeth kept to her bed the next day, reassuring her worried uncle and her sister that she just needed a little more rest. "This court life is far more exhausting than the daily life at home," she noted. "Uncle, please tell Anne I am so honored by the fete, and will be there come the morrow."

But Anne Boleyn had fretted nonetheless and, escorted by Lord Cambridge, had come through the garden door to visit her friend. "You look pale," she noted.

"I am not used to staying up till all hours of the night dancing and gaming," Elizabeth said with a small smile. "I cannot sleep two or three hours and then be at the Mass, perfectly dressed and coiffed, as you seem able to do. I am a country girl, and used to sleeping more than several hours a night."

"Don't you get up with the sun?" Anne wanted to know. "And the sun rises early these days, Bess."

"Aye, but I go to bed early in the evening. Your life is tiring, Anne. I should rather spend my day out on horseback riding from flock to flock than spend my life in idle merriment. Your pardon, dear friend, but I am not used to such a life."

"But you have had fun, haven't you?" Anne asked.

"Aye, I have had fun, but you see me today in my bed recovering from the past few weeks, and tomorrow I know will be busy from dawn to moonset," Elizabeth said.

"Yes! Yes!" Anne agreed. "We are going to have barge races on the river, and archery contests for both the ladies and gentlemen, and dancing, and singing. It will be wonderful! And the feast! I have chosen the menu myself. We will have peacock, swans, game pies, beef, duck, and goose. And subtleties of spun sugar, and marzipan."

"Gracious!" Elizabeth exclaimed. "I am hardly worthy of such a spectacular effort, dear Anne. There are many who will be jealous that you have honored a simple country woman as myself."

"I know," Anne Boleyn said. "Won't it be fun?"

Elizabeth laughed. "You are really very bad, Annie," she told the older girl, "but I believe they deserve it for their behavior towards you. I am sorry that others do not know you as I do. You have a good heart, but you are sorely treated, and much is asked of you. I would wish it were not so," she concluded.

"I will survive. One in my position learns quickly or perishes, Bess. I will not be beaten by them. I will do what I must, and I will be queen one day. And I will birth my lord Henry's son, and he will live, as those poor Spanish Kate bore did not. I am strong!" Then Mistress Boleyn jumped up from her place by Elizabeth's bed. "I must go," she said. "I just came to be certain you are all right. Lord Cambridge swore you were, but I needed to see for myself. Is your costume for tomorrow wonderful?"

Elizabeth chuckled. "You will be very surprised when you see me," she told her companion.

"Will I recognize you?" Anne wanted to know.

"Easily," Elizabeth assured her. "You will see tomorrow."

"Farewell then," Anne Boleyn said, and hurried from the chamber.

Elizabeth Meredith's twenty-second birthday dawned fair and warm. She was awakened by Philippa and Thomas Bolton, both of whom brought her flowers. "How lovely!" she exclaimed, smiling at them both.

"Are you ready to face the day, dear girl?" Lord Cambridge asked her with a twinkle in his amber eyes.

"I am ready," Elizabeth assured him, "and Philippa has promised to come too, haven't you, sister?"

"I have already tried on my costume," the Countess of Witton said. "How you can manage to have a gown made for me, Uncle, when you have not seen me in over three years is amazing."

"You do not change, dear girl," he told her.

"But I might have," she responded.

"Nonsense," he replied. "It is simply not in your nature, dear girl."

"Have you seen my costume, Philippa?" Elizabeth wanted to know.

"I have," her sister answered. "It is quite outrageous, but then it is also quite clever, and 'twill suit you. You are mocking the courtiers who would mock you. The king will very much enjoy the jest. Mother will too, when you tell her."

"I have never been ashamed of who I am," Elizabeth said quietly.

"Nor should you be, dear girl," Lord Cambridge said.

They left her, and Nancy brought Elizabeth's breakfast to her bedchamber. The tray contained a little dish of fresh strawberries with clotted Devon cream, a plate of Cook's wonderfully short scones, butter, honey, and watered wine. Although she would have eaten eggs and meat had they been offered to her, Elizabeth knew Cook was considering her very fitted costume. She ate slowly, enjoying her food, and putting off for just a short while more the time when she would have to be dressed and at Greenwich. When she had finally satisfied her appetite enough, Nancy had her little tub ready. "How am I to wear my hair with the costume?" she asked her young tiring woman. "I don't think it should be down, do you?"

"I'm going to contain it in a gold mesh snood," Nancy said. "You don't want your lovely hair detracting from your wonderful costume."

Elizabeth quickly bathed, drying herself with a large cloth that had been warming before the fire in her bedchamber hearth. Then with Nancy's help she began to dress. First she sat and drew on her creamy white silk stockings. Next came a man's short silk chemise. She pulled on the white breeches, which were slashed, with tufts of lamb's wool peeking from the slashings. A sleeveless jerkin of curly lambskin went over the chemise, followed by an open-fronted white silk doublet with large puffed sleeves. Like the breeches the sleeves were slashed, with tufts of lamb's wool poking through, and the doublet itself sewn with crystal beads. She sat briefly so that Nancy might gather her hair and tuck it into a gold mesh snood. The girl then placed several little pink-and-white-striped bows in Elizabeth's hair. Then the tiring woman knelt to place black leather shoes, cut to resemble sheep's hooves, onto her mistress's feet. Elizabeth stood up.

"Oh, mistress!" Nancy exclaimed. "It is so clever."

"You have the masque?" Elizabeth asked.

Nancy nodded, handing it to her.

Elizabeth held the masque of a pretty lamb's head to her face by its long gilded stick. "What do you think?" she asked Nancy.

"I think"—Nancy giggled—"that you would frighten the flock if you appeared in the meadow that way; but today you will delight the king and his court with your cleverness. Shall I go and see if Lord Cambridge is ready?"

Elizabeth nodded. "And her ladyship too," she said, turning about to peer at herself in the mirror. The costume was perfect, and she smiled. Today's fete was in her honor. Elizabeth Meredith, a simple country heiress from the north. Not a noblewoman of impressive lineage with a great name, but the daughter of one of King Henry VII's loyal knights. She wondered what the father she did not remember would think of it all. When Nancy returned to say that both her ladyship and Lord Cambridge awaited her, Elizabeth moved downstairs to the foyer of the house to join them.

"Dear girl! It is even better than I had anticipated," Thomas Bolton crowed, delighted. He was quite splendid himself in a matching costume of black silk and black sheep's wool. His doublet was also decorated with crystals, and he carried a silver masque. On either side of his head had been affixed curved ram's horns.

"Philippa," Elizabeth said, looking at her sister, who was quite beautiful in a gown of blue-green iridescent silk sewn with crystals. The silk brocade fabric of the underskirt looked like a peacock's tail in design, and she carried a masque of peacock feathers. Her glorious auburn hair was loose about her shoulders.

"It is daring," she said in a worried tone. "Your legs are most prominent, sister. I wonder if you should show them so boldly." Then she laughed at herself. "But no matter! There is no gentleman here for you, so it means little. And the Friarsgate heiress shall certainly be remembered for her wit and her ability to play a clever jest on the court. Most will wear naught but masques, but others will be gloriously costumed."

"Then we are ready," Lord Cambridge said.

Together they walked through the house's garden and the wood beyond the brick wall. They exited onto the lawns of the palace and made their way to where the king sat with Anne Boleyn by his side. She was garbed in his favorite Tudor green, and carried a little mask representing a frog. As they had previously planned, Philippa moved ahead of her sister and uncle. Stopping before the king, she curtseyed low, smiling as she did, although she thought her face would crack at greeting not just the king, but the Boleyn wench as well.

"My liege," she said politely, drawing her masque away just long enough for him to see her.

"Lovely!" the king enthused. "You are a perfect peacock, Countess."

Philippa curtseyed again, then stepped gracefully aside to allow the king a view of her sister and uncle. Both bowed, and then, as they had decided earlier, Thomas Bolton and Elizabeth Meredith danced a gay little dance all the way to the foot of the king's chair, where they bowed once again, drawing their masques aside so he might see them.

"We greet your majesty and Mistress Anne," Lord Cambridge said.

"Bravo! Bravo!" the king cried, clapping his hands delightedly. "How clever you are! Never have I seen such costumes. They are quite marvelous!"

"We hoped it would please your majesty," Elizabeth said.

"You thumb your nose at the court, Mistress Meredith." The king chuckled.

"I simply wish to point out that I am what I am," Elizabeth returned wickedly.

"By the rood," the king said, " 'tis a pity there is no man at this court worthy of you, Elizabeth Meredith. If there were I would make the match myself, but you are your mother's child, more so than your sisters, I see. You must return home to find your fate."

"I am, as my mother before me, your majesty's most humble servant," Elizabeth said, making an elegant leg as she bowed again.

Henry Tudor roared with laugher. "Like your mother, only when it suits you, I suspect, Mistress Meredith."

Anne Boleyn came from her seat by the king's side and linked her arm with Elizabeth's. "Come, and we will show off our costumes," she said. "How daring of you to show off your legs in those breeches. Do you see my uncle of Norfolk glaring at us from across the lawn? He is such a handsome man, but he schemes too much. He worries the king will lose interest in me, and then I will bring nothing of worth to him but a bad reputation. How sad it is for all of us."

"Do you really believe the king will get his divorce and wed you?" Elizabeth asked in a soft voice.

"Aye, one way or another he will be rid of Spanish Kate, and I will be his wife," Anne Boleyn said confidently. "And they all believe it too," she said, her dark eyes taking in the courtiers promenading about the lawn. As they passed her they would bow and nod greetings. "I am queen in all but name only," Anne said low.

The festivities began. The day was bright and the riverside pleasant. Anne had arranged for barge races, and there were several heats between vessels belonging to the nobles until the final race against the king's royal barge. The courtiers gathered along the riverbank, wagering and shouting as the four barges in the last heat raced down the river, their colorful pendants flying in the light breeze. The oarsmen, their chests bared, bent over the oars, their muscles bulging and flexing as they pulled for home. In the end the last race was between the king's barge and Thomas Howard, the Duke of Norfolk, Anne's uncle. At the last moment the royal barge sped ahead, and there was much cheering.

Tables with food were set up near the palace itself. There was, as Anne had promised, peacock, roasted and then refeathered. Swans, geese, capons, and crisp ducks in a sauce of sweet Seville oranges and raisins. There were pies of rabbit, small game birds, and eel. Platters of trout and salmon with carved lemons and watercress were served. There was a great side of beef that had been packed in salt, and was roasting slowly over a large fire pit. There was venison, country-cured hams, and mutton stew. There were silver chargers of the king's favorite—artichokes—bowls of new peas, and lettuces braised in white wine. The breads were hot from the ovens. There were large crocks of sweet butter as well as several wheels of good cheddar cheese, and Brie from France. And when all had been eaten, and the leftovers removed to give to the poor at the king's gates, bowls of sweet strawberries and clotted cream were brought, along with tiny sugar wafers, marzipan fruits, and spun-sugar subtleties. The wine and ale flowed endlessly from huge kegs that had been set up on the lawns near the tables.

In late afternoon the archery contests were announced: first the ladies, and then the gentlemen. Elizabeth acquitted herself quite well, but the prize was taken by her sister Philippa, and presented by the king himself. It was a gold brooch with a small ruby heart. Philippa was most pleased, and wished Crispin had been there to see her little triumph. Then it was the gentlemen's turn, and for the first time that day Elizabeth saw Flynn Stewart. He was extremely skilled and won the contest. His prize, a small bag of gold coins, was presented by Mistress Boleyn.

The twilight was long, and now lanterns were brought and lit. Musicians appeared and began to play. The dancing had begun. Elizabeth was delighted to have Flynn Stewart claim her hand in a country dance. They danced well together.

"Is it wise to allow them to dance?" Philippa asked Thomas Bolton.

"She fancies herself taken with him, doesn't she?" he replied. "No matter. He is a Scot, and unsuitable. She knows it, for your sister is no fool. And we will be leaving in a few days' time to return to Friarsgate. Will you be traveling with us?"

Philippa shook her head. "I am going to Woodstock to see the queen," she answered him softly.

"Is that wise?" he queried her.

"Perhaps not, but I will go anyhow," Philippa answered. "As long as my plans are not known to any they will assume I am returning home, which I will immediately afterwards. I cannot desert her, Uncle."

"She is a foolish woman," Lord Cambridge said, "and overweening proud. She cannot win this battle between them, and he will have his way in the end." Then he turned his head back to watch the dancers, and Philippa joined him.

It finally grew dark. The king had taken up his lute and begun to sing a little roundelay he had written for Mistress Boleyn. Elizabeth thought the tune a pretty one, and suddenly her voice was blending with the king's as she learned the lines of the chorus. Henry Tudor smiled, for he remembered her father's clear voice, and was pleased to see Elizabeth had inherited it. His roundelay sounded even better for the sweet female voice joined with his. It had been a good day, and he felt quite the young man again.

"You sing well," he told Elizabeth when his tune came to an end.

"I hope your majesty did not mind," she returned. "I could not resist. We frequently sing at night in my hall to entertain ourselves."

"You have a natural talent for melody, Elizabeth Meredith," he told her.

The dancing had finally ceased, but the musicians played on, their tunes more for entertainment now.

"I thank your majesty and Mistress Anne for a wonderful day. I shall never forget it," Elizabeth said quietly.

"Your friendship with my Annie pleases us," the king said.

"I am honored by her kindness," Elizabeth replied, and then with a small bow she withdrew from the king's presence. Moving off onto the lawn, she found herself suddenly accosted by a gentleman in a wolf's masque.

"Greetings, lambkin," Flynn Stewart said.

Elizabeth laughed. "Have you come to eat me up?" she teased him.

"Would that I might have that right," he answered her softly.

"But you are a loyal Scot," she replied as softly.

"Given where you live, and your family," he told her, "my nationality should not prevent us from remaining friends, lambkin." He took her hand in his and tucked it into his arm. "We will never be enemies, Elizabeth Meredith, no matter the differences between our countries."

"Nay, we will not," she agreed, "but—"

His fingers stopped her lips, and their eyes met for a moment. "Let those words remain unspoken between us, lambkin," he said. "I think perhaps it is better that way."

To her surprise two tears slipped down her cheeks, but she nodded.

"First love," he told her gently, "is rarely last love, lambkin. You must trust me in this, for I am a man of experience." He moved his fingers from her lips.

"I never said I loved you," Elizabeth whispered softly.

"Nay, you did not, did you?" he responded as softly.

"If you were only just a Scot instead of a king's brother," Elizabeth said sadly.

"But I am a king's brother," Flynn Stewart replied. "And now because it is best I will bid you adieu, lambkin. We will not see each other again." He took her shoulders in his two hands and, leaning forward, placed a kiss upon her forehead. Then, turning, he disappeared into the darkness that was enveloping the palace lawns.

Elizabeth began to cry. It was not fair! It was her birthday, and she should have what she wanted, but she could not. "I want to go home," she whispered to the night. "I want to go back to Friarsgate!" And then she felt a comforting arm slip about her shoulders, and looked into the face of Lord Cambridge. "Ohh, Uncle!" she sobbed.

"He is wiser than you, Elizabeth, but that does not mean his heart is not breaking too," Thomas Bolton told her.

"It is not fair!" she cried.

"Life, dear girl, seldom is," Lord Cambridge said gently. "Your position as the mistress of a large estate has certainly taught you that. You are not one of these no-thought-for-the-morrow courtiers, and neither is he. Come, let us go home now."

"To Friarsgate?" she asked, and he nodded in agreement.

"To Friarsgate," he told her, and together they walked from the palace while the moonlight shimmered on the river behind them, and the lanterns began to burn low on the May-green lawns.

# Chapter 8

❦

Elizabeth slept late the next day. She never wanted to see the court again, but Philippa's wisdom prevailed over her emotions.

"You must remain until the end of the month. You cannot depart until the king is ready to depart," she told her younger sister.

"I cannot bear to see him again," Elizabeth said, and tears filled her eyes.

"What is the matter with you?" Philippa scolded. "Your acquaintance was a brief one. He is not suitable at all, and he knew his place. God's wounds, sister! The man is a Scot, and worse, a Stewart's by-blow. You are behaving like a little girl with her first love. I hope you were not silly enough to be seduced."

"Flynn is a gentleman," Elizabeth snapped back, "and there is nothing wrong with being a Scot, Philippa. And yes, if the first man to engage my hopes can be considered a first love, then he is. And no, I am not like these little maids who come to court all aflutter, only to lose their virtue to some overweening courtier. If passion drove me as it has our mother I should have lost my innocence long since to some handsome shepherd."

"Do not say such a thing!" Philippa cried.

Elizabeth laughed. "Oh, sister, my reputation is pure and will not harm yours, but if I remain away from the court today it will cause no gossip. My moment in the sun departed with moonset. Someone else, something else, will engage the court today."

"You cannot leave Greenwich without bidding the king farewell. I am certain he will have a message for Mother," Philippa said.

"Another amusing tirade about her husband, I have no doubt," Elizabeth murmured. "Do you think Mother was ever his lover?"

"There was a rumor to that effect years ago, but Mother always denied it. One of the queen's Spanish women swore she saw them together, and told the queen out of spite because she was jealous of mother's friendship with Queen Katherine. Mother said it was Charles Brandon, and it had been nothing more than a flirtation. It was before he was married to Princess Mary. The Spanish lady was sent back to Spain with her husband, for the queen believed Mother in the end."

"Did you?" Elizabeth asked wickedly.

"Of course," Philippa said. And then she added, "It was better that I did. How would it have appeared if I had doubted my own mother?"

"You think she did!" Elizabeth said.

"I honestly don't know," Philippa replied. "What I do know is that there are certain ladies of whom the king is most fond now, but not in a lecherous way. Yet they have been known or rumored to have shared his bed at one time. Bessie Blount, the mother of his eldest son. The Countess of Langford, who was briefly his mistress. They called her the Quiet Mistress because she asked nothing of the king for either herself or her family. Even Queen Katherine liked her. But the rumor about Mother was no more than a whisper on the wind, and quickly forgotten, particularly as she hasn't been to court in years. Yet he is openly sentimental of these ladies when they are mentioned, and kind to their families. You are the daughter of Rosamund Bolton, a childhood friend. He and the queen have been very good to Banon, to me, and to my family. I believe he would even find you a husband should you ask it of him, Elizabeth. So you cannot leave the court without bidding the king a gracious farewell. And there is your friend Mistress Boleyn to consider as well."

A small smile touched Elizabeth's lips. "You will not be friends with her yourself," she noted. "But if your sister is, then our connection cannot harm your sons if she becomes queen one day. But is not one of my nephews in the service of her uncle, the Duke of Norfolk?"

"Aye, thanks to the king. When Wolsey fell shortly after Owein joined his household he would have lost his place but that the king told Norfolk to take him, for, he said, a duke could always use another page. Owein might have had to come home but for the king. The

Howards are a very powerful family, Elizabeth. Your nephews serve the two most powerful men in the kingdom."

"I will not leave without making my proper farewells," Elizabeth promised her sister, "but today I wish to be alone with my thoughts."

"Very well," Philippa said, rising from her sister's bedside, where she had been seated. She shook her skirts out. "But do not dream of what cannot be, sister. Consider what you will do now, for you must have a husband. It is rare that Mother and I agree on anything, but it this matter we stand united, and Banon too."

"Go away!" Elizabeth said, and, snuggling back down in her bed, she pulled the coverlet up over her head. She heard her older sister's footsteps crossing the bechamber, and then the door opened and closed. Elizabeth peeked from beneath the covers. Philippa had gone. She heard the murmur of voices in her dayroom—Philippa undoubtedly giving Nancy instructions of some sort. She lay back and considered the day ahead.

It was a beautiful late-May morn. Much too good a day to remain in bed, Elizabeth thought, sitting up and swinging her legs over the edge of her bed. But it was also much too nice a day to go to court. She wanted to go riding. "Nancy," she called.

Her tiring woman appeared in the door between the chambers. "Yes, mistress?"

"Has my uncle gone yet?" she asked.

"It ain't noon, mistress," Nancy replied. "But I think he is just up, for I saw Master Will fetching his tray."

"Go and ask him if I may speak with him," Elizabeth said.

Nancy hurried off, and Elizabeth slid from her bed. Going to the window, she looked out onto the garden below and saw her sister making her way towards the wall gate. Philippa would not miss a moment of the May court, which would be over in just a few more days. *Good,* Elizabeth thought. *She will make my excuses, and I am free for now. Yes! I want to go riding. Does no one ride at Greenwich? I haven't been on my horse since we arrived here.*

Nancy returned. "His lordship says to come along, mistress," she said.

Elizabeth, in her long chemise, hurried from her own rooms down the hall to her uncle's quarters. She found him sitting up in his great bed awaiting his breakfast.

"Good morning, dear girl!" he greeted her cheerfully. "Has Philippa gone yet?"

"Aye, after coming to lecture me." Elizabeth chuckled, sitting on the edge of his bed. "Uncle, I don't want to go to court today. I want to go riding. Can we?"

"An excellent suggestion, dear girl," he agreed. "Aye, 'twill give us a respite from the tedium I find the court has become. Perhaps I am growing older, but I find court less amusing than I once did. I will be glad to depart it."

"Philippa says we cannot go until the king departs. Is that so?"

"Regretfully, aye, it is," he told her.

"But we don't have to dance attendance every day, do we?" she asked.

"Nay," he responded. "I know a lovely path by the river where we may ride this afternoon, dear girl. Ahh, Will, at last! I am perishing from hunger."

Elizabeth saw the small smile flicker across William Smythe's face as he set the tray upon Lord Cambridge's lap and tucked a napkin into the top of his nightshirt. "Cook wanted to have the bread absolutely hot and fresh for you," he said. "The loaf has just come from the ovens, my lord."

"He takes such good care of me, dear girl. Does he not?" Thomas Bolton said.

"Indeed, Uncle, he does," Elizabeth agreed, snitching a piece of bacon from her uncle's plate. "We are going riding this afternoon, Will. Can you join us? You have worked very hard, dashing back and forth to London several times over these last few weeks while Uncle and I have enjoyed ourselves at court. We will soon be returning home. Come and ride out with us today."

"I should like that," William Smythe said.

"Have you told Uncle about the kitten yet?" Elizabeth asked. "Will found the most adorable kitten hiding in our barge. He doesn't know how it got there, but we're taking it back north with us. We call it Domino because it is black and white. I have promised him if his Pussums does not like the little fellow I shall give it a home."

"Pussums is an elderly lady now, and will probably resent the young fellow," Lord Cambridge noted. "Still, I have grown used to having a cat about me, and now there will be one for each lap of an evening. If you want another cat, dear girl, you shall have to find your own, I fear."

"Uncle! You are so good," Elizabeth said, and Thomas Bolton chuckled.

She left him, and Lord Cambridge finished his meal before dressing for their ride. The three horses were awaiting them at the stables, and they rode out into the countryside surrounding Greenwich. At one point Elizabeth raced her horse ahead of her two companions and over a hillock, while they walked their beasts sedately behind her.

"Mistress Elizabeth seems a bit sad today," William Smythe noted.

"I believe given the smallest bit of encouragement she could have fallen in love with the Scots king's messenger, Flynn Stewart," Thomas Bolton noted. "He is more a gentleman than many, Will. But of course unsuitable."

"Because he is a Scot," Will said.

"Aye, and yet nay," Lord Cambridge said. "If he were not the king's half brother he might very well suit. I had thought to find Elizabeth a good English husband, but given the Friarsgate inheritance, I realize that may no longer be possible. What is left to us, dear boy? We must either force her into a marriage with one of our northern English, or she finds a Scot who suits her. But Flynn Stewart's loyalty to the Scots king is too great. Should there be another war, and eventually there will be, he could not remain neutral. Friarsgate has always managed to remain dispassionate in the face of these disputes between England and Scotland. Its isolation has kept it safe from marauding armies. Perhaps a Scots husband, a plain Scot with no important connections, a Scot of good family, would suffice."

"You have someone in mind, my lord?" Will asked, and knew the answer before his master even spoke. Thomas Bolton had obviously given a great deal of thought to this problem of Elizabeth Meredith and the Friarsgate generations to come after her.

"Mayhap, dear boy, I do, but I am not quite ready to reveal all," Lord Cambridge said. His look was thoughtful.

"You have said naught to Mistress Elizabeth, I assume," Will spoke.

"Nay, nor will I. Nor will I speak with my cousin Rosamund yet. I must see if this possible match is the right one for Elizabeth before I even bring it up, dear boy, and you must keep my secret."

"Have I not always kept your secrets, my lord?" Will replied.

Lord Cambridge smiled. "You are a treasure, dear boy, and you well know I could not do without you," he said.

Elizabeth galloped back to rejoin them. "You two are so poky," she said.

"We are simply letting you run off your great energies, dear girl," Thomas Bolton told her. "Will and I are quite enjoying our sedate ramble."

She laughed, and, wheeling her mount about, she dashed off down the road again.

"Ah, youth," Thomas Bolton observed.

Elizabeth felt better for escaping the tedium of the court, and galloping about the countryside. She liked returning home to her uncle's house and eating a rather well cooked meal instead of watching the king and Mistress Boleyn eat and then nibbling what she could find. She particularly enjoyed going to bed at what she considered a reasonable hour instead of staying up half the night. She was a country woman, and content to be so.

She returned to court the following day, and sought out her friend, Anne Boleyn.

"Where were you?" Anne demanded to know. "Your sister would say only that you were resting, as you were not used to the pace of court life."

"You spoke to Philippa?" Elizabeth was surprised.

Anne's little cat smile exhibited itself. "Aye. She came to me, and curtseyed, and said you were home in bed. It was difficult for her, I know, but her manners are really quite flawless, Bess. Does she still support the queen?"

"I do not know if 'support' would be the correct term, Anne," Elizabeth said, careful to protect her sister. "You must remember Queen Katherine has been our mother's friend from early girlhood. My mother's friendship never wavered in those difficult days before Queen

Katherine married the king. Mother brought Philippa to visit court when she was only ten years of age, and from that moment on my sister wanted nothing more than to serve the queen. She did, of course, from the time she was twelve until her marriage. The queen has been good to Philippa. She feels a certain loyalty to her," Elizabeth explained. "If she did not I should not respect her as I do, but even Philippa is impatient with the queen's intractability in the matter of a divorce."

"And when I am queen will she feel the same loyalty for me that she feels for Katherine of Aragon?" Anne wanted to know.

"How can she?" Elizabeth answered candidly. "But she will respect your position as queen. Of that you may be assured. She is ambitious for her sons."

Anne nodded. "I will miss you, Bess, for no one speaks so honestly to me as you do. Must you return to your bleak northern estates?"

"I will wither away, dear Anne, if I cannot go home soon," Elizabeth said. "But I do not consider Friarsgate bleak. It is beautiful, with the green hills tumbling into my lake, and those same hillsides dotted with my sheep. I long to awaken to the song of birds, and a fresh Cumbrian breeze blowing through my windows. Aye, I must go home."

Anne sighed. "To be able to do what you desire is a privilege that I will always envy," Anne Boleyn said softly. "I must do as I am told. When I am queen, however, I shall obey only the king!" she declared.

"Anne, I would beg a boon of you," Elizabeth said. "Will you ask the king if my uncle and I may leave Greenwich before he does? I do not think I can bear waiting."

Anne nodded. "I will ask him," she promised.

"Ask me what?" the king demanded to know as he entered Mistress Boleyn's privy chamber. He bent and kissed her lips.

Anne colored prettily. "Bess would like to go home now, Hal," she said softly. "While I will miss her, I do understand her need to be where she is happiest, for I am where I am happiest when I am with you. We will not leave Greenwich for several more days, and custom demands that having been a part of the court she remain until the king departs. Would you not, I pray you, give her permission to go sooner?"

The king looked at Elizabeth. He reached out and tipped her heart-shaped face up so he might meet her gaze. "You look like your father, but I can see you are like your dear mother in your heart's desire. Friarsgate is where you get your strength, Elizabeth Meredith. I have thought you looked pale these last few days. Unlike your sister, the Countess of Witton, you are not a creature of the court. You have our permission to leave as soon as you may make ready. Tell your uncle to come and bid me farewell today, that you may then go with our blessing for a safe journey, Elizabeth Meredith." He held out his big hand to her and, taking it, Elizabeth kissed it.

Anne watched, and thought that while she counted Elizabeth Meredith her friend, she would not be sorry to see her depart sooner than later. She brought back memories to the king that Anne would prefer he forget. She did not want Henry Tudor living in a happier past. Anne wanted him in the present, happy with her. If only his divorce could be arranged! They would marry, she would give him sons, and they would be happy forever.

"Thank you, your majesty," Elizabeth said in a soft voice. Then she stood and, bending, she kissed Anne's cheeks. "Thank you for your friendship, Anne. I will cherish it always. And I will pray for you, and your heart's desire." Then Elizabeth curtseyed to the king and his companion, backing gracefully from their presence. She hurried to find Lord Cambridge, and told him that once he had made his farewells to the king they were free to depart Greenwich at any time.

"Dear girl!" he exclaimed, "you have your mother's charm when you choose to exhibit it. I shall go immediately. The day is young, and if we hurry the servants we can be packed and ready to depart on the morrow. I shall leave the house open for your sister, for Philippa will not leave until the king departs. And she will probably remain with the court until they go to Windsor in mid-June. But you and Will and I shall go home, Elizabeth! With luck we shall reach Friarsgate by Mid-Summer's Eve, and watch the fires on the hills to celebrate." Then, turning, he moved quickly off.

Elizabeth departed the palace, almost running through the wood that separated the king's enclosure from her uncle's house. Finding

Nancy in the kitchens she told her, "We are to go home. Tomorrow, if we can be packed!"

"Us too?" Lucy, her sister's tiring woman, asked.

"Nay," Elizabeth told her. "You know your mistress."

"Aye, she'll stay till the angel blows his trumpet." Lucy chuckled. "How she loves this court life. She was barely out of childbed with her daughter but that she would come for you, Mistress Elizabeth. I am sorry you have found no husband."

"I'm not," Elizabeth said. "Friarsgate is mine, and mine alone. I'll be upstairs, Nancy. Do not dally." And then she was gone from the kitchens.

Lucy shook her head. "She ain't easy, is she?" she said to Nancy.

"Aye, she really is easy, but all she thinks about is Friarsgate. It consumes her like the court consumes your mistress. It ain't natural, I'm thinking." She rose from the table where she had been seated. "I'd best go up or she'll be jamming her gowns in the trunks in her hurry to leave here." Nancy followed in her mistress's wake.

And while the two young women busily packed, Thomas Bolton found Philippa preparing to play tennis with a friend. He drew her aside. "Your sister has managed to get the king to allow her to leave as soon as possible," he said. "The house is yours until the court departs for Richmond again. And you know the London house is at your disposal as well. Come and have supper with us tonight. If I know Elizabeth, she will have us on the road for home by sunrise tomorrow." He chuckled.

Philippa shook her auburn head. "I am so sorry, Uncle, that I have failed the family," she told him.

"You have not failed, nor have I," he told her. "What we sought to accomplish was a herculean task, dear girl. Elizabeth is not you, with your sophistication, or even Banon, who is content to be a wife and a mother. She is the heiress to Friarsgate, and she takes that responsibility most seriously. It will take a very special man to husband her."

Philippa sighed, knowing he was right. "I wish you good fortune in your quest, dear Uncle." Then she giggled, reminding him very much of the younger Philippa he had once known. "It is a bit like seeking the Holy Grail, isn't it?"

"Do not say it, dear girl!" he exclaimed. "Remember, the Grail was never found."

Philippa now laughed aloud. "I shall miss you," she said, hugging him. "And I will come home early so we may all have a final meal together."

"Excellent! Now I must go and bid adieu to our most noble monarch," Lord Cambridge said, and he hurried from the tennis court. He found the king preparing to leave Mistress Boleyn's apartments for the midday meal. Thomas Bolton bowed with élan. "Majesty!" he said.

"By God, Tom," the king exclaimed, "no one can execute a bow like you! You are the most elegant fellow. You have come to bid us farewell, I assume."

"I have, majesty. As much as I regret my niece's eagerness to return north so quickly, I must accompany her. Rosamund would not approve of her traveling alone."

"And when will you return to us?" the king wanted to know.

"That, your majesty, is a moot point. I am sixty years of age now, and find that travel does not hold the same charms for me that it has in the past. I have become, I fear, like a large tabby who prefers his own hearth," Lord Cambridge admitted with a wry smile and a tilt of his head.

"We will miss your style and your wit," the king replied, "but we understand. Go then with our permission, Tom, and I hope to see you again one day." The king held out his big, beringed hand, and Lord Cambridge kissed it.

When the hand had been withdrawn Thomas Bolton turned his attention to Mistress Boleyn. He kissed her elegant little hand, noting the tiny sixth finger she possessed. Leaning forward, he murmured something into her ear.

Anne smiled broadly, a rare sight indeed, and kissed his smooth cheek. "Thank you, my lord," she said. "It is the perfect solution. Why I did not think of it myself I do not know."

"Sometimes, dear lady, the most obvious answer is the most elusive," Lord Cambridge told her. "I wish you good fortune," he said, and then, bowing a final time, moved away.

"What did he say to you?" the king wanted to know as they moved toward the hall where the midday meal was to be served them.

"He suggested I wear my sleeves a bit longer to disguise the finger on my left hand," Anne Boleyn replied. "His instinct for fashion is most amazing, Hal." She was pleased, for that tiny extra appendage was a source of embarrassment to her.

Thomas Bolton hurried from the palace, almost as relieved as he suspected Elizabeth had been. He would not see this place again, he sensed. When he returned home he would spend the rest of his life in Cumbria. And was it not time? He was no longer a young man, and he was beginning to feel his years. Especially in his knees, he considered with a grin. Entering the house and going to his apartments, he discovered Garr, his valet, and Will already packing. He chuckled. Had none of them enjoyed this visit to court that they were all so eager to depart?

Philippa arrived for the evening meal to discover the traveling cart already fully loaded. She shook her head and laughed to herself. She and Elizabeth were only four years apart in age, yet they were a hundred years apart in attitude. She was a modern woman who understood the ways for her sons to get ahead in society. Elizabeth was content to be a responsible landowner. Neither of them was going to change, but Philippa did want her youngest sister to be happily wed.

"You will be retiring early," she teased Elizabeth and Thomas Bolton as she entered the riverside hall to join them.

"And you will eat and hurry back for the evening's entertainments at the palace," Elizabeth teased back.

"Nay," Philippa surprised her by saying. "Tonight I shall remain with you and our uncle. If you retire early then so shall I. Your travels tomorrow will only take you back to the London house. It will not be a strenuous day, for you will lounge in Uncle's comfortable barge the entire way. 'Tis the day after you will remember where your bottom is after you have ridden for many hours," she teased.

Lord Cambridge winced. "One day there will be a far more comfortable way of traveling," he said. "If I could but live to see it."

"You could travel in one of those newer traveling carts that I have seen," Philippa suggested. "But only a few possess them."

"Thank you, no!" Thomas Bolton said. "They are primitive conveyances, I fear. I shall continue to ride if I must ever travel again, which I shall certainly attempt to avoid. Otterly to Friarsgate and no farther, my dear, darling girls. I swear it!"

The sisters laughed at his declaration, and Elizabeth remarked, "In a few years, dear Uncle, you will grow bored, and the itch to visit court will need to be scratched. Besides, with Banon's five little daughters you may need to come south again, and they shall be far easier to find husbands for than I have proven."

He chortled. "I have not given up on you yet, dear girl," he told her.

William Smythe joined them, and they spent a pleasant evening together eating a good supper, and then the sisters sang together as they had in the days when they were children. Will and Lord Cambridge played a game of chess, while the sisters spoke at length for what would be a final time until they met again.

"If you do wed," Philippa said, "you must know certain things about men and women. I dare not leave it to Mother to explain. Listen to me, Elizabeth, and then keep what I have told you to yourself."

"Do not speak!" Elizabeth said. "I know what I need to know."

"Sheep are not people," Philippa shot back.

"I know," Elizabeth replied, giggling.

"Banon! Banon has spoken to you," Philippa said. "Well, I am glad she saw your need, Elizabeth. Ignorance is not bliss, but I assume you are wise enough to pretend ignorance when you at last have a wedding night." She did not wait for her youngest sister to confirm her conclusion.

Elizabeth did not enlighten her otherwise. She might be ignorant, but she did not want to discuss such matters with her oldest sister. She rose from her seat. "I think I will retire," she said. "We depart early." She kissed both of Philippa's cheeks. "Thank you," she said to her. "I will bid you farewell now, for I doubt you will arise as early as we will. I think I have actually enjoyed being with you, sister. We have both grown older and hopefully wiser with the passage of time."

"Aye," Philippa agreed. "Give Mama my dearest love. Tell her I wish she might see her grandchildren."

"If you would bring them north she could," Elizabeth reminded her sibling. "She will not travel south, but you might come to us, if only once. She misses you, Philippa, and she has never gotten over what you did, despite the fact that I am a far better chatelaine than you would have ever been. When your daughter is older, come to see us, sister, I beg of you."

Philippa had the good grace to look discomfited by her sister's gentle chiding. "Perhaps next summer," she said, "when Mary Rose is closer to her second birthday."

"I know Mama would like it, and you can stay at Friarsgate, so you will not have to go into Scotland. Mama has made Claven's Carn more habitable, but it is still rough in comparison with my manor house. Do not allow your love for court to change your mind, Philippa," Elizabeth warned. "The court will always be there for you. Mama will not. Farewell, sister." And without waiting to allow Philippa the last word, Elizabeth turned and went upstairs.

Seeing her go, Lord Cambridge and Will Smythe rose from the game table by the window.

"It isn't even dark yet," Thomas Bolton complained. "These long twilights and longer days can be so deceiving. But if Elizabeth has retired then I must do so too, dear Philippa. Your sister will be ready to depart at sunrise, and she will brook no tardiness from me. Return for the evening's entertainments if you will."

"Perhaps I shall," Philippa said. "I know I said I wouldn't, but if you are all going to bed I might as well go back to the palace. I shall take a dark lamp, Uncle, to facilitate my return." She hugged him. "Goodbye! I will miss you, but then I always do."

He kissed her on both of her cheeks. "And I you, dear girl! My felicitations to Crispin, of course." He paused as if considering something, and then he said, "You must come north next summer, Philippa. You are your mother's firstborn, and she cannot help but favor you. She has not seen you since you forsook Friarsgate. By next summer your heir will be half-grown. She has never seen him or your other children. Without her you should not have all you have today. Remember that when you consider delaying your visit to Friarsgate. The king and the duke will release your sons from their service under the circumstances if you ask. Do not fail me. Do not fail your mother." He kissed her forehead. "Farewell, dear girl." And he left her standing in his hall to disappear upstairs.

"God bless your ladyship," William Smythe said, kissing her hand and bowing low.

"Thank you, Will," Philippa said. "I have been properly lectured, haven't I?"

"Indeed, my lady, you have. But it was done with the love his lordship has for all of his family. I believe you know that," Will answered quietly.

"Godspeed on your journey home, Will," Philippa said.

"Thank you, your ladyship. Farewell." And he departed the hall.

Philippa stood alone for a long moment. It had been a most interesting month, and with her sister's leaving she realized that perhaps she was ready to return to Brierewode in a few days' time. She missed Crispin. She missed little Hugh and her baby daughter. But tonight, she decided, she would return to join in the festivities that were sure to be swirling about the king and his little paramour, Mistress Boleyn.

And before she departed, she must speak with Henry and Owein on the matter of discretion. Her two older sons had displayed rough manners of late, and it must be curbed. Anne Boleyn would eventually go the way of all the king's whores. But for now she held the power, and it would not do for either of the Earl of Witton's sons to be accused of ill-advised and imprudent behavior based on others' opinions. Why had no one ever explained to her the difficulties of being a mother? With a deep sigh of resignation she hurried from the house and back to the palace.

When she awoke in her bed late the following morning she learned that her uncle and sister had indeed departed at first light.

They were fortunate in the weather, for the day had dawned fair, warm, and windless. They had caught the early tide upriver just before dawn, reaching Lord Cambridge's house on the city's outskirts early. They had decided that rather than remain overnight they would continue on that same day, but they stopped long enough to break their fast and gather their men-at-arms for their travels. Will did not remain with them, but rode ahead to book their accommodations at a suitable inn along their route.

In the lush Warwickshire countryside Elizabeth hardly heeded its great castle, although she did comment on the green meadows. Staffordshire's terrible roads remained dry, and she did not notice them at all. She exhausted everyone with her fast and furious pace as she galloped across the flat countryside of Cheshire. She was somewhat slowed as they moved through Lancaster, where the roads traversed great forests of towering trees. The wildness of Westmoreland's hills set her heart to racing faster despite the rains that fell, for they crossed it in a day, and were finally into Cumbria.

At Carlisle they stayed overnight at the guesthouse belonging to St. Cuthbert's, where Elizabeth's great-uncle, Richard Bolton, was its prior. Despite nearing his seventieth year he was still a handsome man, with his startlingly blue eyes and snow-white hair.

"Cousin Thomas," he greeted Lord Cambridge. "Have you returned with our lovely Elizabeth bringing good news? Elizabeth, my child, you look radiant. Is it some fine young man that brings such a sparkle to your eye?" He smiled warmly.

"Nay, sir," Elizabeth replied pertly. "I fear I will be a great disappointment to Mama, for I have found no husband. If I look happy it is because I am so near home again, and happy to be so."

Prior Richard shook his head. "Perhaps then your fate is and has always been here in the north, my child," he told her. "Cousin Thomas, you look worn. It would appear such long journeys are no longer for you."

"Alas, cousin," Lord Cambridge answered him, "I agree."

They ate a simple meal with their relation, and then Elizabeth retired to the female quarters of the guesthouse while her male relations sat talking over a decanter of wine.

"I remember Philippa returning from court that first time, and declaring she would go back. She would not, she told me, be shackled to some country bumpkin," the prior said with a smile. "And now you have the opposite difficulty with Elizabeth. It always had amazed me the differences in Rosamund's daughters. You had no luck at all then?"

Lord Cambridge shook his head. "Nay, but then I did not really think I would. It is possible that I may have a solution to this problem, but I am not yet ready to discuss it. I hope, however, when I am that you will support me. You know I only want what is best for Rosamund and her daughters. I have not ever failed them."

Nay, you have not," Prior Richard agreed. "I don't suppose you will give me even the merest hint," he half teased.

"A Scot, and that is all I will say," Thomas Bolton replied.

Richard Bolton's elegant eyebrow raised itself in amusement. "Indeed," he said. "More wine, cousin?"

Lord Cambridge's beringed hand held out his goblet. "I don't get drunk," he told his older cousin, and the prior burst out laughing as he poured the dark red wine into the silver cup. "And I have said all I will for now," Tom Bolton declared, downing the wine and then rising. "Good night, Richard."

"Good night, Thomas. I shall pray for you. You are obviously going to need my prayers," the cleric said with a chuckle. "You are attempting to create a miracle."

The following morning after the early Mass and a meal of oat stirabout, bread, cheese, and ale, they departed Carlisle for Friarsgate. Again the day was fair, as most of the days had been since their departure from Greenwich. Elizabeth attempted to set a quick pace, but Lord Cambridge refused.

"Do not bother to race ahead, dear girl," he told her. "We cannot possibly reach Friarsgate until tomorrow sometime. We will overnight at St. Mary's Convent, as we did when we departed to go south. They are expecting us. I do not intend hurrying all day long, only to be caught between there and Friarsgate come dark, a perfect target for some marauding borderer." He shuddered. "God alone knows what they would do to us."

"Swear we will leave the convent before the Mass," she demanded of him.

"I swear," he said with a smile, and he kept the promise, leaving a substantial donation behind them as they departed St. Mary's the following morning even before the sunrise. The sleepy portress was surprised by both the early departure and the gift.

Elizabeth could scarcely contain her exuberance. She galloped ahead of them most of the day, two men-at-arms in her wake. She knew instantly when she crossed the borders of her own land, stopping for a moment to rest her mount. And when she topped the crest of the hills surrounding her home and saw the lake glittering in the sunlight, she wept, silent tears of joy slipping down her face. Friarsgate! Her beloved Friarsgate! She would never leave it again.

Then she began to scan the scenery. The fields were fertile with growth. Her flocks and herds looked healthy. Everyone was working diligently. Her one and a half months' absence had not been detrimental to her estates, as she had feared before she left. She moved her horse down the hill road, waving to her people as she came. Was not this a hundred times better than King Henry's court? Oh, yes! It was a thousand times better. She reached the house, and Maybel came to greet her, for Will had ridden ahead to warn the manor of her coming.

"Child, bless me, it is good to have you home again," Maybel said, hugging her.

"I will never leave Friarsgate again," Elizabeth declared as they went into the hall arm in arm. "The court holds no charms for me, dearest Maybel."

"But did you find a good man?" Maybel wanted to know.

"Nay, I did not," Elizabeth admitted. "There was one, but he was not suitable."

"And why not, I should like to know?" Maybel demanded as they sat themselves before the little fire in the hall.

"His first loyalty would never be to me or to Friarsgate," Elizabeth said sadly.

"What? No welcome for me, old woman?" Lord Cambridge joined them, kissing Maybel heartily on her weathered cheek.

Maybel chuckled. Then she grew serious. "You was our last hope, Tom Bolton, and the lass says the only lad she found was unsuitable. Was Lady Philippa right then?"

"She was," Lord Cambridge said, "but all is not lost, dear Maybel. I am never without ideas or resources. We shall see if what I have in mind can be accomplished."

"You're a wicked fellow, Tom Bolton," Maybel declared, "but you has always had the best interests of this family at heart. I will wait to see what you can do."

"He hasn't even told me," Elizabeth said. "Where is Edmund? I want all the news of Friarsgate. Is he in my privy chamber?"

"You are just home, child," Maybel said, "and my Edmund has had a long day. Let him have his evening meal, and you will speak with him tomorrow. All has been well, I swear it."

At that moment Edmund Bolton, Friarsgate's steward, came into the hall. He went directly to Elizabeth and kissed her upon the forehead. "Welcome home, my child," he greeted her quietly.

"Maybel says all has been well," Elizabeth said. "We will speak in the morning. For now I shall tell you all my adventures, including the fete that Mistress Boleyn gave me on my birthday. We wore costumes, and as always Uncle Thomas outdid himself, and we were a great success."

The servants began bringing the meal into the hall. Elizabeth, her family, and Will gathered about the high board. It was a simple country meal: a roasted capon with a stuffing of bread and dried fruits, two whole broiled trout displayed upon a platter of cress, a platter of lamb chops, fresh peas, tiny new carrots in a creamed dill sauce, fresh cottage loaves, newly churned butter, and a half-wheel of sharp cheddar. There was good brown ale, and when they had eaten their fill there came a bowl of newly picked peaches.

"I did not eat a meal at court that could compare to this," Elizabeth told Maybel, her eyes sparkling as she took another ripe peach.

"I see travel and weariness have not claimed your appetite." Maybel chuckled.

"Tell us of the court," Edmund said.

Elizabeth began a detailed recitation of her travels. Now and again Thomas Bolton would add his own colorful commentary. They chuckled at her wicked descriptions of the courtiers she had encountered, and laughed until the tears rolled down their faces when she explained how she and Lord Cambridge had attended her birthday fete costumed as sheep.

"What did the king say?" Maybel wheezed.

"He is a clever gentleman, and he caught the jest," Elizabeth said.

"What did your hoity-toity sister have to say?" Maybel asked.

"At first she was a bit taken aback, and said she would not attend," Elizabeth said, "but Uncle Thomas knew she would never miss such a fete, and besides, the gossip that would ensue if she did not come could ruin her."

"Aye, her ladyship has always had an eye out for herself," Maybel responded.

"Nay, she thinks not of herself now, but of her sons, who are already in service at the court. Henry is a page to the king, and Owein to the Duke of Norfolk."

"I thought she had one with the cardinal," Edmund remarked.

"He has fallen from grace," Thomas Bolton said.

"A poor man's son who climbed too high," Edmund said. "It was bound to happen eventually. He did not stay where he belonged, and got above his station."

"He was a brilliant man, Edmund," Lord Cambridge said, "and a loyal servant to the king. His crime was that he could not give the king what he wanted."

"Tell us about Lady Philippa's gown," Maybel said.

"She was garbed as a peacock," Elizabeth said, and went on to explain.

The evening grew late for the country, and Elizabeth went gratefully to her bed.

When she had departed the hall Lord Cambridge explained the visit from his point of view. "I will find her a husband, although I know she is glad we did not. She may be twenty-two years of age, but she is yet young and knows nothing of passion. It is time she learned."

"Will you send to Rosamund?" Edmund wanted to know.

"Not yet," Lord Cambridge said. "Let Elizabeth enjoy being home without having her mother and Logan fussing over her supposed failures. There is time yet for a husband and children."

"The young Scot who was here through the winter," Edmund began. "His father has written to say the sheep he bought for Grayhaven seem to have taken to their new home well. With Elizabeth's permission he wants to send his son back to Friarsgate to learn more about our weavers and their looms."

"Indeed," Thomas Bolton said. This was surely a sign that what he had in mind could be accomplished. "What did you reply?" he asked as casually as he dared.

"I didn't see no harm in it," Edmund replied. "I wrote to the master of Grayhaven that he should send his son back here, but that to learn about our weavers he might have to remain through the autumn, possibly the winter too."

" 'Twas wise, I believe," Lord Cambridge said. "He seemed a pleasant enough fellow, and intelligent to boot."

"When will you be returning to Otterly?" Maybel wanted to know.

"In a few days I shall send dear Will to see how the builders are coming along," Lord Cambridge answered. "I shall not return until I can move into my new wing. And Will must be certain we are private this time. As much as I adore my darling Banon, her brood is much too noisy and active for a man of my years."

"If Elizabeth weds and has bairns"—Maybel chortled—"you'll not be able to hide yourself away at Friarsgate any longer. Are you certain you would have her wed?"

"For her sake, for my darling Rosamund's sake, and especially for Friarsgate, aye! Elizabeth must be wed, Maybel. As for me, I shall be a snug as a bug in a rug with my new and absolutely private apartments. But I shall come now and again to Friarsgate." He yawned, stretched, and stood up. "I am weary with all the traveling and excitement I have endured over these past two and a half months." He yawned again. "I shall find my bed. Good night, Edmund. Good night, Maybel."

He walked from the hall, his facile mind turning. A plain Scot. Baen MacColl certainly fit that description. He had not thought it before they left for court, but now Thomas Bolton was reconsidering his position. Elizabeth needed a husband. She needed a man who would be as much involved in Friarsgate as she was. A man who would defer just enough to her to make her believe she continued to have complete autonomy over Friargate. A good man like Sir Owein Meredith, her father, had been.

There had been an attraction between them, Lord Cambridge knew. Could he see that it was rekindled? Encouraged to grow into a love between them? And would the Scot love Elizabeth enough that he could overlook the differences that separated their two countries? Baen MacColl was no Flynn Stewart. His loyalties would be to the father who had taken him in as a lad. He might be the master of Grayhaven's eldest child, but as a bastard he could not inherit. Would the father consider giving him his freedom in exchange for wealth and respectability? Prior Richard was right: He was going to need a miracle. Strangely, the thought did not deter him. He had lived a good life and been generous to all. Surely God would now give him this miracle. Thomas Bolton intended praying harder than he had ever prayed, because this was right. He just knew it!

# Chapter 9

❦

Colin Hay, the master of Grayhaven, looked at his eldest son and said, "I'm sending you back to England, Baen." He was a big man, standing three inches over six feet, with black hair and leaf-green eyes. Despite his fifty-two years he was a handsome man who gave the appearance of one twenty years younger. He looked more Baen's brother than his father. "I've written to Friarsgate and had back a reply. You'll go for the summer and autumn, and if you need to remain longer, you will."

"Why?" Baen asked. "I'm barely home again, Da." He stood an inch taller than his parent, but had the same wide, high forehead, long, straight nose, and generous mouth. From a distance they were often mistaken for each other.

"I want to learn more about this weaving you told me about when you returned a few weeks ago," Colin Hay said. "These Friarsgate folk are kept busy the winter long at their looms, and the cloth they weave brings in an income. You will learn everything there is to know about this industrious endeavor, Baen. Then we will attempt to set up a similar undertaking here at Grayhaven. It will be your responsibility, for your brothers, good lads both, have not the instincts for trade or industry."

"When am I to go?" Baen asked his father. He wondered if the lovely Elizabeth Meredith would have returned from court. And if she had, was she a married woman now? Of course, he had no right to think about her, but he had not been able to get her out of his mind. Her sweet mouth. Her golden hair and luminous hazel-green eyes. He almost sighed aloud with the memory. He wondered if she had thought of him.

"You can depart tomorrow," the master of Grayhaven said. "Return when you know what you need to know, lad."

So Baen had ridden out from Grayhaven the following morning with his dog, Friar, and for the next few days he rode from dawn until darkness. He carried wine in his flask and oatcakes in his pouch to sustain him. His horse grazed the night hours away wherever they stopped. Friar hunted rabbits. His woolen cape and his dog kept him warm in the fields where he bedded down. And with Friar by his side he was safe from marauders and wild beasts. Down from his Highland home he came, bypassing Edinburgh and riding across the Lowlands to finally cross into England. When he at last topped the hill and looked down into Friarsgate's valley, he felt an odd sensation in his chest that he couldn't comprehend. It was if he were coming home. Friar, seeming to recognize where he was too, barked noisily and dashed excitedly about.

The first to welcome him back was the priest, Father Mata. He was coming from his church. " 'Tis good to see you again, laddie," he said. "Edmund will be in the house now with Elizabeth. Today is their day for checking the figures on the flocks."

"Mistress Elizabeth has returned from court?" Baen asked, dismounting. "And has she brought a fine bridegroom with her, Father Mata?"

"Nay, alas, there is no husband," the priest said, shaking his head.

"Perhaps she will find one among her neighbors," Baen said without conviction.

"We have few neighbors, and none near," the priest replied mournfully. "I do not know what the lady Rosamund will do now. She made Elizabeth the heiress of Friarsgate, but we always anticipated the lass would one day wed and breed up a new heir or heiress for Friarsgate. It would appear that will not happen now, and what will become of Friarsgate? The lady will quarrel with her daughter when she learns this truth, but they have kept it from her so far, for anger will not solve the problem."

They had reached the house now, and a lad came to take Baen's horse. The priest went in with the Scot, and they walked to the hall. There they found Lord Cambridge, who stood up, smiling broadly at the sight of Baen MacColl.

"Dear boy!" he exclaimed. "Welcome back to Friarsgate. It is good to see you once again. Come and sit with me. How fortunate I am still here to greet you. Alas, the workmen building the new wing at Otterly have been wretchedly slow."

Baen joined Thomas Bolton, and a servant brought them both goblets of wine. The priest had disappeared from the hall. "Your visit to court was not a successful one, Father Mata tells me," Baen began. "I am sorry, but if I recall, you did not think it a good idea, but went because Mistress Elizabeth's mother desired it."

"It was a stratagem that worked for the two older sisters," Lord Cambridge said, "and my cousin Rosamund hoped it would succeed for Elizabeth. It did not."

"What will you do now, my lord?"

"I am thinking about it," Thomas Bolton said. "Now, tell me, dear boy, why has your father sent you back to us? Are you in the market for additional stock?"

"He would like me to learn about Friarsgate's weaving trade," Baen answered. "I think he hopes to give me a purpose in life, as I cannot inherit, being his bastard. He is a good man and loves me, I know, but is concerned with my future in this world. There is only so much to be had at Grayhaven, as Jamie and Gilbert must come before me."

"He would appear to be a good man, your father," Lord Cambridge observed, sipping his wine. This boded well. If the master of Grayhaven loved his bastard enough to care about his future, perhaps something could be arranged. Mayhap Colin Hay would not object to giving his oldest-born to England. Now, of course, Thomas Bolton thought he must encourage the budding attraction he had seen the previous winter between Baen MacColl and Elizabeth. She did seem to have a predilection for Scotsmen. Hopefully her little flirtation with Flynn Stewart hadn't broken her heart too badly. And then there was, of course, the little matter of convincing his cousin Rosamund to approve such a match. At this point, however, she should be delighted for any son-in-law who would love Elizabeth and help her care for Friarsgate.

Maybel came into the hall now, greeting Baen, who stood up, coming forward to stand before her. "I had heard you had arrived," she said.

"You are welcome. I have prepared a wee chamber upstairs for you, as you will be with us awhile. Is this the pup you took with you several months ago?" she asked, giving Friar a pat. "You've taken good care of him, laddie."

"Aye, I couldn't leave him behind," Baen said. "We have become rather good friends, Friar and I. You are as pretty as ever, Mistress Maybel, if I may be allowed to note it." His gray eyes twinkled at her as he took her hands in his and kissed them.

Maybel chuckled. "Go on with you, laddie," she told him, coloring, pulling her hands from his, and giving him a friendly swat. "You're a proper rogue, I can see."

He grinned at her. "Tomorrow is Midsummer's Eve Day, Maybel. Will you dance about the fire with me?"

"Indeed I will"—she chortled—"and be the envy of all the women for having such a handsome young fellow by my side."

"Baen MacColl, welcome back to Friarsgate!" Elizabeth came into the hall. She had a look in her eye that told her uncle she was happy to see the Scotsman again.

He took her hand in his, slowly raising it to his lips to kiss it. "It is good to see you again, Elizabeth Meredith," he told her, and she blushed prettily.

*Yes,* Lord Cambridge thought, delighted. *The attraction is still there, and with a bit of encouragement we shall fan it into a love that will last a lifetime. What matter that he is a Scot? I will wager his father would be happy to see him wed to a girl like Elizabeth. Settled. Comfortable for the rest of his life. He is a man of the land. Why did I not see it before?* He almost purred like a cat with his pleasure at the situation unfolding before him. He had promised to find Elizabeth a husband, and he had, though none of the others knew it yet.

"Oh, you have brought Friar with you!" Elizabeth exclaimed, and knelt to fondle the half-grown dog.

"He insisted on coming," Baen said, kneeling next to her to pat the pup.

"You have taken good care of him," she noted.

"He's becoming an excellent herder," Baen told her.

They stood simultaneously.

"I'll have Maybel show you to your chamber," Elizabeth said. "We have room to spare. The meal will be served shortly." She turned. "Uncle, the ship has made several trips to the Netherlands since we departed for court. The cloth we had woven last winter is all spoken for, but as usual there are complaints about the scarcity of the Friarsgate blue fabric. Perhaps it is time to increase our output come winter. Edmund tells me the wool crop will be most bounteous this year. We'll be shearing shortly."

Baen followed Maybel from the hall, fascinated by this conversation. Elizabeth was just back from court, and already her adventures, whatever they might have been, were obviously forgotten in her passion for her home and her industry. He climbed the stairs, Maybel ahead of him, moving slowly.

"My knees," she complained, "are not what they once were." They reached the corridor above, and she hurried down the dim hallway. "Ah, here you are, laddie." She flung open a door and ushered him inside. "Plenty of room, and a bit more private than a bed space in the hall," she said. "Settle yourself, and then come back down." She shut the door behind her as she left him.

Baen looked about. It was not a large chamber, but it was clean and comfortable. There was a small fireplace on the wall opposite the bed, which had heavy natural-colored linen curtains hanging from brass rings. At the foot of the bed there was a wooden chest. To the right of the bed was a casement window. There was also a table to his right with a small brass ewer and china pitcher upon it. He placed his saddlebags in the chest and poured water from the pitcher into the basin to wash the dust of the road from his face and hands as his stepmother, Ellen, had taught him. Then he returned to the hall, where he found Elizabeth and her family already seated at the high board. He hesitated, unsure.

"Come and sit next to me, dear boy!" Lord Cambridge called to him, waving him forward. "I will wager that you are hungry after your travels."

Baen came and sat next to Thomas Bolton. "A good meal is welcome," he told them. "I travel with oatcakes in my pack, and nothing more." He took the bowl the older man passed him and ladled a potage of meat and vegetables onto the plate. He was handed a chunk of bread. Knowing the blessing was already spoken, he crossed himself and set about eating. He wolfed down the potage and was offered a platter with slices of country ham. He took several, added a wedge of cheese and more bread, which he spread with butter, using his broad thumb. His goblet was kept filled with good brown ale. He did not speak, but concentrated upon his food. He remembered to take several chunks of meat from the stew and drop them beneath the table, where his dog, Friar, lay at his feet.

"I do so like a man with a good appetite," Lord Cambridge murmured as Baen finally seemed to be satisfied for the moment.

"So do I," Elizabeth chimed in. "Nothing is more aggravating to the mistress of the house than to have those at her table picking at their food. It does not please Cook either." She reached for a peach from the bowl now on the table. It was good to be home. It was good to be wearing clothing that allowed her to breathe naturally. It was good to have her boots on her feet instead of those dreadful but beautiful court shoes. She turned to the Scot. "I understand your father wishes to learn how we weave and market our cloth, Baen."

"Aye," Baen replied. Was it possible she was more beautiful?

"Tomorrow you will ride out with me, and we will inspect the flocks, which I always do just before the shearing. Over the next few weeks we will show you how we store and prepare the wool prior to weaving. It keeps us busy throughout the autumn weeks. The threads must be woven and dyed and put on spools before the cloth can be made. Some dye the cloth after it's woven. I do not. It is a very laborious process. Your cotters need the temperament for such an industry or they will not be able to do it."

He nodded. As she spoke he considered that perhaps his father's clansmen and -women might not have the patience for such work. But he would learn everything she could teach him, if for no other reason than to be near Elizabeth Meredith. She challenged him to a game of Hare and Hounds. He accepted, laughing when she beat him, teasing her when he prevailed. The hall was comfortable with its evening fire. The dogs were scattered about the floor, sleeping. He suddenly realized that Lord Cambridge and his secretary were no longer in the hall.

Maybel and Edmund were snoring in their chairs. To all intents and purposes he and Elizabeth were alone.

"Did you enjoy the court?" he asked her, knowing the answer before she spoke, but eager for conversation with her.

"A little bit," she admitted, "but it is a life I could not bear if I had to live there all the time. The clothing is beautiful. The conversation amusing. But they do little other than play games and dance attendance upon King Henry. In general I found it boring, but I did make one friend: the king's friend, Mistress Anne Boleyn."

"They say she is a witch," Baen remarked.

Elizabeth laughed. "Aye, the gossips would. They can well understand the king's need for a son and his desire to rid himself of Queen Katherine. What flummoxes them is that he is in love with Anne. That he will not consider a French princess as a new wife, but must have this Englishwoman with her common bloodlines for his queen."

"What is she like then?" Baen was curious.

"Striking in appearance, but certainly no beauty," Elizabeth began. "She has a good heart, but her uncle, the Duke of Norfolk, manipulates her, and Anne is frightened, although you would never guess it, for she covers her fear well. I feel sorry for her, and am happy I am who I am."

"And who else did you meet at court?" he asked her.

"Another Scot like yourself. He is King James's half brother," she explained.

"What was he doing at King Henry's court?" Baen queried her.

"He is his brother's personal messenger between the English court and the Scots court. His name is Flynn Stewart, and we became friends, for, like me, he was an outsider."

Baen felt a surge of jealousy. "Did you kiss him?" he demanded to know.

Elizabeth smiled a slow smile. "I did," she admitted. "Several times," she added.

"And who else did you kiss?" he wanted to learn.

Elizabeth laughed. "No one. Just Flynn. I am no wanton."

"Yet you kissed him," Baen insisted. "A stranger. A mere acquaintance."

"I seem to have a weakness for Scots," she teased him wickedly. Then she arose from the game table. "I'm going to bed. My day begins early. Good night, Baen. I am glad you are back with us."

He sat there after she had left him. He was glad to be back too. But he had to control his emotions when he was around Elizabeth Meredith. He was certainly old enough to know better, and he could not be the man for her, though he wished he could. His birth wasn't good enough for her. He had naught to offer. Naught but the love he realized was growing in his heart. Elizabeth deserved a man who would bring something to Friarsgate besides his heart. For several long minutes he stared into the fire, and then he got up and retired to his own chamber.

Maybel opened her eyes. She had not been sleeping at all, but listening and observing through half-closed lids. She had seen the look on Baen MacColl's face. It was the look of a man in torment. Was she imagining it, or did the laddie have feelings for Elizabeth? And Elizabeth, never touched by love, was oblivious to him. Maybel didn't know whether she should be upset or not. She would have to watch closer over the next few weeks. Perhaps she would even discuss this matter with Thomas Bolton. Reaching out, she poked her husband. "Wake up, old man. It is time to go to bed," she said. Edmund grumbled and awoke just enough to stumble to their chamber, where he fell into his bed, asleep before his head hit the pillow.

The following day Elizabeth was up early, and with Baen MacColl by her side. They rode out to inspect the flocks in the miles of meadows belonging to Friarsgate. The ewes were plump with thick coats, the lambs born this past winter fat with their mother's milk and the green grass they were now eating as well. The rams who oversaw each flock stood slightly separate from their flocks like monarchs, surveying all. Each of them was large, with a woolly coat and some had fine horns.

"Your meadows are wonderful," Baen said. "No wonder your flocks are so healthy. The Highland meadows are not nearly as lush. This Friarsgate of yours is almost magical, Elizabeth."

"It is, isn't it?" she replied with a smile. "There is no place on earth like it, and no place I should rather be than right here. I will never leave it again, Baen."

They returned home in early evening. The fires were already beginning to spring up on the hillsides in celebration of Midsummer's Eve. Tables had been set out before the house, and the servants were even now hurrying to bring the food. There were barrels of ale, and all the Friarsgate folk were invited to celebrate with Elizabeth. The benches were soon filled with men, women, and children eating and drinking. Every family had brought their own trenchers of bread, wooden cups, and spoons. The trenchers were filled with mutton stew, fragrant with onions and carrots. There was capon, and trout from the lake. And fresh loaves, newly churned butter, cheese, and fresh fruit. The drinking vessels were filled again and again with good Friarsgate ale.

The children ran about, excitedly gathering the last bits of wood for the great fire that would shortly be lit a little way distant from the house. The feasting meant little to them. It was the excitement of the fire and the dancing that would follow. The air had a warm moistness to it. The skies were luminescent with the high-summer twilight. Here and there in the firmament stars began to show.

And then the lady of Friarsgate stood up. "Who wants to help me light our fire?" she asked, and the children surrounded her all begging to be the special one. She turned to Baen. "Who would you choose?" she asked him, motioning him forward to join her.

He looked at the noisy group of children, and then his eye lit upon a little girl who had been pushed to the rear of the pack by her siblings. Her forlorn look told him of her disappointment at being too small to be noticed, but he noticed. She had blond braids like Elizabeth, and he imagined that once Elizabeth had looked like that. Stepping into the crowd of children, he lifted her up. "Here is a bonny bairn to help you, lady!" he said, cradling the little girl in the crook of his arm. The smile that lit the little maid's features warmed his heart.

"A fine choice, sir," Elizabeth praised him. Then she said to the child, "Put your hand on mine, Edith, and together we shall light our Midsummer fire."

Baen was surprised that she knew the bairn's name. There were so many youngsters crowding about them, how could she keep them all straight? The child in his arms leaned forward and put a firm little hand on Elizabeth's hand. The torch touched the pile of faggots once, twice, a third time. The flame sprang up to light the night, and the Friarsgate folk cheered.

"Nicely done, lassie," he told Edith, setting her down once more. The bairn flashed him a sweet smile. "Thank you for choosing me, sir," she said. Then she curtseyed and ran off to find her mother, flushed with her triumph.

"How kind you are," Elizabeth said softly.

"I could see how desperately she wanted to be chosen, yet she had little hope of it, being the smallest," he said. "It is difficult to be ignored when you so very much want to be noticed. Was it not that way for you when you were the youngest of your sisters?"

"Once we were very close," Elizabeth told him. "It was only after Philippa came back from court that first time that things began to change. She could scarcely wait to return as a maid of honor. It was all she thought about, and frankly it was very irritating."

He chuckled. "I should like to meet this oldest sister of yours," he said.

Elizabeth shook her head. "Nay, you would not. She is nobility now. A countess, and she never forgets it. But I should do Philippa an injustice if I did not say how kind she was to me at court. She tried her best."

The musicians had begun to play, and a circle was forming about the fire. Baen took Elizabeth's hand, and they joined the group. They danced boisterously about the flames for some minutes, and above them the skies began to darken slightly. The fire crackled and shot sparks into the air. One country round dance led into another until Elizabeth was breathless with her exertions. As the evening began to deepen finally into a short night, couples began to disappear into the darkness. The circle of dancers grew smaller, and the flames shot higher, casting shadows all around. She wanted to go into the shadows with a man, which she had never done. Reaching out, Elizabeth took the Scot's hand and walked from the fire into the blackness.

His hand tightened around hers. "What are you doing?" he asked softly.

"I've never left the fire with a man on Midsummer's Eve," Elizabeth said. "I'm twenty-two, Baen. Don't you think it's time?"

"Do you know why couples flee from the fire, Elizabeth?" he asked her.

"So they can make love," she answered him candidly. "Would you like to make love to me, Baen?" Elizabeth asked low.

He stopped short. He could not see her face, and only that he had her hand in his could he even know she was by his side. "Elizabeth, you told me earlier that you were not wanton, and yet now you would suggest that we explore passion together. I must understand exactly what it is you are asking of me before we proceed further."

"Don't you want to kiss me?" she countered.

"Very much," he replied.

"Then why don't you?" Elizabeth wanted to know.

"Did you not once tell me that kissing leads to cuddling, and cuddling led to passion?" he demanded to know.

"I want you to kiss me," she said. "I am twenty-two, an old maid with little chance of marriage, no matter what they say, and I want to be kissed, Baen MacColl. I want to be kissed in the darkness on Midsummer's Eve. But I want those kisses from a man I like and admire, as I do you." She turned to face him, slipping her arms about his neck, pressing against him seductively.

He could feel the pressure of her breasts against his chest. Her slender body against his hard body. He closed his eyes briefly, enjoying the sensations she was engendering within him. Her lips brushed over his.

"Kiss me," she whispered against his mouth. "Kiss me!"

And he did. One kiss melted into another and another. She sighed, her warm breath touching his face. He caressed the sweet face he could not see for the pitch-black engulfing them. He took that face between his hands, kissing her forehead, her eyelids, her nose, her cheeks, her chin before returning to her ripe mouth to drink the addictive nectar of her lips once more. It was a testament to his great restraint that he touched her with tenderness when he really wanted to push her down onto the meadow grass and possess her completely. Finally he groaned, "We have to cease, Elizabeth."

"Why?" she demanded. "I like kissing."

Gently he disentangled her from about his neck, and, holding her two hands in his, he pushed her gently away. "Because I am beginning to desire the cuddling," he told her.

"I think I am too," she admitted boldly.

He laughed. "You are becoming a very bad wench, I fear," he told her. "What am I to do with you, Elizabeth Meredith?"

"Kiss and cuddle me, Baen?" she suggested wickedly.

"What if we find we want more than the kissing and the cuddling, lass? I could never shame you, Elizabeth. I have not the right to you," he told her seriously.

"Why not?" she asked defiantly. "No one else wants me."

"My birth does not match yours, lass. You know that," he said quietly.

"If I were one of the village lasses, Baen, would you take me further into the darkness and make love to me?" she queried him. She drew him closer, slipping her arms about his neck once more. Was she so unattractive that he could not desire her? And why did she want him to? She wasn't a tease.

"Elizabeth," he said helplessly, feeling his need for her rising with every passing moment. Aye, if she were anyone else he would have her on her back in a trice!

"Pretend I am one of them," she begged him. "Do not think of me as the heiress to Friarsgate, Baen. Think of me as a pretty girl who would kiss and cuddle with you on Midsummer's Eve. Is that so difficult?"

He wasn't a saint, damnit! And he wasn't some green boy who couldn't stop when the passion flamed too high. The wench wanted to be kissed and cuddled. She was desirable, and by the rood, he wanted her! Wordlessly he led her deeper into the darkness, past several shadowed haystacks, until at the far end of the meadow he stopped before the last cone of hay. He drew her down into the pile of sweet-smelling grass and began to kiss her once more: deep, passionate kisses that left them both weak with pleasure.

The hard body pressing her down into the hay set her pulse racing wildly. His mouth demanded from her emotions so new she wasn't certain she even understood them. His tongue pushed into the sweet cavern of her mouth, seeking, stroking, fierce with his need. She intertwined her tongue with his, moaning with a strange new need that was arising within her. She felt a sticky wetness between her thighs.

Baen cradled Elizabeth in the curve of his arm. His fingers skillfully undid her shirt, and he slipped his hand within to caress her two small, round breasts. She gasped, surprised, but she did not pull away from him. The two breasts came alive within the enclosure of his palm. They grew firm, and the dainty nipples puckered beneath the stroking of his big hand. "Sweet! Sweet!" he murmured in her ear, and she sighed with her open pleasure. "You've never been touched before, have you?" he whispered.

"You know I am a virgin," she managed to say, although the actions of his hand were rendering her dizzy with enjoyment.

"Some virgins have kissed and caressed, yet not permitted their maidenheads to be plucked, lass. You, however, have never known a man's touch, have you?"

"Nay," she said. "Not until now. Is there more, Baen? Tell me there is more!" she pleaded with him. She had never imagined the feelings she was now experiencing, and she was certain she was going to die if he did not give her more.

In answer he opened her blouse wider and lowered his dark head, his mouth closing over one of her nipples to suck.

"Oh, God!" Elizabeth half sobbed. The hungry drawing on her breast sent a shudder of hot delight through her. She mewled with pleasure as his tongue licked at her, and with each stroke of that tongue she was drawn into a new world. "More! I want more!"

He moved to her other breast and treated it as prettily as he had the first. He could feel her heart thundering beneath his ear. Unable to help himself, he slid his hand beneath her skirt and moved it up to brush the inside of her thigh with a sensuous motion. He expected to be rebuffed, but he was not. She pressed down hungrily against his hand as he cupped and gently squeezed her plump mons within his palm. And feeling the moisture on his skin from her, he knew he had to cease this love play or there would be no stopping for either of them. What madness had made him play this game with her? He was the older, the more experienced, she but an eager virgin. He should have known better, but the truth was, he could not resist the invitation she had so freely offered.

"Elizabeth, we must stop," he told her.

"Why? Oh, please don't stop, Baen! 'Tis wonderful!" she told him.

Reluctantly he withdrew his hand from beneath her skirts and gave her lips a quick kiss. "Elizabeth, I want you. All of you! But I will not ruin you for the man who will one day have the incredible good fortune to be your husband, lass. This was Midsummer madness, but there is little harm done." His strong fingers relaced her blouse shut. He stood up, pulling her with him. "Come. If we are gone much longer the worst will be thought of us. I will not have your reputation sullied, lass." He was glad for the darkness, as walking was at first difficult.

Elizabeth was not certain that she could walk at all. Her legs felt weak. She clung to his arm as they moved back across the meadow towards the fire. Her time in Baen MacColl's arms had been a revelation to her. She realized now that she could never give herself to just any man. It had to be a man she liked. A man she could love. Flynn Stewart had been so charming. He had briefly stolen her heart. But Elizabeth knew now, as Flynn had gently pointed out to her, that he was not a man to settle down. And she knew that only a man who could love Friarsgate as she did would be the man for her. Was it possible that Baen could be that man? She was beginning to realize that they had more in common than she had previously considered. She understood her mother and her older sisters just a little better now, she thought. But would they understand her and the decision she would make regarding a husband?

"Why do you say your breeding does not match mine?" she asked him quietly.

"You know I was born on the wrong side of the blanket," he began.

"So were two of my great-uncles: Edmund Bolton, who is my steward, and his younger brother, Richard, the prior of St. Cuthbert's. They are good men, and respected despite their birth. My great-grandfather recognized them both and gave them his name gladly. It was before he was wed to my great-grandmother," Elizabeth said.

"My mother was nothing more than a cotter's daughter," he continued.

"Your father, who recognizes you, is the master of Grayhaven," Elizabeth countered. "My father was a Welsh boy whose cousin, a steward in the household of Jasper Tudor, took pity on him and gained him a place as one of his master's pages."

"I was told your father was a knight in service of the Tudors," Baen replied.

"It took him years of devoted and loyal service to gain his rank, and he was landless," Elizabeth explained. "When he met my mother he possessed naught but his horse, his armor, and his weapons. He was a poor man, Baen."

"I possess nothing but Friar," Baen responded. "Everything else I have is my father's. My horse, the clothing I wear."

"Yet you are respected and loved by that same father, who would, I suspect, give you anything you asked him for that he could give you without robbing your brothers. And your brothers accept and respect you too. You have said it," Elizabeth said.

"I owe my father my duty," Baen told her.

"I am pleased to hear it. I count loyalty among one of the greatest virtues in a man," she told him bluntly. "Now please do not tell me ever again that you are not worthy of me, or of anyone else."

"Your kissing has improved," he said mischievously.

"Perhaps it is due in part to Flynn Stewart," Elizabeth teased him back. "He was most assiduous in his instruction of me."

"I think no one has ever spanked you, Elizabeth Meredith," he growled.

"Fortunately for me, we are now back where all can see us, and so I shall be spared your further threats," she mocked him with a grin.

"One day . . ." he said menacingly.

"I suspect I may look forward to it," she told him wickedly. "Do you spank as well as you kiss and cuddle, Baen?"

He roared with his laughter. "You will be the judge, for eventually I suspect you will force me to violence."

"Probably I will," Elizabeth agreed sweetly.

Thomas Bolton had watched them return with interest. He had, of course, seen them slip from the fire, as had many other young couples. He had never known his niece to leave the fire, at least according to Maybel, who had seen them go too. How far had the flirtation gotten? There was a bit a straw in Elizabeth's hair, but she did not have the look of a woman satisfied. The Scot was a gentleman then, despite the temptation placed before him. Interesting. He would speak with Elizabeth in the morning. He had to learn whether her feelings made it worth pursuing his solution to the family's problem.

"You are plotting, Uncle," Elizabeth said, coming to sit next to him on the bench.

"What makes you say such a thing, dear girl?" he wanted to know. He patted her soft hand with his.

"Your eyebrows are crinkled, as they always are when you are considering a problem," she informed him. "Midsummer's Eve is not a night for serious thoughts."

It was certainly after midnight. The morning of a new day. *Time enough,* he thought. "Do you like the Scot?" he asked her bluntly.

Elizabeth smiled. "You saw us leave the fire," she replied.

"You have not answered my question, dear girl. Do you like Baen MacColl?"

"Aye, I do, Uncle," Elizabeth admitted honestly. "You know I have always had a weakness for Scots." She chuckled.

"Would he make you a good husband?" Thomas Bolton asked her candidly.

Elizabeth colored, but then she said, "Aye, he would. But he is a Scot. Friarsgate must remain English, Uncle. I may play at kissing games with Baen, but even I understand this is just the same difficulty as with Flynn Stewart."

"Nay," Thomas Bolton said. "It is not. Flynn is a son of the late king. Half brother to the current king of the Scots. He owes all his loyalty to the royal Stewarts. But Baen is the bastard of a man with less land than you possess. He may be the eldest son of his father, but he cannot inherit, for he has two legitimate younger brothers who will."

"His loyalty to his father is every bit as strong as is Flynn's to his king," Elizabeth said. "He told me he has nothing. That everything he possesses is his father's."

"His father loves him?" Lord Cambridge queried.

"Aye, he does," Elizabeth said.

"Then he should jump at the chance to better Baen's position in the world," Thomas Bolton said quietly. "He did not know this son until he was twelve, and though he has loved, taught, and sheltered him these past twenty years, Elizabeth, he might be willing to let him go if his going meant becoming your husband."

"What you mean is becoming the lord of Friarsgate," she responded.

"You will always be the lady of Friarsgate, dear girl, and Baen does not strike me as a man who would force you from your place," Lord Cambridge observed.

"Give me time to learn this for myself," Elizabeth said. "He has just returned, and we have many months ahead of us to be together. I would be certain we are suited, Uncle. And I would want this knowledge you have gained between us alone. My mother and Logan should not know quite yet."

"I must inform your mother that you are home again sooner than later, dear girl," he said. "You know she will be curious."

"Tell her you have an idea, Uncle, and ask for time to explore it," Elizabeth replied with a little smile.

"Now who is plotting?" He chortled.

"Do you think he would wed me?" Elizabeth asked her uncle softly.

"He would be a fool not to, dear girl," Thomas Bolton replied.

"Will you go home to Otterly soon?" she queried him.

"I have sent William to see how far along the builders are. I fear I may be forced to rely upon your hospitality awhile longer, dear girl. Will you mind it?" He smiled at her warmly, his brown eyes full of his love for her.

"Nay," she answered. "I think I may need your guidance—and your protection when Mama and her Logan come over the border to scold me."

"Let us have it over sooner than later, my angel girl," he said to her. "I will write her tomorrow. She will come, I am certain, for I cannot keep her away, but we will reassure her together. Then she will go back to Claven's Carn, and you will have the rest of the summer and autumn months in which to seduce your Scot." Lord Cambridge chuckled.

"Uncle! What makes you think I mean to seduce him? I am a proper virgin," Elizabeth declared indignantly.

"Hah!" he barked a laugh. "You have a mother and two older sisters, all known for their passionate natures. And I know quite well that Banon and her Neville were sharing a bed in the months before their marriage. I turned a blind eye to them, for I realized Banon was binding her Neville with the unbreakable cords of love."

"I did not know that," Elizabeth said slowly.

"You were a little girl, and not supposed to know of such things," he replied. "And your mother was in bed with Logan before they wed."

"I certainly did not know that!" Elizabeth exclaimed.

"You must follow your heart and your instincts where Baen Mac-Coll is concerned, my pet. Neither will disappoint you," he assured her.

"Uncle, you surprise me," Elizabeth said.

Thomas Bolton chortled. "It seems to me that your mother and each of your sisters has said something along those lines to me at one time or another. I may have no wife or mistress, dear girl, but I understand love quite well." He arose from the bench where they were seated. "It is growing damp, and I am too old to remain outdoors of a summer's night. I am going to bed."

"I will come too," she told him. "Tomorrow is not a holiday, though most will be slow to their tasks, I suspect. When do you think Will is coming back?"

"He should be gone no more than a few days," Lord Cambridge said as they walked towards the house. "I will send a message to your mother tomorrow, but I will word it in such a way that perhaps Logan will remain in his own home when she comes here to Friarsgate."

"It would be best," Elizabeth agreed. "If my stepfather ever knew that I was considering a Scots husband he would have all his friends' sons calling upon me." She sighed. "He waited all those years for Mama, and yet he does not understand that I want to love and be loved too."

"It is your mother we must convince, dear girl. She will make her own brazen Scot understand that your heart must lie where it must lie."

*   *   *

A messenger was dispatched to Claven's Carn the following morning, and several days later Rosamund Bolton Hepburn returned to Friarsgate in the company of that same messenger. Her husband was not with her, but her stepson, John Hepburn, was. Lord Cambridge hurried to greet his beloved cousin, enfolding her in a warm embrace.

"My dearest girl!" He kissed both her cheeks. "You are as radiant as ever. Welcome home to Friarsgate." He led her into the hall, where Maybel was waiting to greet the woman she had raised. Lord Cambridge let them hug and sit together to chatter. After a short time, however, Maybel arose slowly.

"I must see to the meal," she said, and bustled off.

Lord Cambridge now rejoined Rosamund, handing her a goblet of wine and sipping from his.

"I suppose I shall need this," Rosamund said quietly. "Where is Elizabeth?"

"Out in the meadows making her weekly count of the sheep, as she should be," he answered. "She's a good chatelaine, cousin."

"Without a husband. Without an heir," Rosamund responded. "Was there no one at court who would have suited? Whom my daughter could have accepted and loved?"

"No one," Lord Cambridge said. "She had a mild flirtation with a bastard of the late James Stewart who is his brother's messenger to Henry's court. The king sends you his regards."

"Not the queen?" Rosamund wondered.

"The queen was not with the court, but sent to Woodstock. Mistress Boleyn rules in her stead. The king is utterly besotted," Lord Cambridge explained.

"Poor Katherine! For all her royal breeding, her great piety and devotion to God, she has had a far harder life than many a humble woman. I know she considers it a penance, and thinks her soul the better for it," Rosamund said. "I am sorry for her. Had it been her court I have no doubt a suitable husband could have been found for Elizabeth. You say you have a possible solution to this conundrum. I beg you, tell me what it is."

"Baen MacColl has returned to Friarsgate," Lord Cambridge began.

"The Scot who was here last winter? Why has he come back?" Rosamund wanted to know. She sipped thirstily at her wine while her other hand worried the dark green fabric of her skirts. "What does he want?"

"His father, the master of Grayhaven, sent to ask if he might return and learn how to set up a small industry, as we have done. Edmund saw no harm in saying he might come. A small attraction sprang up last winter between him and Elizabeth. It still exists. The man cannot inherit from his father, for he has two legitimate brothers. Elizabeth would accept him as a husband if she could but convince him. Baen's loyalty to his own father is deep, however."

"A Scot would be master of Friarsgate?" Rosamund said slowly.

"I doubt Baen has any loyalties except to his family," Lord Cambridge said quietly. "He is not a political creature."

"Scots always become nationalistic when faced with an English war," Rosamund said. "Logan and I have been fortunate, but should war break out between our two countries in our lifetime, I do not know what we should do, Tom."

"You would barricade yourselves in Claven's Carn, and wait till it was over and done with, dear girl. Besides, the English always make for Edinburgh in a war, and that is on the opposite side of the country from both Friarsgate and Claven's Carn," he reminded her. "We have always been relatively safe here."

"But what do we know of this Baen MacColl, Tom? Really know?" Rosamund wondered aloud.

"We know he is a good man," Thomas Bolton said. "Stay with us for a few days and observe him yourself."

"Does he want to marry my daughter?" Rosamund asked her cousin.

"My dear girl, the subject hasn't even come up," Lord Cambridge said. "Nor should it until Elizabeth decides the time is right," he cautioned.

"Are you telling me that this Scot has evinced no interest in marrying my daughter?" Rosamund demanded to know.

"He is not a presumptuous man, dear girl. He thinks himself not worthy of her," Lord Cambridge responded, attempting to mollify her outrage.

"But she intends to convince him otherwise," Rosamund said.

"I fear she does, dear cousin," he answered her.

"I am sorry she did not find a good English husband at court," Rosamund began. "But I question why this particular man?"

"Because, Mama," Elizabeth Meredith said, entering her own hall, "ever since the Earl of Glenkirk I have always had a weakness for Scots." She hurried to her mother and embraced her warmly. "Welcome home, Mama."

Rosamund hugged her youngest daughter; then she set her back so she might look into her face. "You are in love with him?"

"I suppose I am," Elizabeth said, "but I am not really certain what love is, though perhaps I am learning."

"Has he taken advantage of you?" Rosamund wanted to know.

Elizabeth laughed aloud. "Nay, Mama, but I have certainly taken advantage of him, though he resists me and prates about honor, and how he is unworthy."

Rosamund sighed. "I shall take your advice, cousin, and remain for a few days to observe this reluctant Scot," she said.

"Please, Mama, say nothing to him. I do not wish him frightened off," Elizabeth said softly. "I really do like him."

And Rosamund found that she liked Baen MacColl too as she came to know him over the next few days. He was a bit rough, but in an odd way he reminded her of Owein Meredith, Elizabeth's father. He was thoughtful. He had a great care and respect for the land. He treated the lady of Friarsgate with consideration, just as Owein had done. But he was a Scot. And not just a Scot. A Highland Scot! Why did he have to be a Scot? It was obvious to her mother's eye that Elizabeth did care for this man. The night before her return to Claven's Carn she confided her concerns to her cousin.

"I don't know what to do, Tom. For the first time in my life I honestly do not know what to do. Help me."

Thomas Bolton sat quietly in his chair stroking the half-grown Domino, who was lounging in his lap purring loudly. "You set the example, dear one. You wed a Scot," he said. "Elizabeth isn't like most girls her age. She feels a great sense of responsibility to her position. She would not be happy sitting by the fire weaving and mothering her bairns, Rosamund. She has become Friarsgate, and she needs a man who will not be afraid of that, or try to take it away from her, attempting to make her into something she isn't. Do I wish he were English, or a borderer? Does it really matter, cousin? She is falling in love with him, and she has never loved any man. And he has fallen in love with her. Last winter, I suspect. But he, too, carries a strong sense of responsibility for who and what he is. What will happen? I do not know. But I am of a mind to let fate and nature take their course, Rosamund. And that would be my council to you."

"But how will Elizabeth resolve his concerns? And how will she gain his promise to remain neutral in the face of a conflict between their two countries?" Rosamund asked her cousin. "We cannot have Friarsgate caught between warring parties."

"Let them find their own way, dear girl. They will do it together, because their love for each other will surely overcome all else. Elizabeth will convince her reluctant Scot to take his place by her side. Of that I am certain. And his father should not object to having his bastard wed with an heiress, even if it means he will lose him."

Rosamund giggled. "Logan is going to be furious," she said. "He will be disappointed that Elizabeth did not choose one of his friends' sons if she is to wed a Scot."

"He will survive the disappointment, dear girl," Lord Cambridge said dryly. "Ah, I remember him when he sought to make you his wife. He was brazen. Dashing. Dangerous! But now, content with you and his lads, he has become a rather ordinary and dull fellow, I fear. That seems to happen to most men once they are wed. Why did you bring John with you? He has spent all his time with Father Mata, and we have scarce seen him at all."

"Mata is taking him to Prior Richard in a few days," Rosamund said.

"Logan has relented? Dear girl, why did you not say so sooner?"

"Logan has not relented. He has just come to realize that John's fate lies away from Claven's Carn, but he still has hopes that after his novitiate, before he takes his final vows, John will change his mind," Rosamund explained.

"But he won't," Lord Cambridge said, "and so your eldest son becomes his father's heir, eh? John will make his own destiny even as Elizabeth will make hers."

"Even as I made mine," Rosamund said softly. "Thank you, Tom."

# Chapter 10

Before she departed the following morning, Rosamund sought out Baen MacColl and spoke with him. He towered over her, and she could suddenly see some of the attraction that Elizabeth felt. He was very masculine. "Do you hear news of Glenkirk?" she asked him quietly. "How is the earl?"

"Well, but older, they say, than God himself," Baen replied. "I have not seen him out riding recently. They say he leaves most of the business of Glenkirk to his son, Lord Adam. The earl has not been well in many years now, lady. His memory is faulty, it is said, but he is still well thought of by all. My father is friends with Lord Adam. Did you know the earl, lady?"

"Once," Rosamund said. "Long ago. I am pleased to learn the earl remains in good health. Should you see Lord Adam when you return home, please tell him that Rosamund Bolton sends all at Glenkirk her kind regards." She smiled up at him. "I think you a good man, Baen MacColl. I am glad you have returned to Friarsgate. I hope you will gain all you desire while you are here."

"Thank you, lady," he said. Her smile was dazzling, and her words kind. "Mistress Elizabeth has been very kind and helpful."

"My daughter, I think," said Rosamund, unable to resist, "has a weakness for Scots, Baen MacColl. Since I am wed to one myself, I can hardly object." There! She had given her tacit approval of him. He did not understand the true meaning behind her words, of course. It was up to Elizabeth now, but Rosamund had come to realize over the last few days of her visit that she would not object to Baen MacColl as a son-in-law. "Farewell, sir," she concluded the conversation, and she gave his arm a friendly pat.

Thomas Bolton had heard all, and now he came forth as if just entering the hall. "Are you ready to leave, dearest cousin?" he asked her. "Allow me to escort you to your horse. I sent ahead yesterday to your good lord to let him know you were returning home. You will be escorted to the border by Friarsgate men, and met by your own Claven's Carn folk. I have not a doubt dear Logan will ride with them. Do not fret about Johnnie. We shall see him safely to St. Cuthbert's, my precious girl." He took her arm and drew her from the hall.

"You heard, you sly fox!" She chuckled.

"I did. Not all, but enough to know you will not forbid a match between the bastard of Grayhaven and the heiress of Friarsgate," he told her. But he had heard all, and the knowledge that a small flame still burned secretly in her heart for Patrick Leslie had almost brought him to tears. But then, did one ever forget such a great love?

They found Elizabeth awaiting them outside of the house. "I will ride a ways with you, Mama," she said, and mounted her own horse.

Lord Cambridge bade his cousin a most effusive good-bye. "Who knows when we shall meet again," he told her dramatically.

Rosamund laughed down at him from her saddle. "Dear Tom," she said, "I have not a doubt it will be sooner than later. When will you return to Otterly?"

"Will arrived last evening. My wing is but half-finished. That wicked daughter of yours had convinced the builder to put in another door between my private quarters and the rest of the house. Will remained while it was removed and bricked up. Banon has been severely admonished, and the builder as well. It would appear I shall not be able to return home until sometime in October, if the snows hold off, of course," he explained. "I shall send a most stern missive to Banon regarding this matter, you may be assured." He took Rosamund's hand in his and kissed it. "Travel in safety, dearest girl, and tell your good lord that I send him my most affectionate regards."

The two women and their escort rode away from the house. The day was cloudy, muggy, and hinted of rain.

"I like your Scot," Rosamund told her daughter as they traveled along. "If you can bring him to the altar, I will not object, Elizabeth."

"Thank you, Mama. What will you tell Logan?" she asked her parent.

"Nothing for the present," Rosamund said. "Surely you do not wish to be inundated with Scots suitors of what your stepfather will consider more suitable births while you are attempting to bring Baen around? No. I shall tell Logan that there was no one at court who was suitable, but that Tom is considering several other families he had not previously considered. If Logan asks me who they are I shall simply say I did not inquire, as I trust my cousin implicitly, since he succeeded in matching your two older sisters so very well." Rosamund chuckled. "Your stepfather will not dare to press the issue further, for he trusts me completely, bless him."

"Poor Logan." Elizabeth grinned. "Does he realize how shamelessly you manipulate him, Mama?"

"Of course not!" She laughed. Then she grew sober once more. "These Scots are prideful, Elizabeth. Remember that as you maneuver your own game. I like Baen. He would make you a good husband, and he will not usurp your authority, as your father did not attempt to steal mine. But his loyalty to the father who took him in is great. In the end, you may have to appeal to the master of Grayhaven if you wish his son as your husband. If that happens you must ask Logan to intercede for you, for only a Scotsman will understand another Scotsman, my daughter."

"If he does not love me enough to remain with me," Elizabeth said softly, "then I do not want him. I am not some prize to be bestowed."

"Elizabeth! That is exactly what you are, and must appear to be. If the master of Grayhaven is to give up his oldest son it must be because the life you can offer Baen is better than what he can offer him. You have the advantage. Do not throw it away because of your own pride, I beg you!" Rosamund said low.

"He must love me enough to stay by my side, Mama," Elizabeth said firmly. "The decision must be his, and no one else's."

Rosamund said no more. Arguing with her daughter would accomplish nothing but to make Elizabeth's determination firmer. To her surprise Elizabeth remained with her until they reached the unmarked place where England flowed into Scotland. Sure enough, there was Logan Hepburn waiting with half a dozen clansmen to escort his wife home.

The laird of Claven's Carn dismounted and came forward to greet them. He took his wife's hand and kissed it. Their eyes met, and the passion that still existed between them was palpable, yet they spoke not a word. Logan turned to his stepdaughter. "Did you bring back a husband, lass?" he asked her bluntly. The vibrant blue eyes looked at her with interest.

"Nay, none of those court dandies are suited to the life Friarsgate has to offer, Logan," Elizabeth answered him, "but Mama will tell you all the news. If we ride hard I will be able to complete at least half a day's work when I get home. Good-bye, Mama. Thank you for coming. I love you!" Elizabeth blew them kisses, and then with a smile she turned her horse back for home.

"Good-bye, my darling," she heard her mother call after her.

She was relieved to have escaped further cross-examination by her stepfather. Logan was Rosamund's problem. That other Scotsman was hers. Her mother was right: Baen was prideful. But he wanted her. Elizabeth might be unskilled in the ways of men and women, but she knew when a man wanted a woman. And she intended on torturing her big Scot until he could no longer resist her blandishments. He was already hers, though he knew it not. Smiling, she hurried her horse home, her Friarsgate men following.

Her fields were green with grain, she noted, pleased. The hay was almost all cut, and drying before being stored for the winter. Her beasts were fat. They would begin shearing next week. Many sheared earlier, but Friarsgate sheared their sheep just after Midsummer's Day. There was time through the remainder of the summer and autumn to grow back the fleece the sheep would need for the winter months. And the wool they harvested from the later shearing could be spun into longer and stronger threads. It was part of the secret of their particularly fine wool. Their flocks were great this year. They had lost no beasts to disease or to any predators.

Strangely the hall seemed a little emptier that evening without

Rosamund. She had for so long been the heart and soul of Friarsgate. As they sat talking after the meal Edmund remarked that he was not feeling well, and then suddenly fell from his chair to the floor. Maybel shrieked her dismay, but Baen jumped forward to pick up the unconscious man.

"This way," Elizabeth said quickly, leading him up the stairs to the chamber Maybel and her husband shared. She flung open the door.

Baen was quickly behind her, and laid Edmund gently upon the bed. Maybel pushed the younger man aside and began loosening her husband's shirt, clucking and fussing as she did.

Edmund opened his eyes. "Lea . . . leave . . . me be," he muttered.

Baen gently moved Maybel away from her husband and, leaning over, spoke into Edmund's ear. "Where does it hurt?" he asked him.

"Head," Edmund ground out. "I c-c-can't seem to m-move."

Baen nodded. "You must rest, Edmund, and let Maybel take care of you. You will feel better tomorrow. You have been working very hard."

"Aye," Edmund said, and his eyes closed again.

"What has happened to him?" Maybel begged Baen. "He has always been so strong. What is the matter with him?"

"I do not know what they call it," Baen said, "but I have seen this before in old men, Maybel. With God's blessing he will regain the use of his limbs, although he will never be as strong again as he was. With some the power of speech is lost too. He is fortunate there. Keep him warm, and give him watered wine if he is thirsty. Sleep is the best healer that there is."

"I will prepare a carafe of wine," Elizabeth said. "I will put a sleeping draft in it so poor Edmund can rest. Stay by his side. I will hurry back."

"As if I would leave him!" Maybel huffed with a bit of her old spirit.

The two younger people left the bedchamber to hurry downstairs.

"Poor Edmund," Elizabeth said. She called a servant and sent the man to her apothecary cabinet with instructions on what to bring back. "What could have caused this? He is not a man to be ill."

"I cannot tell you what caused it, but I heard once that it is an eruption within the head. It can cause death if it is severe. I do not think

203

it is that severe with Edmund, but it is unlikely he will regain his full strength again," Baen told her.

Elizabeth nodded. "I will need your help then," she said. "You came to learn our ways with the sheep and the wool. Now you will have to take Edmund's place for me until he is well again, but I will teach you myself what you need to know, Baen."

"I will do whatever I can to help you, of course," the Scot answered her, "but I cannot step into Edmund's shoes. It would be presumptuous of me. What would your Friarsgate folk think of such overweening conduct from me? They would resent me, and rightly so, Elizabeth."

"If you are right he will be well soon enough," Elizabeth said. "Besides, if you have my authority they will accept it. Please! Until Edmund is well again. I have no one else, Baen. Edmund has never had anyone to assist him, nor have we ever considered a time when he could not do his duty." She looked up into his handsome face, her eyes filled with worry and concern. "Please!"

He nodded. "Very well," he told her. "But only until Edmund is well again."

"Thank you!" she cried and, flinging her arms about his neck, kissed him.

"Nah, nah, lass!" he admonished her, but he was smiling, and he did not push her away when she snuggled even closer. "Would you cause a scandal?"

"Do you think we could?" she asked innocently.

"Elizabeth!" He unwrapped her arms from about his neck. "Here is Albert with your herbs. I think Maybel will feel safer once you have mixed your potion."

Elizabeth took the small container from Albert, giving him a wink as she did. The middle-aged man could not restrain his grin. "Thank you, Albert," she said sweetly. Then she set to work adding just the right amount of a powered substance to the wine, gently shaking the stoppered carafe to mix it in. "I will take this to Maybel. Please remain in the hall until I return," she told Baen. "We must talk further." Then she hurried off, the carafe of wine in her hand. Reentering the bed-chamber where her steward lay, she set the carafe upon a small table and poured a draft into an earthenware cup. She gave it to Maybel, saying, "See he drinks all of it," and she waited while the older woman gently coaxed her husband to finish the wine. Elizabeth took the cup back and set it by the carafe of wine.

Edward was quickly asleep, and Maybel turned to look at her young companion. "What is the matter with him?" Her voice quavered. "What will happen to him, Elizabeth? Is he going to die? And who will help you with Friarsgate now?"

"Baen says he has seen this kind of thing before. It is an eruption within the brain. It will take many months for him to recover, but Baen thinks he will. Edmund Bolton is my blood kin as well as my steward," Elizabeth said. "His position is his, but I have asked Baen to take over his duties until Edmund can manage them once again. Do you think I have made the right decision, Maybel? Edmund has never permitted anyone to help him, nor has he trained any to take his place one day."

"What man wants to think of his own mortality?" Maybel asked in a broken voice. "Baen MacColl is a good man. Edmund would approve your choice, Elizabeth. Thank you for your kindness, my child."

"Kindness? Maybel, you and Edmund are my family!" Elizabeth cried.

Maybel shook her head wearily. "If you had a husband," she said, "I believe Edmund and I would retire to that cottage of ours. But how can we leave you to manage Friarsgate alone?" She paused as if considering her next words, and then she said, "The Scot is a good man, Elizabeth. And I see that you like each other. Many a marriage has been celebrated on less than that. If your mother would approve it, child, Baen MacColl could be the answer to your problem."

Elizabeth smiled. "I have Mama's permission to pursue him, Maybel, and I intend on doing just that."

The older woman gave the girl a wan smile, and nodded. "Does he know it?" she asked. "He seems a strong and independent man."

"Not yet," Elizabeth admitted with a twinkle, "but he will soon. I think he will be more comfortable, Maybel, knowing you approve my decision to put him in Edmund's place temporarily. If I sit with your man will you go down to the hall and tell him?"

Maybel arose from her place by her husband's bedside. "Aye. He's the kind of man who would not impose himself where he is not wanted. I will tell him I am grateful for his aid in our troubles." She moved towards the door to the chamber. "I will not be long, lass."

Elizabeth sat by the bedside of Edmund Bolton. He was sleeping peacefully now, but the right side of his mouth was pulled down and crooked. His hands were frozen, partly open, the right one more so than the left. He did not move, and only by the rising and falling of his chest did Elizabeth Meredith know that her great-uncle lived. To see Edmund helpless and frail was somewhat of a shock, for he had always been so hearty and robust a man. But he was no longer young, Elizabeth realized. He was past seventy now by a good year.

Elizabeth sighed softly. How foolish she had been. She had not taken the passing of time seriously. She had not considered that each year she added to her own age those around her were also growing older as well. Edmund and Maybel would not be with her forever. Had they not earned their rest in their own dear little cottage that they rarely visited these days? And Friarsgate. Her beloved Friarsgate. None of her nieces or nephews were suited to inherit it. What had she been thinking when she had so obdurately refused to consider marrying?

Yet she knew. Her mother had found love thrice in her lifetime. Philippa and Banon had found love in their own marriages. And Elizabeth Meredith would not, could not settle for any less than what they had. But until Baen MacColl had come into her life she had seen no hope of finding a man to love, a man who would love her enough to accept her as she was. The lady of Friarsgate. However, Baen did. Now her only problem would be in convincing him to stay with her. She had her mother's permission to bring him to the altar if she could. And even now Maybel was convincing him how necessary he was to Friarsgate, to them all.

And indeed the old woman was. She had taken up his hands and kissed them both before bursting into tears. "Thank God and his blessed Mother Mary that you are here to aid us, laddie. We should be lost without you," she told him, sobbing.

Instinctively Baen had put his arms about the weeping woman. "There now, Maybel, do not greet. Your Edmund will be all right with

God's good help. I am here to help, and I will until he can get on his feet again. How is he now?"

"Sleeping," Maybel said. "Elizabeth gave him the draft and is sitting with him while I have come to thank you. But I must return now," she said, moving from the comfort of his strong arms.

"Is there anything we can do to make him more comfortable?" Lord Cambridge asked. He had come into the hall shortly after Edmund had been carried upstairs.

"Thank you, Thomas Bolton," Maybel said. "I believe all is being done that can be done for now." Then she hurried back to her husband.

"Well, dear boy, I thank heavens you are with us," Lord Cambridge said. "For all the ladies of Friarsgate think they can manage, each has needed a man at one time or another," he said. "Poor Edmund, but alas he is not a lad any longer, I fear. None of us is, of course, but he is the oldest of the Boltons."

Elizabeth returned to the hall and requested of Albert that the evening meal be served. Father Mata arrived from his church, where he had been schooling some of the younglings in the Latin of the Mass. Elizabeth told him what had transpired, and then said, "Eat first, Mata, and then go to Maybel. I know you well, and you will remain the night by Edmund's side with an empty belly if I do not make you eat now."

The priest said the blessing, and then gobbled his meal of lamb stew with carrots and leeks, trout with butter and parsley, and bread and cheese. Then, rising, he made for the stairs. Several minutes later Maybel entered the hall, and Elizabeth beckoned her to the high board to eat. She finished her meal as quickly as the priest had, and disappeared back to her chamber, where Edmund lay silent. Thomas Bolton and Will Smythe excused themselves from the hall after a single game of chess, leaving Baen and Elizabeth alone. The servants cleared the remnants of the evening meal away, and the hall was suddenly empty but for the Scot and the lady of Friarsgate.

"Let us sit by the fire," Elizabeth invited him, offering the tapestried chair with the high back. When he had seated himself she sat down in his lap. "Isn't this nice?" she asked him, snuggling against him.

"Aye," he agreed, his arms slipping about her. "Are you attempting to seduce me, Elizabeth?" The delicate fragrance from her hair was enticing. White heather, he thought, and smiled to himself.

"Aye, I am attempting to seduce you, Baen," she told him boldly. "Do you mind?" She looked up into his face.

"Lassie, lassie," he said almost mournfully, "I do not think this is a good idea."

"Why not?" she asked frankly. "Don't you want to be seduced?"

"If you were anyone other than who you are, Elizabeth, I would gladly succumb to your sweet blandishments," he told her. Why was she torturing him so? And why was he allowing her to do so? He had to resist her.

"I am no one special," she countered. "I am just plain Elizabeth Meredith." His arms were so warm and comforting. She could live in them forever, she realized.

"You are a wealthy landowner, and I the bastard of a Highlander. We have been over this before, Elizabeth, and I know you understand what I am saying," Baen replied, attempting to remove her from his lap, but, defying him, she burrowed deeper.

"Of course I understand you, but it does not make any sense, Baen." Her fingers played with the laces of his shirt. "I am wealthy and English. You are poor and a Scot. We both know it, but why should such a thing stop us from desiring each other and acting upon those desires?" The shirt laces loosened, and she slipped her hand beneath them to find the smooth skin of his broad chest and caress it.

He felt her fingers stroking him. Then she twisted in his lap, and, lowering her head, she began to kiss his flesh and lick at one of his nipples. "Elizabeth!" he pleaded with her, but he couldn't bring himself to make her stop. The little feathery kisses were exciting and oh, so sweet! Finally he pulled her up, and his mouth met hers in a fiery kiss. His big hand unloosened her single thick braid and tangled in her soft blond hair. He couldn't stop kissing her. Their mouths fused together again and again and yet again until Elizabeth was moaning with undisguised satisfaction.

Her lips felt bruised, and still she did not want him to cease. When he began to kiss her throat she could hear a roaring in her ears. She felt him opening her shirt as she had opened his. He was kissing her breasts, and she was crying out with the pure pleasure that was suffusing her whole body. "Oh, Baen," she moaned.

Why wasn't she telling him no? Why wasn't she defending her honor and crying for her servants to drag him off and beat him for his presumption? The scent of white heather arose up from her body to assail him again. He buried his face between her small breasts. "Elizabeth! Elizabeth!" he whispered against her beating heart. God help him! He was falling in love with her. Nay! He *was* in love with her and had been for months. To be holding her in his arms, to be kissing her . . . it was more than he had dared to hope.

Her fingers wove themselves into his dark head. The touch of his mouth on her skin was utterly intoxicating. And she wanted more. But what more was there? Could she tempt him tonight into revealing the mysteries of passion? She sighed happily.

And it was that soft sound of utter contentment that brought him to his senses. He might be in love with her, but he had no right to make love to her. And he was an experienced man ten years her senior who knew that unless they stopped this delightful activity right now, disaster was going to befall them both, but especially Elizabeth Meredith. He closed his eyes for just one more moment of pleasure. Then, lifting his head, he said sternly, "Enough, Elizabeth. This can only lead to seduction."

"Aye," she drawled. "Don't you want to be seduced, Baen?"

He laughed in spite of himself. "What am I going to do with you, lassie?" he despaired. "You surely know better."

"I only know what is best for us, Baen," Elizabeth told him.

"Us? There can be no us, lassie," he said in a suddenly hard voice.

She jumped from his lap, surprising him. "There most certainly can be an us, Baen MacColl. I am the lady of Friarsgate, and I want it! And I usually get what I want!"

"Damn it, why will you not understand?" he demanded angrily.

"Why will *you* not understand?" she snapped back, stamping her foot at him. Her hazel-green eyes scanned him, and she saw the hard bulge between his thighs. "You want me!" she accused him. "And if you dare to give one of my servants that which I want, I will murder the girl, Baen MacColl! Do you understand me? If you would satisfy that itch I have caused, you must satisfy it with me alone!"

"You will kill me before this is done," he said half angrily.

"You must kill me with pleasure first, Baen," she whispered against his lips, her hands reaching down to stroke him boldly as she slipped back onto his lap.

"I don't believe you are a virgin at all!" he accused her. "You behave like a wanton, Elizabeth Meredith!" He forced her out of his lap again.

"There is but one way to find out, Baen MacColl," she challenged him wickedly.

"Go to bed!" he commanded her. God's blood, how he wanted her!

"Alone?" she asked softly, her lips pursing temptingly. "Would you not come with me, Baen, and lie by my side? I want you to make me a woman, and you want me."

In answer he flung himself out of the hall and heard her mocking laughter behind him. Damn her! Damn the little tease! What in the name of all that was holy was she thinking of, behaving so? If she kept up like this he was going to eventually succumb, but if he did it would be her own wretched fault. He rubbed his distended member, for it ached, but he would not satisfy himself on another.

Elizabeth had watched him go, and she had laughed in hopes of forcing him back to silence her with his kisses. Kisses that would eventually lead to more. But Baen was an honorable man. Still, she had proved to them both that he could be tempted. Yet she had to admit she was satisfied with the results of tonight's encounter. As unfortunate as Edmund's sudden illness was for him, it had proved providential for her. Baen could not escape being with her now. She would have him. Oh, yes, she would!

Outside there was a strong rumble of thunder. The storm that had been threatening all day was ready to break. There came a gentle patter of rain upon the windows that over the next few minutes grew into a hard downpour. Elizabeth moved through her house, seeing that all the doors leading to the outside were firmly barred, snuffing the candles, making certain the public fires were banked. The dogs in the hall didn't even move as she stepped over them and, climbing the stairs, went up to her own bedchamber. Nancy was waiting for her.

"You should have gone to bed," Elizabeth said. "You know I can take care of myself," she told her tiring woman.

"But I'm supposed to take care of you," Nancy replied with a smile. "You're a grown girl now, and must accept all that goes with your position as lady of Friarsgate. Besides, 'tis my duty to look after you, mistress. If I did not have this duty I might be out in the fields or in the kitchens or helping the laundress. I prefer caring for you."

Elizabeth laughed. "Very well then," she acquiesced, and let Nancy prepare her for her bed.

"How is Edmund?" Nancy asked.

"I think in the morning we shall know better," Elizabeth answered her, and explained what Baen had told her.

"Poor old fellow," Nancy sympathized. "Friarsgate won't be the same without him. You have your work cut out for you now, mistress."

"The Scot will help. Edmund wants him to take his place until he is strong enough again to act for himself," Elizabeth said softly.

"He's a right handsome lad," Nancy responded with a small grin. "We've all flirted with him, but he don't seem to like the lasses. Yet I don't think him like Lord Tom and his William. Mayhap he has a sweetheart in the Highlands, and is being true to her, the lucky girl."

Elizabeth said nothing, getting into her bed and bidding her tiring woman a good night. She had never considered that Baen might have someone else. Well, it didn't matter. He was going to be hers. Still, the thought niggled at her, and the next morning as they rode out together to the shearing sheds she asked him bluntly, "Do you have a woman of your own at Grayhaven, Baen?"

"Nay," he answered her, and then he realized that if he had said aye, she would have left him in peace.

"Good!" she said sweetly. "I should hate to have her disappointed by you."

"If I had such a lass," he queried, "how would I disappoint her?"

"By marrying another," she told him.

"I will never wed," he said quietly.

"Why not?" Elizabeth demanded of him.

"Because I have naught to offer a wife," he responded.

"You are wrong," Elizabeth said, "but I will not argue the point with you now."

"I am relieved to hear it." He chuckled.

"Do you know why we shear our sheep later than most?" she asked him, changing the subject completely and quickly.

"Aye, but tell me again." He was relieved to be off an uncomfortable topic.

"The fleece is thicker, the hairs longer and stronger," she answered him. "This allows the fabric to be woven tighter, which makes it warmer and more resistant to the rain. Our fabric is prized in northern Europe."

"Do I not recall Tom saying you regulate the production of the Friarsgate blue?" he asked her.

"Aye. It's a better blue than anyone else makes, and much in demand. We keep the price of it higher by making just a little each year. So far no one has been able to match the color. I'm thinking of trying the same process by which we get the blue with green and possibly a golden color as well," Elizabeth told him.

"Your eyes sparkle when you speak of your wool," he told her.

Elizabeth laughed. "Now you understand why a gentleman of the court would have made a disastrous husband for me. I must be involved in my work. Oh, I will give my husband children, and gladly. But I will never sit passively by a fire."

"It will take a rare man to live with you, Elizabeth Meredith," he said.

"It will take a brave man to live with me," she admitted.

"Aye," he agreed, laughing, "it will indeed."

She left him at the shearing sheds to watch the process, and rode back to the house. The *Bold Venture* was due back from northern Europe soon, and Elizabeth was anxious to learn how the market had gone this season. She spent much of the rest of the day in her library working on her books. Now that Edmund was unable to do it the task must fall to her.

The old man was showing small signs of improvement this day. His voice was stronger, and no longer strained. The paralysis in his left hand had disappeared, but his right hand was still crippled like a bird's claw. Father Mata had carried Edmund to the hall and settled him in a chair. William Smythe had brought the game table forth and now sat playing Hare and Hounds with Edmund. Maybel, who had been up all night, was catching up on her sleep. She was not young either anymore.

Lord Cambridge popped his head into Elizabeth's library. "Where is the Scot, dear girl? I thought you would not let him out of your sight," he teased her.

"He's learning about the shearing," she replied.

"Do you think it will help him when he decides to shear you?" Tom Bolton chuckled wickedly.

"I think it far more likely I will shear him first," Elizabeth told her delighted relative. "He is a man of strong loyalties, and I will have to seduce him before he will see reason, Uncle. I am certain to shock him, as he does not think virgins should resort to such tactics. But I have a mother who brought her lover into this house, and I have two older sisters who are wed. I have gained enough knowledge to know something of what I am doing, Uncle."

"Indeed," Thomas Bolton murmured. "And would you like to share your plans with me, dear Elizabeth? Or am I and the rest of your family to be surprised?"

"Do you not enjoy surprises, Uncle?" she teased him mischievously. "I know for a fact that you do, and so I shall keep my strategies to myself."

"God's blood, I believe the poor man has no idea of what a scheming wench you are, dear girl." Lord Cambridge chuckled. "But do not be overconfident. He is a clever fellow, and could outmaneuver you if you are not careful."

"Nay," Elizabeth said softly. "His heart is too pure, Uncle."

Thomas Bolton smiled knowingly. "Why, Elizabeth, dear girl, I believe you have fallen in love with that big, bonny Scot."

"Perhaps I have," she replied. "Now leave me be, Uncle. I have a page of sums to enter into my ledgers before I am free to come into the hall. How Edmund did it all I will never know. I thought myself hardworking, but he has done so much more than I could have imagined, and made it look easy."

Lord Cambridge nodded, and, blowing her a kiss, left her.

When Elizabeth finished, her fingers were stained with the black ink. She left the little library and hurried upstairs to her chamber. Entering it, she was surprised to discover that Nancy had a bath waiting for her. "Bless you!" she said.

"Don't touch your garments with those ink-stained paws of yours," Nancy cautioned. She helped her mistress from her clothing. "I'll need to pour just a bit more hot water from the kettle, and then you get right in," she instructed.

Elizabeth nodded and waited as her serving woman made certain the bath temperature was just right. Then, stepping into the oak tub, she sank down into the water. "Ahhh," she said, and a smile lit up her features.

"You have little time to dally," Nancy told her. "It will soon be time for the meal, but I somehow thought you would like your bath now instead of later."

"Aye, entering numbers, line after line of them, is tiring. I should rather be out riding across my fields. When Edmund is well enough . . ." She stopped in midsentence, sighing. "I must stop thinking nothing has changed, Nancy. Edmund is an old man. When he is well he and Maybel must retire to their cottage. He has stewarded Friarsgate for over fifty years now." She soaped her fingers and rubbed them with her cloth.

Nancy nodded and, taking up a brush, scrubbed Elizabeth's long back. "Aye, he's an old man now, and I know he's been having dizzy spells for the last year, but he would not tell Maybel or you, mistress. He feared you could not do without him, as you had no husband to take over for him."

"I have been so selfish," Elizabeth said. "I have thought only of what I wanted, and not of the good of those who serve me and in doing so serve Friarsgate. I have been a poor chatelaine, Nancy, but I did not realize it. This is going to change. It has to!"

"You've always done right by us," Nancy soothed. "None here would call you a bad mistress. There!" she said, handing a washing cloth to Elizabeth. "Do the private bits, and you're finished. The sun is low on the horizon, and soon those in the hall will be ready for their food, and you must be there to say the blessing."

Elizabeth did as she had been bidden. Then, arising, she stepped from the tub and began to dry herself off. As Nancy bustled about the chamber gathering fresh garments, the lady of Friarsgate glanced at herself critically. Would Baen MacColl find her body attractive? Would it be as tempting to him as any woman's was? She hoped so.

Nancy handed Elizabeth a clean chemise. She put it on. Two petticoats followed, then a black linen skirt and white blouse. She fitted a wide leather belt about her narrow waist. Sitting, she let Nancy brush out her long hair and rebraid it. Then she slipped her bare feet into a pair of black leather slippers and hurried from her chamber. She stopped first to see how Edmund was doing. He had been returned to his chamber and was now sleeping.

Maybel arose and hurried forward when Elizabeth entered. "He is weary, I fear, but a bit better. He can move his left hand again. Only the right remains useless."

"When he is well enough," Elizabeth said, "you are going home to your own cottage, Maybel. Edmund has served Friarsgate well and long. It is time for him to rest, and you too. I know my mother would agree with me. I sent a messenger to her this morning telling her of Edmund's illness, but I also told her it was not necessary for her to return. You and I will care for Edmund."

Maybel nodded slowly. "Who will manage the house for you?" she asked.

"You will pick your successor, but I do favor Albert," Elizabeth replied.

Maybel nodded again. "The cottage will need cleaning," she said as if to herself.

"Then we will send someone to clean it," Elizabeth told her with a smile. "Come now, and let us go down to the meal. We will send a serving wench up to watch over Edmund while you are gone." Elizabeth slipped her arm through Maybel's.

The hall was full with Friarsgate folk, the men-at-arms who guarded the manor, servants, and a peddler who had asked shelter for the night. Elizabeth took her place of authority at the high board. "Give the blessing tonight, Father Mata," she said.

"The eyes of all wait upon thee, o Lord," the priest began.

"And thou givest them their meat in due season," came the hall's reply.

The priest continued, ending the blessing with, "Glory be to the Father, and to the Son, and to the Holy Spirit."

"As it was in the beginning, it is now and ever shall be, world without end, *Amen!*" came the chorus from those in the hall. Then came the scraping of the benches as they all sat.

Baen found himself seated on Elizabeth's direct right, in the place that had been Edmund's. He was just vaguely uncomfortable, but no one seemed to object.

"What did you learn watching the shearing today?" Elizabeth asked him.

"That sheep are quick, and they can be very ornery when parting them from their fleece," he answered with a grin. "But you were right. The fleeces are wonderful."

She nodded, helping herself to the fish and tearing a piece off of the warm cottage loaf. "I don't know whose idea it was to shear just after midsummer, but we've always done it that way here at Friarsgate." She began to eat, and he did too.

Wine was poured into their goblets. A fat capon stuffed with bread, onions, and sage was served to them. Elizabeth tore the bird in half and placed half on his wooden plate, along with several slices of ham. He said nothing, but he was surprised, for she was treating him like an equal. But glancing surreptitiously about him he could see no one was surprised by her actions. Mumbling his thanks, he began to eat. She added several spoonfuls of new peas, and more bread. He ate and he drank, and, looking about the hall, he imagined for the briefest moment what it would be like to be master of all this. It would be wonderful, he thought, to be the lord of Friarsgate with Elizabeth, the lady—his lady—by his side. Then he pulled himself back to reality, banishing the warm glow that had temporarily bathed him. "You must not serve me," he said to Elizabeth as she put several chunks of cheddar cheese on his plate.

"Why not?" she asked him.

"I am not worthy of this place, or of you," he told her.

"Is not that my decision to make, Baen? After all, I am the lady of

Friarsgate," Elizabeth told him. "You must put aside this unassuming and quite frankly irritating humility with me. It does not suit you, and I will wager your father would agree with me. I have told you that I mean to have you for my mate."

"Your speech is too bold," he said low.

"Because you will not say what is in your heart I must be bold," she replied.

"How do you know what is in my heart?" he asked her. "I have not spoken out of turn to you, lady."

"Your stormy gray eyes tell me what I need to know, Baen," Elizabeth told him softly. "When I was at court I learned to read the expression in eyes even as lips said something entirely different. I might have fallen in love with Flynn Stewart, King James's half brother, but for what I saw in his eyes. Now I see in your eyes that you want me, that you love me, but you will not speak. So I must. I want you for my husband."

"I cannot!" he groaned low. "You know I cannot! My first loyalty must be to my sire. You have been surrounded by love your entire life, Elizabeth. You do not know what it was like for me in the house of my mother's husband. He hated me even before my birth. Had my mother not protected me from that same hour he would surely have left me out on a hillside to die. And had I been devoured by wolves I believe it would have pleased my mother's husband quite well. But as she lay dying she told me of my father, and how I came to be conceived. And in the hours after her burial I forever left the cottage where she had lived in such misery, and went to Colin Hay. It is true I am his image but for my mother's eyes. There was no doubt I was his son. He might have refused to acknowledge me, and I would have understood. He might have, out of a sense of guilt, given me a place in his stables, and I would have been grateful. But he embraced me and took me into his house. My stepmother chided him for a randy lad, and laughed. She tipped my face up, looked into it, shook her head, and said that she had always wanted many laddies, and I was surely the easiest come into her world. I owe the Hays of Grayhaven my loyalty, Elizabeth, and I give it to them gladly. Jamie will one day inherit. But Gilly and I have only what our father gives us. The sheep are for me, and I must make them profitable for him. There can be no love for me. No wife."

"Eat your supper," she advised him quietly. "You have distressed yourself, Baen. In each match made there is one stronger than the other. I see I am to be the stronger, as my sister Banon is in her marriage." She smiled sweetly at him.

"You will break my heart if I let myself love you," he told her.

"Nay, you will break mine if you leave me for your family," Elizabeth said. "Nonetheless I must love you. There has been none before you, nor will there be any man after you, Baen MacColl. It is our fate to love each other."

He turned away and began to eat again. But his food had grown cold and his appetite had disappeared. She was offering him paradise, and he could not take it. If he were wise he would leave Friarsgate tomorrow, but he could not. His father had sent him to learn, and he still had much to learn from Friarsgate about their weaving industry, and how they sold their cloth to their best advantage. He did not believe that Grayhaven was big enough or had enough sheep or grazing land to do what the Friarsgate folk did. But possibly he could adapt what was done here to fit a smaller holding. And perhaps they might even ship their wool through Friarsgate. He had to remain. He could not disappoint the father who had given him this opportunity.

"You have not finished your supper," Elizabeth said.

"I am no longer hungry," he replied.

"You are too big a man to miss a meal," she responded. Then she buttered a piece of cottage bread, put a piece of cheese on it, and handed it to him. "Eat it," Elizabeth commanded him, "or I will feed you myself." She poured more wine into his goblet.

Her caring touched him. "You will make a good mother one day," he told her.

"I know," Elizabeth Meredith said. "And we are going to have the most beautiful bairns, Baen MacColl." Then she smiled brilliantly at him.

"How can I love you, and then leave you?" he asked her low.

"You will do what you must," she told him quietly. "I do not think you should have to choose between your father and me, but if it should come to that, then whatever you decide I will accept, for I will have no choice." But she didn't believe her words.

"Nay, you will not," he responded seriously. He was going to love her despite the futility of it. He knew it. And she was encouraging him onward to their eventual doom. He knew that too. But the attraction between them was too strong now for either of them to deny it. "How can I not love you, Elizabeth?" he asked her.

# Chapter 11

✦

*I*t was madness. They both knew it. What had encouraged her to speak so openly to him this evening? But she knew. Baen MacColl was a man of honor. He would love her to his death, but he would have never said a word to her, so she had no choice but to speak her own heart. She wondered about his father, this man known as the master of Grayhaven. Did he really demand such fealty from his bastard son? Or was Baen's sense of duty to his sire overstrong? She had to learn the truth. Of course, she had already made up her mind about their situation. And she had a plan.

Thomas Bolton had teased her about seducing the Scot, but that was exactly what Elizabeth had in mind. She would entice him into her web. They would become lovers, and then he would never leave her. She felt not the slightest modicum of guilt over her design. The master of Grayhaven did not really need Baen MacColl. But Elizabeth Meredith did. And when the die had been cast, she would cajole him into a handfast union, which was good for a year and a day but no more. But at the end of that year, or even sooner, she would have convinced him that she, and not his father, was the fate for which he was destined. They would then wed under the auspices of the church. Elizabeth smiled to herself, well pleased. Her scheme was flawless.

They remained in the hall that evening. She played a game of chess with Will, and then declared herself fatigued. "I must see to Maybel and Edmund before I sleep."

Baen watched her leave the hall. His head was filled with confusing thoughts. She was not nobility, but she was the heiress to much land. His father was minor nobility, but his mother had been nothing more than a cotter's daughter. Her father had been a knight. Yet her mother was a country woman, even as Elizabeth was. Perhaps in blood they were evenly matched. Perhaps? Her mother seemed to like him. Lord Cambridge had not opposed the friendship Elizabeth Meredith had for Baen MacColl. Indeed, all at Friarsgate appeared welcoming of him. Did he dare to hope he might gain her as a wife? Become of man of means?

But what would Colin Hay say to such a match? Would he even consider allowing his eldest son to marry Elizabeth Meredith? His father was not overly fond of the English. Yet Baen could see little difference between his family and Elizabeth's. Both were people of the land, with a love of country and a respect of Holy Mother Church. But if this miracle were to happen he should have to relinquish his loyalties to his homeland, to his family. He would no longer be a Scot. But could he be English? It was a difficult conundrum, and he was probably better off the way he was. Baen MacColl, the master of Grayhaven's bastard. Brother to Jamie and Gilly.

Friar came and pushed a wet nose into his hand, whining. Baen looked down at the animal and smiled. Friar wagged all over in his enthusiasm to communicate. "I know. I know," Baen told the dog. "You want to have a run before we bed down for the night, eh, boy?" He stood up. "Don't let Elizabeth bar the door on me," he said to William Smythe. "I'm just taking the dog out, but I will be back."

"Aye," Will answered him, nodding.

When the Scot had disappeared from the hall, Thomas Bolton, who had appeared to be napping in his chair, said, "She has begun her campaign to woo him." He did not open his eyes. "I believe he loves her."

"But his loyalties would be divided if they wed," Will replied.

"She will require only fealty to Friarsgate, and to herself," came the response.

"But what if England and Scotland go to war again? You know there is always that possibility," Will said. "Not so long ago King James was killed, and his infant put on the throne. It is bound to happen again."

"Aye," Lord Cambridge agreed, and now he opened his eyes. "But wars between England and Scotland rarely reach our small corner of England. They go south from the east side of Scotland, or north from the east side of England. We are far to the west."

William Smythe smiled. "You are determined to have her marry this Scot, aren't you, my lord?"

"Would you not agree they are a perfect match, dear boy?" was his answer. "He would never have done for Philippa or for Banon, but for Elizabeth? Aye! How odd," Thomas Bolton considered, "that my darling Rosamund's girls should all be so different. Philippa was enamored of the court from the moment she arrived there. She is a noblewoman to her delicate fingertips. And my adorable Banon is a shining example of country gentry with her Neville husband. But as for Elizabeth, she is a farmer, with her estates and her sheep. She needs a strong man of the land for her mate, and Baen MacColl is that man." He chuckled. "It was not so long ago, dear Will, that the Boltons of Friarsgate were nothing more than a wealthy farm family. It was my darling Rosamund who took them from the obscurity of Cumbria into the court. But of her three daughters only Elizabeth wanted Friarsgate and its responsibilities. And Elizabeth is a plainspoken country woman. Friarsgate is in good hands with her, but we all know she must have a husband, and children to carry on after she is gone one day. If Baen MacColl is her choice, then by God, dear boy, she shall have him no matter what we must do to make it happen! Now pour me some wine. I am exhausted with this difficult line of thought." He sat back in his chair, a languid hand reaching out for the goblet that William Smythe poured. He sipped at it. "Ahh, yes! That is much better," Lord Cambridge declared.

"How will you manage this marriage?" Will wanted to know.

"I? Dear boy, I will have nothing at all to do with it except to sit back and let Elizabeth manage the entire thing, for that is what she will do, you may be certain. Rosamund approves of the Scot. I certainly favor him. Their blood is almost equal, I have reconsidered. Her father was a knight. His is lesser nobility. It is enough."

"But what of the master of Grayhaven?" Will persisted.

"The man would be a fool not to allow his bastard, particularly a beloved bastard, to wed with a landed heiress, even if she is English. It will all work itself out, dear boy, and I am eager to let it. I want to be home at Otterly by autumn. You must go back and see that my wing is completed on time with no more interference from Banon. I will have my privacy. Think on it, Will! Peace and quiet at long last. We shall spend the winter as snug as two mice in a full granary. When we were in London I found a cache of books and manuscripts for sale. They belonged to some elderly noble whose heir was obviously an uneducated barbarian. I purchased them and had them shipped to Otterly. We shall spend our days cataloging my find. It is a veritable treasure, dear Will!"

"You do not believe your further aid is needed then?" Will said.

"Nay. Elizabeth has the whole situation well in hand. In a few weeks we shall travel home, and all will be well."

Baen MacColl reentered the hall, Friar bounding ahead of him.

"Dear, dear boy, you have enjoyed your romp with your dog?"

"Aye," Baen told him. "The evening is fair, sir. The air here has a softness to it that I do not find in my Highlands."

"It comes from the sea," Lord Cambridge murmured. " 'Tis why my nieces have such fine skin. Elizabeth in particular. Otterly is farther from the sea, and Philippa's home at Brierewode not near the sea at all. Do you not find Elizabeth lovely, dear boy? She is the fairest of Rosamund's daughters."

"Aye," Baen said. "She is lovely." He flushed with the words.

Seeing it, Thomas Bolton knew he had made his point. He arose, setting his goblet aside. "I must find my bed, for I am fairly exhausted, dear boy. Elizabeth has not come down, and may not. Would you see the house is safe for the night?"

"Aye, my lord, gladly," Baen answered, bowing slightly.

"Good night then, dear boy," Lord Cambridge said, and linked his arm through Will Smythe's as the two men left the hall.

Friar had settled down by the fire, his eyes closed. Baen went to the front door of the house and set the bar across it. He walked through the main floor of the dwelling, making certain that all the fires were banked and the candles snuffed out. Satisfied that all was well, he sat down for a moment before the warm hearth. It felt so natural to do the tasks that would belong to the master of the house. But of course he was not the master here. And he couldn't be. He owed an allegiance to his father first. With a sigh he arose and went upstairs to his bedchamber.

Opening the door, he saw the fire burning in the small hearth, casting black shadows on the walls. He did not bother to light his taper, for he could see well enough to disrobe. Stripping to his natural state he washed himself in the basin left for that purpose. Then, turning, he walked across the room to his bed. The coverlet suddenly flipped back.

"Get in," he heard Elizabeth's voice command, and then she raised herself from the mattress. "You will catch a chill, Baen," she said in a gentler voice.

He stood there, shocked, more mindful of his nakedness than he had ever been in his entire life. He grabbed at the coverlet to shield himself.

Elizabeth giggled. "I have already seen everything you have to offer, Baen, and it is most impressive, I must say." Then, tossing the coverlet off, she displayed herself completely to him.

"You're naked," he croaked. He could not take his eyes from her. She was slender where a man would want a woman slender, and sweetly rounded where he would want her rounded. Her skin was pale, like rich cream, and her blond hair spilled over her shoulders like a waterfall. Her hazel-green eyes met his gray ones directly.

"Get into bed, Baen," she repeated.

He backed away from her. "Are you mad, lass?" he wanted to know.

"Did you not believe me when I said I wanted you for my mate?" Elizabeth asked him quietly. Actually her heart was hammering, and she did not feel nearly as bold as she was portraying herself to be. He was a very big man. Big all over. Still, she knew from her sisters what was involved in a man's coupling with a woman. She had just never realized that a manroot could be that large.

"If I get into that bed, Elizabeth," he said in dark tones, "there will be no going back for either of us. You cannot cry rapine in the morning."

"Why would I?" she questioned him. "You are my mate."

"If you are a virgin I will ruin you for any husband," he said.

"I am a virgin, and I want none other but you," she told him.

"I cannot remain with you once my business here is complete. I must return to Grayhaven, lass," he attempted to reason with her. "My sire has my loyalty, as he must."

Elizabeth held out her hand to him. "Come," she said softly.

"If I do . . ." he began.

"You will take my virginity, and then that barrier between us will be over and done with, Baen, my hinny love," Elizabeth answered him.

He swallowed hard. Then, gathering up strength from the depths of his soul, he turned his back on her and walked away from the bed. "Nay, lass, I will not dishonor you," he told her.

Elizabeth jumped from the bed, her feet making a thumping noise as she did. She threw herself at him as he turned, startled. Her slender body, her small, soft breasts, pressed against his hard body. Her hands reached up to take his face between them. "Do not dare run from me, Baen MacColl!" she cried. "It is not worthy of you!"

His control broke. His arms wrapped about her. His dark head lowered, and he kissed her with a violence that sent a thrill through her from the top of her head to the soles of her feet. "You are a bold witch, Elizabeth Meredith, and whatever happens now between us is on your own head, damn it! Do you understand that?" A single hand caressed her face, cupping it.

Her heart was going to burst through her chest. She was melting with the heat the conjunction of their two bodies produced. "Yes!" she whispered fiercely. "Yes!"

"Then so be it!" he groaned, and, picking her up, carried her back across the room to the bed, where he laid her gently before joining her. "I have wanted you almost from the first moment I saw you," he admitted.

"I know," Elizabeth told him. "You were not very good at concealing your feelings, Baen MacColl. It was very flattering, and when I was sent off to court I had a new confidence because of it." She pulled his dark head down to hers and gave him a slow, sweet kiss.

"I didn't teach you to kiss like that," he said, jealousy rising at her expertise.

"Nay, you didn't," Elizabeth said, smiling up at him. "You were my first kiss. I have kissed others since, but I shall never kiss another again," she promised him.

"You will have a husband one day," he said.

"Do you think me so without honor, Baen, that after giving my virginity to you I should take another man?" Elizabeth responded. "You are my man. There will be no other." Her hand tangled in his dark hair, and she caressed the nape of his neck with delicate fingertips. "You will have to tell me what to do," she murmured in his ear.

He shuddered and closed his eyes briefly. This had to be lunacy, he considered tersely. But then Elizabeth was placing little kisses across his face. Baen shook his head in a gesture of surrender. There was no denying his arousal. He was mortal, not some saint. She was soft. She was perfumed. And she was oh, so willing to be loved. And he did love her. He opened his eyes and looked down into her lovely face. "Has anyone told you it may hurt the first time?" he asked her softly. His big hand smoothed the soft blond hair from her forehead.

She nodded, and he could see the small fear in the back of her eyes.

"You must let me take my time and prepare you, sweetheart," he said.

Elizabeth nodded solemnly. "I trust you, Baen," she told him.

He smiled gently. "Touch me," he told her. "Let your pretty hands explore me. You will find it difficult to fear that which you know, Elizabeth. A man likes to be touched every bit as much as a woman," he explained to her. Then he lay on his back.

She propped herself on her side and looked closely at him. Her first impression of bigness was confirmed. Was his manroot larger in this light? Shyly she ran a hand over his chest. His skin was smooth and warm. The hand slipped to his taut belly, but then drew quickly back. She had never before seen a grown man fully naked. He said nothing. Lowering her head she began to kiss and lick the nipples on his chest, as she had once before. He sighed pleasurably. Emboldened, she now climbed upon him, her bottom resting on his belly. Her two hands smoothed over his broad chest. She feathered little kisses across the hard flesh.

Reaching up he took her two small breasts in his hands and began to play with them. He fondled the twin globes gently. Leaning forward, he licked at them. He teased the nipples until they stood hard with her budding passion. When she bent forward to kiss him on the mouth, Baen wrapped Elizabeth in an embrace and rolled her onto her back again. She gasped, and he soothed her with little murmurs and kisses. She quieted, but then tensed as he caressed her as she had him. Boldly his hand moved to tangle itself in the nest of golden curls between her milky thighs. "Easy, lass," he whispered to her. His finger slid along the pouting slit of flesh, and Elizabeth trembled.

"I have never been touched there before," she confided.

Her words were a most potent aphrodisiac, for he believed her. He was the first! He pressed the first joint of one finger between her nether lips. She was moist there, but not yet ready. He sought for and found the tiny nub of flesh that he knew if stimulated properly would excite and pleasure her. He touched it, and she trembled as if sensing the mystery about to be revealed. He rubbed that tiny bit of flesh with his fingertip.

Elizabeth stirred restlessly beneath his hand. What was he doing? Why was he doing it? But instinct suggested she not forbid him, and instinct prevailed. She felt the tiniest of tingles in that secret region of her body, and as he continued to stroke that sensitive bit of flesh she sensed a burgeoning of not just her flesh, but something else to which she could not give a name. And then suddenly it was wonderful! She gasped. "Oh!" she was surprised to hear herself cry out. "Oh! Oh!" Their glances met, and she could see the delight in those gray eyes that his actions were offering her pleasure.

"You like it?" he asked eagerly.

"Yes!" she managed to gasp. "Oh!" His finger had penetrated her to the knuckle. "Baen! What are you doing?"

"Making certain you are ready," he groaned. Then his mouth found hers. He was burning up with his impatience to have her. To fill her full with his manroot and hear her cry of surrender as their two bodies became one entity. And Elizabeth was very ready, he realized. Her juices were flowing copiously, soaking his big hand. He withdrew his finger from her, sucking it, tasting her, and he thought his lust would explode then and there.

Her breath was coming in short, sharp pants. She was somewhat shocked to see him sucking on the finger that had so recently been within her. "Baen?" She felt fear beginning to well up within her.

"I can't stop now, Elizabeth," he half sobbed. "I can't!"

She swallowed hard. "I know," she acknowledged. "Just do it! Please!"

"Ah, God, sweetheart, don't be afraid," he pleaded with her. "I will love you as sweetly as I can." His big hands spread her wide, and he slid between her legs. She was so delicate, he suddenly realized.

She felt the head of his manroot penetrating her, and stiffened. She had not dared to look, but it felt as if she were being pierced by an iron rod. She struggled to maintain her composure, for she had initiated this encounter. But God's blood! He was so big!

"If you fight me, even without meaning to, it will hurt more than I want it to," he said, and he shuddered. Then he pushed firmly against her resistance.

Elizabeth drew a deep breath. She wanted this. She wanted him! And, reassuring herself, she did what Banon had told her would give her man pleasure. She wrapped her slender legs about his hard torso, gasping, "Hurry!"

He needed no further encouragement. Drawing himself back just slightly, he plunged deep into her fair body, feeling her virginity tear and give way before his passionate onslaught. Elizabeth's cry of sudden pain was like a knife to his heart. He stopped a moment to let her body grow used to this invasion. Then he began a slow and carefully measured rhythm, moving himself back and forth within the tight, hot passage that had welcomed him.

Beneath his sweating male body Elizabeth Meredith was filled with a surprising sense of power. She held him in her arms as he labored over her, almost weeping as her fears subsided and her own desires began to overwhelm her. "Oh, Baen!" she cried. "Oh, my love! My darling!"

He couldn't get enough of her! And the sweet words of her building passion but roused his lust for her more. "Elizabeth! My angel! My own!" he sobbed, kissing her wet cheeks tenderly.

"Don't stop!" she innocently begged him.

"I don't think I can," he groaned low. "I have never had such a need!"

"You see!" And he heard the triumph in her voice. "I told you we were meant to be mated, Baen MacColl! Oh! Oh!" She was growing dizzy with the pleasure now beginning to race through her body.

The knowledge that his own passions were stoking hers filled him with an incredible sense of power. He had wanted her. Now he needed her. She was necessary to life itself. She shuddered beneath him, and, unable to sustain himself further, he loosed his love juices into her fevered young body, growling into her ear as he did so, "Now, you border witch, are you satisfied?" And to his surprise she answered him.

"Not yet, hinny love! This is but our beginning."

He fell away from her, laughing, a sound that was part amusement and part relief. "Elizabeth! Elizabeth! What am I to do with you?" he asked her.

"Love me more!" she told him, flinging herself atop him so that their bodies met.

"You are newly breached, sweetheart," he said. "And I need some sleep."

"Do you not want to make love to me again?" she asked him.

"I will need some sleep in order to recover my strength," he explained.

"I have seen the stallion mount several mares in succession out in the fields," she told him, sounding puzzled.

"As much as I would like to be the stallion, I am but a man," he told her. "And you should not be found in my bed on the morrow, sweetheart."

"Aye," she agreed. "What is between us should remain between us only for now." She slipped from the bed and donned her chemise, which he had not seen before. Then, going to the door, she turned and smiled a sweet smile at him. "Good night, Baen," she said, and was gone.

He lay back in his bed, considering the last hour and what he had shared with Elizabeth Meredith. She had boldly seduced him. He almost laughed aloud again. And he had allowed himself to be seduced, even though he knew better. But there was no going back. He could not change what had happened, and the truth was, he didn't want to change it. He loved the brazen baggage. He loved the lady of Friarsgate. Then his thoughts grew sober. It could not happen again. He owed his father his loyalty, and it was a loyalty he could not share with Elizabeth Meredith.

But Elizabeth would not be deterred. She entrapped him in a barn the following day, and before he knew it he was fucking her lustily in a stall full of sweet-smelling hay. She shamelessly pulled him beneath a hedgerow in a sheep meadow one afternoon, and they coupled despite his laughing protests. She teased him wickedly with little touches and kisses when no one else was looking. She came to his chamber each night, and he could not refuse her. He felt complete now only when he was with her. When he was filling her with his passion. When she lay beneath him crying out with her own need. It was madness, yet neither of them could cease indulging in their desperate hunger for each other. Elizabeth was certain her plan was succeeding. Soon he would be hers forever!

"I will surely get you with child," he warned her one night as they lay, limbs entwined, in his bed. "I don't want you shamed by a bastard, as my mother was shamed. I don't want the child ridiculed by the circumstances of his birth. I will have to leave you soon, sweetheart. We do not speak of it now, but you know it."

"Handfast with me," Elizabeth said casually. "That way if you return to your father's house, any child that comes of our love will be legitimate. A handfast is good for only a year and a day, Baen. If I do not have a child in that time then there is no harm done to anyone. Soon it will be Michaelmas, and many handfast secretly then. If you would leave me, then a handfast between us will protect me."

"You know I must go," he told her unhappily. "I have never made a secret of it."

"You could come back," Elizabeth said. "I do not believe your father needs you more than I do, Baen. He has two legitimate sons. If you were not so stubborn you would see that. We are equals in so many ways, my darling. Are you telling me that the master of Grayhaven is such a tyrant that he would forbid you marriage to an heiress with good lands? That he doesn't want you to be happy?"

"I warned you!" he growled at her. She was confusing him.

She pulled his head to hers and kissed him passionately. "Aye," she agreed. "You warned me, but I did not believe that once we became lovers, you could so casually cast me aside. I am not some cotter's daughter or tavern wench!" Her hand reached down to fondle him, and he grew instantly hard within her warm, taunting fingers. Then Elizabeth boldly mounted him, feeling his length slip into her love passage, filling it with his bulk and his heat. "Can you so easily desert me, my love?" she demanded of him, riding him, seeing the lust rising in his stormy gray eyes.

His hands reached up to crush her two breasts. "We will handfast, you hot-blooded border bitch, because I love you, and to protect any fruit of our passion. But my first loyalty will always be to he who sired me and acknowledged me as his own." He rolled her over and began pumping her fiercely.

Elizabeth cried out, half with anger, half with pleasure. "You bastard!" she hissed at him, and he laughed.

"There has never been any doubt of that, sweetheart," he told her.

The air crackled with their determination and energy as they made passionate love. Their need for each other had but grown over the weeks since Elizabeth had first come to Baen's bed. They both admitted to being in love, but it made no difference. Their loyalties were divided, and neither would give way to the other.

"I hate you!" she cried in the throes of her desire for him.

"Liar!" he mocked her, kissing her hungrily until her mouth was bruised.

Elizabeth struggled to restrain her tears. Then she realized he had not gone yet. There was still time, and she would handfast with him to bind him even closer. She let the passion they shared sweep over her like a great wave of water, and cried out with her satisfaction at the same moment he cried out with his.

What had begun in secret between them was now an open affair. There was no one at Friarsgate who did not know the lady was in love—and in bed—with the Scot. Maybel fretted to Lord Cambridge, who was preparing to return home to Otterly.

"She has wantonly thrown away her virtue, Tom. Who will have her now?"

"She wants none but him, my dear," Thomas Bolton said gently.

"A Scot? What will Rosamund say?" the old woman worried.

"She encouraged Elizabeth to it, so relieved was she that her daughter had finally found a man she could love, and share Friarsgate with, Maybel."

"Even now he plans to return to Scotland," Maybel said. "I have heard him say it. Now that Edmund can take up some of his duties again he will go."

"Aye, he will go," Elizabeth said coming upon them, "but you and Edmund will go to your cottage to live, for my great-uncle can no longer bear the burden of this estate. I am not such a fool that I do not know that. If Baen leaves me, I will manage my lands without help. Have I not trained all my life for this role?"

"And who will take care of you?" Maybel wanted to know. "You are strong even for a woman, my child, but you are not invincible."

"Nancy takes care of me, thanks to you," Elizabeth said, hugging the older woman warmly. "And Jane has directed the housemaids while you nursed our Edmund. You trained her yourself, Maybel, and she is quite competent, you must agree." She turned to Lord Cambridge. "When will you leave, Uncle?"

"Two days after Michaelmas," he said. "Will writes that my wing is now ready for habitation, and my books have arrived from London. But I do love Michaelmas here at Friarsgate, dear girl. So I will not go until October first."

"I am sorry you must go at all," Elizabeth told him, "for I do enjoy your companionship, Uncle. Soon I shall be alone with only myself for company," she said seriously. "But I shall be so busy I shall probably not notice my lack at all. Is Edmund awake, Maybel?"

"Aye, and anxious to see you," Maybel replied.

"I'll go to him now, and tell him of my plans," Elizabeth said, and departed her hall.

"What is to become of her?" Maybel said, shaking her grizzled head. "The land consumes her. She loves the Scot, but she will let him go from her. And what is the matter with him that he would leave her when he loves her too? His sire must be a monster to demand such loyalty of the lad."

"I think," Lord Cambridge told Maybel, "that both Elizabeth and Baen are confused. She cleaves to Friarsgate as if it were the most important thing in her life, and he clings to his sire for the same reason, when the truth is they should be pledging their loyalty to each other. I do not think the master of Grayhaven would forbid his son a rich wife. Even a rich English wife. But I suspect Baen, in his misguided loyalty for his father, will say naught of Elizabeth to the fellow. Still, I do believe that love can surmount much that is foolish in this old world, dear Maybel. Let them be parted for the long, cold winter months. If the spring comes and neither has overcome their stubbornness, then we must do something ourselves to bring about this happy union for everyone's sake, but most especially for Elizabeth and Baen."

"Why is it that you always make problems that are difficult seem so simple to correct, Thomas Bolton?" she asked him wryly.

"It is a gift, dear Maybel," he told her with a grin. "It is my fate to bring happiness to all who surround me, all whom I love." And Thomas Bolton chuckled.

"You mock yourself, Tom Bolton, but you speak the truth," Maybel told him. "Never have I known a kinder and more generous man than you are. What a shame that the Boltons should die with you."

"That too is fate," Lord Cambridge said quietly.

Michaelmas, celebrated on the twenty-ninth of the month, was a perfect late-September day, with bright sunshine and clear blue skies. A pole was set up before the house, and atop it Elizabeth had set one of the beautiful kid gloves with its pearl embroidery that she had worn at court. Around the pole visiting merchants would set up their booths to ply their wares. In order to participate they had to swear before Father Mata that they would give a portion of their profits to the church. Elizabeth paid her servants for their year's labor, warning them not to lose their wages in careless gambling or purchasing shoddy products from the fair's booths.

In midafternoon, as the fair was at its height, she found her lover and led him away from the festivities to stand beside the lake. "It is time," she told him quietly, taking his hands in hers and facing him, "for us to handfast ourselves to each other, my darling Scot. In God's presence beneath the blue sky I gladly take thee, Baen MacColl, as my husband for a year and a day. May Jesu and his dear Mother Mary bless us."

"And in God's presence beneath this canopy of blue sky I gladly take thee, Elizabeth Meredith, for my wife for the term of a year and a day," he replied. "May Jesu and his sweet Mother Mary bless us."

"There, now that was not so difficult, was it?" she teased him.

"Nay," he agreed, "it was not."

"And we will tell no one of our handfast," she said. "Will you swear it?" Now when he remained with her they would all know it was because he loved her better than his father, and not because she entrapped him into a handfast union, Elizabeth thought.

"Aye," he said. "I swear it." He was already ashamed, knowing that soon he would depart Friarsgate for Grayhaven, and it was unlikely he would ever see her again. And in a year and a day she would be free to wed a man who was worthy of her. His heart was breaking with this knowledge, but he had warned her, hadn't he?

William Smythe had returned to Friarsgate the day before Michaelmas to escort his master back to Otterly. Now, on the morning of October first, the two men and their escort prepared to take their leave of Elizabeth.

"It has been a very interesting year, dear girl," Thomas Bolton declared. "I am most devastated to have failed you in your search for a husband."

"I am not an easy girl, Uncle. Do not all say it of me? I have already chosen my own mate, and despite your most delicate discretion you are well aware of it," Elizabeth said with a smile. She patted his velvet-clad arm.

"He will return to you," Lord Cambridge said encouragingly.

"If he leaves me, Uncle, he need not return," Elizabeth replied quietly.

"Do not be foolish, niece," Lord Cambridge warned her. "He must work out his loyalties in his own time, and if you do not force the issue he will. And he will return, for even a fool can see he loves you." Thomas Bolton kissed her on both cheeks. "Now bid my good Will farewell, dear girl."

"I will miss you, William Smythe," Elizabeth said. "Go with God, and take care of my uncle as you have done so well these past nine years." She kissed his cheek.

Lord Cambridge's secretary and companion bowed low. "Listen to him, Mistress Elizabeth. We but seek your happiness."

"Come along, Will!" Lord Cambridge, now mounted, called. "I am eager to return home! Good-bye, dear girl!"

Elizabeth watched the two men as they rode off from the house surrounded by their men-at-arms. She loved Thomas Bolton and would miss his amusing presence in the hall. And Edmund and Maybel had departed yesterday for their own cottage. Still weak and not fully recovered, Edmund had ridden in a cart with his wife. Maybel had wept, of course, as if she would never see Elizabeth or the house again.

"You but go down the path a piece," Elizabeth said, laughing.

"I know! I know!" Maybel sobbed, "but I have spent most of my life in this house looking after the lady of Friarsgate. And Edmund has stewarded the estate since he was barely out of boyhood."

"So it is time then for you to go home, and look after each other, and enjoy the days remaining to you," Elizabeth said. But she knew her house would be very lonely without Maybel and Edmund. She had written her mother, and Rosamund had fully approved Elizabeth's decision, not that she had needed Rosamund's permission. She was the lady of Friarsgate, and had been for eight years.

Two days ago it had not been so, but today there was a distinct nip in the air. It was autumn. October. And before they knew it winter would be upon them. And she would spend the long nights wrapped in her handfast husband's arms making sweet love. She sought Baen now, having last seen him in the hall bidding her uncle good-bye. Returning to the hall she asked Albert, "Where is Master Baen?"

"Gone to the stables, lady," was the answer.

Elizabeth turned and hurried from the hall to the stables. He was saddling his horse. "Good!" she said. "We must check the outlying meadows today and be certain their shelters are ready for winter, stocked, and secure. But I think we should keep the flocks closer this year. It is just an instinct."

"I am leaving, Elizabeth," he said quietly. He tightened the girth about his horse.

"When?" Surely she had not heard him aright. He was not going to leave her.

"Now. Today. It is better I go before the weather sets in. Already they will have seen snow on the heights of the bens in the Highlands," he told her. He fastened the tabs of his saddlebags. "With your uncle gone it is a good time for me to leave as well."

She would not beg, Elizabeth thought, her heart hardening. "Why not remain until St. Crispin's?" she asked him. "We would give you a fine sendoff then."

He shook his head, but then, stepping forward, he put his arms tightly about her. "I do not want to go," he said, "but you know that I must."

Her heart cracked, and then she did what she had sworn to herself she would not do if the horrible day ever came: Elizabeth Meredith began to cry. "No! You do not have to go, Baen. You do not! You are my husband. How can your loyalty to your father be greater than your loyalty to me? I am your wife!"

"We handfasted to give any child we made a name," he said.

"Do you truly believe that was the only reason, Baen?" she cried. "You love me!"

"Aye, I do love you, and nay, 'twas not the only reason I handfasted with you, my hinny love. I did it because more than anything in the world, I wanted you for my wife."

"You would put your loyalty to a man who didn't even know you existed for the first twelve years of your life above me?" she sobbed bitterly.

"A man who for the last twenty years has sheltered me, and treated me as if I had been born on the proper side of the blanket and not the wrong," he reminded her. "Aye! My father is my first loyalty, and I have made no secret of it, Elizabeth. You have known from the first that once I had learned those things I needed to know to set up a cottage industry at Grayhaven that I would go. I never deceived you. If I deceived anyone it was myself. In loving you, in handfasting with you, Elizabeth, I dreamed briefly what it could be like to have a wife and a purpose of my own. I thank you for it."

His words were kind, yet cruel. Elizabeth struggled to regain her composure. For a moment she rested in his arms, her cheek against his doublet, the steady sound of his heart in her ear. Then, swallowing hard, she stiffened her spine and pulled away from him, looking up into his handsome face. "Do not go," she said softly. It was a plea, yet it was not a plea.

"I must," he replied. Then his hand reached out and he cupped her face. "In a few months you will have forgotten me, sweetheart. And in a year you will be free to wed a proper man," Baen said in a clumsy attempt to comfort her.

Elizabeth shook her head at him. "You are a fool, Baen MacColl, if you really think that I could forget you. And a bigger fool to believe I would wed another. Ever!"

"Elizabeth—"

"If you leave me you can never come back. Do you understand, Baen? If you go I do not ever want to see you again," Elizabeth said in a hard voice.

His hand dropped away from her face. He stepped back wordlessly and, turning, took the bridle rein of his horse. His dog crept from the shadows to join him.

"Never!" she cried as he walked through the stable doors. "Ever!" she shouted as he mounted the animal. "I hate you, Baen MacColl!" she shrieked as he began to move off.

He stopped and, turning, looked at her, his face a mask of anguish. "Yet I love you, Elizabeth Meredith," he said to her. And then, kicking his mount, he cantered from the stable yard and towards the road to the north, Friar loping along by his side.

She watched him go, the tears she had attempted to stem pouring down her face. Elizabeth began to shake, and then she crumpled to the ground on her knees, sobbing. A lone stable boy, seeing her, ran to her side.

"Mistress, be you all right?" he asked her, frightened. He had never seen the lady cry. And she was crying so bitterly. He was young, but he recognized the sound of misery when he heard it.

Still in shock at what had happened, but aware of her position, Elizabeth put a hand on the boy's shoulder and pulled herself to her feet. "I'm all right," she said in a shaking voice. "Saddle my horse, lad, for I have a long day ahead of me."

Trained to obey, the boy hurried to do his mistress's bidding, and then he watched her as she rode off towards the high meadows. All the day long Elizabeth Meredith did what she had been trained to do. She inspected each shelter in each meadow to make certain that it was stocked, or see if it needed to be stocked with winter supplies. She looked over her flocks and spoke with her shepherds, giving them instructions to move nearer to the manor house and barns in the next few days. "I sense a bad winter ahead," she said, and the shepherds took her at her word. After all, she was the lady of Friarsgate, and who would know better than she?

When she finally reached home, it was almost dark. Above her the sky was darkening to a strong deep blue. The sunset stained the western horizon with its vibrant shades of red and orange. A young crescent moon hung above it all. She dismounted, tossing her reins to the same lad who had saddled the animal for her earlier in the day. Then she hurried into her house. All was silent but for the crackling fire.

"Albert!" she called, and the serving man hurried forward.

"Yes, lady?" he inquired politely.

"You have served me well," Elizabeth told him. "I am appointing you steward of the hall. You and Jane will see to my comfort from now on. I have much else to do and cannot be bothered. Is supper ready yet?"

"Yes, lady," Albert replied, struggling to maintain his composure at this elevation in his rank. "Will Master Baen be joining you shortly?"

"The Scot left this morning to return north," Elizabeth said in a cold voice. "I am hungry. Bring me food at once!"

"Yes, lady," Albert said in a calm voice. He had known Elizabeth Meredith all her life, and he easily recognized her anger. "I shall serve you myself immediately. You have but to be seated at the board." Why had the Scot gone so precipitously? He dashed off to fetch his mistress's meal, and to relay his new knowledge. In the kitchens as he piled a tray high with a vegetable potage, some slices of ham, bread, butter, cheese, and a dish of newly stewed pears, he repeated what he knew.

"Gawd almighty!" Nancy swore softly. "They was lovers! Her heart will be broken. How could the villain leave her?" She stood up from

the table, where she had just finished her meal. "I'd best go and prepare a nice bath for her. She'll be in want of soothing. Take that tray,
Albert, and I'll bring a fresh carafe of wine."

The two servants hurried upstairs to the hall, where Elizabeth sat
in solitary splendor awaiting her supper. They placed the dishes and
plates before her, and, taking the wine from Nancy, Albert poured
their mistress a full goblet while his female counterpart scuttled off to
prepare the bath.

"Leave me!" Elizabeth said to Albert. "I'll call if I want anything."
She looked at the dishes brought. She had not eaten since early morning, yet she seemed to have little appetite. She speared a piece of ham
and laid it on her plate. She sliced herself a wedge of cheese and pulled
a chunk of bread from the cottage loaf. The ham seemed too salty. The
cheese was dry, and the bread, even generously buttered, stuck in her
throat. Only the wine tasted good. Ignoring the pears, which usually
were favorites with her, Elizabeth drank the entire carafe down. Briefly
she felt content. So Baen MacColl was gone. *Well, good riddance!* She
didn't need him. Let him run home to his father, the sainted master of
Grayhaven, like the child he was. He was a fool, and she had no tol-
erance for fools. He had walked away from her, from Friarsgate, from a
life of his own. And for what? An old father who had two other sons
perfectly capable of caring for him. *Fool!*

She wanted more wine, and she saw another carafe in the middle
of the board, but when she reached for it, it wasn't there at all, and the
two carafes become an empty one. Elizabeth giggled, tipsily lurching
to her feet. There would be wine on the sideboard in her chamber. She
stumbled, but her legs didn't seem to want to go in the right direction.
She practically fell into a chair by the fire. It was so quiet. Why was it
so damned quiet? Oh. Yes. She was alone. Lord Cambridge was gone
home, and Will with him. And Baen MacColl had left her. Elizabeth
began to weep again, and it was there that Nancy found her.

The young serving woman put a strong arm about her mistress,
prodding her up out of her chair. "Come along, Mistress Elizabeth, 'tis
past time you found your bed," she said. "I have a nice bath for you,
but I think not tonight. 'Tis straight to sleep for you, I'm thinking.
Come along now." Gently she pushed and pulled Elizabeth from the

hall and up the stairs to her chamber. Safely inside the room, she began to loosen the garments her mistress was wearing and pull off her boots.

"He's left me, Nancy," Elizabeth said mournfully.

"So you said, mistress," Nancy said.

"We were lovers." Elizabeth giggled.

"I know," Nancy responded.

"You do?" Elizabeth seemed surprised. "How do you know?"

"You ain't slept in your bed for weeks, mistress. You've been sleeping in his. 'Twould follow that two healthy young people sharing a bed were lovers," Nancy said dryly.

"Why did he leave me, Nancy?" Elizabeth was swinging back to maudlin now.

"You'd know that better than me, mistress," Nancy said. She gently pushed Elizabeth into her bed, tucking her feet beneath the coverlet and pulling it up.

"He's a fool," Elizabeth muttered.

"Yes, mistress." Nancy blew out the taper stick. "Good night," she said.

"A bloody Scots fool," Elizabeth mumbled, and then she was silent.

Listening carefully, Nancy heard her mistress's even breathing. *Poor thing,* she considered as she left the room. Robbed of her virtue by a duplicitous Scot. Unfit to be any man's wife now. What was going to happen to Friarsgate now? What was going to happen to them all?

# Chapter 12

*⁓⁕⁜⁕⁓*

lizabeth Meredith awoke with a throbbing head. In all her life she had never had such a headache. She groaned softly. Why did her head hurt so? She struggled to marshal her thoughts. Then she remembered. Her uncle was gone home to Otterly. Maybel and Edmund were retired to their cottage. And Baen MacColl had deserted her. She was alone, and last night she had finished an entire carafe of wine by herself. Her mouth tasted like a stable floor. Suddenly her stomach rebelled. There was no time to get out of her bed. Elizabeth leaned from the bed, almost screaming with the pain that knifed through her head. Grabbing at the chamber pot, she vomited the contents of her belly into it. Then, setting the chamber pot on the floor again, she lay back. Her forehead was speckled with sweat. She felt clammy all over. She was going to die, and she resolved then and there never to drink wine again. Elizabeth closed her eyes.

"Are you awake, mistress?"

How long had she dozed? Had she slept at all? "I'm suffering from too much wine, I fear," Elizabeth answered in a weak voice.

Nancy swallowed a giggle, then, seeing the chamber pot's contents, said, "I'll empty this. You'll live. No one ever died from a single carafe of wine." She picked up the vessel and hurried from the room.

Elizabeth closed her eyes again. She still had her headache, but she was actually feeling a little bit better. She didn't think she could do the book work awaiting her today, but a ride in the fresh air might help her. She considered getting up, but she wasn't really quite ready for that, she decided. The sun was streaming into her bedchamber, and it hurt her eyes. "Nancy? If you are there, close the draperies."

241

"You'll feel better if you get up," Nancy said as she drew the heavy fabric across the casements. She came over to the bed. "Let me help you, mistress." She pushed pillows behind Elizabeth's back, aiding her to sit up. "How is that?"

"My temples throb," Elizabeth complained, "but it is no worse sitting up than lying back," she admitted to her serving woman.

"You need a bit of food in your belly," Nancy said.

"The thought of food is distressing. I do not think I can eat," Elizabeth said.

"Some nice bread," Nancy coaxed. "I'll go fetch it." She bustled off, returning shortly with a single slice of warm bread, which she gave to her mistress. Then, fetching a hairbrush, she began to slowly and gently brush Elizabeth's pale hair as the girl ate the bread a morsel at a time, chewing it slowly, then swallowing. "Is that better?" Nancy queried as the bread was finished.

Elizabeth considered a moment, and then said, "Aye. It seems to have settled the roiling in my belly. Thank you." She closed her eyes again as Nancy continued to wield the brush. Then, opening them once more, Elizabeth said, "I am going riding. Get my breeks. What time is it?"

"The morning is half gone. 'Tis past ten," Nancy said. She set the brush aside. "Are you strong enough to ride out, mistress?"

"Because I am a fool," Elizabeth said, "doesn't mean I can entirely shirk my duties as the lady. We have much preparation ahead of us before the winter sets in, lass." She threw back the coverlet and swung her legs over the side of the bed. "When I return later, have my bath hot and ready for me." Then, ignoring the ache behind her eyes, Elizabeth got out of her bed.

Nancy scurried about, quickly gathering her mistress's clothing. As was her habit Elizabeth dressed herself quickly, lastly pulling her boots on over a pair of knitted stockings. Nancy climbed on the bed behind her and braided the long blond hair up neatly. Without another word the lady of Friarsgate was gone from the room.

In the days that followed Elizabeth was up early, and either out or in her privy chamber keeping her accounts. Other than to direct her servants or shepherds, Elizabeth hardly spoke at all. She sat alone at her high board each night, ate her meal, and was gone to her chamber. Sometimes she would remain by the fire afterwards for a short time. St. Crispin's Day came, and bonfires were lit that night to celebrate, but there was no feast in the hall for its single occupant. On All Hallows Eve the hall was silent, as usual. The cook served a dish of crowdie, a sweet apple cream dessert. Elizabeth waved it away.

"Give it to the servants as a treat," she told Albert. She knew that within the dessert had been placed two marbles, two rings, and two coins. Whoever found the rings would find love and marriage. Elizabeth laughed bitterly thinking on it. Whoever found a coin would be rich. She was already rich, for all the good it did her. And those finding one of the two marbles would lead a cold and lonely life. That privilege was already hers. As for those who found nothing, it was their fate to lead a life of uncertainty. There was no uncertainty in her life. She would grow old alone.

The following day it was customary to hold a feast in honor of all the saints. That night her hall was filled with the Friarsgate folk, as she would not punish them for her stupidity. There was a roasted boar, which everyone loved. The next day, All Souls, prayers were offered for the dead, and the children went a-souling, singing and asking for soul cakes, which had been previously prepared and were given them. Martinmas followed on November twelfth, and again the hall was filled with her folk, who this time were treated to roast goose. On the twenty-fifth of the month St. Catherine's feast was celebrated with cathern cakes in the shape of the wheel upon which the saint was martyred.

The days were growing much colder and shorter, the nights long and dark. Elizabeth had overseen all the preparations necessary to protect her flocks and her folk. She had ridden out almost every day on some purpose or another. She had collected the herbs and flowers she would need to make fresh teas, salves, and poultices for her apothecary. It was her duty as the lady to minister to any in her care who grew sick. But no matter how busy she kept herself she was still bitter at Baen's defection, and so very lonely. She still could not believe that he had deserted her when he loved her.

A messenger came from Claven's Carn inviting her to spend

Christmas with her mother, her stepfather, and her half brothers. Elizabeth sent him back with a message that she thought it unwise to leave Friarsgate with winter upon them. But the truth was that she had not felt well at all since Baen had gone. The thought of traveling into Scotland was unpleasant. She did not believe she could bear the happiness that surrounded her mother at Claven's Carn.

A long, newsy letter arrived from Otterly. Lord Cambridge asked after her health, and sent his regards to Baen. The new wing of the house was perfect. He was safe from Banon and her noisy brood, and once more had his privacy. A small gallery had been built connecting the main house to Thomas Bolton's snug wing. But the doors at either end of the gallery had but two keys that fit their locks. And Lord Cambridge carried these keys on his person at all times. The door at the far end of the gallery was fitted into the paneling on both sides, so unless one was aware there was a door, one could not find it. It opened into a secret passage that opened into a little-used hallway in the main house. Banon had no idea it was there, and Thomas Bolton had no intention of telling her until he lay on his deathbed. Hopefully that would be many years hence.

He was sharing his secret with Elizabeth, he said, in case he be struck down suddenly. She smiled reading this, almost hearing his voice, ripe with glee at having outfoxed her sister Banon. His library was coming along beautifully. He had found some rare manuscripts among his cache from London, including one by Master Geoffrey Chaucer. Will had come upon it among some lesser works, the dear, clever boy.

*I shall not invite you to the Christmas festivities here at Otterly,* he wrote her. *If you were caught by the weather and forced to remain here, Banon's brood would put you off having an heir for Friarsgate entirely. Besides, I know that you are happy with everything the way it is now, and will be settling down for the winter.* He asked after Edmund and Maybel. And then he closed, sending her his dearest love. Elizabeth put the parchment aside, feeling the tears behind her eyelids. She was feeling so fragile lately.

Then, looking up, she said to the Otterly messenger, "I will send you with a reply tomorrow. Go to the kitchens and eat. There is a bed space in the hall for you." Going to her privy chamber, Elizabeth considered what she would say to her uncle. In the end she simply wrote that Master MacColl had returned north in the autumn.

Reading the missive several days later, Lord Cambridge pursed his lips. It was what Elizabeth hadn't said that intrigued him far more than what she had. She could dismiss her lover so casually? He shook his head. She was hurt, of course, because she had been foolish enough to make his love a choice between her and his father. But when the spring came Baen MacColl would come south again, Lord Cambridge was certain. He loved Elizabeth Meredith, and she loved him. She would forgive him, and all would be well once more.

The twelve days of Christmas came, and for the first time in memory there was no celebration in the hall at Friarsgate. Elizabeth herself went from cottage to cottage on Christmas morn, delivering the gifts she had for her folk. But there were no gifts for her, nor feasting in her hall. Twelfth Night came and went. The snows had finally come, and Elizabeth knew that her cotters were busily weaving the fine cloth that helped bring wealth to them all. But there was little for her to do now. Her books were in order. There was, praise God, no sickness among them.

Candlemas was celebrated on February second. She presented Father Mata with a supply of fine new candles for the church in the new year. Reports were beginning to come to her that the ewes were starting to drop their lambs. Then one night Elizabeth heard the howling of wolves. The next morning she ordered the flocks moved even closer to the house and barns than they had previously been.

Dressing one morning she said to Nancy, "You must speak with the laundress. She has of late begun to shrink my garments. My gowns are becoming too close fitting."

"The laundress does not wash your gowns, mistress," Nancy said. "I look after them myself, and am most careful. But now that you mention it I have noted that your bodices are stretching across your bosom too tightly these days. And you are developing a belly beneath your skirts." The words were no sooner from her mouth when Nancy gasped with the realization of what she had just said. "Mistress! I believe you are with child," she gasped.

Elizabeth reached out to steady herself. "With child?" she repeated.

"When was your last moon link?" Nancy said, realizing that it had to be several months since she had prepared bleeding clothes for Elizabeth or taken stained chemises to the laundress. There could be no other explanation.

Elizabeth sat down heavily. "With child," she said. What was the matter with her that she had not realized it? Of course she was with child. Although she knew her mother had ways of preventing conception, she had never needed to know them. Rosamund would have told her youngest daughter when she married. But all summer and into the early autumn she and Baen had made love at every opportunity. She blushed, remembering the many places where they had lain, lustily indulging their passion for each other. He was a virile man, and the women in her family were noted for their ability to produce healthy offspring. Aye, she was with child. Elizabeth began to laugh, and she laughed until the tears rolled down her pale cheeks.

"Mistress." Nancy's voice quavered. "Are you all right?" The serving woman thought it odd that Elizabeth found this news so amusing. The heiress of Friarsgate was carrying a nameless bastard child. Surely there was no humor in that.

"We must send for my mother," Elizabeth said. " 'Tis cold, but clear. A messenger is to ride with all haste to Claven's Carn and fetch her back to me."

"Will you write a message?" Nancy wanted to know.

"Nay. Just tell him to say I need my mother immediately," Elizabeth replied.

At Claven's Carn, Rosamund Bolton Hepburn queried the Friarsgate man. "Is my daughter all right? What has happened?" Elizabeth wasn't the sort of girl to send for her mother except under the direst of circumstances, and perhaps not even then.

"My lady, I know nothing more than what Mistress Elizabeth's tiring woman, Nancy, told me. I was to fetch you with all haste. But I can tell you that my mistress appears well."

"What the hell is the wench up to now?" Logan Hepburn, the laird of Claven's Carn, demanded to know of his wife.

Rosamund shook her head. "I do not know, but Elizabeth would not send for me in the dead of winter without cause."

"I'll go with you," he replied, and was surprised when she did not argue with him. She was worried, and Rosamund was not a woman to jump at shadows. "If the weather holds I'll ride down to St. Cuthbert's and pay John a visit while you see what it is your daughter wants. When I return we will come home."

"Is tomorrow too soon to leave?" Rosamund asked him.

"I can be ready," Logan Hepburn said. She was worried.

They departed Claven's Carn even before first light the following morning. Rosamund could reach Friarsgate the same day if she traveled early and long. Once over the border her husband left her with their clansmen to travel on to St. Cuthbert's monastery, where his eldest son was now studying for the priesthood. He had a longer journey than Rosamund, but having made the journey once before he knew he could find shelter tonight with a border farmer who was related to the Hepburns. He traveled alone, leaving his clansmen to escort his wife. Shortly after dark they reached Friarsgate.

Rosamund hurried into the hall to find Elizabeth already at the high board eating.

"Come in, Mama!" The younger woman waved the older forward. "Albert! A plate for the lady Rosamund."

"What is the matter?" Rosamund demanded, flinging her fur-lined cape at a servant and sitting down next to her daughter.

"How good you are," Elizabeth said. "You came immediately, didn't you?"

"You have never been a child to ask for my help, Bessie," her mother said. "When you do then I know it is a serious matter."

"Do not call me Bessie," Elizabeth said softly, but there was an edge to her voice.

"Tell me," Rosamund repeated.

"I know how you have fretted that there was no heir of my body to follow me here at Friarsgate. I wanted you to know, Mama, that come the spring there will be an heir, or perhaps an heiress, for Friarsgate. Are you not pleased?"

Rosamund heard her daughter's words, but at first she could not absorb what Elizabeth was telling her. But then the import of her daughter's announcement exploded in her brain. She gasped, and then she said, "What have you done, Bess—Elizabeth? What have you done?"

"I fell in love, Mama. Was that not allowed? You loved my father. You loved Lord Leslie. You love Logan. Philippa loves Crispin. Banon loves her Neville. Even Uncle Thomas loves his Will. Am I not permitted the same privilege? 'You must marry, Elizabeth. We need a husband for you, Elizabeth. Friarsgate must have an heir, Elizabeth.' Did you not all say it to me over and over and over again? So I went to court to please you all, but there was none for me there. Did you expect me to find a man of the land among those boring perfumed courtiers, Mama?"

"It's the Scotsman, Baen MacColl, isn't it?" Rosamund said.

"Of course it is Baen MacColl, Mama. Was he not perfect for me? For Friarsgate? But he would put his parent above me, and above what I had to offer him."

"He has taken advantage of you!" Rosamund cried.

Elizabeth burst out laughing. "Nay, Mama. I took advantage of him. I seduced him boldly, and without a thought for what might come of our passion. I thought—nay, I believed—that because I loved him, because he said he loved me, that he would come to understand we were meant to be together here at Friarsgate. But none of it meant anything to him. His damned father, this master of Grayhaven, is more important to Baen than I am. Than Friarsgate is! He could have been the master here, but he chose to remain his father's bastard. I never want to see him again!" Her voice was shaking.

"Did he know you were with child when he left you?" Rosamund wanted to know.

"I didn't realize it until just a few days ago. Baen left the same day my uncle returned to Otterly," Elizabeth said. "We had handfasted ourselves, yet he still went."

"He must wed you properly," Rosamund said quietly.

"Children of a handfast union are legitimate," Elizabeth said.

"There can be no cloud of any kind tainting this child's right of inheritance," Rosamund told her daughter in a suddenly hard voice. "My uncle Henry Bolton's last wife bore many bairns, but only the eldest was a true Bolton. Still, my uncle did not deny her brats for fear of being ridiculed, though all knew he was a cuckold. But they bear the name Bolton, and so under the law are Boltons. I will not have one of them suddenly arriving at Friarsgate to take it from us, Elizabeth."

"Did you not hear me, Mama? I never want to see Baen MacColl again!"

"Do not be ridiculous, Elizabeth," Rosamund snapped. "You will be properly wed in the church so that none of Mavis Bolton's brats—should any still be alive, or near—can claim our home. When is the bairn due?"

"In the spring, I suppose," Elizabeth said in a surly voice.

Rosamund drew a long, deep breath. "When were you last linked with the moon?" she demanded of her daughter. "We must know if this child will come early or late." Her brow furrowed in thought. "If he left at the beginning of October then you had to be with child then," Rosamund considered. "So probably by August." She looked for Albert and, finding him, motioned him towards her. "Find Mistress Elizabeth's woman for me," she said.

"Yes, my lady," the steward said. Standing so near he had heard everything that had transpired between the two women. Had he not been recently elevated to his position he would have been eager to share what he had overheard. But he was the steward of the hall, and a man in his position did not gossip. Finding Nancy, he sent her back to the hall. She undoubtedly knew of her mistress's condition, but had said nothing. Such a woman of discretion would make a good wife for the steward of the hall, Albert thought.

Nancy curtseyed to Rosamund. "My lady?"

"Can you recall when my daughter was last linked with the moon, Nancy?"

" 'Twas just after Lammastide," Nancy said. "I remember because Mistress Elizabeth did not feel well, which is unusual for her. And Master MacColl carried her to her chamber for me to care for that evening."

Rosamund nodded. "You know?"

Nancy flushed and nodded. "Aye, my lady."

"How long have you known?" Rosamund wanted to learn.

"Why, only in the past few days, my lady," Nancy answered. "Mistress Elizabeth was complaining that the laundress was shrinking her garments of late. But I care for my mistress's gowns. Then I noted that her bodices were tight these days, and that she gave evidence of a belly. The words were no sooner out of my mouth when I realized what it was I had said, and said so to my mistress. She was surprised, but then she agreed it must be true." Nancy curtseyed again to Rosamund.

"Thank you, Nancy. You may go and prepare your mistress's bedchamber for her now. You must see she is well taken care of in the next few months."

"Yes, my lady," Nancy said, curtseying a third time and hurrying off.

"Logan will go north to Grayhaven as soon as possible and make the arrangements with Lord Hay," Rosamund began.

"You can do what you want," Elizabeth said. "I will not marry the man because I am carrying his child. He left me, Mama. His father was more important to him than I was. When it came time to make the choice he chose his sire over me. My son will never do that!" She reached for her goblet.

Rosamund stayed her hand. "You were a fool to make his decision a choice, Elizabeth. Can he not love his father and you? You know how to care for Friarsgate, but you know nothing of a man's heart, or how to win it."

"Friarsgate is all that has mattered to me since I gained memory, Mama," Elizabeth told her parent. "I do not need a husband for Friarsgate."

"Perhaps not," her mother said dryly, "but you surely need a husband for your child. And a handfast union will absolutely not do. You are not nobility like your oldest sister, but you are an heiress of some worth. Not some milkmaid or cotter's lass. Your marriage must be celebrated in the church, my daughter."

"If you send my stepfather to bargain with the master of Grayhaven he will certainly quarrel with him, Mama. Logan has always been most kind to me."

"Then Thomas Bolton must go with him," Rosamund decided. "And I will have to ride on the morrow myself to Otterly to fetch him." She chuckled ruefully. "He will not be pleased to be forced out of his snug home in February and told he must travel north into Scotland. But he will do it because he loves his family, Elizabeth. Remember that. Family is all that truly matters in this world in which we live. The child you now carry in your belly is family, and his father must have the opportunity to love him even as you will love him."

"We all say 'him,' " Elizabeth noted. "What if it is a girl?"

"Then we will love her as well," Rosamund said. She beckoned to Albert. "Who is the housekeeper now?"

"Jane, my lady, Maybel's cousin," he answered her.

"Tell her to prepare me a bed and then fetch me a hot meal. And tell my captain I would see him when he has finished his food," Rosamund said.

"At once, my lady," Albert replied with a bow from the waist.

"And, Albert, I do not have to tell you to remain silent," Rosamund murmured.

"You do not, my lady," came the quiet response.

"And no one is to tell Maybel or Edmund that I have been here and gone, Albert. You will see to it, I know."

"Of course, my lady." Albert hurried off.

"You have not told Maybel of your condition, of course," Rosamund said. "Do not until I tell you that you may. And when Logan comes, which he surely will before I am back from Otterly, you will tell him nothing. I will speak to him myself. He will not be pleased with you at all, Elizabeth. It is better that I am here when you disclose the nature of your need."

"You don't have to ride to Otterly to fetch my uncle, Mama, nor send him and Logan north to deal with the master of Grayhaven," Elizabeth said. "I will not have Baen MacColl for a proper husband, and that is that." She reached for her goblet and drank deeply from it.

"This matter is not one for any discussion between us, Elizabeth. You are with child by this Scot, and you will marry him. It makes no matter that you are angry, or that you feel betrayed. You will do what is best for Friarsgate because you are its lady, and because you are my daughter. You know your duty, Elizabeth. When I became aware of your passion for this land and your abilities to care for it I gave it to you. Do not disappoint me now by behaving in a thoroughly childish way."

"If he really loved me he wouldn't have left me," Elizabeth muttered.

"Perhaps that is so," Rosamund agreed, "but on the other hand, perhaps he was torn between the two people he loved best, and confused as to what to do. So he chose what was most familiar to him. The fact that his loyalty is so strong bodes well for you. He did not strike me as a man to avoid his duty. This situation has convinced me that neither of you has a great deal of common sense. And why didn't you simply come to me, my daughter, and ask me to arrange this marriage in the first place?"

"I am not a child, Mama," Elizabeth said.

"In matters such as this you certainly are," Rosamund snapped. "It makes no difference that you are the lady of Friarsgate. Any marriage you contract must be arranged by me." A steaming dish was placed before her. Rosamund looked up with a smile. "Thank you, Albert," she said, giving him a smile.

"I have spoken with Jane, my lady, and your captain will join you shortly," he responded. "Is there anything else I can do to serve you?"

"You have been most helpful, Albert," Rosamund told him, and then turned back to her meal. She had just finished when the captain of her clansmen came into the hall. "Ah, Jock, here you are. I want half of your men to escort me to Otterly tomorrow. Pick those you want to go, and the rest will remain here to await the laird's coming," she said.

"Just half, m'lady?" he questioned her.

"The countryside between here and Otterly is as safe as any, and it is winter. As we must remain overnight I do not want to burden Lord Cambridge too greatly with our care and feeding," Rosamund said with a small smile.

The captain nodded. "Very good, m'lady. What time will you want to depart?"

"Just at dawn. 'Tis a long day's ride over the hills, but we should be able to reach Otterly by sunset," Rosamund told him.

He bowed, and was gone.

"Are you angry at me, Mama?" Elizabeth asked.

"Come and let us sit by the fire," Rosamund suggested, and the left the high board. "Nay, I am not angry with you, sweeting. But you have rather put the cart before the horse now, haven't you? You must love him very much."

"I love him not at all!" Elizabeth declared.

Rosamund laughed softly. "You always were a bad liar, Bessie," she said. "Do not fear. We will negotiate a marriage contract that will allow him nothing but what you would willingly give him. If he loves you as I suspect, it will mean nothing to him, and he will sign it. His father may be a bit difficult to convince, but I think Logan and Tom will manage the master of Grayhaven between them quite nicely."

Elizabeth couldn't help the giggle that escaped her. "Baen is certain to understand, but I wonder if his proud old Highlander of a father will."

"In the end," Rosamund said wisely, "he will consider the advantages his son will gain by marrying you. You have said Lord Hay loves Baen. Then he will let him go, Elizabeth. If only you had consulted me on this we would have had it settled by now."

"I thought he would stay," Elizabeth said sadly.

Rosamund reached out and, taking her youngest daughter's hand in hers, said quietly, "I know he must regain your trust, my child, but do not make it too difficult for him. Just enough so that he will not lose his respect for you." She patted the hand in hers. "He is a most bonny laddie, Elizabeth. Is he big all over?"

"Mama!" Elizabeth blushed. Then she said, "Aye."

Rosamund smiled. "You will be outrageously happy once you come to terms with each other." Then, standing, she said, "I'm off to bed, daughter. I have a long, cold ride ahead of me tomorrow." She bent and kissed Elizabeth on her forehead. "Good night."

Elizabeth sat by her fire for several more long minutes. Then, standing, she got up and went down to the kitchens. A serving wench was scrubbing the large wooden table while another finished a pot in the stone sink. "Where is Cook?" she asked.

Both girls looked up, startled, but one's eyes darted toward the pantry briefly.

Elizabeth grinned. She could now hear the low grunts and heavy breathing of a man laboring mightily over a woman. "Tell Cook I will want food ready at dawn so my mother and her men may have some sustenance along their way."

"Yes, mistress," the girl at the table said. She was obviously grateful Elizabeth had not ordered one of them to fetch the cook, who each night after his duties were done took one of the kitchen wenches into the pantry and lustily swived her. Cook did not like to be disturbed when he was at his pleasure.

Elizabeth grinned again, and returned to the hall to begin her nightly preparations. She snuffed the many candles, saving a single taper to light her own way upstairs. The fire was burning lower, the dogs snoring before it. A cat had taken its place in the chair where her mother had earlier sat. All was quiet. And then suddenly she felt a tiny fluttering deep in her belly. It was as if she had swallowed a butterfly. She stood stock-still, a look of amazement upon her face. Then her hands went to her belly in a protective gesture as a tear rolled down her cheek. It was real. The child was real! Reaching for her taper, Elizabeth Meredith slowly climbed the stairs from the hall to her own bedchamber, where Nancy was waiting for her.

"You look pale," Nancy said as her mistress entered the room. "Are you all right?"

"I felt the bairn move," Elizabeth half whispered, setting the taper down.

"Well, bless it!" Nancy said smiling. "I have heard it called the quickening. I saw your mother settled in her bed. She's still a beautiful woman. I remember her when she was lady here." She helped Elizabeth from her clothing but for her long chemise, which was also her night garment. "Go and wash your face and hands now before I tuck you into your bed. You need as much rest as you can get." She bustled about putting her mistress's things away.

Elizabeth followed Nancy's advice, and was then tucked into her bed. When she awoke the following morning she learned that Rosamund had departed earlier. Stretching slowly, she let her gaze wander to the casement windows. The sun was shining. She was relieved that her mother would have a good day in which to travel to Otterly, which was a long and full day's ride.

And Rosamund was equally delighted to have the burden of her trip lightened by good weather. It was wickedly cold, but there was no wind at all. It was several hours before she lost feeling in her toes and fingers. They passed by the convent of St. Margaret just at the noon hour. Rosamund heard the bells in the convent church tolling for sext. She debated stopping. Her cousin, Julia Bolton, was a nun in this convent. She had resided there since she had been weaned from her wet nurse, her stepmother and father, Henry Bolton, not wanting the bother of her care. Rosamund had met Julia, who was known as Sister Margaret Julia, twice. She was a sweet-faced woman with a sharp intellect, and had risen to be second in rank at her convent. Rosamund had liked her. She was nothing at all like her father, but then Julia Bolton could never remember ever having seen the late Henry Bolton in all of her life.

"Are we stopping?" the captain asked Rosamund, for he knew her cousin was at St. Margaret's.

"Nay," Rosamund said, shaking her head. "We cannot spare the time. If it were summer it would be another matter, but I want to get to Otterly by dark."

She had refused the basket of food the Friarsgate cook wanted her to take, explaining they had no time to stop and eat. If they grew hungry they would consume the flat oatcakes the Scots all carried. There would be one brief respite from their journey so their horses might rest for a few minutes and be watered. And so that any who needed to might relieve themselves. The sun was setting in a glorious burst of red, red-orange, orange, and gold when they reached Otterly. A messenger had been sent on ahead earlier to advise of their coming. He was awaiting them, and guided them to the small private entrance of Lord Cambridge's wing.

Rosamund dismounted and hurried inside, where a servant was waiting to escort her to a charming little hall where Lord Cambridge awaited her. The captain and her men would stable the horses and be fed in Otterly's main hall. She was not surprised to find her middle daughter waiting with her cousin. "Banon! How lovely," she said, hugging this second child she had borne. "Ahh, I see you are breeding again. When is this one due? How many is it now? Eight?"

"Soon," Banon replied. "Aye, eight. What is the matter, Mama?"

"Dearest cousin!" Thomas Bolton stepped between the two women, embracing Rosamund. "Come, my darling girl, and sit down.

God's wounds, but your lovely little hands are frozen! Will! Some wine, dear boy, before my cousin perishes. Banon, my pet, bid your mama farewell. You shall see her later. It is almost dark, and your servant has remained to escort you back to your part of the house." He smiled benignly.

"Damn it, Uncle! You come and go without exiting the premises. Why do you make me?" Banon was not pleased.

"Because, dear girl, you and your noisy brood would abuse your privilege, as you did before. I must have my privacy. Now run along," he said, patting her shoulder and gently pushing her out the door into the foyer.

Rosamund chuckled. "You have her completely in hand, Tom. I always wondered how you would manage with my clever Banon." She sipped her wine slowly. The feeling was beginning to return to her hands and feet with a tingling and burning sensation. She sighed as she began to relax.

"You did not ride down from Scotland in the middle of February simply to pay me a social call, my darling girl," Lord Cambridge said. "I echo Banon's query. What is the matter? Is Logan all right?"

"For now Logan is visiting John at St. Cuthbert's, and hoping that his eldest son has changed his mind. I know he has not, but if he had he would find himself in a quarrel with *my* eldest son, who now sees himself the next laird," Rosamund said. "But it has nothing to do with the Hepburns, Tom. It is Elizabeth."

"Elizabeth? Is she all right, dear girl?" he asked, his look concerned.

"No, Tom, she is not all right. She is with child. Baen MacColl's bairn," Rosamund told him.

"And he has left her." Lord Cambridge looked irritated. "The fool. He loves her."

"He departed from Friarsgate the same day you did, Tom. She had no sooner bid you farewell than he rode out to return to Grayhaven," Rosamund said. "He knows nothing of his coming child. Elizabeth didn't realize it until a short while back. Her whole attention is on Friarsgate, the sheep, the wool trade. And with Edmund unable to carry part of that burden now, it has all been up to her. She has never been a girl to think of herself when others needed her. When she realized her condition she sent for me, though why I cannot fathom, since she doesn't want to take my advice. Why is it that two of my three daughters have persisted in being so stubborn where men are concerned? When I remember how Philippa howled and snarled at us over that foolish incident with Giles FitzHugh; and yet she found perfect happiness with Crispin."

"And became a countess," Lord Cambridge murmured.

"Elizabeth will never be a countess," Rosamund said with a small smile, "but she loves this Scot, and he her. Yet she says she will not have him. Her belly grows bigger each day, and she rages that he left her for his father, and she will not have him back. Well, I will not have it, Tom! She will wed Baen MacColl, and the next heir to Friarsgate will be legitimate and carry its father's name."

"I agree, darling girl. I agree fully with you," Lord Cambridge said. "And while I am delighted to see you, this is a dreadful time of year to travel. Could you not just have written all of this to me?"

"I need your help, Tom," Rosamund said softly.

"Dearest cousin," he began, "you know I will do anything for you."

Rosamund smiled archly at him. "Anything?" she purred.

"Of course! Any . . ." A look similar to that of a trapped animal suddenly appeared upon his face. "Rosamund," he quavered.

"I need you to go to Scotland, Tom," she said. "We must leave tomorrow."

"Scotland? At this time of year?" he croaked. "It is cold, cousin. Scotland? It will snow, and I shall be frozen to death."

"You cannot freeze to death until you and Logan reach Grayhaven. If I send Logan alone to speak with the master of Grayhaven he will surely lose his temper and quarrel with the man. We need Colin Hay's complete understanding and cooperation, Tom. Logan adores Elizabeth. When he learns of her condition he will be ready to start a feud between the Hepburns and the Hays. And her attitude will only encourage him to mayhem. You must travel with my husband and see that Baen MacColl is brought back to marry my daughter. Logan cannot do this alone. He needs you. I need you. Elizabeth needs you. Besides, you were there when she began her affair with the Scot. Do not tell me you did not know what she was doing! Elizabeth is not a subtle girl."

"My dear Rosamund, surely you aren't blaming me for Elizabeth's naughty behavior?" Lord Cambridge looked just slightly offended. "Your daughters, as you well know, are most strong-willed girls."

Rosamund chuckled. "You did not answer my question, Tom," she said.

"You must accept part of the blame for this yourself, darling girl," he countered. "Did you not approve of Baen MacColl? Yet you did not share with Elizabeth the secret you possess for avoiding . . . er . . . um . . . the complications of one's naughty behavior."

Rosamund shook her head. "Nay, I did not. I did not believe she would bed him before marriage, Tom. If I had I should have given her the secret. Aye, I am equally to blame, but you are too!"

"We have both been too anxious to see Elizabeth happy at last," he admitted. "And, darling girl, she is so very happy when she is in the company of her Scot."

"Then you will go," Rosamund said, "and promise to never rue the day we were reunited as a family, Tom."

He laughed aloud. "Darling girl, I can barely remember the time when we were not together, nor do I wish to remember it. We have loved each other from the moment we met, and I regret naught of our time together. Aye, I will go. I will travel north, in the company of that handsome husband of yours and his brawny clansmen, through the foul winter weather. We will bring back Master MacColl to stand in Friarsgate Church before Father Mata, with Elizabeth by his side, to be united in matrimony. But I must tell you that I thank heavens Elizabeth is the last of your daughters, darling girl! I do not believe I have many more adventures left in me," he concluded with a gusty sigh.

She laughed and blew him a kiss. "Thank you, Tom."

"Are you hungry?" he asked her. "Of course you are. You have ridden the day long. Will, shall we show my cousin the secret of entering the main house?" Lord Cambridge chuckled. "I usually join Banon and her family for the evening meal."

"I believe that Lady Rosamund will keep your secret, my lord," Will said with a small smile. "And it is time."

Thomas Bolton rose from his chair and took his cousin by her arm as she stood. "Come along, darling girl. Only one other person knows my secret, and that is Elizabeth." He led her from the room and into the gallery, one wall of which was all windows. The facing wall was hung with portraits of Lord Cambridge, his late sister, their parents, Rosamund, and each of her daughters. The gallery appeared to have but one entrance, but at the far end Thomas Bolton reached out to touch the paneled wall and a small door sprang open. They moved through it, Will drawing the door shut behind them. "This way," Lord Cambridge said as they walked down a narrow interior corridor that was obviously a secret passageway.

"Tom, you are wickedly clever," Rosamund told him, and heard him chortle.

After they had gone a short distance Lord Cambridge stopped and, reaching out again, pressed his fingers against a small, practically hidden catch. A second door flew open, and they stepped out into Otterly House. "Can you see anything in the wall?" he asked her. "I believe my entry is quite invisible, darling girl."

Rosamund peered closely at the paneling in the corridor wall. She could see nothing that gave evidence of a door in the wall. She shook her head. "It is ingenious, Tom," she told him admiringly.

"This corridor is in what was my original wing of the house. When I lived here I was constantly besieged by Banon's brood. They could not seem to leave me in peace. Now that I am gone they come here not at all. It allows me the perfect entry without being seen. And the servants rarely come except to clean. I believe Robert Neville hides here now and again, poor fellow. Banon is a dear girl, but she has little control over her daughters, as you will shortly see. Listen. You can already hear the shrieking."

They entered the hall at Otterly. Banon's five daughters, ranging in age from nine to three, were chasing one another about in a rough game of tag. "Grandmama!" they cried with one voice upon seeing her.

Rosamund held out her arms to them, laughing as they swarmed her.

"So my mother now knows the secret, but I do not," Banon grumbled at Lord Cambridge.

"Otterly is still my house, dear girl," he replied quietly.

"Oh, Uncle, I did not mean to be rude," Banon cried, "but you know I hate secrets, and this is one you seem to very much enjoy keeping."

"A man must have his privacy, dear girl. One day when your brood is grown I shall share my knowledge with you. Until then I pray you accept my decision in the matter." He patted her cheek. "You have always been my favorite, Banon, which is why you are my heiress. Be satisfied with that."

She sighed. "I have no other choice, I fear. Now, tell me," Banon said, slipping her arm through his, "why has Mama come?"

He lightly swatted the little hand on his arm. "Bad child! She will tell you herself if she chooses," Lord Cambridge scolded her.

Banon laughed.

Robert Neville came forward to greet his mother-in-law. He was a quiet man who quite obviously adored his wife and children. And he was content to allow Banon to rule their home, for it allowed him more time for gentlemanly pursuits. "Rosamund, this is a pleasant surprise," he said, kissing her hand and bowing.

"Thank you, Rob," she answered him. "I apologize for appearing at Otterly with scant notice, but there is a small family emergency that must be attended to. I needed to come for Tom." She turned to her granddaughters, who had started to quarrel over some silly matter. "Girls! Girls! Stop at once!" Her usually gentle voice was sharp, and the little girls looked at her openmouthed. "Your behavior is not acceptable at all. Katherine, as the eldest it is up to you to keep order among your sisters. Instead you lead them in bad behavior. This will not do."

"But Grandmama," Katherine Neville, age nine, whined, "they will not obey me. And it is her fault!" she said, pointing at one of her sisters.

"Why should I obey you?" eight-year-old Thomasina demanded to know.

"You listen to your sister because she is your elder by one year and ten days, if memory serves me," Rosamund said. Then she turned back to Katherine. "But you must set a good example, and not bully your sisters simply because you are the eldest."

"Did our mother and her sisters get on better than we do, Grandmama?" Thomasina asked pertly.

"Indeed they did," Rosamund said quickly. "Now go and wash your hands and faces, my pets. When you do you will be welcome at the high board tonight."

The five little girls looked to Banon, who nodded her approval, and so they ran off to do their grandmother's bidding. "You have asked them to the high board so you will not have to discuss Elizabeth," Banon said.

Rosamund nodded. "After the meal I shall tell you all," she promised.

Banon made a face, but was forced to be content with her mother's decision.

It was a happy table that evening. Led by Katherine Neville, Thomasina, Jemima, Elizabeth, and Margaret Neville exhibited their best manners. And when the meal was over and they were dismissed by their parents, they kissed each of their relations good night and retired without a word of complaint.

"Your behavior has been excellent, girls," Rosamund told them as the left the hall.

Katherine turned and curtseyed with a smile to her grandmother, but Thomasina, turning, grinned and winked mischievously before scampering after her siblings.

Banon waited patiently for several minutes after her daughters had departed the hall, but finally she could bear it no longer. "What has happened at Friarsgate?" she demanded of her mother.

And so Rosamund explained quietly and in detail.

When she had finished her recitation Banon said bluntly, "Well, I would have never thought Bessie had such passion in her, Mama. 'Tis true that Katherine was already in my belly on our wedding day, but at least Rob and I knew we were getting married. Do you think Logan and Uncle Thomas can bring this Scot back? And what if she does as she has threatened and refuses to wed him?"

"For once in her life," Rosamund said, and there was a distinct edge to her voice, "your youngest sister will do precisely as she is told. We will protect her position in the marriage contract that is drawn up, but she will marry Baen MacColl so that her child may know its father and Friarsgate have its next generation. Whatever is or is not between them they must settle themselves, but marry they will."

"Or that dear boy Logan will set the Highlands aflame with his outrage," Lord Cambridge said drolly. "If I must make a trip north to Scotland in the dead of winter, my darlings, I do believe I should enjoy myself. I have not a doubt that Logan Hepburn will see to it that I do, and provide me with a variety of amusements. Now," he said, rising, "I must leave you. Will and I have to see to my packing. If I am to appear before this master of Grayhaven it must be in my finest garments so that I may convince him to release his son to us. It will not do that I look less than my absolute best. We do not want him to think badly of our family. Good night, all." He blew them several kisses as he left the hall.

"The master of Grayhaven is in for a rare treat," Robert Neville said with a grin. "I doubt he has ever met anyone like Lord Cambridge."

"Nor is he ever likely to again," Banon agreed. "Let us hope this Highlander survives his encounter with my uncle."

"Let us hope Logan survives his travels with him," Rosamund said, chuckling. "He likes my cousin, but Tom has always confounded him. And takes great delight in it."

"I hope this Baen MacColl is worth all the trouble we are going to for Elizabeth," Banon said. "You have met him. Is he, Mama?"

Rosamund smiled. "He is. Bessie is going to be very happy, when she ceases being angry at us and at herself for ever letting him go."

# Chapter 13

❖

$C$olin Hay, the master of Grayhaven, stared at the man who stood before him smiling broadly. He was a peacock of a fellow in his scarlet velvet breeches with cloth of gold showing through the slashings. His striped gold-and-scarlet silk stockings sported a single garter of sparkling red crystals sewn upon a golden ribbon which adorned one shapely leg. His scarlet velvet doublet had full padded sleeves and a fur collar, and was trimmed in rich marten. The shirt beneath had a ruffled edging on the collar and sleeves. His hat had a stiff turned up brim, and was embellished with an ostrich plume.

"My dear sir," the vision said in the plummy tones of a well-bred northern Englishman, "I am delighted to meet you at last." A beringed hand, freed of its pearl-trimmed glove, was thrust towards the master of Grayhaven.

Colin Hay took the soft hand and shook it, for to do otherwise would have been intolerably rude, and he had no quarrel with this fellow. Yet. The handshake surprised him for it was firm and hard. He had not expected such a handshake from such a creature. "My lord," he said. The man was obviously nobility. Then his gaze swung to the peacock's companion, and he relaxed, recognizing the garb and stance of a border laird. He held out his hand again, this time towards his fellow Scot. "Sir."

Logan Hepburn shook the hand offered him firmly. "My lord. I am Logan Hepburn, the laird of Claven's Carn. My companion is Thomas Bolton, Lord Cambridge of Otterly. We are kin through my marriage to Tom's cousin Rosamund Bolton."

"Of Friarsgate?" Colin Hay grinned. "You're both welcome to Grayhaven," he said jovially now that he knew who they were and could place them. Wine!" he shouted to his servants. "Come and sit by the fire, gentlemen," he invited them.

"Gladly!" Lord Cambridge said. "Your weather is not disposed to be kind to travelers, my dear sir. I thought at least twice I should die of the bitter cold. Were it not of the greatest importance that we see you immediately I should be safe at home cataloging my library." He sat in a wood chair directly next to the fire.

A servant brought goblets of wine, and when the three men were finally all settled by the hearth, Colin Hay asked, "Why have you made such a journey in the dead of winter, sirs? I agree with Lord Cambridge. It is not a good time of year to travel."

"Where is your son?" Logan Hepburn asked.

"Which one? I hae three," the master of Grayhaven said.

"Baen," Logan Hepburn replied. "Baen MacColl."

"Baen will be out with his sheep right now," Colin Hay replied, "but he'll be back by dark, when he's certain his shepherds are safe with their flocks for the night. He fights a losing battle, for the sheep no longer thrive here. They did at first. 'Twas a good idea, but it does not seem to be a successful one now. He is disappointed. Do you wish to sell him more sheep, my lords? You have wasted a trip if that is your purpose, I fear."

Thomas Bolton chuckled. "There is only one little ewe sheep he must have whether he will or nay. But 'twill be to his advantage, I assure you, sir."

"Tom!" Logan Hepburn looked decidedly aggrieved. "This is no laughing matter. This is serious business we come upon."

"What is it then?" Colin Hay demanded to know. "You surely do not need my son's presence to tell me what you must."

"It would be better if he were here too," Lord Cambridge responded, now serious himself. " 'Twill save the telling of it twice. Might you send for him? 'Tis a long time until the night falls, sir."

"Aye, send for him, and let us get this over and done with," Logan Hepburn said.

"To satisfy my own curiosity if for no other reason," Colin Hay said, beckoning a serving man to him. "Ride out and fetch my son Baen," he told the servant. "Tell him I want him in the hall with all possible haste."

The man bowed and hurried off.

"I don't suppose you would have a bit of cheese?" Lord Cambridge said. "We have not eaten since dawn, when we dined on some rather dry oatcakes that had been hiding in the bottom of a clansman's saddlebag. They had the taste of old leather," he said, shuddering delicately and sipping from his cup.

" 'Tis almost time for the meal," the master of Grayhaven replied. "We eat our main meal at noon in winter, for other than Baen few venture out after that. Have you ridden far?"

"From Claven's Carn in the west borders," Logan said.

"And I several days farther from Otterly," Lord Cambridge said.

"It must be an important matter that you would come at such a time, and so far," the master of Grayhaven answered. What was this all about? And why did they insist that Baen be with them when they explained? A servant girl with a big belly wouldn't merit such a visit. And then Colin Hay remembered the lady of Friarsgate, and how every time his son spoke of her—which was rare indeed, for Baen had been almost taciturn since his return from England this time—but each time he would mention this girl his eyes were soft with the memory of her. What was her name? But he could not remember it, if indeed he had ever known it. The peacock appeared to be dozing now. The border laird sat staring into his wine goblet. They waited.

It was almost an hour later when Baen came into his father's hall. "Da! Are you all right?" he asked as he entered, and then he saw Thomas Bolton and Logan Hepburn. He grew pale. "Elizabeth?" he croaked. "Is she well?"

The peacock was immediately on his feet. "Dear, dear boy!" he exclaimed effusively, embracing Baen warmly. "It is delightful to see you, although I should have preferred it be in a warmer clime."

"Elizabeth, Tom! Is she all right?" Baen repeated.

"She is as well as can be expected," Lord Cambridge offered with a teasing grin.

"She's got a big belly, and 'tis your bairn!" Logan Hepburn said without any preamble. "You'll come back to Friarsgate and make it right!"

"I can't!" Baen said low, his voice anguished.

"And why not?" Logan demanded angrily.

"You know the duty I owe my father," Baen began.

"My stepdaughter is no serving wench, damn it!" the laird of Claven's Carn snapped. "She's the heiress to Friarsgate, and this child should be the next heir to the estates. You cannot desert her, Baen MacColl! I will not allow it."

"Nor will I," the master of Grayhaven said suddenly. "Do you mean to tell me, you mutton-headed fool, that you would leave the girl because of some foolish idea in your head regarding your loyalty towards me?" His open palm made contact with the side of Baen's head. "Do you love her?"

"We handfasted. Is that not good enough?" Baen asked in pained tones.

His father smacked him again. "Do you love her?" he demanded.

"Aye, but Da—"

"Then you will wed her properly in the church, and give my grandchild a name. You'll nae sire a bastard as I did, Baen. I love ye. I've loved you from the first you turned up at my door and I saw my own face staring back up at me in the person of a frightened yet defiant lad. But ye're my bastard, and there is nothing here for you at Grayhaven. Especially now that the sheep are failing. Why should you not have a wife and bairns of your own? And a home of your own? Ellen wanted it for you, and I do too. You'll be the lord of a fine manor."

"Nay, he'll not," Logan Hepburn said. "He'll be the husband of the lady of Friarsgate, and no more. The father of the heir. No more unless she permits it. I'll not lie to you, Lord Hay. Elizabeth is very angry that Baen left her. She would have raised her bairn alone but that when her mother learned of her condition, she would not have it. But Friarsgate belongs to the lady even after she weds."

"I understand," Baen said.

"I dinna," his father spoke up. "Who controls the land for the lass now?"

"Elizabeth has controlled Friarsgate since her fourteenth birthday,"

Lord Cambridge began. "She is a fine steward of her own lands, as was her mother before her marriage to dear Logan. She has never had any intention of giving control of her lands to a husband. Baen knows this. Because of his loyalty to you he tried to stay his attraction towards my darling niece. But she would not have it, for Elizabeth is a strong-willed lass, Lord Hay. She wanted your son, and she boldly seduced him."

"She seduced you?" Lord Hay was at first disbelieving, and then he laughed. "She sounds like a fine hot-tempered wench to me. A man gets strong sons on a lass like that." Then he grew serious. "If he weds her, what part will he play at Friarsgate?"

"As we have said, he will be the lady's husband, a respected position, my lord, you will agree. But she will award him as part of the marriage settlement the position of steward of Friarsgate. Until recently her great-uncle held that place, but he is no longer able to do his duty. The infirmities of old age have finally overtaken him."

"Why did you leave her?" Lord Hay demanded of his son.

"It was the most difficult thing I have ever done, Da, but my first loyalty must lie with you," Baen said. "You took me in when my mother died. I was a stranger, but you accepted me readily. You have loved me and treated me equally with Jamie and Gilly. I owe you my life, Da. And I have learned duty and loyalty from you."

Colin Hay's green eyes filled with tears. Impatiently he wiped them away with his fist. Then he hit his son a third blow with the same fist. "You owe me naught, you mutton-headed fool! A man loves his bairns and does the best he can for them. Sending you away to wed with this lass you love is the best I can do for you, Baen. You know there is nothing for you here. Jamie must come first, and then Gilly. I can barely provide for either of them. This is a golden opportunity for you, and you must take it, my son."

"I will be English then," Baen said.

"Nay," Logan Hepburn said in a kindlier tone. "You'll be a borderer, lad. 'Tis true we raid one another's cattle and sheep when we can, but a borderer is a borderer no matter what side of that invisible line he calls home. We're not quite English, nor are we quite Scots. The wind blows from a different direction in the west part of the border."

"My son will not be abused? He'll be respected as the lady's husband? Obeyed as her steward?" the master of Grayhaven wanted to know.

"He is already well respected there, my lord," the laird of Claven's Carn replied.

"Pray God then that no war separates us," the master of Grayhaven said softly. Then he turned to Baen. "I want you to go back to Friarsgate and wed with its mistress. I want you to do for your bairn what I could not do for you, Baen. Give my grandchild its proper name. And if you would truly please me, my son, I would ask that you finally accept my surname as your own."

"I have always been content being Baen MacColl," the younger man said to his father with a small smile.

"Be Baen, son of Colin Hay, now. Not some nameless Colin, but Colin Hay," the master of Grayhaven said quietly.

Baen nodded slowly. "I have always been proud to be your son, Da," he told his father. "And I suppose in England, Hay will be a better surname for my children than MacColl. If I can gain Elizabeth's love once again I promise you there will be more than one child at Friarsgate in this next generation."

"Then you will go with my blessing, Baen," Colin Hay told his son. "And take those damned English sheep of yours with you before I eat them!"

"Da! Those aren't eating sheep," Baen protested.

"All sheep are for eating," the master of Grayhaven said, roaring with laughter.

Colin Hay's two legitimate sons now entered the hall. They gawked at Lord Cambridge, having never seen anyone in such fine garb in all their lives. He gazed back at them, thinking them handsome young fellows, but then they did look a bit rough.

"Come and meet Lord Cambridge, lads, and the laird of Claven's Carn." Colin Hay beckoned his sons forward. "And congratulate your brother, Baen, for he is to be wed."

James and Gilbert Hay whooped in a combination of delight and surprise.

"It's that English girl, isn't it?" James said.

"Aye," Baen answered him quietly.

His two younger brothers eyed each other knowledgeably, nodding. But the words on their lips remained unspoken in the presence of their guests.

"As soon as Baen can gather his flock I'm sending him back to England with the sheep for his dower," the master of Grayhaven said.

James and Gilbert hooted derisively, for they had thought their elder's preoccupation with his sheep amusing.

"I thank you both for your good wishes," Baen said to them dryly.

"If you take the sheep," James said, grinning, "what will we serve the guests at my wedding to Jean Gordon?"

"Let the Gordons worry about that," Baen replied. "Besides, your wedding isn't for another few years. The bride has to grow up first," he mocked his brother. "At least mine is a woman grown."

"With a bairn in her belly?" Gilbert Hay asked slyly, unable to restrain himself despite the black look his father shot him. But why else would these two gentlemen have come to Grayhaven in the dead of winter, he thought, except the lass was breeding?

But Baen laughed at his youngest brother's jibe. "Aye," he acknowledged, "but I handfasted her in the summer, Gilly. Now I'll return with our father's blessing to wed my Elizabeth in the church."

"Will you come back to Grayhaven?" Gilbert Hay asked, suddenly serious.

"Nay," Baen said. "Elizabeth has her own lands, and I will steward them. I will have no time to return to Grayhaven, for my duties to Friarsgate will fill my days."

"But we'll never see you then," Gilbert said softly.

"You can come and visit me, Gilly," Baen told him. "Da has you betrothed to Alice Gordon, Jean's sister, and she is but a wee girl barely out of leading strings. You will have time to travel, and the Hays of Grayhaven will always be welcome at Friarsgate. Is that not so, Tom, Logan?"

"Aye," the laird of Claven's Carn agreed. "The Scots are always welcome at Friarsgate, unless, of course, they come in large numbers uninvited." He chuckled.

The other men laughed.

James Hay stepped forward and embraced his eldest brother. "I wish you well, Baen," he said enthusiastically. Secretly he was relieved to see his eldest brother well settled and soon to be gone. He had been a very little boy when Baen had arrived in their midst, and their youngest brother not even born. From the time he was old enough to understand their place in their father's life, James Hay knew he was his father's heir, though he was his second-born son. But he also knew that Colin Hay loved Baen best of all his sons, though he would never have said it, and he treated his lads with an equal hand.

Their father had always been concerned with finding a place for Baen. Now one had been supplied, and James Hay, while wishing his brother good fortune, would not be sad to see him gone from Grayhaven. Gilly would miss him more, James knew, but then Gilly had always looked up to their oldest brother. Not to Grayhaven's heir, but to Baen. James Hay loved his brother Baen, but he had always found it disconcerting that even though he was their father's heir, Baen came first with so many others. He smiled broadly at Baen now, for his elder's departure was like a great weight being lifted from his shoulders. But he also felt a little ashamed to think it.

It would be several days before Baen MacColl was ready to leave Grayhaven. March had begun, and the weather was raw and wet. The master of Grayhaven gave his son a covered cart to transport the few lambs that had been born the previous month. They were still too young to travel with the flock, and there was still snow on the ground. It was not the best time of year to move the animals, but Baen was anxious to get back to Friarsgate, and to Elizabeth. The sheep had not thrived well over the long months, although it had at first seemed they would. At least a third of them had died, been poached, or taken by wild beasts. But once back at Friarsgate, Baen knew, they would do well once again. He and Friar would bring the flock home safe.

The master of Grayhaven had read over the marriage contract his son was to sign. He was not pleased by the strict terms Elizabeth Meredith was imposing upon her husband. Baen would have no rights to the manor should she die in childbirth. The land would revert to her mother then. Should she produce an heir or heiress, and then perish, the estate became the child's, and her mother its legal guardian. If the child should then die, again Friarsgate returned to Rosamund Bolton, and not Baen MacColl. Elizabeth appointed him her steward, but all decisions made with regard to Friarsgate must be approved by her. As her husband and the manor's steward he would have a respected position. He would be given a small portion in coin for himself and that was all.

" 'Tis too harsh," Colin Hay said. He turned to Logan and Lord Cambridge. "Have you read this? She is not an easy woman."

"The women of Friarsgate are very proprietary where their land is concerned," Logan offered.

"She loves him," Lord Cambridge said. "Trust me, dear sir, she will relent eventually, and this shall be rewritten."

"Why is she so angry with him?" Colin Hay wanted to know.

"She is angry at herself more than your son," Thomas Bolton said. "You see, dear boy, Elizabeth prides herself on being coolheaded and logical. She has never made a decision that she did not carefully consider. But then she fell in love, and she made a fatal mistake often made by those in love, even men: She asked her lover to make a choice between her and something else he loved. In this case, you. It was foolish, of course, and afterwards when he had left her she knew it, but it was done.

"I have been convinced all along, and Logan will tell you it is so, that had my cousin Rosamund approached you regarding a marriage between your eldest son, Baen, and her youngest daughter, Elizabeth, you would have been amenable. It would have been worked out to everyone's satisfaction. But from the time Rosamund's eldest child refused to accept her position as the heiress to Friarsgate, and Elizabeth told her mother she wanted it for her own, my niece has listened only to herself. She was twelve then.

"When she was fourteen her mother turned Friarsgate over to her legally, although if the truth be known, she had been caring for it since the day it was promised her. She oversees every facet of the estate, until recently with her steward, Edmund Bolton. But Edmund is an old man now, and his health is poor. Elizabeth asked Baen to take his place until Edmund was well again, although we all knew Edmund would never again accept that responsibility. When your son left her in October she took up the reins herself."

"You say her mother would have approved a match had we negotiated one," the master of Grayhaven said. "Why has a husband not been found for her before? What is the matter with the lass?" Colin Hay wanted to know.

"There is nothing the matter with Elizabeth," Baen spoke up.

"But why was she not wed previously?" his father demanded to know.

"Being as mutton-headed as your son," Logan Hepburn said, "she didn't want a husband who would try to wrest her authority from her. Her sisters found husbands at court, and we sent her last year. But none would do for her. She wanted a man who would love Friarsgate, and work by her side, yet not try to take it from her. That man turned out to be Baen MacColl."

"Are you content to sign this marriage contract?" the master of Grayhaven asked his eldest son. "The terms are not favorable to you."

"I'll sign it," Baen answered. "I love her, and I always will. With God's blessing Elizabeth will eventually forgive me deserting her to return to Grayhaven, Da."

"I'll want a proxy marriage performed before you depart," the master of Grayhaven said. "That way I'll know my son is protected to some extent."

"Agreed!" Logan Hepburn replied. "That way all we'll need is Father Mata's blessing at the church rail to finish it."

"And I shall be the bride," Lord Cambridge said mischievously. "I have always wanted to be the bride," he chortled.

Colin Hay looked somewhat askance, but having grown used to Thomas Bolton over the years Logan Hepburn laughed loudly. "Aye, Tom, and a lovely bride you will make, I have no doubt at all. When she ceases being angry Elizabeth will be both flattered and grateful to you."

"Elizabeth is not to know," Baen said quietly.

"What?" His father and his father-in-law, speaking in unison, looked startled by his words.

But Thomas Bolton understood. "Ah," he said. "How well you

know her, dear boy. Of course. My lips shall be sealed in the matter until I am told otherwise."

"Well, I don't understand," the master of Grayhaven said.

"Nor I," Logan Hepburn concurred. "What nonsense is this, Baen?"

"Elizabeth needs to feel that the decision to marry me is all her own. I will gladly agree to a proxy wedding here at Grayhaven for my protection, and so my father and brothers may participate. But Elizabeth is not to know. Not now. Perhaps not ever. I do not want her any angrier than I know she already is. And I do not want her feeling that her hand was forced in this matter. She is the lady of Friarsgate, and has always maintained a certain dignity. She will consent to wed me, but she must come to that conclusion by herself."

"The lass must be brought to heel immediately, Baen, or you will have no peace in your house," Logan Hepburn declared, and Colin Hay nodded in agreement.

"Have you ever been able to bring Rosamund to heel?" Baen asked wickedly.

"That's different!" Logan insisted.

"Nay, 'tis not, and Elizabeth is Rosamund's daughter," Baen said with a grin. "You have weaseled your way around your wife even as I will weasel my way about my darling Elizabeth, Logan. And I will have peace in my home as you do in yours."

The laird of Claven's Carn chuckled. "You're right, of course," he said.

"I know," Baen responded. He turned to his father. "Will you send for the priest then, Da? If he can come at once we can leave in another two days. I am anxious to get back to Friarsgate. The trip will not be easy."

The priest came the following day. The situation was explained. Father Andrew witnessed the signing of the marriage contract, and then performed the ceremony with Lord Cambridge, resplendent in his scarlet clothing, standing in for the bride. Afterwards the master of Grayhaven held a small feast in honor of the marriage just celebrated. He sat at his high board with Thomas Bolton to his right, the priest and the laird of Claven's Carn to his left. They watched as his piper played and his three sons danced to the spritely tunes, their laughter and affection for one another obvious as they vied back and forth for their father's approval. And the night came, and the hall emptied slowly until only Colin Hay and his son Baen remained, seated together by the fire, their wine cups almost empty.

"You'll not be back," the master of Grayhaven said to his firstborn.

"I know," Baen answered.

"I'm proud of you," Colin Hay said, "even if you are a mutton-headed fool. You might have been happy with your lass these last months but that you came home, lad. And for what? For me? The da who never even knew of your existence until you were already half-grown? I've never understood why your mother never told me. Why she let herself be wed to that miserable Parlan Gunn when he would not even pretend you were his and give you his name. He would have had a fine son in you, Baen."

"I think she thought it was for her parents' sake she marry Parlan," Baen replied. "They had arranged the marriage. Parlan had taken her with little dower. He had been good to them. And by pretending not to know who you were but for your Christian name she believed she was protecting you. Had Parlan known he would have extorted you, for he was a venal as well as a cruel man, Da. Only when she knew she would no longer be there to protect me did she reveal her secret, and only to me. Her parents were dead by then, and she had no one else to shield."

"I remember that day you came to my door. You were thin with your hunger, and your clothing was threadbare. But you were mine, and I never had a moment's doubt when you told me who had borne you, and mothered you," Colin Hay said, tears of remembrance in his eyes. "You flinched, I remember, when I reached out to draw you into the house. You were afraid, but you never admitted to it, lad." Reaching out, the master of Grayhaven ruffled his son's black hair, which was so like his own. "They've been good years we've shared together, lad."

"I'll miss you, Da," Baen told his father. "I'll miss Grayhaven."

"You'll have the memories, lad. Cherish them, for they are yours alone. And make new memories. This Friarsgate is a fair place, you've said."

"Aye, it is. The hills rise all about it, and the lake spreads out before it. The meadows there are greener than anywhere else I've ever been. And there is peace there, Da. A wonderful, gentle peace that enfolds it all. I have loved it since the first moment I laid eyes on it," he told his sire.

"It sounds to me like home," Colin Hay said softly.

"Aye, it is," Baen admitted.

"Then that is where you belong, lad. Not here at Grayhaven, but at Friarsgate, with a lass who loves you, and your bairns about you," his father told him.

"Will you come one day and see us, Da?" Baen asked his father.

Colin Hay shook his head. "Nay," he said. "In my youth I served in the Earl of Errol's household. While it was exciting to be involved in the king's court, I missed my home terribly. Once I returned I vowed to never again leave it. Everything I have is here. I visit now again with old Glenkirk, for he was briefly at court with his children when I was there. He enjoys speaking of the old days, as most elderly men do."

"Children? I thought the earl had but a son," Baen remarked. "Lord Adam."

"He had a daughter too once," Colin Hay said. "A beautiful fiery little lass named Janet. I begged my father to make us a match, but then they were gone from court to Europe, for the earl was an ambassador for King James. 'Tis a long story," he concluded with a smile. "Nay, I shall not go down into England, Baen, and you will not come north again, I know. We shall say our good-byes tonight, my son. Ours is not an unusual situation. Most children bid farewell to a parent at marriage, and never see them again in this life. For twenty years I have had you by my side, and it has pained me knowing I could give you nothing more but my love and respect. That everything else I had must go to Jamie because he is my legitimate son."

"He's worthy of you, Da," Baen said. "He's a good son to you, and always will be. And Gilly too. I'll miss you, but I know you'll be safe with my brothers."

"You speak as if I'm an old man," the master of Grayhaven snapped.

"You're past fifty," Baen teased him.

"Not so old that I can't appreciate a pretty lass, or give her pleasure, lad. I hope you'll have the same good fortune when you reach my age." His father chuckled. "Now speak to me of Elizabeth Meredith, for you have said so little of her."

"She is a tall girl, and slender, but rounded also," Baen began. "Her hair is like golden thistledown, and her eyes are a hazel-green. She has a little nose, but slim. And a mouth that was surely made for kissing. She is wise, and her people love her. She loves the land too, Da, with a passion I am almost jealous of but that she loved me the same way too. But Elizabeth is stubborn, and she can be determined beyond anyone I have ever known. I can well believe she was prepared to raise our child alone, for she has no fear of anyone or anything except perhaps the Lord God."

"I am sorry then that I shall never meet her," Colin Hay said. "She sounds like a most worthy young woman. I can hear in your voice how much you love her, Baen. But do not allow her to overrule you, lest that love be killed."

"It will take time to regain her trust," Baen said slowly, "but I believe her love for me has not wavered."

"You will soon know, but for good or evil she is now your wife," his father answered. And then Colin Hay stood up. "I'm going to bed," he announced.

"Will you see us off in the morning?" Baen asked his father. "We leave at dawn."

"Aye," the master of Grayhaven told his son. "I will see you off." Then he turned abruptly and left the hall.

Baen watched him go. He sighed, and then he too departed the hall to find his bed, for the dawn would come sooner than later. And it did. It seemed to him he had scarce laid his head down when Jamie was shaking him awake. Groaning, he pulled himself from the bed in the chamber he and his brothers had shared. Jamie was a morning person, but Gilly was not. Swearing under his breath, he muttered at his brother for waking him so soon.

"Baen will be leaving," Jamie explained. "Do ye not want to bid our brother farewell? Will we ever see him again? Get up!"

Baen listened to them squabbling back and forth as he washed, scraping the beard from his face, for Elizabeth liked him clean-shaven. It would be many days before he saw her, but he was already eager for the sight of her. He ran the wooden comb through his unruly locks, then pulled on the rest of his garments, dressing warmly, for the ride would be a long one today, and who knew where they would shelter this night. Then, his brothers trailing in his wake, Baen hurried down into the hall.

The servants were already bringing the meal to the board. Trenchers of fresh-baked bread filled with hot oat stirabout. A platter of ham, poached eggs, cottage loaf, butter, and a sweet berry jam. Logan Hepburn and Lord Cambridge entered the hall to join them. There was yet no sign of Colin Hay. They ate heartily, quaffing down mugs of ale along with their food. And when they had finished, the master of Grayhaven came into the hall, dressed for riding.

"I'll go with you a few miles to the edge of my lands," he said. "I ate earlier."

"Then we'd best get started," Baen responded, touched that his father would ride with him. "I'll see to the loading of the lambs into the cart."

"I'll help," Gilbert Hay said.

Within a short time they were ready. Several shepherds would go with them as far as the borderlands. A messenger would be sent ahead so that when they arrived there would be Friarsgate men waiting to take over. It would be many days, however, before they got there. Baen bade his brothers a tender farewell, embracing them each a final time.

"Now you can be certain 'tis all yours," he murmured to James.

"You knew?" James Hay was surprised.

"I would have felt the same way if our positions had been reversed; but had I remained here, Jamie, my loyalty would have always been to Da, and then you," Baen told him. "Now you're the eldest."

"You're a good man," James Hay said, "and while I always knew it . . ." He paused.

Baen nodded, then turned to his youngest brother. "Now, youngster, I expect you to behave yourself, obey our da, and Jamie when his counsel is good. Try not to spread your seed about too much, for I know how much you like the lasses, and that you are already a father several times over," he teased.

"I don't want you to go," Gilbert Hay said in a muffled voice. There had never been a time in his sixteen years when Baen hadn't been there for him.

"You're not Da. Come down into England and see me," Baen told the lad. Then he hugged him hard.

Gilbert Hay nodded, and then, turning, he ran off before they could see him cry. James Hay stood quietly as the men mounted their horses. He raised his hand in farewell as they moved off. The flock of sheep and the wagon carrying the lambs had already gone ahead. He watched as they rode slowly away, smiling as Baen turned once to raise his own hand to salute his brother. James looked relieved, Baen thought, smiling. As if he could not be certain his oldest brother was gone until he had seen him ride off.

They were fortunate in the weather, for spring was coming. They managed to leave the Highlands behind after several long days of travel. There was no new snow to impede their progress, although one day they traveled in an icy mist for hours. Lord Cambridge, usually amusing, was not that day. At the boundary of his lands Colin Hay bade them a final farewell. He embraced his son one last time, and there were tears in his eyes. Then, with a nod, he turned and rode away. He would never again speak to anyone of the son he had sired on a cotter's daughter one summer's afternoon in the fragrant heather. The memories of Baen would always be painful to him, for he loved this eldest son of his, bastard or not, best of all. But his conscience was clear, for Baen would now have a good life. "You'd be proud of him, Tora," he said softly as he rode away.

The travelers were both careful and fortunate in their accommodations, staying at either religious houses or farmhouses each night. Their generous donations, paid in advance, assured their welcome, allowing them to keep the flocks safe. Each evening when they stopped they would unload the lambs from the cart. The little creatures would scamper off, bleating for their mothers and, finding them, settle down to suckle contentedly. They crossed from the east side of Scotland to the west as they traveled south towards England.

And then finally the terrain began to look more familiar to Logan Hepburn. "We're on my lands now," he said suddenly one afternoon as they rode.

"Dear boy, how can you tell?" Lord Cambridge wanted to know. This had probably been the worst adventure he had ever undertaken, and he silently vowed that other than an occasional trip to Friarsgate he would not ever travel again. Never in his life had he been so dirty. Never in his life had his garments stunk so completely. "Are we near Claven's Carn?" he asked hopefully.

"It will be near dark, but aye, we can reach it by nightfall," the laird of Claven's Carn said, and he smiled. Rosamund. His warm and loving wife would be waiting. He would sleep in his own bed at long last. He was flea-bitten from the bedding they had been offered in their travels. He preferred the warmer months, when a man could sleep on the moors on the sweet grass or in the fragrant heather. Raising a hand, he signaled to one of his clansmen, who rode up next to his chieftain. "Ride ahead, and tell the lady Rosamund that we will be home for supper," he said.

The clansman nodded, and then rode off.

Logan turned to Baen. "Tomorrow we'll ride on to Friarsgate. The shepherds can come more slowly. It's important you and Elizabeth settle your differences as soon as possible. The bairn should be born happy."

"With your permission I will send my father's people back from Claven's Carn," Baen answered him. "The sheep can remain in your care until I can get my own Friarsgate shepherds to fetch them."

"Aye, 'tis a more practical idea than changing the guard at the border," Logan agreed. He noted the new proprietary tone of Baen's voice, and smiled to himself. This man might give all due respect to his prickly stepdaughter, but he would be the lord of Friarsgate in the end.

"You sent a messenger to dear Rosamund?" Lord Cambridge queried.

"You will have a fine dinner, Tom, and a comfortable bed in which to sleep tonight," Logan promised him with a grin.

"It had best not be too comfortable or I shall never arise from it," Thomas Bolton said almost irritably. "I want to go home to Otterly."

"You're closer now, Tom, than you were several weeks ago," Baen remarked, and he too grinned. "Just a few more days, my friend, and you will be safe back in that nest of your own making. I hope you will invite Elizabeth and me for a visit soon."

"Not too soon," Lord Cambridge said tartly. "It will take me weeks to recover from this little adventure we have had. But I do believe I was a great help in convincing your dear rugged father to release you to Elizabeth. And I did make a most delightful bride, although none, alas, shall ever know it. Once again I have done my dear cousin Rosamund a great service, and saved the day for the last of her daughters."

His two companions laughed, and Thomas Bolton joined them. They were all feeling much better with the sudden realization that the worst of their journey was now almost over. Within the next few days it would all be settled. Elizabeth and Baen were united in matrimony, and the next generation to the Friarsgate inheritance could be born with no stain on his or her escutcheon.

There was, of course, the temptation to ride ahead in order to reach Claven's Carn sooner, but mindful of the flock of sheep they traveled with, Logan kept no more than the same daily pace they had done each day. The sun had already sunk behind the western horizon when they finally reached the laird's keep. The sheep were driven into a safe enclosure and the lambs unloaded to find their mothers before the three men entered the dwelling, walking slowly into the hall. The Hepburn sons looked up, delighted to see that their father had returned. They rushed forward to greet him.

Rosamund came forward, a smile of pleasure upon her beautiful face. She walked directly into her husband's arms, taking his face between her two hands and kissing him. "Welcome home, my lord. You have been successful, I see, and brought me a new son-in-law." She stepped away from him now. "Tom!" She hugged her cousin, kissing his cheek. "Thank you!"

"Darling girl, you have no idea what I have gone through for you in order to give dearest Elizabeth the happy ending she is entitled to have," he told her. "I am tired. I am dirty, and the garments I wear will give the fire pause when I dispose of them. But, aye, we have been successful, and brought the bridegroom home." He kissed both of her cheeks, and stepped back with a satisfied smile.

Rosamund now turned to Baen. "Do you love her?" she asked him bluntly.

"Aye," he answered without hesitation. "I did from the first."

"Good," Rosamund answered him. "You will need the patience of a saint to deal with my daughter until her ire at your departure last October can be cooled. She did not want us fetching you, foolish girl. But I will not have my grandchild born on the wrong side of the blanket."

"He will not be," Baen answered her.

"So"—Rosamund smiled—"you are convinced you got a son on her."

"The Hays have the tendency to throw lads, madame," Baen told her.

Rosamund laughed. Then she said, " 'Tis no longer MacColl?"

"My father has asked that I be Baen Hay, and I am happy to honor his wish now. Hay is a better border name," Baen answered, "though some may call me the MacColl."

"Aye, a wise man," Rosamund agreed.

The servants brought in the food, and Rosamund led the men to the high board. They ate a hearty well-cooked meal, and afterwards the mistress of Claven's Carn moved to her cousin's side and murmured something in his ear. Tom Bolton's face was suddenly wreathed in smiles. He hugged her and hurried from the hall.

"What did you say to him?" Logan asked his wife.

"I told him if he would follow Tod he would be led to the kitchens, where a hot tub was awaiting him. He will also find fresh clothing. Perhaps not to his taste, and certainly not stylish enough, but clean. He'll have no choice, for as soon as he doffs his garments I have given orders that they be burned immediately," she told her husband.

Logan and Baen burst out laughing, but their laughter was short-lived.

"And when Tom has finished his ablutions, Baen will use the water next, and then you, my darling Logan," Rosamund told them. "You will not infest my clean beds with your nits and fleas. And I will be washing your heads," she said firmly. "Now I must go to the kitchens, for Tom will surely be ready for me." And she bustled off.

"So you love her," Logan murmured. " 'Tis a good thing, for these

Friarsgate women are strong-minded and willful. There is little use in arguing with them."

Baen chuckled. "My stepmother, Ellen, was much like that," he said. "Da adored her, though he had his other women now and again."

"I wouldn't advise you to follow his example," Logan warned.

"Nay, my da married Ellen for sons. She was his third wife. But he did respect her, and they were fond of each other. She knew when he strayed, but she also knew he would come home again, and nothing would change. It is different for me. I love Elizabeth Meredith with every fiber of my being. There can be no other woman for me."

"I'm glad to hear you say it. I have no daughters of my blood, but Elizabeth was just a little girl when I married her mother. She does not recall her own father, and I think of her as I would my own child," Logan said. "I want her happy."

"So do I," Baen replied, "but even I know it will take time to regain her trust again. I know now that I've been a fool."

"Aye," Logan drawled, "you have. Be sure and tell her that. Women like it when a man admits he has made an error in judgment. It makes them feel so wise and so justified in their own actions."

A servant came to tell Baen that the mistress was ready for him now. Baen did not argue, but followed the man to the kitchens. Without a murmur, he stripped off his clothing and climbed into the tall oak tub. To his surprise the water was still quite hot. Rosamund handed him a cloth and soap. Then, climbing up on the tub steps, she plied a brush until he thought she would scrub the skin off his body. Finally she washed his thick, dark hair, her fingers digging into his scalp, swiftly pulling the nits from his black locks.

"Well," Rosamund finally said, "you're finished. At least you won't stink when you wed my daughter. I'll ride with you tomorrow to Friarsgate. Elizabeth is in a rather prickly mood these days," she informed him.

"Is she well?" he asked anxiously as he climbed from the tub and she wrapped a piece of toweling about him.

"Aye, she carries the bairn easily," Rosamund told him. She handed him a clean linen shirt with which to clothe himself, and a pair of dark-colored breeks.

He pulled the garments on gratefully. "Madame, I thank you," he said.

"Send my husband down," she told him with a grin. He had big feet, she noted, but then he was a big man with a big heart. Elizabeth was a fortunate girl, although right now she knew her daughter was not thinking kindly of her Scot.

Baen made his way back to the hall, informing his host that his wife awaited him in the kitchens. Then he was led by a servant to a bed-chamber, where he found Thomas Bolton snoring on a trundle. He had obviously left the bed for the larger man. Baen fell into it and was quickly asleep. He did not dream.

They departed Claven's Carn in the early morning even before the sunrise, although the sky about them was already light with the com-ing day. With hard riding they would reach Friarsgate in early evening. Now Baen was anxious to arrive at his destination. Thomas Bolton considered that in another two or three days he would be back at Ot-terly. As for Logan Hepburn, he was anxious to conclude this business with his stepdaughter and return home with his wife. With Rosamund's three daughters all safely wed, his life would shortly return to normal. They did not spare the horses, stopping briefly at midday to rest them, and to eat and relieve themselves.

There was just the barest hint of warmth in the air as they rode. The skies above them were a flat and cloudless blue. The sun was warm upon their shoulders. The hills about them were beginning to show patches of new green amid their winter browns. The day waned, and the sun began to sink beneath the western horizon. Reds, oranges, and golds mingled together in a glorious daub of fiery colors. Pink and mauve clouds edged with golden light drifted over-head, and now there was no breeze stirring at all. Finally the skies above them began to fade into a deeper and deeper blue. And then below them as they topped the hills the twinkling lights of Friarsgate shone in welcome.

They stopped for a moment, and seeing Baen's face Rosamund knew that Friarsgate would be in safe hands as long as he stood by Eliz-abeth's side. The look upon his handsome countenance was one of pure love. His eyes swept over the meadows, the house, the lake, with something akin to joy, as if he could not believe he was here at last, and here to stay forevermore.

"We did not send a messenger ahead," Rosamund said quietly.

Baen turned, flashing her a grin. "You want my arrival to be a surprise," he said.

"I thought it best," Rosamund replied. "She will be in the hall, and cannot hide away from you if we arrive unannounced. I will want the wedding tomorrow, Baen. The quicker it is over and done with the better for Elizabeth, and for you."

"Aye. Whatever we have to settle between us will be best done when we are finally wed," he agreed.

"My dear Rosamund, may we please continue on," Lord Cambridge said in a voice that bordered on the pitiful. "My poor bottom has finally revolted with my weeks in the saddle, and I want my supper!"

With a chuckle she waved them on and they descended the hill to the house.

# Chapter 14

$\mathscr{E}$lizabeth Meredith looked up, startled, at the noisy entrance into her hall. She flushed upon seeing Baen MacColl, and struggled to her feet. "So," she said scathingly. "They have managed to drag you from your father's side. Well, you have wasted your time. I've decided I'll not have you. Our handfast charade will have to do until it expires, and I will raise my own bairn without your help. Go away!"

Baen looked at Elizabeth with her big belly and thought her the most beautiful woman in the world. He walked swiftly to her, sweeping her into his arms and giving her a long, satisfying kiss. "I have never missed anyone in my life the way I have missed you, Elizabeth."

She reared back with surprising agility for a woman in her condition. Her small hand flashed out, smacking his cheek. "You dare? You dare to kiss me, you rogue!" Her voice had a very sharp edge to it. "I told you if you left me to not return! I hate you!"

"Dearest girl, do not say it!" Lord Cambridge cried, his gloved hand flying to his heart in a gesture of deep destress. "I have traveled for weeks now into the icy winter Highlands and back to restore this fellow to you. Do not, I plead with you, tell me that it has all been in vain." He sank into a chair, reaching out for the goblet of wine a servant brought him.

The barest of smiles flitted across Elizabeth Meredith's face, and then it was gone. "You mock me, Uncle," she responded. "Have I not said from the moment I knew I carried this bairn that I was capable of raising my child alone? I do not need this man."

"What?" Baen said. "You seduce me, you vixen, let me go away, and now you play the injured party? You have boldly used me to get an heir for Friarsgate, Elizabeth, but the bairn is mine as well as yours. 'Twas my seed that took root in your womb."

"Impudent bastard!" Elizabeth cried. "You did not cry off when I seduced you!"

He caught her hand and kissed it, drawing it to his heart. "I would have been a bigger fool than I have been, Elizabeth, had I refused you," he told her, his gray eyes twinkling at her.

She snatched her hand from his gentle grasp. "Villain! Scots knave! Scroundrel and blackguard!" She hurled the epithets at him.

"Did you not call me something similar once?" Logan Hepburn remarked to his wife wryly.

"Aye, I believe I did," she cooed back at him with a grin.

"I am going to bed!" Elizabeth said furiously.

"You most certainly are not!" Rosamund countered. "You are going to sit at your high board with your husband by your side and see we are decently fed. We have ridden all day on a handful of oatcakes and are hungry, my daughter."

"He is not my husband!" Elizabeth shrieked.

"Did you or did you not handfast with him last summer?" Rosamund said.

Elizabeth glared at her mother sullenly. "Aye," she muttered. "But a handfast isn't a real marriage. 'Tis just a promise to marry, and I've changed my mind."

"Well, I haven't," Rosamund said. "Tomorrow morning Father Mata will formalize the union you contracted with Baen MacColl while in the throes of your lust on a summer's night. My grandson will be born on the proper side of the blanket, for he is the next heir to Friarsgate, damn it!"

"How can you be certain 'tis a lad?" Elizabeth snapped.

"Because Hays usually throw sons," Baen said to her. He put a hard arm about her thickened waist, drawing her close to him, and his big hand caressed her belly, feeling the child within move strongly as he did so. He grinned, pleased. "Aye, 'tis a lad," he said. " 'Tis our son you carry, Elizabeth. Yours and mine."

She had felt the child inside her move with the touch of its father's hand. For a moment feelings of tenderness threatened to overwhelm her, but then Elizabeth hardened her heart against him once more. "You'll never have Friarsgate," she snarled at him.

"I don't want it," he replied. "I want you. I want our son and the other children we will have. Friarsgate is yours. You are its lady, and nothing can change that."

"A husband can change that," she said. "Do you think I am a fool, and do not know the law, Baen? A woman becomes chattel once in the hands of a man. My mother suffered that, but she escaped. I will not be any man's possession!"

"Sit down, Elizabeth," Rosamund told her daughter. "Sit down and read the marriage contract that Baen willingly signed, and that you must now sign." She turned at the sound of a familiar footfall as her daughter sank heavily into a cushioned chair. "Ah, Mata, here you are. Come and witness Elizabeth's signature. You will perform the marriage in the morning. Logan and I want to return home as quickly as possible. We have left the boys alone, and the boys do quarrel when we are not there to mediate."

Elizabeth had spread the parchment out into what now passed for her lap. Her hazel-green eyes scanned the document. Baen was to hold the position of her steward, which was, she thought, honestly fair, but other than that nothing was to change. Friarsgate remained hers, and hers alone. And if she died it returned to her mother or her heir. Relief poured through her, and her heart stopped hammering in her chest. She drew a deep breath and said, "Someone find me a quill with which to sign this." She arose and went to her place at the high board. When the inked quill was brought to her she signed the marriage contract, sanding it afterwards to fix her signature. She said nothing more, affixing her seal into the hot wax she poured on the document. Then she shoved it towards the manor priest. "Keep it safe, good Father Mata," she told him.

The meal was now brought to the table, and Elizabeth was surprised at the bounty of her board, for her guests had not sent a messenger ahead. It was obvious that her servants had been expecting company, even if she had not been. Baen took his place at her right hand. She glanced at him from beneath her thick lashes. He was so handsome. She wondered if their son—their child, she corrected herself—would look like him. She had noted the name of her bridegroom on the marriage document. Baen MacColl Hay. So he was at last taking his father's surname. Hay, she decided, would be a less contentious name here in the borders.

He watched her carefully during the meal. Her appetite was good, he was relieved to see. The bairn would be born strong and healthy from a mother who ate as Elizabeth did. But then, she had always had an appetite that surprised him on a woman. He noted she watered her wine heavily. Curious, he thought.

When she saw his interest she said, "Pure wine does not agree with me now."

They were the only words she spoke directly to him during the evening.

After the meal, when they all sat together by the fire, Elizabeth said, "We must send for Edmund and Maybel. I cannot wed without them by my side. They were with you at my birth, Mama. They should be here when I marry."

"Send to them tonight then," Rosamund said. "I will not linger another day."

"Nor I," Lord Cambridge said. "Another day of hard riding, and I can be home at Otterly tomorrow night. I have missed my Will, and I have missed my home. I want my own bed, and meals to please my palate, and long days in my library. I shall have to undo everything dear Will has done in my absence, for he will not have cataloged to suit me. And I shall have to do it surreptitiously, lest I hurt his feelings. In the end he will believe he has done it all for me, and I shall thank him profusely."

Elizabeth laughed. "Uncle, you are ever the sly fox." Then she slowly rose to her feet. "Now I have done all that is required of me I shall depart to my bed. Good night."

"Shall you join her?" Thomas Bolton asked mischievously of Baen when he believed Elizabeth was out of their hearing. His amber-brown eyes twinkled.

"I think it wise I wait until Elizabeth asks me back into her bed," Baen answered.

"Never!" Elizabeth snapped, for her hearing was very sharp and then she was gone.

Logan chuckled.

"I think you are very prudent," Rosamund told him, throwing an annoyed glance towards her husband. "No matter what the marriage contract says, you must convince my daughter that you will keep to your bargain. And then when she has stopped spitting at you like an angry cat you will have to woo her all over again. But when you win her for good, Baen, it will be a victory worth having, I promise you."

"Aye," Baen told his mother-in-law. "Elizabeth is an incredible prize, lady, and well I know it. But she has never been easy."

His companions laughed, and Rosamund admitted, "Nay, she never has." Then she signaled to Albert, who hurried to her side. "Has the lady sent a messenger to Edmund and Maybel's cottage?" she asked him.

"Yes, m'lady, on her way to her chamber," the hall steward replied.

"Then we may retire too," Rosamund said. "Baen, you know where Elizabeth's chamber is, of course. Sleep in the room next to hers. The one before her door," she said. "It has a connecting door for the time when you are forgiven," Rosamund concluded with a small smile.

He nodded, and then replied, "I will see to the house then, madame."

"That is as it should be," she told him, and with a nod of her head turned away, taking Logan's arm as they exited the hall.

"Well, dear boy, 'tis almost done now," Lord Cambridge said. "You are the perfect husband for her. I knew it from the beginning."

Baen laughed and sat down opposite the older man. "You are a fraud, Tom," he told him. "You hoped for one of those overbred gentlemen of the court, not the bastard of a Highland chieftain. But I thank you for your kind words."

"I considered the possibility of a nobler match," Lord Cambridge admitted, "but the truth is there are more bastards at court, and while their blood is finer by far than yours, you are the nobler man, Baen. The moment I realized it I strove for a match between you and Elizabeth. You surely knew you had my approval and my cousin's."

"I knew," Baen answered him quietly.

"I admire your loyalty and devotion to the master of Grayhaven. I hope you will now transfer those same emotions to Elizabeth. If you had only come to me and asked, I should have arranged for the family to speak with your father. But Elizabeth was no better, and she was childish in her unspoken insistence that you choose between her and your sire," Lord Cambridge said. "Why did you not speak out?"

Baen sighed. "I did not really feel I was worthy of the heiress of Friarsgate," he replied. "As much as I loved her I thought she should seek a greater name than mine."

"Yet you allowed her to seduce you, which you had to know she did to keep you by her side," Thomas Bolton remarked.

Again the tall Scot sighed. "It was dishonorable of me, I know, but I could not resist her. I have never known a woman who could bring my blood to a boil, but she can. I will never leave her again, Tom," Baen promised.

"Dear, dear boy," Lord Cambridge said with a smile, "it is most unlikely my darling Elizabeth will let you. She is certain to punish you for what she deems your disloyalty, but in time she can be brought around. No one is happier than I that this situation has resolved itself so well, but then I knew it would. I have successfully settled a trio of headstrong girls. I can hardly believe it of myself." He stood. "Good night, dear boy! I will see you in the morning." And Thomas Bolton almost skipped from the hall, so pleased was he with how everything had turned out.

Watching him go, Baen smiled. Lord Cambridge would always remain his favorite uncle, he thought, chuckling to himself. He arose and made his rounds, seeing that the fires were all banked and the candles snuffed but for the taper he carried. Then, climbing the stairs, he found his chamber and went to bed. He was awakened even before the sunrise by the hall steward, Albert, shaking his shoulder gently.

"Master, 'tis time to arise. The lady has ordered the ceremony be said directly after prime, and 'tis in but half an hour," Albert told Baen.

Baen swung his long legs over the bed and sat for a moment, gathering his thoughts. "Are there any flowers in the meadow or on the hillside yet?" he asked.

"Nay, master, but there is a bit of dried white heather hanging in the pantry," Albert answered.

"Find Nancy, and ask her if she can spare a blue ribbon. She is not to tell her mistress, Albert. I would surprise my bride."

"I understand, master," the older man said. He was pleased that his mistress was to marry the Scot today. The Friarsgate folk had come to like and respect him. He hurried from the bedchamber to do Baen's bidding.

Finding a pitcher of water in the warm ashes, Baen washed himself as best he could, and then dressed himself in his best breeches, carefully tucking his linen shirt into the waist of the garment. He did not own a doublet, but he donned his sleeveless leather jerkin with the horn buttons. Over it he set a length of red-black-and-yellow Hay plaid, pinning to it the clan badge his father had given him when he turned sixteen. The falcon on it had garnet eyes. He found his boots had been cleaned, and drew them on, pleased. He might not be an elegant gentleman of a noble house, but he would make Elizabeth a presentable husband nonetheless. Running his fingers through his thick locks to neaten them, he left the bedchamber and proceeded to the hall.

"You are prompt," Elizabeth greeted him. She was wearing a pale blue velvet gown with an extra panel in it. It had puffed sleeves tied with cream-colored ribbons. Her breasts, fuller than he recalled, swelled dangerously over the neckline. Her belly could not be hidden. Her lovely blond hair was pulled back and twisted into a soft knot affixed with silver hairpins at the nape of her graceful neck. She wore a pearl-trimmed French cap atop her head, and about her neck a rope of large pearls.

"So are you," he replied. "How lovely you look this morning."

She colored but then said in a sharp tone, "Do not think you can wheedle me, sir. You deserted me, and came back only because you were dragged. Will you run back to Scotland once the priest has wed us?"

"I will remain by your side always, Elizabeth," he responded. "And I did not desert you, which you well know. I never made any pretext of remaining at Friarsgate. You knew I had to return to Grayhaven," he said.

"I was with child!" she cried.

"A fact you were not even aware of at the time," he countered. "You could have written to me. I do read and write, as you know."

"I hate you!" she muttered angrily.

"And I love you," he told her.

"Master?" Albert was at his side. In his hand was a bouquet made from three sprigs of dried white heather tied with a blue ribbon.

"Thank you," Baen said. Then, turning to Elizabeth, he handed her the bouquet. " 'Tis the best we can do. Nothing is yet in bloom. I don't even know the month now."

She took his offering, gazing at it, tears coming to her eyes, which she hurriedly blinked back. " 'Tis April," she said low. "April fifth."

"A good month, and a good day for a wedding," Baen told her.

"Ah, here you are," Logan Hepburn said, coming into the hall. "I have come to lead you to the church, Elizabeth. With your permission, of course. Rosamund and Tom are waiting for you in the hall," he said to Baen.

When the bridegroom had departed Elizabeth held out her little bouquet to her stepfather. "I want to hate him," she said, "and then he goes and finds a way to bring me a bridal posy. How could he, Logan? How dare he be kind to me? He's only marrying me because you and Uncle Thomas dragged him back here."

"He's marrying you because he loves you, Bessie," Logan told the girl.

"Don't call me Bessie!" she sobbed.

He took her by the arm. "Come along, you impossible little shrew. The priest is waiting. Baen loves you, Elizabeth. Do not be foolish, and do not be so stubborn that you will not admit to be true what you know in your heart is true." And the laird of Claven's Carn firmly led her from the hall.

The day was gray and chill as they walked from the house to the little church. The hills were shrouded in a silvery mist. It hung above the waters of the lake like bits of torn, thin pieces of fabric. There was no wind at all, and the lake itself was like dark glass. Reaching the church Logan stopped outside of it to allow Elizabeth to compose herself, for she was still sobbing intermittently.

Finally he asked her, "Are you ready now?"

The girl nodded and swallowed her last sob. Within her the baby turned, and her hand went to her belly in a protective gesture.

Inside the church Rosemund, Lord Cambridge, Maybel, Edmund, Albert, Nancy, and Friar were waiting. The laird of Claven's Carn led his stepdaughter to her bridegroom and then joined his wife. Father Mata began by offering up the first holy office of the day, which was called prime. When he had concluded the short service he set about to marry the young couple before him. Elizabeth let her gaze wander, looking at the beautiful stained-glass windows her mother had commissioned for the church. If the day had been a bright one they would have reflected their myriad colors about the stone walls and floor of the small edifice. Baen squeezed her hand gently, and she was drawn back to the service. She realized the ceremony was coming to an end, yet she did not recall giving any responses. But she must have, or the priest would not now be wrapping their hands together with the holy cloth, blessing them, declaring them husband and wife. But he was. She flushed to think that, while she had been here, she remembered little of her own wedding.

"You may give your wife the kiss of peace," Father Mata said solemnly.

Baen gently brushed her lips with his own, his hands holding her shoulders as he did so. "Wife," he said low.

Elizabeth did not answer him. She wasn't ready for this. Why had she let them force her to the altar? She grew pale and swayed slightly. His arm went about her.

"Put your hand in mine, Elizabeth," he said. "You need your breakfast. Our son is hungry. That is all it is." Then he led her out from the church, and they walked slowly back to the house.

When they had gained the hall again he seated her at the high board, calling to Albert to bring them food immediately. Rosamund came and sat next to her daughter, taking Elizabeth's cold hand in her own and warming it. Baen put a goblet of cider to her lips, and she drank thirstily, her eyes meeting his, then quickly looking away.

"Mama?" Elizabeth's usually strong voice quavered.

"You are fine, Bess . . . Elizabeth," her mother said. "Your bodice is too tight, and you are hungry." She reached behind the girl to loosen her laces. "There. That should help. A woman in your condition cannot be too fashionable, even on her wedding day." She smiled at her youngest daughter and stroked her cheek.

Elizabeth nodded, grateful, and drew a long, deep breath. She was beginning to feel warmer again. The sweet cider was settling her belly. She was appalled at having shown such weakness before Baen. He must never think she was one of those fragile creatures who must be managed for their own good. "I am better now," she said in her usual strong voice. "Albert, the breakfast. My guests must leave soon if they are to gain their own homes by nightfall."

The servants dashed into the hall with their platters and bowls. Trenchers of oat stirabout were placed before each of them. Today the hot oats were dressed with cinnamon and sweet raisins. A platter of eggs poached with a dilled cream sauce was brought, and another of sweet country ham. There was cheese, butter, jam, and newly baked cottage loaves still warm from the ovens. Wine, ale, and cider were offered.

Logan Hepburn raised a toast to his stepdaughter and her husband, wishing them a long life together and many healthy children. Lord Cambridge stood next, raising his goblet to "a task well done." Even Elizabeth couldn't help but smile at his remark. Edmund stood, saying he and Maybel had seen Elizabeth born, and were happy they were alive to see her married and soon a mother. But finally the meal was over. It was almost half after eight, and the wedding guests prepared to leave Friarsgate. Elizabeth and Baen walked their guests outside. A light rain had begun to fall.

Lord Cambridge shuddered with his displeasure as he embraced his niece. "My dear girl, he is really quite a beautiful man. Do take good care of him. And make your peace as soon as possible, for your sake and the child's." He kissed her on both cheeks, holding her just a moment more against him. Then his amber eyes looked down into her face. "You chose well, Elizabeth, and he was your choice."

"I wish you weren't going," she told him, almost childlike.

"Dearest girl, if I am gone much longer Will will think I have deserted him. No! I must go home. I am not a young man, Elizabeth, though there are few to whom I should admit such a thing. It has been a long, hard winter on your behalf. Now it is up to you." He kissed her again, this time upon her forehead, and, turning away, mounted his horse. Thomas Bolton was at once surrounded by the Friarsgate men-at-arms who would accompany him in safety over the hills home to Otterly. "Rosamund, my darling girl, adieu. Dear Logan, your companionship was delightful. Baen, take care of the heiress. Now I must leave you all. Farewell! Farewell!" His horse moved away from them, and with his troop about him Lord Cambridge turned eager eyes towards Otterly.

"Darling, I will be back in a few weeks," Rosamund told her daughter. "By my calculations you should deliver your child in mid-June. I shall return at the end of May. Baen, do not permit her to work too hard now that you are here."

"I am perfectly capable of managing my lands," Elizabeth snapped.

"Of course you are," Rosamund agreed, "but the bairn cannot take the strain of your dashing about now. You must rest until he comes."

"Like you did?" Elizabeth said candidly.

Rosamund laughed. "Try," she said, embracing her daughter.

"Listen, if only this once, to your mother, Elizabeth," Logan Hepburn said. Then he helped his wife into the saddle before climbing upon his own horse. Immediately the Hepburn clansmen joined them. "Remember," he told the bride standing by his stirrup, "that he is allowed to beat you, but you may not beat him."

Elizabeth gasped, and then, realizing he was teasing her, giggled.

"Ah," Logan said, "that's better, lass. You've been too dour this morning, but I am heartened that you see me off with a smile. Baen, take care of her. God bless you both," the laird of Claven's Carn said, and then he signaled his party to move off.

Elizabeth and her bridegroom stood in the doorway of the house and watched for a few minutes as the last of their guests rode off. Inside the hall again Maybel and Edmund joined them. Edmund looked considerably better with the spring than he had in many weeks. But his arm still hung useless by his side.

"Come by the fire," Elizabeth coaxed them both. "I am sorry to have sent to you so late last night, but Mama insisted the wedding be celebrated early this morning so she might return to Claven's Carn.

Edmund, my husband will now hold the stewardship of the estate, according to the marriage contract. Will you guide and advise him? I am still the final authority, however," she reminded them all.

Edmund nodded. "I'll come tomorrow," he said.

"No," Baen told him. "I'll come to your cottage, if you do not mind. I would like to ride out to see the flocks, and it is time to count the new lambs."

Edmund nodded. "You're always welcome, Baen," he told the younger man.

Maybel and Elizabeth were speaking in low tones as the men discussed estate matters. After a time Albert came to say the cart was waiting to transport the senior Boltons home to their cottage. The little dwelling was within easy walking distance of the main house, but Edmund was not strong enough to walk it now. The elderly couple departed, wishing the newlyweds happiness.

When they had gone Elizabeth said tartly, "The deed is now done. We are not nobility to waste our day in celebration. There is work to be completed."

"I agree," he told her. "But first we should remove our wedding finery."

She nodded. "Aye. We have no coin to waste on frills and furbelows, sir."

They walked up the stairs to their bedchambers.

Elizabeth was surprised to find him in the room next to hers. "You are here?" she said. "Who said you might sleep here?"

"Your mother," he told her, "but if you would prefer I choose another chamber I will do so, Elizabeth."

She appeared to be considering his words, but then she said, "Nay. It matters not to me where you lay your head. I ask only one thing of you, Baen. Do not futter your light skirts there. Take them to the barns."

"Like you took me?" he said wickedly. "And you know well, Elizabeth, that I have had no other Friarsgate woman but you."

"But you have had other women," she pressed him.

"Aye. I am ten years your senior, and no monk," he replied.

"Well, I don't care if you have other women," she told him.

"Aye, you do," he said with a teasing grin. "But I have excellent self-control, wife. Until you are ready to share yourself with me again I shall remain celibate."

"I will never lie with you again!" she insisted heatedly.

"Aye, you will," he taunted her. "I love you, Elizabeth Meredith Hay, even if you did use me deliberately to get an heir."

"Aye, I did!" she told him.

He laughed. "You are a poor liar, wife. You only wanted your pleasure."

"And you are wasting the morning in argument with me when you should be working," Elizabeth said. Then she slammed angrily into her chamber to change her garments. She couldn't wait to get out of her wedding gown. She longed to get into the large, loose garment she had taken to wearing since her belly had burgeoned. It would soon be time for the plowing. The frost was not yet out of the fields, but almost. She needed to decide which fields would be planted with what particular grain. It was good she had learned to rotate her crops, lest the earth be made useless. Nancy silently helped Elizabeth with her clothing. The young tiring woman had learned when to speak and when her mistress was brooding.

"This day is no different from any other," Elizabeth informed Nancy as the servant, standing behind her, tied the neck of her gown closed. "I'll be in my library."

"Yes, mistress," Nancy replied as Elizabeth hurried from her chamber. She looked about the room. Was the master to sleep in here with his wife? She wasn't certain, but she decided to change the sheets and freshen the bed nonetheless.

Elizabeth had gone immediately to her library, which served as her workroom. A warm fire burned in the hearth, and the room was quite cozy. *I will sit by the fire for just a few moments*, she thought. Outside, the rain was now falling heavily, and she wished her guests had not been in such a hurry to depart. But it was April, and April was known to be a wet month. She put her feet towards the flames, and felt the soles warming.

She was married. Married to Baen MacColl. Hay, she corrected herself silently. No matter what she had said, Elizabeth was relieved that there would be no question about the legitimacy of the child in her belly. It was the next heir to Friarsgate. Unless, of course, it was an heiress, because Baen was never going to get into her bed again. He had served his purpose, and gained her as a wife for his trouble. Eventually he would realize she was quite serious in her intent not to cohabit with him, and he would take a mistress.

No! He would not! She would not let him. The thought of another woman lying in his strong arms, tasting his heady kisses, sent a wave of jealousy rolling over her. No! If she was to be celibate, then so must he. Despite what he claimed to her, to all who would listen, he had wanted Friarsgate. She was certain of it. How could he not want it? What a coup for the bastard of a Highland chieftain with nothing to recommend him but his handsome face. Well, he had Friarsgate now. Not quite as he had anticipated it, she was certain, but he would ride about the estate and be called master by her folk. His child would inherit it one day.

She rose heavily and seated herself behind the large table she used when she was working. Drawing out a map of her fields, she studied them carefully, deciding which field would be planted with what crop. They were going to need more hay this year, she decided, marking the meadows that would grow it. Three fields to the west she decided to have planted with rye to replenish the soil there. Corn would go here, barley, and wheat there, she marked the fields. And several fields would be left to grow onions and shallots; peas, beans, and cabbage. Though leeks were considered unhealthy by many, they had always been grown at Friarsgate since the time of Elizabeth's Welsh father. But she grew them in her own kitchen garden along with parsley, sage, and other herbs. Finally she was satisfied with her planning scheme. She would have to consider whether they needed any seed. Usually they grew enough for the following year's crop.

There was a knock upon her door, and it opened to reveal Baen. He stepped into the chamber and asked her, "Is there anything in particular you would have me do today, Elizabeth? I shall see Edmund tomorrow, and speak with the shepherds then."

"Come in," she beckoned him. She was feeling stronger now that she was doing something familiar. She was the lady of Friarsgate, no matter that she had a husband now. "Come and see what I have planned for the fields, and give me your council."

He walked around the table to stand next to her and looked down at the map. "Why are these fields not to be planted?" he asked her, curious.

"Each year I leave several fields fallow and plant rye. It replenishes the soil," she explained. "Doesn't your father do that?"

"We don't have fields such as yours, and 'tis all he can do to get a living out of what he has," Baen said. "By the way, I haven't had the time to tell you until now, but I brought you a dower portion."

"Indeed?" A smile played about the corners of her mouth.

"Most of the sheep I bought from you last year, and their lambs," he told her.

"Just most?"

"Those that weren't lost by one means or another," he said.

"Stolen? Eaten by your father's cotters, or wolves? How many remain?"

"Actually about two-thirds of the flock," he told her.

"You are a well-propertied man, husband," Elizabeth responded, pleased.

"Well, they were yours to begin with," he said.

"But you purchased them honestly," she quickly replied.

"Several of your shepherds rode out early this morning for Claven's Carn. It will take them a good day and a half to bring the flock home," he explained. "The lambs were too young for the journey, and so we put them in a straw-filled wagon."

" 'Twas well done!" she exclaimed, very pleased.

"I expect they will be glad to be back at Friarsgate," he said with a rueful grin. "Our Highland pastures are not the lush meadows of Friarsgate. The sheep had a harder time of it, I fear."

"How many lambs?" she asked him.

"A dozen, no more, though the ram was vigorous," he murmured.

She flushed, nodded, and then said, "I would like you to see if we kept enough seed for the fields." She rolled up the map parchment. "Take this with you when you visit the seed storage." She handed it to him. "And if you have the time you might begin visiting the cotters who weave. Edmund can tell you who they are. Learn how much cloth each wove this winter. I must begin preparing for the shipment to our factor in the Netherlands. The cloth market is always happy to see Friarsgate wool arriving." Then she turned away dismissively.

Baen walked from the library. She was all business, his bride of just a few hours. He wondered if other newlywed couples spent their wedding day as they were. She masked her anger well, but such icy hauteur from a girl he knew to be a passionate creature amazed him. He would have a difficult time, he could now see, in winning her heart back, but he had no intention of giving up. Elizabeth was not going to forgive him easily, but then he had never been anything but honest with her. He made no secret of the fact that he would return to Grayhaven. Why was she angry at him for being loyal? He shrugged. She had to come around eventually. Didn't she?

The next few weeks passed, and each day but for the Sabbath was like the last. They arose, broke their fast, and worked. The main meal of the day was at the noon hour. They ate, and worked until sunset. A final light meal was served, and then Elizabeth would disappear upstairs into her chamber. She rarely spoke to him except to issue orders or discuss the business of the manor with him. He had attempted to engage her in a game of Hare and Hounds on several evenings, but she had refused him. She was not openly hostile to him, and she listened to his advice when he spoke. But there was no rapport between them as there had once been, and she made no effort to cultivate one.

And with each passing day Elizabeth's belly seemed to grow larger and larger. She was beginning to waddle about very much like the ducks in the barnyard. She was beginning to wheeze slightly when she walked. And her temper was growing shorter and shorter as the weeks went by. Baen was beginning to look forward to the return of his mother-in-law.

"This bairn you put in my belly is going to be a giant," Elizabeth said irritably one evening. The stairs were hard for her now, and she was avoiding them for the moment.

"My father is a big man, I am a big man, and my brothers are too. Still, Ellen, my stepmother, was tall and slim like you. She birthed

Gilbert easily, for I was there," he told her cheerfully. "Our son will be a big man."

"It had best be a lad," Elizabeth snapped, "for a girl this big would never find a husband, and be considered odd. And do not tell me your sister is large."

"Nay, Margaret is small and delicate," he answered her affably.

"She's a nun, isn't she?"

"Aye. Like your cousin," he remarked.

"I think I should like to play a game with you," she said. "Can you play chess?"

"Aye, I can. I'll get the game table," he said, hurrying to do so.

"I am restless tonight," Elizabeth remarked.

He set up the game table between them and offered her her choice of pieces. She surprised him by taking the black. It matched her mood, he thought wryly. "So I am to be the white knight," he said, amused.

"Isn't that what my family thinks?" she snapped at him.

"I didn't have to come back," he replied sharply.

"But you did, didn't you? The lure of Friarsgate could not be denied," Elizabeth murmured sweetly.

"The marriage contract I signed says even if you die, and our child with you, God forbid"—he crossed himself—"Friarsgate will return to your mother. There was no advantage to marrying you, Elizabeth, but that I love you. But loving you becomes more difficult with each passing day. Your tongue is sharper than a sword. Aye, I left you, but then I always told you I would, for I am an honest man. I owed an allegiance to my father, and I thought you understood that. Until he released me from that loyalty I could not—would not—desert him. You might have sent to me and told me you were with child. You might have asked my father to favor a marriage between us. But you ignored your condition, and only when your mother saw it was my father called upon."

"I am a woman," Elizabeth cried. "Respectable women do not ask men to marry them, Baen! You were supposed to ask me!"

"Respectable women do not seduce their stewards, yet you did. And how could I ask you when my loyalty lay elsewhere? When I had nothing to offer you? God's blood, Elizabeth! You're the heiress of Friarsgate!"

"The pieces are set up," she said coldly. "Shall we play?"

"Nay, damn it! We shall not!" he shouted, sweeping the game board clean with his big hand. Then he stormed angrily from the hall.

Surprised, Elizabeth watched him go. She had never before seen Baen exhibit any sort of anger, but his choler had been high, and his temper was hot as he left her. He was always leaving her, she thought self-pityingly. The tears began to roll down her cheeks. Well, why would he remain? She was fat, and not pleasant to be around at all these days. She was hardly the bold girl who had debauched him all those months back. What had ever possessed her to do such a thing? she asked herself for the hundredth time. She would have been better off an old maid than what she was now. The child within her stirred restlessly, and Elizabeth wept all the more.

When he returned to the hall he found her asleep in her chair. Baen stood watching her for several long minutes. She was so beautiful, even with her big belly. Sadness overtook him. He had hoped that by now her attitude would be softening towards him. They could not live their lives at each other's throats. Not once their son was born. A boy learned the important things he needed to know from his father, but if he had no respect for that father there would be great difficulty. And unless Elizabeth's stance towards him changed, there was little likelihood of his son respecting him. The lad would be the next heir to Friarsgate, and he would be treated from his birth with much deference. But in just a few short years that child would understand what existed between his parents. Better it be love.

Reaching out, he touched her shoulder to waken her. "Elizabeth," he said softly, "let me get you to bed." And he picked her up in his arms and walked across the hall.

She stirred in his arms, her eyes fluttering open. "What are you doing?" she asked him sleepily. "Where am I?"

"You fell asleep by the fire," he explained. "I'm taking you to your chamber."

"I can walk," she protested, struggling faintly in his grasp as he began to ascend the stairs. "I am not an invalid!"

"The stairs are difficult for you now," he replied, his arms tightening about his burden. "You are tired, lass. The burden of your lands is great, I know."

"I am capable of it even with my belly," she retorted.

"Aye, you are. I have never known a stronger woman, Elizabeth." They had reached the top of the stairs. He moved quickly towards her chamber, kicking at the door with his booted foot.

Nancy was there almost immediately, opening the door, gasping as Baen entered with his wife.

He set her down gently. "She fell asleep in the hall," he explained. Then he kissed Elizabeth on her forehead, and without another word left her.

"Ain't he sweet," Nancy said. "He's the best-tempered man I've ever known, mistress. You're a lucky woman."

"I want to go to bed," Elizabeth said low. "Get me out of this tent I'm wearing."

Nancy said nothing more, but her grin said everything. Elizabeth was hard-pressed not to slap her. She struggled out of the enveloping garment, washed herself in the basin on the table, and climbed into bed. "I'll want a bath in the morning," she told her servant.

"You can't possibly climb into that tub now," Nancy protested.

"Then bring the small one we used as children. And several extra buckets. I'll stand in it, but I must wash myself. The scent surrounding me is not a pleasant one," Elizabeth said. "Good night, Nancy." She closed her eyes. She couldn't turn over onto her side, for her belly was simply too large now. She heard the door close as Nancy left her. Elizabeth lay wakeful now. Baen had spoken some hard truths this evening, and for the first time in weeks she had listened. She had seduced him because she wanted him for her husband, and now he was. Had been for six weeks. Why was she still angry at him? He was an honorable man, but she was still not certain despite his avowals that he really loved her. And she did want to be loved, even as her mother and sisters were loved.

She accused him—and she knew wrongly—of wanting Friarsgate. But he had never really exhibited any venality towards her lands. Indeed, he treated her with the respect due her station, and always had. He did his duties as her steward, and her people liked and respected him in turn. She had heard them addressing him as master. What was the matter with her that she could not forgive him? The bairn within her stretched himself, and she winced with the slight pain. Her hands went to her belly, and she rubbed it soothingly. The bairn quieted.

"Ah, you are going to be like your da, young Tom," she said softly. She had decided to name a son after the uncle she loved so. Both of her sisters had added Thomas to their sons' names, but they were Henry Thomas and Robert Thomas. Her son would be Thomas Owein Colin. She did not know her father-in-law, and it was unlikely she would ever meet him, but she knew he would be pleased that his first grandchild bore his name. And her mother would be pleased that Elizabeth honored the father she did not remember. Her hands smoothed about her belly as she tried to imagine what the child would look like. Would he be his father's image? Or would he look like her? Finally her eyes began to grow heavy again, and she slept.

And in the chamber next to hers, Baen lay restless. For the briefest moment as he carried his wife upstairs she had relaxed in his arms, her blond head against his shoulder. All her anger was gone for those few moments, and the Elizabeth he loved had rested safely in his arms. And it had been wonderful! He wanted it to be like that all the time. He wanted their old relationship back. And whatever he had to do to attain that goal, he was going to do. But finding the key to the conundrum that was Elizabeth was not going to be an easy one. He slept at last.

As the month of May drew to a close, Rosamund rode over the hills from Scotland into England to be with her youngest daughter when she gave birth to her first child. She was amazed at how Elizabeth's belly had grown since she had seen her last. And the poor girl's ankles were swollen dreadfully. Hugging Elizabeth, she scolded her gently.

"You should not be on your feet so much now, child," she said.

"I have work to do, Mama. You know that." Elizabeth replied.

"I will wager all your books are up-to-date, the lambs counted, the wool shipped off to Holland, and I can see the fields are thick with new growth. You are managing admirably, Elizabeth, but you are soon to give birth and must spare yourself now for a short time. I have seen

Edmund, and he is well enough to help out a bit, and he wants to help out. And Maybel is not going to allow you to give birth without her. Does Baen do nothing to help you?"

"Baen is an excellent steward," Elizabeth found herself defending her husband. "He is gone from morning till evening, Mama. Never has Friarsgate had a better man."

"I am happy to hear it," Rosamund said with a small smile. "Then you are getting on better, Elizabeth?"

Elizabeth was silent, and then she said, "I want to, but I cannot forgive him, Mama."

Rosamund shook her head. "I have never known such a foolish girl as you, my daughter. Is there nothing I can say to you?"

"If he would only stop defending himself, Mama," Elizabeth wailed.

Rosamund shook her head. "Of all my children you are the one who has suffered the lack of my company. You did not like Claven's Carn and so I let you return to Friarsgate to Maybel's care. I should not have. You are too independent, Elizabeth."

"You were independent!" Elizabeth protested.

"I was indeed, but I knew when to retreat from an impossible position. You do not. Well, you and Baen must work it out between you, my daughter," Rosamund decided. "Now tell me how you are feeling?"

"I sometimes think this will never be over, and that I shall never see my feet again, or be able to sleep on my side," Elizabeth admitted.

Rosamund laughed. "I know," she sympathized.

"But none of your bairns was as big as this one, I'm sure," Elizabeth said.

"Baen is a big man, but you will birth the bairn well, and I will be with you," Rosamund promised her child.

"I am so glad that you are here, Mama!" Elizabeth said.

"I am glad I am here too, Bessie, and do not scold me. In my heart you will always be Bessie to your mother," Rosamund said with a smile.

# Chapter 15

&#10087;

Rosamund watched in distress as Elizabeth and Baen attempted to mend their difficulties. Actually she admired her son-in-law's patience with her daughter, who could not, it seemed, resist snapping at him at every opportunity. Several times she almost remonstrated with her daughter, but realizing it would only make matters worse, and that Elizabeth would consider that her mother was taking a position in Baen's favor, Rosamund bit her tongue in defeat. She had thought Philippa difficult in the matter of marriage, yet Philippa had been easy compared to her youngest sister. But then Philippa had a goal in mind, and having attained it was content. And Banon had never resisted the idea of marriage. She found her Neville, and was happy to settle down as wife and mother.

"Do you love Baen?" she asked her daughter one afternoon as they sat in the little walled garden belonging to the house. It was filled with rosebushes now coming into bloom, and the air was fragrant with them.

"I thought I did," Elizabeth admitted. "I should not have lain with him if I did not love him." Her hand went to her belly.

"But do you love him now?" Rosamund persisted.

"I do not know."

"Either you love him, or you don't love him," Rosamund said impatiently. "You had best consider it, Elizabeth. One heir is not enough for Friarsgate, and 'tis better to couple with a man you love."

"At last I am beginning to understand Philippa," Elizabeth said sharply.

Rosamund laughed, not in the least offended. "Her reluctance was your gain, daughter. You are as passionate about Friarsgate as I am. My first husband was a strong child, and yet he was felled by the spotting sickness. Children are fragile."

"This bairn will not be. He is a great lazy lump of a lad, and if he is not born soon, I think I shall go mad. And as for having another, Mama, this is surely not the time to consider that," Elizabeth said.

"He is a good man," Rosamund said.

"I know it," her daughter admitted.

Several days passed, and Rosamund thought her daughter was surely due to birth her child, but Elizabeth showed no signs of it. And then on Midsummer's Day Rosamund was awakened by the sounds of a woman shrieking. Jumping from her bed and pulling her cloak about her, she hurried from her room to Elizabeth's chamber, from where the sound came. Her daughter stood in a puddle of water, and Nancy was staring, frozen. Immediately the older woman took charge. "Nancy, tell Cook to have plenty of hot water and the clean clothes ready. You have prepared them in anticipation of this birth?"

Nancy stared at Rosamund, puzzled. "M'lady?"

"Really, Bessie, you didn't make the clothes? What else haven't you done while you have sat complaining these past few weeks?" She turned back to the tiring woman. "Go to the kitchens and tell the cook that Mistress Elizabeth is about to go into labor. Then find the laundress and tell her we need clean clothes. She will have them, I am certain. Tell Albert to find the birthing table. It should be in the attics. Bring it to . . ." Rosamund paused, deciding where the table should be brought. "Bring it to the hall, and set it up by the fire. Is the cradle prepared for my grandchild?"

"The cradle!" Elizabeth exclaimed.

"Really, daughter, it is not ready? I am glad you are such a fine mistress of Friarsgate, but now you have another responsibility to consider as well, and you must care for it in an even better fashion. The cradle will be in the attics too, Nancy. Go along, girl! Hurry!"

"I am having my baby?" Elizabeth quavered.

"Yes. Your waters have broken, and now the child will be born," Rosamund said.

"When?"

"When he decides to be," Rosamund answered with a laugh. "Some labors are quick. Others are not. Are you in pain?"

Elizabeth shook her head.

"Let us get you out of this wet garment," her mother suggested. "Then we will go down to the hall." And Rosamund helped her daughter from her wet chemise and into a clean one. She sat Elizabeth down and brushed her long blond hair out, then braided it into a single plait. "Your father's hair was like this," she told her daughter.

"Mama?" Elizabeth's voice was suddenly plaintive. "I am afraid."

"Nonsense!" Rosamund said briskly. "I have birthed eight bairns with little or no difficulty. You are a healthy lass, and your confinement has been a good one. Come along now and we will go down to the hall. Since you have neglected to make the necessary preparations for this birth, then I must. Shall I send for your husband? He was out early, I see."

"Baen is very reliable," Elizabeth said as they slowly descended the stairs. "Edmund says we are very fortunate in him. Where is Maybel? I want Maybel!"

"I will have Albert send a lad to fetch her," Rosamund said quietly, assisting her daughter into a high-backed chair by the fire. She took a goblet of wine from the intuitive servant who hurried to their side, nodding a small thanks. "Drink this. It will help," she told Elizabeth. I will see to what needs to be done while you wait for your labor to begin." Then, as the younger woman nodded, Rosamund moved away.

Several manservants came into the hall, struggling under the weight of the oak birthing table. Albert followed, carrying the old cradle, which was blackened with age. Both Rosamund and her deceased brother had lain in that cradle, as had their father and his brothers before and after him. Her own daughters had been rocked in it. She felt the tears pricking at her eyelids and blinked them back. Time, it suddenly seemed to her, was passing by so quickly.

"Send a lad for Maybel," she said to Albert. "And have someone find the master."

"At once, my lady," he said, and shouted to a young serving man to attend him.

Elizabeth watched as everyone about her moved quickly to their tasks. The large birthing table was scrubbed by two red-cheeked serving girls. Then it was carefully dried by hand. Several pillows were set on it at one end. The cradle was first carefully dusted, then polished. Maybel bustled into the hall and, seeing the cradle, beamed as she brought forth a new mattress she had spent weeks making. She laid it in the cradle's bottom. Her eyes met those of Rosamund first, and the two women smiled as if in some secret understanding. Then she hurried over to Elizabeth.

"How do you feel, my chick?" Maybel asked the young woman.

"Nothing is happening," Elizabeth said.

"It will soon enough." Maybel chuckled. "The laddie obviously has manners, and is but waiting for all to be ready for him." She took the empty cup from Elizabeth. "I'll fetch you a bit more wine," she said solicitously.

Rosamund, now with Maybel's aid, soon had the hall in readiness for the birth. Nancy had returned from the lower regions of the house with a large pile of clean clothes. She set them upon a small table which already had a large basin and a small pitcher of olive oil. Servants were placing several pitchers of hot water in the coals of the hearth. There was wine on the sideboard. There was a hushed expectancy now in the hall as they awaited the arrival of the next heir to Friarsgate.

Albert came to Rosamund's side. "The cook wants to know what he is to do about the dinner today?" he asked her.

"Everything is to be as usual," Rosamund replied. "The family will need to eat."

"Very good, my lady," he replied.

"Now go and ask your mistress the same question," Rosamund gently admonished the hall steward. "You should have gone to her first, and then consulted me."

"I apologize, my lady," Albert murmured, flushing.

"I understand," Rosamund returned quietly. "You were a lad when I ruled in this hall, but it is my daughter who for so many years now has held sway." Then she watched as Albert moved to Elizabeth's side and spoke to her, then, nodding, moved away.

Towards midmorning a look of surprise crossed Elizabeth's face. "Mama!" Her tone was an urgent one. "I felt a pain."

"Then your labor is beginning," Rosamund responded calmly. "Come, stand up, and let us walk together for a bit. It will help you."

For several hours Elizabeth's pains came slowly. Then towards late afternoon they began to come with greater frequency, and they were harder, lingering longer, it seemed. It was the longest day of the year, and the servants were anxious to get outside to join the revelry of the summer's night. The Midsummer fires were already springing up.

"Where is my husband?" Elizabeth demanded petulantly.

"Here, wife," Baen answered her. He had come into the hall earlier, but had been wise enough to keep out of the way. "How may I help you, love?" He knelt by her side, and took her small hand in his.

"Stay with me," Elizabeth said, to his surprise. Her mood had barely softened over the past weeks, even after her mother had come.

"I am here, and I shall go nowhere," he replied.

"Put her on the birthing table," Rosamund said to Baen. "It is time."

"Is the bairn to be born now?" Elizabeth asked her mother.

"He will come in his own time," Rosamund answered, "but I believe you have done all the walking and sitting by the fire that you should. Now you must encourage your child forth, Bessie."

"Do not call me Bessie!" Elizabeth wailed. "Ohhhhh! That hurts, Mama."

"Of course it hurts," Rosamund said calmly. "You are about to push a bairn forth from your body. There must be pain if there is to be joy, daughter."

The long summer's twilight lingered until it was almost midnight, and then it grew briefly dark. The pains were coming faster and remaining longer, one barely fading away before the next. Elizabeth could feel a fierce pressure in her nether regions as her child struggled to be born. Droplets of sweat beaded her smooth forehead. Tendrils of blond hair, no longer fully constrained by her plait, hung limply about her face. A sharp pain, like a knife slicing into her vitals, tore through her. She screamed piteously with the hurt, her eyes like those of a trapped animal.

"Mama!" she cried.

"You are doing very well, Elizabeth," her mother's calm voice reassured her. But Rosamund was not as assured as she appeared. Her eyes met those of her son-in-law. She stood up. "I need to walk about a moment, dearest," she said. "I will come right back," she told her daughter. She patted Elizabeth's cheek and moved away.

Baen was quickly by Rosamund's side. "What is it?" he asked her.

"The child is very big," Rosamund said, "and it is her first birth."

"How can I help?" he wanted to know.

"Have you ever helped an animal to be birthed?" she queried him.

"Aye. One of my father's prize heifers had difficulty with her first birthing. I put my hand up her to help the calf along."

"Then you must, I think, do the same with Elizabeth's bairn. If we could just get the head and shoulders free I believe she could do the rest," Rosamund told him.

"The child is ready?" he wanted to be reassured.

"Aye, and growing tired with his efforts, I have no doubt," she responded. "That is dangerous for them both, Baen."

He nodded. "Then let us bring my laddie forth from his mother's body," he said.

They returned to Elizabeth, who was but half-conscious now. She opened her eyes. "What is the matter? Am I going to die, Mama? Is my bairn all right?"

"The lad is big," Rosamund began.

"I knew that," Elizabeth replied. "Did I not tell you he was big?"

"You need help in birthing him. You are growing weary with your efforts, and so is the bairn. Therefore his father must help him into the world, Elizabeth, and then you will complete the birth yourself," Rosamund explained.

"No!" Elizabeth cried. "I can do this myself!"

"In God's name, woman!" Baen roared at her. "I can take no more of this! I love you, Elizabeth. Do you understand what I am saying? I love you! I apologize to you for leaving you last October. I should have had the wit and the courage to ask my father if he would let me go. As it turned out he was more than willing, and my own foolishness cost me your love. I am sorry. But I will not allow your stubborn nature to cost you your life and that of our child! Now let me help you."

Elizabeth was, for the first time in her life, rendered speechless. She collapsed back upon the hard bolster behind her back, watching as her husband washed his hands in the basin, and then covered one hand and part of his arm with olive oil.

"Tell me when you feel the next pain coming," he said to her.

She nodded, and a moment later cried, "Now!" She was on her back with her legs up and apart. Fascinated, she watched as he bent, and then his hand pushed into her as the full thunder of pain rolled over her.

Baen had seen the child's head crowning when he had bent down. Gently he slipped his thumb and a finger about the baby's head, and slowly drew it forward. He felt Elizabeth's body yielding to allow the infant to move ahead and through the opening her body was making for it. She shrieked as its head broke forth from her, and then its shoulders. Her husband looked up at her, his heart breaking at the sight of her tears.

"When the next pain comes try to push the rest of the bairn out, Elizabeth," he instructed her quietly. "The worst is over, lass, and he's beautiful!"

"You haven't seen all of it," she moaned. "He could be a she." Then she winced with the rising pain, and bore down with all her might as the rest of the bairn came into the world. They caught him in a clean cloth, and Rosamund opened his little mouth to clean out any extraneous matter. The baby coughed, and then began to howl. Baen was grinning from ear to ear.

"We have a son," he told Elizabeth, leaning down to kiss her. "Everything is exactly where it should be, and of a good size too."

Pale and exhausted, Elizabeth looked up at him. "Did you mean what you said? That you were sorry you deserted me? That you still love me?"

"Aye, I meant every word," he vowed, the stormy gray eyes filled with his love.

"Then I forgive you, Baen," she whispered to him, and then she gasped as another pain, but this one less intense than the others, racked her. Her startled eyes went to Rosamund. "Mama? I still have pain."

" 'Tis the afterbirth, and nothing more," Rosamund said, taking up a small basin. "When you have passed it Baen must take it out and bury it beneath an ash or an oak."

"Why?" Elizabeth demanded to know.

"So your son may have all the qualities of that tree," Rosamund responded. "Its beauty, its strength."

"What time is it?" Elizabeth asked.

"Almost dawn," her husband told her. "The sky is already light with the coming day. You have done well, Elizabeth," he said.

"I want to see Thomas," she said to them.

"Thomas?" Rosamund smiled.

"Thomas Owein Colin Hay," Elizabeth answered, looking at Baen. "With your permission, of course, husband."

" 'Tis a fine name for a lad, wife," he agreed with a smile.

And Elizabeth smiled back at him. It was the first real smile she had given him since his return. What had happened? And then he realized that in his fear for her and for their son, he had offered her an apology, and said in so many words that she had been right all along. Baen almost laughed aloud at the simplicity of it all. An apology! Why had he not considered it before? Because they were both right, he decided, and they were equally stubborn. But it mattered no longer. She had smiled at him, and solicited his opinion in the matter of naming their firstborn son.

"Thomas for your uncle, Owein for your father, and Colin for Baen's father," Rosamund said. "Aye, 'tis a fine name."

The afterbirth was expelled into the basin and handed to Baen. He restrained a shudder, for it was certainly not a pretty thing. "I'll bury it now, and then we will announce our son's birth," he said. "With your permission, of course, wife."

Elizabeth nodded, and accepted the now swaddled bundle that Maybel handed her.

"Oh, he's a good laddie, he is," Maybel cooed. "A finer bairn I have never seen born, my dearie. He's his father's spit, and that is for certain."

Elizabeth looked down at her son. Then she looked up at Maybel, and her mother. "Thank you for being here with me," she said softly, and then her attention became totally absorbed by her child. His hair was dark and covered his round head. "His eyes are blue," she noted.

"They may change eventually," Rosamund told her.

"Something has changed, Mama," Elizabeth said softly.

"Aye," Rosamund said with a smile.

"He apologized! Did you tell him to do it?"

"Nay, I did not," Rosamund replied. It would have never occurred to her.

"He loves me!" Elizabeth said.

"Aye, he does, very much, but then you surely knew it, Elizabeth," her mother said quietly. "Have you made your peace with him now?"

Elizabeth nodded, and then she said, "I am so tired, Mama."

"Aye, you would be," Rosamund agreed. "Your labor was a long one. Not the longest I have known, but long enough. You need to rest now, daughter. When Baen comes back he will carry you to your bed." She removed the infant from his mother's charge. "Where is the cradle rocker?" she wanted to know.

A girl of twelve stepped forward. "Here I am, my lady," she said.

"You must rock him most gently," Rosamund instructed the girl as she set Thomas Hay into his cradle.

"Yes, my lady," the girl replied.

"She's Alfred's niece," Maybel informed Rosamund. "Her name is Sadie."

"Take good care of my grandson, Sadie," Rosamund told the girl, who nodded vigorously.

The two women, with Nancy's aid, began the business of cleaning all evidence of the birth from Elizabeth. By the time they had finished Baen returned to the hall, and he carried his wife up to her bed for a well-deserved rest. When he returned to the hall he found Rosamund and Maybel seated together at the high board, breaking their fast. Father Mata had just entered the hall, and congratulated Baen on his son's arrival.

"When will he be baptized?" the priest wanted to know.

"Will your father come down from the north?" Rosamund asked Baen.

Baen shook his head in the negative. "He'll not leave his lands. But perhaps I can get my youngest brother to come. I should like him to stand as my son's godfather, along with Lord Cambridge," Baen answered her. Then he turned to the priest. "The lad appears to be strong and healthy, Father. I believe we can wait a few weeks, can we not?"

The priest nodded. "I am here should there be an emergency, Baen," he said.

"Then we will set the baptism for Lammastide. That will give a messenger time to ride north and bring Gilbert back with him," Baen decided.

"And I shall go home tomorrow," Rosamund said. "But we should send someone to Otterly today to inform my cousin of his namesake's safe arrival on this earth. Now, someone find the master chamber's cradle, for when my daughter awakens it will be time to put her son to her breast. She is too weak to come into the hall each time young Tom needs to be fed. The baby and its rocker must be with her. Has she chosen a nursemaid for the child?"

"As if I should allow anyone else to look after that precious bairn!" Maybel declared indignantly. "I am not so ancient that I cannot care for him."

"But Elizabeth will need your counsel to chose another, for you must be in your own home each evening with Edmund," Rosamund said. "What if you grew ill, and there was no one to look after the lad?"

"Well," Maybel allowed, "there is Grizel. She is Sadie's mam, and widowed. Sadie is her youngest. She would serve quite well."

"Will you speak with her then, dear Maybel?" Rosamund asked.

Maybel laughed, shaking a finger at Rosamund. "Do not think to cozen me, my lady." She chuckled. "Remember, I raised you, and I know all your tricks. I am not so foolish that I do not realize I could use the aid of a younger woman."

Rosamund leaned over and kissed the old woman on her cheek. "Thank you." Then she beckoned to Baen and the priest to sit down. "Come and break your fast," she said. "It has been a long night for us all. Baen, you must get some rest when you have eaten. And Mata, why are you looking so worn?"

"I spent the night praying for Elizabeth's safety, and that of the bairn," the priest said quietly. "Surely you do not believe that you were the only ones helping the lady of Friarsgate along," he teased them.

"Then you are both entitled to some rest," Rosamund declared.

"There is work to be done," Baen protested. "The hay is ready to cut."

"Edmund can oversee it today," Rosamund told her son-in-law.

He did not argue. He was more tired now than he could ever remember being in all of his life. It was as if he had given birth to his son, he thought, a faint grin breaking forth on his handsome face. He ate quickly, and then excused himself. Upstairs he went into the chamber where he had been sleeping, and then, anxious for Elizabeth, he opened the door connecting their two rooms for the first time and stepped inside.

Elizabeth lay on her back, not yet asleep, but her eyes were closed as she tried to gain that state. She was exhausted, but still excited by the birth of her son. Hearing the door she opened her eyes to see Baen. "Have you eaten?" she asked him, and she smiled.

He sat down on the edge of the bed and, taking her hand, kissed it. "Aye. Your mother says I must get some sleep, and Edmund will see to the haying," Baen told her.

"You should," she agreed. "You were with me all the night long. Is he not the most beautiful bairn?" She was glowing with her happiness. Happiness she had never thought to experience.

"Aye, he's a fine lad," Baen said. "And you were so braw, my sweet wife."

"You saved us, Baen," Elizabeth said suddenly serious. "I could not have birthed our son without your help. I had grown so weak, and if you had not helped him forth from my body I know we would have both died. And I did not want to die. Not before I told you that I do love you."

"I knew it without you saying it, Elizabeth," he replied. "After all, you have always had a weakness for Scots, haven't you?" Baen teased gently.

She giggled. "Aye," she admitted, "I always have, husband."

He leaned forward, and their lips met briefly. "Go to sleep now, my love."

"Stay with me," she pleaded softly. "I think I will sleep better in your arms, Baen, than I will alone."

And that was how Rosamund found them when she peeped into the chamber an hour later. Baen was lying with his back to the headboard, his arms protectively about Elizabeth, whose head was on his chest. His head rested atop her blond head. Both were sleeping soundly. Rosamund closed the door to the chamber as quietly as she had opened it. She could go home tomorrow knowing that a permanent peace had been forged between her youngest daughter and her husband. It was a great relief, and her heart was lighter than it had been in months. She went to the small library and, taking some parchment, wrote to Thomas Bolton, inviting him to his godson's baptism on the first day of August. She smiled, almost hearing his protest at being disturbed yet once again, but the trip between Otterly and Friarsgate was hardly a great one. He would come. And Banon and her husband would come, but when Rosamund wrote to her middle daughter she insisted that her grandchildren, but for the two eldest, remain at home. And she, Logan, and their sons would come. And she would write to her uncle Richard Bolton, asking that he send John for the baptism of his new niece. John Hepburn might not be her blood, but he was Logan's eldest son. It would be a wonderful family day.

Elizabeth was saddened to see her mother depart the next day, but she knew Rosamund's place was at Claven's Carn. The daughter had noticed that when her mother was at Friarsgate this time the servants deferred to her in a way that Elizabeth felt took from her position. She had been lax in her discipline in the last days of her confinement. It was time for the Friarsgate folk to be reminded again who the lady of the manor was. Within a few short days after young Tom's birth she had Baen carry her to the hall, where she spent her days. And a week after that she was in her library again. And then she was walking and riding once more as her strength increased. By the time the day for the baptism arrived Elizabeth was her old self again.

"Dear girl!" Lord Cambridge said when he saw her. "You are in love! How simply marvelous! Is love not marvelous, Will?" he asked his secretary, who had accompanied him.

Elizabeth laughed. "Uncle," she said, kissing him, "you are ever the romantic." Then she kissed Will. "I can see you are taking good care of him. Thank you. He is my favorite relation. Come in! Come in!"

Banon and her Neville arrived shortly thereafter.

"Jemima is most put out that you would not include her," Banon told her sister. "And I have never looked so well after a confinement as you do. My new bairn was a boy too! We have named him Henry, after the king."

"I have not the accommodation for your family," Elizabeth said, not in the least disturbed by her sister's complaint. "Mama thought it best only the two eldest come. If we had included Jemima, then my name-sake and your youngest daughter would have wanted to come. As it is our brothers are sleeping in the stables."

"Why do you not simply enlarge the house?" Banon wanted to know.

"Actually we are considering it," Elizabeth said.

"So I finally get to meet this Scot you married," Banon responded. "Where is he?" She looked about the hall.

"He is the biggest man in the room," Elizabeth said proudly.

"God's wounds, Bessie!" Banon exclaimed. "He is gorgeous! How on earth did you manage to get him?"

"I seduced him," Elizabeth answered her older sister. "And please do not call me Bessie!"

"You didn't!" Banon sounded just slightly shocked. "I would have never thought it of you." She giggled.

"Well, I did," Elizabeth said with a grin. "The proof of my naughti-ness is currently in Uncle Thomas's arms."

Banon's eyes grew large as she looked at the baby Lord Cambridge held. "He's huge!" she exclaimed. "And you birthed him when?"

"The morning after Midsummer's Day," Elizabeth said.

"God's blood! It's a wonder he didn't kill you. None of mine have been that big at so young an age," Banon told her sister.

"Baen helped me. He drew the bairn's head and shoulders from my body," Elizabeth exclaimed to Banon's openmouthed amazement.

"He didn't!"

"He did."

Banon shook her head. "I never thought you would find a man to suit you, and to suit Friarsgate, but 'tis obvious you have, Elizabeth." She put her arms about her sister, hugging her. "I am so happy for you! I can't wait till Philippa sees him. Is she coming?"

"Nay. I wrote to her myself, but she says she is too busy attending to the queen while the court is in progress. Katherine was sent to Moor Park in Hertfordshire, and has since been removed to Bishop's Hatfield. The king does not wish to see her face again, Philippa writes, and the princess has been removed from her mother's custody now."

"Poor lady," Banon sympathized.

"Foolish lady," Elizabeth said. "Anne told me she would be queen, and it would appear that she may be one day sooner than later. I do admire Philippa's loyalty, however. It has never wavered."

Banon nodded. "Aye, but then she believes her small success is owed to the queen's patronage. I am glad I am not at court. I am quite content to be a country wife."

"Philippa's good fortune is owed to our uncle," Elizabeth said, "as is all of ours."

Banon nodded again in agreement.

Thomas Owein Colin Hay was baptized shortly thereafter in the same church in which his mother had been. He had two godfathers standing for him: the man for whom he was named, and his uncle Gilbert Hay, who had come down from Scotland as Baen had predicted. The baby howled as the holy water was laved over his dark head, and it was considered an excellent omen, for the devil had been driven from the child in that simple act of baptism. His mother, his father, and his relations smiled, well pleased.

"He's a braw laddie," Gilbert Hay said, looking down at the infant in his arms. "Da will be pleased when I tell him."

"I wish he had come with you," Baen said.

"Och, you know Da. He rarely goes off his own lands. He's been up at Glenkirk of late. The old earl is not well. They think he may not last another winter, but who knows? He's a tough old man," Gilbert remarked.

There was feasting in honor of Thomas Owein Colin Hay. Long tables were set before the house. There was venison, lamb, and beef roasted. There was trout, and salmon broiled in wine. There were artichokes for the high board, peas, and braised lettuces for below. There was bread, sweet butter, and several kinds of cheeses. There were jellies, and spun-sugar subtleties shaped like lambs. There was even an enormous cake soaked in marsala wine with enough slices for everyone. And the Lammas Day traditions were all observed as well. The Friarsgate folk admired the new heir, and then they ate and drank. And after the sun had set and the infant was put in his cradle, Sadie by his side, there was dancing and singing.

Finally the Friarsgate folk returned to their own homes. The servants cleared away all evidence of the celebration as the family adjourned to the hall. Alexander Hepburn had disappeared with his brother James into the darkness. Gone hunting for pretty maids, Elizabeth thought with a smile. She watched as her half brothers, twins Thomas and Edmund, played hide-and-seek with their nieces, Katherine and Thomasina. The four were so close in age that they seemed more brothers and sisters.

"A most splendid day!" Lord Cambridge enthused. "Your table is most munificent, dear girl, and my namesake a fine young fellow. I have enjoyed myself quite nicely, and Will too. We shall come again, perhaps next spring."

"You and Will are always welcome, Uncle," Elizabeth told him. "And I want young Thomas to know you as my sisters and I have."

Sweet wine and sugar wafers were now brought around, and the family remained, gossiping. Logan Hepburn reached out and took his wife's hand. Rosamund smiled back at him in return. They both knew she would not come to Friarsgate as often now as she had in the past. With Baen and Elizabeth in charge the manor was safe and in good hands. And there was a male heir, the first in several generations. He was glad, for he loved Rosamund more today than he had when he had first seen her as a child, more than when he had lusted after her and she had fallen in love with another man. More now than he ever had. He wanted his wife all to himself.

The hour grew late. Banon and Robert Neville took their daughters and went upstairs. Lord Cambridge and Will had been the first to retire. Rosamund and Logan bade Elizabeth and Baen a good night.

Logan had seen the twins settled in the hayloft of one of the barns. In the first barn he had gone into he had heard a great deal of giggling and voices from the loft above, and knew where his two older lads had gotten to, with two Friarsgate lasses undoubtedly. He grinned, pleased, at the same time hoping no damage would be done to the girls in question.

Finally Baen and Elizabeth found themselves alone in their hall. Together they laid the timber across the front door. Together they walked about seeing to the fires in the hearths and snuffing out the candles. Standing at the foot of the stairs, they embraced, kissing slowly. His big hand smoothed her cheek as he smiled into her eyes. Then together they ascended the staircase to their bedchamber. Nancy had been sent to her bed earlier, and so they undressed each other. It was the first time since Baen had left her the previous autumn that they had made love, and each was a little shy of the other.

She helped him off with his breeches and jerkin, then unlaced his shirt. Her blond head bent to kiss the warm flesh of his chest as she pressed the shirt from his shoulders and it slipped down his tall form. He shuddered as her mouth feathered little kisses across his skin. Then, pulling her up, he turned her about and unlaced her gown. It was silk, the blue of the sky today. It was Elizabeth's favorite color, and it suited her. He pushed the gown down to her waist, unlaced her petticoats, and then lifted her from the tangle of fabric. Only her chemise remained, and Elizabeth smelled sweet in his embrace.

"I have longed for this moment for months," he told her.

"I have longed more," she admitted. "Sit down." And when he had she took off his boots, putting each of his legs between her two and pulling firmly. Then, turning about, she unrolled his stockings down his legs and over his feet. "You have such big feet and toes," she remarked with a small smile.

"Now you sit," he said. And he removed her shoes, stockings, and garters, his hands slipping up her legs beneath her chemise to caress her warmth.

Elizabeth murmured a sigh of contentment, standing quickly, pulling him up, and unlacing the linen drawers he was wearing beneath his breeches today. He did not usually wear such a garment. He was completely naked. "Now," she said wickedly to him, "I mean to have my way with you, sir."

"First, madame, we must be equals in this matter," he replied, drawing her chemise over her head so that she was naked too, "for I mean to have my way with you too, Elizabeth Meredith Hay, my love, my wife." His arms tightened about her as their bodies pressed against each other. "Do you know how much I want you?"

"Aye," she responded to the question, her hazel-green eyes twinkling. "Your desire is already in evidence, my love. Much, much in evidence."

His dark head descended, and he gave her a slow, deep kiss, his tongue pushing easily past her lips to plunge into her mouth. Together their tongues danced in a ballet of wet longing. Elizabeth sighed a long sigh. His hands cupped her face and he spread kisses across it, his mouth brushing her closed eyelids, her cheeks, returning to her mouth to drink the nectar of her rising passion. Raising his head he whispered to her, "I love you! I love you!"

Tears crept from beneath her thick lashes, but her eyes remained closed. "I have never been so happy, Baen. Swear to me that you will never leave me again. Swear!"

"Open your eyes and see the truth of my vow," he told her, and when their eyes met he said, "Only death will ever part us, Elizabeth, and that I cannot control, but I will always love you. Even from beyond the grave! And I will never leave you again, except should death call me. But my love will always be with you." Then, picking her up, he laid her in their bed, which smelled fresh with lavender.

Elizabeth held out her arms to her husband, drawing him down into her embrace. "I love you, Baen, son of Colin." And she smiled sweetly into his face.

He cradled her now with an arm, and a large hand reached out to caress her breasts. They were fuller now than he remembered, and then he thought of his son, who nursed lustily at those beautiful breasts. His tongue snaked out to lick at one of her nipples. Almost at once a droplet of milk oozed out. Unable to control himself, he closed his mouth over the nipple and suckled it, swallowing the liquid that poured forth into his mouth, almost choking him. Was it wrong? he wondered. But he could not cease, and Elizabeth did not forbid it. Even when he had drained the breast dry he was unable to tear himself away from it for a few moments. It was one of the most exciting experiences he had ever known.

His fingers pushed themselves between her nether lips, and he found her wet with her own desire. He played with the sensitive flesh, rubbing at the jewel of her sex until she was whimpering and her juices were flowing even more. He met her gaze and put those wet fingers in her mouth. Her eyes widened with surprise. "The taste of you is intoxicating, wife," he growled. "I must have more!" Then his dark head pushed between her thighs, and he began to greedily feast upon her.

Elizabeth cried out with surprise, shocked to feel his tongue on her most secret flesh. Then she realized she was enjoying the sensations he was creating within her. She heard herself begging him not to stop, and he didn't. Her fingers kneaded the thick, dark hair on his head, digging into his scalp. His tongue moved to lick at her thighs, and then pushed into her love channel. She almost screamed with the thrilling little shivers racing down her spine. "Baen!" She cried his name, but he was so lost in his lust for her that he barely heard her voice.

Now, unable to restrain himself any longer, Baen mounted his wife and drove himself deep into her warmth. He was consumed by her, and did not hear her cry of pain, for she was still sore from the birth of their son almost two months ago. But she wanted him every bit as much as he wanted her. Elizabeth wrapped her legs about his thick torso, her fingernails raking down his back in her desire as she caught the rhythm of their shared desire. Never, she thought dreamily, had their pleasure in each other been so great. "Baen! Baen!" she cried his name aloud, and the infant in the cradle by the fire stirred.

"Let go!" he groaned in her ear. "I cannot wait much longer, wife! Let go!"

"Together!" she hissed at him, squeezing his lance within her.

He cried out even as her head began to spin with lust fulfilled, and her body was racked with deep, strong shudders as his pent-up love juices exploded to fill her. Their short, hard pants of mutual satisfaction burst forth as he rolled off of her and lay by her side. Reaching out, he took her hand and, bringing it to his lips, kissed it.

Young Tom began to complain of his hunger.

Elizabeth struggled from their bed and, going to the cradle, lifted her son out. Coming back to the bed she laid him upon it and changed his nappy. Then, picking him up, she sat down upon the edge of their bed and put her infant to her full breast.

"Will he be satisfied?" Baen asked, feeling just a small modicum of guilt.

"For now, but he'll waken in a shorter time, I fear," Elizabeth admitted.

"Find a wet nurse," Baen said.

"Why? I am capable of feeding him," Elizabeth protested. "I don't want him in a village cottage where he could grow ill."

"Bring the wet nurse here," Baen replied. "She can live within the house and feed him here. I do not want to futter my wife with my son nearby. Nor do I want to share your beautiful breasts with him, Elizabeth."

"Not yet, Baen," Elizabeth said. "By Twelfth Night, I promise."

"By Michaelmas," he countered. "I will wait no longer."

"You said you would not leave me ever again," she cried, and the infant at her breast protested the timbre of her voice.

"I won't," he said pleasantly. "I'll just beat you for disobeying me," Baen told her with a wicked smile.

"You wouldn't!" Elizabeth cried.

Again he smiled. "Do you wish to test my word, wife?"

Elizabeth looked hard at him. He did appear to be quite serious.

"Friarsgate belongs to you, but you, my darling, belong to me. In the eyes of the law, and in the eyes of the church," he said.

"That is not fair!" Elizabeth said.

"No, it is not, but I will invoke my husbandly privilege if you do not obey me. You do not want me finding a wet nurse and bringing her into the house, do you? Better you ask Maybel's advice, and share the chore with her. You know I love you, and I love our son, but I will not share my bedchamber longer than necessary with our bairn. Shall I speak to Maybel, or will you? Tomorrow, Elizabeth."

"I never knew you were a bully, Baen," she muttered, cradling young Tom against her chest. "I would not have married you had I known."

"Nor did I know what a little shrew you can be, Elizabeth, my love, but I would have wed you anyway," Baen responded.

Elizabeth laughed. "Damn me, husband, if we are not well matched, for I say we are. But if we futter so often we could find ourselves with another bairn. Is that what you want, Baen? More children?"

He grinned. "Aye," he drawled. "But let us make a daughter next, Elizabeth."

She laughed. "I cannot become enceinte if I am nursing, it is said," she teased him.

"Michaelmas," he repeated, and a single big finger reached out to stroke their son's dark head.

In the morning before her mother departed Elizabeth sought her out. "Tell me the secret you possess to prevent a child too quickly," she said.

Rosamund smiled. "Ask Nancy, my darling, for I have already given her the recipe. She is shocked, of course, but also curious to see if it will work. It will."

"Baen wants me to find a wet nurse for young Tom, Mama," Elizabeth told her mother. "One who will live here in the house."

Rosamund nodded. "Humor him, but begin your special elixir immediately."

"I will nurse young Tom until Michaelmas," Elizabeth said.

"Do not believe that old wives' tale about nursing woman being infertile," Rosamund warned her daughter. "It is not necessarily true. I was still nursing you when I became enceinte with your brother who perished."

"Oh, dear!" Elizabeth murmured.

Rosamund grinned conspiratorially. "Heed my advice, Elizabeth. Today." Then she kissed her daughter. "Farewell, my darling. I am content that I finally leave Friarsgate in two pairs of most excellent hands."

"Because of Baen?" Elizabeth said with a small smile.

"Aye, but also because Friarsgate now has a new heir, and the hope of more to come," Rosamund Bolton Hepburn said with a smile.

# Chapter 16

❧

A year and a half had passed since young Thomas Hay's baptism. Friarsgate was locked in another winter. Candlemas had passed, and the lambs were being born once more in the February snows. Elizabeth and Baen were locked in a struggle to keep the manor safe and prosperous, for this particular winter was proving a cruel one. They were therefore very surprised when on the last snowy day of the month a messenger arrived at their door. As he was brought into the hall by Albert, who took his cloak, Elizabeth saw that the man wore the royal livery. A sense of foreboding gripped her.

"Come in, sir, and welcome," she greeted him, signaling a servant for wine.

The messenger came directly to her and bowed low. "Have I the honor of addressing the lady of Friarsgate?" he asked.

"I am she," Elizabeth replied.

"I bring you a message from the queen, madame," the messenger responded.

"Queen Katherine? What can she possibly want with me?" Elizabeth said aloud, voicing her thought.

"Nay, madame. The princess of Aragon is no longer queen. 'Tis Queen Anne from whom I come." He reached into his doublet and drew forth a packet, handing it to Elizabeth with another bow.

"You will be hungry, sir, and tired," Elizabeth said as she accepted the packet. "Albert will show you to the kitchens for a hot meal, and then he will give you a warm bed space here in the hall. You must remain with us until the weather clears."

"I was instructed to return directly from you with an answer to the queen," the messenger told Elizabeth.

The lady of Friarsgate nodded. "Of course," she said, "but you shall not go until the storm is over, sir."

"Thank you, madame," the messenger said and, turning away, followed Albert out of the hall.

"Queen Anne?" Baen looked puzzled.

"My only friend at court, Anne Boleyn. She did vow she would be queen one day," Elizabeth said slowly. "I shall not know anything until I have read the letter she has sent to me." She looked down at the packet in her hand for a long moment. Then she broke the red wax seal and unfolded the oiled parchment. There was Anne's familiar careless scrawl. Elizabeth focused her gaze on the words.

*I am his wife as I said I would be. And I am to be crowned in June. I will tell you all when I see you, and you cannot refuse my command. I am your queen now. I am surrounded by the ambitious, and those who formerly professed to despise me now toady to me in an effort to gain my favor. I pretend to give it, but you know me better, dear Elizabeth. I need your friendship now more than I have ever needed it. But I do not beg. You are commanded to court, my lady of Friarsgate. I want you here in time for my coronation, and other things. You will arrive no later than the twentieth day of May. We will be at Greenwich as we always are. Return my messenger with word of your plans.*
*Anne R.*

Elizabeth reread the letter once, and then again. Her face was pale with her distress. If there was one place in the world she did not want to be it was court.

"What does it say?" Baen's voice broke her thoughts.

"I am commanded to court," Elizabeth said softly.

"By whom?" he demanded to know.

"By Queen Anne. He has married her, which means he has obtained his divorce from Queen Katherine, poor foolish lady," Elizabeth said. "Philippa must be beside herself, and I think it odd she did not write to me or our mother. Certainly a messenger would have stopped by here on his way to Claven's Carn. Knowing my oldest sister, she is being loyal to the end, yet torn by the situation because of her sons' careers. Philippa is very ambitious for her lads."

"You will not go, of course," Baen said.

"Nay, I will go, husband. I have been commanded to court, and there is no excuse for refusing a royal command," Elizabeth told him. "I do not want to go, but I will." She sighed. "How like Anne to demand my presence because she is feeling alone. She is a strange creature. Her heart is good, but few know it. Yet she will demand my presence without any thought for how my life will be conflicted."

"You were friends with her? I have heard her called the king's whore," Baen said.

"Nay, she was not his whore. Had she been, Queen Katherine might still have her place, for the king is a fickle man, and should have discarded Anne long since, as he did her sister, Mary. But he does need a legitimate son, and refused even to consider the princesses who are available because of his passion for Anne Boleyn," Elizabeth said.

"Does he not love her?" Baen asked.

"I do not believe this king capable of the kind of love we share, that my mother and my sisters share with their husbands. He has but one paramount desire, and that is for a legitimate son and heir. He has proved himself capable of siring a son with Bessie Blount, and many say Mary Boleyn's son is his. The king and his counselors, of course, deny that paternity, for to admit it would make any marriage with Mistress Anne null and void on the basis of consanguinity, and any child she bore him bastard. I think it is very possible, although she says it not in so many words, that Anne may already be with child."

Baen shook his head. "I thought you despised the court, Elizabeth. Did you not swear you would never return?"

"I do, and I did," Elizabeth admitted, "but the choice has been taken from my hands, Baen. The queen commands. I must obey."

"Could you not plead your belly?" he said hopefully.

"I wish I could," she replied, "but I cannot."

"When will you go?" He did not look happy.

"Certainly not until late April," Elizabeth said.

"You must get your uncle to accompany you," Baen decided.

Elizabeth shook her head. "Nay. Not this time. Besides, he has become more and more content to remain at Otterly. I know what I face this time. When I send the messenger back to the queen I shall ask that she send me an escort to bring me to Greenwich, for I cannot travel alone."

"I should go with you," he said.

"And who would steward Friarsgate if you did? Edmund cannot take the burden up ever again, Baen, and you know it. Besides, what would you possibly do while I am dancing attendance on the queen? You are not a courtier, and the only Scots there are those attached to King James's ambassador," Elizabeth said.

"Are you ashamed of me, lass?" he asked quietly.

"Nay! And how can you even ask such a question of me, husband? I love you, Baen, and I am proud to be your wife. I picked you for myself, did I not? I am not going to court to pay a social call upon the king and his queen; I am going to comfort my friend, who, for all her bravado and temper tantrums, is obviously frightened. Long ago when my mother was a girl at the court of King Henry VII, she was befriended by Queen Margaret and the Princess of Aragon. They were of an age together in the house of the king's mother. And afterwards, when the princess was ignored and frightened, abandoned by all, and left destitute even by her own father, the king of Spain, my mother sent her small purses to aid her survival.

"This is the basis of my family's friendship with Katherine of Aragon. This is how my eldest sister gained her place in the queen's household, and thus was able to climb into the ranks of the nobility herself. But when I went to court several years ago the queen was already out of favor. I did not even pay my respects, for she was gone then. Unlike my sisters, who enjoyed the court, I felt gauche and very much out of place. I could not control my tongue, which is what brought me to Anne's attention. She is clever herself, and likes clever friends. She befriended me, Baen, and for the short time I remained at court that friendship made my life quite pleasant. Not so much so that I did not long to return home as quickly as possible, of course. But at least I was no longer sad.

"But while the king favored Anne, many at court—my own sister included—did not. They were all sure the king would tire of her as he had many others. Most could barely conceal their scorn for her, and went out of their way to slight her when they dared. But I judged Anne Boleyn on the girl herself. Her family and her pedigree meant nothing to me. I liked her. She was clever and witty, unlike most others but a few. She made the king laugh with her keen and shrewd intelligence. She is musical, and the king loves music. She is a wonderful dancer, and the king loves nothing better than a good dancer. And seeing another girl come to court who like herself did not really fit in, she reached out to me and brought me into her circle. She treated me with kindness. She is vain, and she is selfish. She is determined in her desires and her need to have her own way, but we became friends, Baen. Like my mother I place a great store by loyalty. My friend, the queen, has called for me. I will go, and that is the end of it, my dearest husband."

"How long do you think you will be gone from me?" he asked her, and he reached out to bring her into the circle of his strong arms, his lips brushing the top of her blond head. "I cannot bear the thought of being without you," Baen told her.

"Do not say it!" Elizabeth cried softly. "I must obey, and yet I hate having to leave you, to leave our wee Tom, to leave Friarsgate." She buried her head in his chest.

"How long?" he repeated.

She shook her head. "I do not know. Anne can be difficult and quixotic when she wants her own way. Hopefully my presence will calm her, and I shall be able to leave her again after a few weeks."

"If you do not return within a reasonable time I will come after you," Baen told his wife. "This queen has the world at her feet, especially if she carries the king's heir. She does not need my wife more than our son and I do."

"I love it when you are so masterful," Elizabeth teased him with a small giggle.

Baen chuckled. "Are you wheedling me, wife?" he teased back.

"You are becoming too clever for me, husband," she replied.

"Nay," he said softly. "I shall never be as clever as you, Elizabeth."

"If you know that," she responded quickly, "then you have at least become wise, my darling, and that could make you dangerous." Her hazel-green eyes twinkled mischievously up at him.

His hand slipped wickedly into her shirt to caress a plump breast. He tweaked the nipple while pressing kisses onto her face. Slowly, slowly he pulled her back until he felt the seat of the chair facing the fire against the back of his legs. He sat, bringing her onto his lap as he did so. He nibbled on her earlobe, whispering to her in very explicit terms exactly what he intended on doing to her in the next few minutes.

Elizabeth felt the heat rush into her cheeks at the murmured words, but she was already growing weak with her need. Had she known the delicious delights of the marriage bed, she thought fuzzily, she would have married far younger than she did. But perhaps it would not have been so wonderful with another man. Perhaps it was just because her husband was a lusty Scot named Baen.

"Tell me what you want me to do to you," he said, his hand now sliding up her leg, his fingers slowly caressing the inside of her silky thigh.

"Everything you promised me," she answered him breathlessly.

"Everything?" he asked her.

"Everything!"

"Right now, and right here in the hall?" he taunted.

"Aye! Right now, and right here in our hall!" she replied fiercely.

The fingers entwined themselves in the curls covering her mons, lightly brushing it in a teasing motion that sometimes tickled, sometime pulled. And then a single finger followed the faint groove down her slit. Down and up it moved until she was quivering with her anticipation.

"Mistress." Albert's voice pierced her consciousness. He was standing somewhere behind them.

"Yes, Albert?" she said calmly, although her heart was hammering wildly.

"The messenger is being fed. Is there anything else I may do for you right now?"

"Nay, Albert, go and have your supper," Elizabeth said.

"Thank you, mistress." he replied, and they heard his footsteps retreating behind them.

"Do you think he saw?" Elizabeth fretted.

"Saw what?" Baen mocked her. "His master and mistress cuddling with the dog at their feet before the fire."

"Your hand up my skirt, you devil," she retorted.

Baen's big finger slipped between her nether lips. "Nay. He could hardly see over this high-backed chair. I was proud of you, Elizabeth. 'Twas well done, wife," he praised her with a grin. Then, finding his objective, he began to play with it, rubbing, teasing, pinching it just enough to make her squeal softly with her excitement. Friar's ears twitched slightly at the sound, and he raised his head up, but, seeing nothing requiring his attention, the dog went back to sleep. "Look at me, Elizabeth," Baen suddenly commanded.

Her gaze locked onto his, her eyes widening as he pushed two thick fingers into her love passage and began to gently frig her. His look was one of the pleasure he was giving her, and she sighed. He bent to kiss her mouth, one kiss blending into another, hot and wet, until she moaned against his lips, "I want it all, Baen! I want it all!"

He withdrew the two fingers and sat her up, helping her to straddle him. She loosened his garments, freeing his love lance, hard with his desire for her. "Do you think we have time before the messenger comes into the hall?" she whispered. She was burning with her need for him.

He nodded in the affirmative, sighing as her hands caressed him. She unlaced his shirt, pushing it open so she might kiss his chest and lick at his nipples, while her two hands played with his stiff manhood. Finally, able to bear no more teasing, Elizabeth mounted Baen, her legs resting on either side of him as she lifted her skirts and then gracefully sank down on his love lance with a gusty sigh. His big hands slipped beneath her buttocks, fondling them. He leaned forward to kiss her, whispering to her as he did so.

"Fuck me well, wife. I am so hot for you at this moment that I care not who comes into the hall."

Elizabeth obliged him, beginning with a gentle walk, progressing next to a trot, then a canter, and finally she galloped them both home. She bit her lip so hard to keep from crying out that it bled, and he sucked the blood from it even as he filled her with his passion juices.

She collapsed upon his shoulder, gasping with her own pleasure as he groaned aloud.

"Woman, no other has ever given me the delight that you do!"

Elizabeth smiled at the declaration. She lay recovering against him for a few minutes, and then she slipped off his lap, drawing her skirts down about her, lacing her blouse back up, and smoothing her disheveled hair with her hands. "We will, of course, continue this discussion later in our bed, sir," she told him.

"At your pleasure, madame," he assured her.

"And yours, sir," she said with a smile.

"How will you satisfy that naughty itch of yours while you are away from me?" he wanted to know. "Will you take a lover, like so many of the fashionable court ladies?"

Elizabeth pretended to consider his suggestion. "Perhaps I shall," she said. "And you, Baen? Will you make one of the maidservants your lover?"

"Nay, a milkmaid or shepherdess, I think," he replied with a grin. "I far prefer an outdoors lass."

She swatted at him, and, laughing, he ducked. "Scots villain," she cried. "I shall know if you are untrue to me!"

Reaching up, he pulled her down onto his lap, kissing her soundly. "There is absolutely no other woman in the world for me, Elizabeth, my wife. I should sooner spend the rest of my life a celibate than have another. But you? Will you be tempted by a charming courtier now that you know what passion is all about?"

Elizabeth punched his shoulder hard. "Nay, and how can you even ask me such a thing? I hated the court, and all of the pompous gentlemen who looked down on me for being more in love with my lands than with them. Only the king was kind to me, because he had grown up with my mother and holds her dear."

"What of your other Scot?" Baen asked.

Was that jealousy she heard in his voice? Elizabeth wondered. "I had forgotten him," she lied. "He was a pleasant fellow, I will admit, but it is unlikely he is still there. I told him he must ask his brother, King James, for a wife with lands. He probably did, and is long gone from King Henry's court. Nay, there is only one Scot for me, and you are he, my love!" Then, kissing him hard upon his mouth, she jumped up from his lap. "The others will be returning to the hall any minute. Straighten your garments, sir!"

"Do you mind that I am jealous?" he asked as he put his clothing aright.

"I am flattered to know that you still love me," Elizabeth said.

"I will always love you," Baen told her.

The storm was gone by the following morning, and the sun was shining brightly over the snowy landscape. Elizabeth had written the message she was sending to the new queen the evening before. Now she handed it to the royal messenger, who was ready to make his return journey. She gave him a silver coin for his troubles, and he thanked her effusively. He had been well fed twice. His horse had been well cared for and was ready. His saddlebag was filled with food for at least the first few days of his journey south. He rode out and was surprised to meet the manor's steward once he was out of sight of the house. "Sir?" he asked, curious.

"Did you stop at the manor known as Otterly on your way here?" Baen asked him.

"Nay, sir, the night before I arrived I sheltered in a farmer's barn along the way," the messenger answered. "I had passed Otterly the day before."

"Ride hard today and you will reach Otterly by nightfall," Baen advised him. "Ask to speak with Lord Cambridge, and give him this." Baen put another packet into the messenger's hand. "Tell Lord Cambridge that the steward at Friarsgate asked that you be sheltered the night. Lord Cambridge has spent much time at court, and you may speak freely with him about your reasons for coming to Friarsgate." He offered the messenger a large copper.

"Nay, sir, the lady has given me a coin," the messenger said politely.

"You are not a rich man; take it," Baen insisted, and the messenger did not demur again, instead agreeing to reach Otterly by nightfall and bring Lord Cambridge the message from the steward at Friarsgate. Baen watched him depart down the snowy track.

The sunset was a bloodred smear on the horizon, and the sky almost black above it when the royal messenger arrived at Otterly. He was ushered into the hall and requested to see Lord Cambridge.

"I will send for my uncle immediately," Banon said, beckoning to a servant. "Fetch Lord Cambridge," she told the man.

"Thank you, mistress," he replied, enjoying the warmth that now seeped into him, taking the chill of the long day's ride from his cold bones. He sipped at the hot cider put into his hands by another servant, watching, amused, as the children in the hall played noisily about them.

After almost a half an hour Thomas Bolton came into the hall. "A messenger?" he said. "From whom?"

"Friarsgate, although this fellow wears a royal badge," Banon said.

Lord Cambridge came up to the messenger. "In whose service are you?" he asked quietly.

"The queen's, my lord. Queen Anne," came the reply.

Banon screamed, surprised, startling her children, who looked nervously towards their mother. "Queen Anne?" She gasped.

"Aye, mistress," the messenger said.

"I had best take this fellow to my wing to learn all, dear girl," Lord Cambridge said. And what had the messenger been doing at Friarsgate? he wondered.

"Nay, Uncle! He will tell us all here. I shall not wait until you decide to share his news with us. I could not bear it," Banon said.

Thomas Bolton looked about him. Even Robert Neville looked curious. "Oh, very well, my darlings," he said. "But give me a goblet of wine first. I fear somehow that I shall need it." He settled himself in a tapestry-backed chair by the fire. "Come, sir"—he waved a languid hand at the messenger—"sit down and tell us all." He gestured towards a small settle opposite him, smiling as a wine goblet was placed in his hand.

The messenger sat down gingerly. He was not used to being asked to sit, but it was certainly more comfortable to tell his story thusly.

"Leave nothing out, dear boy," Lord Cambridge told him. "We want to know why you went to Friarsgate, and how Anne Boleyn managed to become queen, and why you have come here to Otterly on your return, for 'twas not by chance."

"Nay, my lord, 'twas not. The lady of Friarsgate's husband, the steward of the manor, stopped me on the road south and gave me this packet for you"—he handed it to Thomas Bolton—"and told me to stop the night here, saying it was at his request you shelter me," the messenger explained.

"I am the lady's uncle," Lord Cambridge said, "and Otterly is my home. Go on now, dear boy, and tell us the rest, the juicy meat of the reason for your journey in such wretched winter weather."

The messenger began his tale, being interrupted now and again by Lord Cambridge, who wanted every detail. Not being a person of importance, the man could tell them little other than the facts he knew, the gossip he was privy to, but Thomas Bolton was able to fill in, thus gaining a reasonably accurate picture of the situation. When he had finished, the messenger looked to Lord Cambridge questioningly.

The older man nodded slowly, and then said, "Banon, have one of your servants take this good man to the kitchens for his supper, and see he is supplied with a warm place to sleep the night. He has a long journey ahead of him. And see there is food for his travels on the morrow," he instructed her.

"Yes, Uncle," Banon said quietly. She signaled to one of her serving men and, after instructing him, sent the messenger from the hall with thanks. Then she turned to her uncle, saying, "What does Elizabeth's husband say?"

The older man cracked the seal on the letter handed him. He spread the parchment out, smoothing the creases in it, and read it slowly through. "Your sister has been commanded to court by the new queen," Thomas Bolton began. "She is not pleased, but she will, being your mother's daughter, of course, obey."

"And Baen wants you to go with her," Banon deduced.

"Nay. He says Elizabeth will not ask me because she does not wish to impose upon my kindness and hopes her visit will be a short one. How she has matured in these past few years," he said with a fond smile.

"But you will go," Banon said.

"Nay, I will not," Thomas Bolton replied, surprising them. "I shall go to Friarsgate as soon as the snow is gone, and Elizabeth will tell me then what it is she desires of me. Fortunately styles have changed little, and the gowns made for her last time will do for this visit, with alterations, of course. Motherhood does tend to enlarge a lady's girth," he murmured diplomatically.

"Indeed, Uncle, it does," Banon told him with a laugh. She was almost plump now with her many children, but still quite pretty.

"And I shall have Will arrange for her accommodation along her route. She will be going to Greenwich without a doubt. She will be fine, dear Banon. She is the lady of Friarsgate. She has a husband, and she goes to court at the request of the queen, her good friend. Who knows what advantage that will give her, as it certainly gave your mother?"

"Philippa must be furious." Banon chortled mischievously.

Lord Cambridge laughed too. "Aye. Now for her sons' sakes she must eat a rather large slice of humble pie, I fear," he said. "But she will. If Philippa learned one thing from your mother it is that family is everything. And since this new queen favors her, Elizabeth must help smooth your sister's new path. If not for Philippa, then for her lads. Who knows? Having Philippa in her debt may be of use to Elizabeth one day."

"I should be terrified to have Philippa in my debt," Banon said. "I can only imagine how very grand she is now after all these years as a countess."

"She was quite charming when we saw her two years ago," Thomas Bolton said.

"Aye," Banon said shrewdly, "while there was still hope that her patroness would regain her vaunted position. But now? Uncle, I shudder to imagine her state."

He smiled wisely. "Philippa, like Rosamund, is a survivor, dear girl."

"When must Elizabeth go south?" Banon asked.

"Baen does not say, but certainly as soon as spring breaks," he replied. "I will depart for Friarsgate in another few days, the weather permitting. I shall learn everything once there so that when I return I can tell you. And Elizabeth will, of course, stop here on her journey south, so you may speak privily with her then," Thomas Bolton said. Then he stood. "I must return to my own wing and tell dear Will all that has happened. He will be perishing with curiosity, as would I were our positions reversed, which—thank God—they are not." He departed the hall.

"The women in your family do have a knack for making friends with the mighty," Robert Neville noted to his wife. "I am very glad you never did, dear heart. I should not be happy if you were commanded to court."

"Nor would I," Banon admitted. "Poor Elizabeth. I can only imagine how much she hates even the thought of her visit. Uncle says she was most unhappy at court but for the kindness of Anne Boleyn. Yet much evil is spoken of this woman even here in the north so far from court."

"Blame that on Northumberland and his family," Robert Neville said astutely. "The old earl always blamed Anne Boleyn for his son's unhappy marriage. He claimed she put a curse on Lord Percy's union because she could not wed him, when the truth was that the king forbade the match because he wanted the lady for himself."

Banon shuddered. "Too much intrigue, Rob. I am glad I was overshadowed by Philippa during my tenure at court. You are the only thing good that came from my stay." She smiled at him lovingly. "You and our marriage and all of our children."

Robert Neville put an arm about his wife. "Thanks to you I far exceeded my family's expectations, Banon," he told her, returning her smile. "Who would have expected a younger son in a minor branch of the Nevilles to wed an heiress? Certainly not my kin." He chuckled.

Banon laughed. "Oh, Rob," she told him, "I hope it is not wrong to be so happy! I want Elizabeth to be as happy with her Scot. I must ask Uncle to see if Baen will ride as far as Otterly with Elizabeth. I can only imagine how furious this royal command has made her."

But strangely, while annoyed to have her life disrupted, Elizabeth was not angry. Anne Boleyn was a very proud woman. The proudest Elizabeth had certainly ever known. If she wanted Elizabeth with her, there was a very good reason for it. *Our acquaintance was not a long one,* the lady of Friarsgate considered, *but a strong friendship was forged between us. I will go to her. I wrote to her when I wed. I wrote to her when young Tom was born. She even sent him a fine silver ladle for a baptism gift.*

*Her purse was never great, so I know that was a sacrifice for her. I do not like the court, but I do like Anne. She will not keep me long.*

Elizabeth and Nancy began unpacking the beautiful garments that Thomas Bolton had had made for her several years ago. Her bosom had increased in size, and she had gained at least a half inch in the waist with her son's birth. They set to work altering the gowns, and Elizabeth hoped that styles had not changed greatly since her last visit to court. She wished she had Thomas Bolton's advice, for he would surely know. She was not unhappy, therefore, when Lord Cambridge arrived at her door some two weeks after the royal messenger had gone his way back to court.

"How did you know I needed you?" Elizabeth greeted him with a hug. "Come into the hall. The April rains have begun. Are you too wet?"

"Dear, dear girl!" He kissed her cheeks, and then stared at the little boy looking up at him with large eyes. "Can this be my namesake, Elizabeth? God's wounds, dear girl, he is practically as big as Banon's little son, and not half his age. I see he is taking after your delicious Scot. Where is the good fellow?"

"In the kennels. His Friar sired a fine litter of pups, and he is choosing one for young Tom," she told him. "I have been commanded to court," she said without further ado. "Anne Boleyn is the king's new wife, and she wants me for whatever reason."

"I know. Baen sent a message to me with the royal messenger, but do not be angry, dear girl. He was concerned for you."

"I will not ask that you come with me," Elizabeth said.

"And I will accept your decision unless you change your mind, my dear," he told her. "Have you gotten out your fine gowns yet?"

"Nancy and I have been working on them for many days now. You have your ear to the court despite the distance between Otterly and London. Have the styles changed greatly, or will my barely used wardrobe do, Uncle?"

"We must have a few more French hoods made, for they will now be all the rage, I guarantee you, dear girl," he replied. "Your gowns were quite stylish three years ago, and will be just as fashionable now. Perhaps something new in green, though."

"I am better in a darker green than light, Uncle. Anne says she is to be crowned in June. Which of my gowns should I save for that day? Though I will certainly not be among the queen's train I know she will want me there, and I would do her proud."

"Then you must have a new gown, and it will be Tudor green to honor the monarch," Lord Cambridge said.

"No," Elizabeth answered him. "It must be some other color, for they will all be wearing Tudor green that day in an effort to catch the king's favor. We must think on this, Uncle, and do something extremely clever."

"Dear girl!" he exclaimed. "You are thinking like a courtier."

Elizabeth laughed. "Nay, Uncle. I am being practical, I swear it!"

At that moment Baen entered the hall and greeted his wife's uncle. He brought with him a small black-and-white border collie pup, and Friar trotted by his side. "Tom! Would you like one of these fellows for you and Will? Friar sired eight of them on his mate. I don't believe you and Will have a dog, do you?"

"I do not believe that Pussums would tolerate a dog," Lord Cambridge said, "but then she is very ancient now, and she accepted Domino without question. But he is a young fellow, and can annoy her. Is one of your pups a quiet creature?"

"The runt is a wee female," Baen said. "She's gentle."

"Perhaps I shall take her then when I return home. I do so admire these border pups of yours, dear boy. But now all my energies must be devoted to preparing Elizabeth for her return to court. We need to fashion a gown she may wear to the coronation."

"You mean all those gowns she had dragged out will not suit?" Baen asked, surprised.

"Nay, dear boy, her gowns are quite fine, yet she needs one special gown for the queen's special day. But I have traveled for hours and must be fed before I can even begin to consider this difficult conundrum," Lord Cambridge told them. "She must stand out from all the Tudor green that will be worn that day, yet not overshadow the queen."

Baen shook his head. " 'Tis a world I am just as glad not to be a part of," he said honestly. "I'm but a simple Highland Scot, Tom."

"Dear boy," Lord Cambridge said, raising an eyebrow, "there is nothing at all simple about you. I could teach you all you needed to know to exist at court in a trice, and your own native intelligence would serve you well too." He chuckled. "A simple Highland Scot indeed!" He turned back to Elizabeth. "When are you leaving?"

"When the queen sends my escort. I sent back to her that she must. That I could not travel without an escort, and that my own people were all needed at Friarsgate," she said. "Perhaps she will decide I am not worth the trouble, and I shall not have to go at all," Elizabeth teased them. But was she teasing?

" 'Tis a great honor, Elizabeth," her uncle said quietly. He looked about the hall contentedly. Friarsgate was always so welcoming, and had always seemed so to him.

For the next few days Elizabeth's gowns were prepared for packing. The alterations were completed, the gowns and bodices inspected for any sign of stain or wear. They were brushed. Any beading needing repair was fixed, as were hems. And Lord Cambridge considered the gown his niece should wear to the new queen's coronation.

"You are most beautiful in blue," he finally announced. "The pale washed blue of a clearing sky after a storm. Pale blue with cream and gold," he decided. "We must send for Will. I have a bolt of the fabric we will need, and he knows where it is. Your man must go immediately in the morning at first light if Will is to be here the day after."

So William Smythe was sent for and returned promptly, bearing with him the required fabric. When he learned the purpose of the fabric Will agreed most heartily with Lord Cambridge that Elizabeth's coloring best suited this shade of blue. Together the two men began work with the manor seamstress to fashion the perfect gown for Elizabeth.

"Uncle! You sew?" Elizabeth was astounded, for she had never known him to possess this particular talent.

"Dear girl, you do not think I can keep abreast of the latest fashions for my own wardrobe this far from London without occasionally doing some of my own alterations," he replied. "The ability to repair a garment is paramount for a gentleman."

"I am once again in awe of you," she told him, and he flashed her a grin.

The fabric that Will had brought from Otterly was not plain, but rather it was a beautiful brocade with a design of pendant flowers and leaves woven into it. The gown's neckline was square, bordered with silver and gold embroidery. From shoulder to wrist the sleeves were narrow, with bell-like cuffs turned back at the lower edge. The cuffs was plain cream colored watered silk. The long brocade skirt of the gown was funnel shaped. About her waist Elizabeth would wear a thin gold chain from which hung a small gold mirror, its golden back embossed with a quarter moon made from mother-of-pearl, and several sapphire stars.

Beneath the gown a chemise of the most delicate creamy lawn had been made. The sleeves of the chemise, which showed from beneath the gown's deep-turned back cuff, were wide, with a dainty ruffle of golden lace at the wrists. It had a round neckline because Tom had dictated that modest but elegant simplicity would please the king. "In the end it matters not who the queen is," he told his niece wisely. "It is the king in whom the power of life and death rests. The king, dear girl, though you must never say I said it, was most inordinately fond of your mother when they were young. And he holds a most paternal fondness for her daughters."

"His wife is just a few years older than I," Elizabeth murmured.

Lord Cambridge chuckled at her sharp observation. "Something that of course you would never say aloud outside of this hall, dear girl."

"Yes, Uncle," Elizabeth said meekly, and then she laughed.

"You will wear pearls with this gown, and only pearls," he instructed her. "And the pearl-edged French hood with its cream lawn veil, dear girl. You will stand out in such a gown, yet you should not overcome the queen's coronation garments."

And at last everything was packed for traveling. Nancy would once more go with her mistress. Realizing this, Albert, the hall steward, came to his mistress and asked if she would permit him to marry the lady of Friarsgate's tiring woman.

"I must think on it," Elizabeth told him, and then she took her servant aside privily. "Albert has asked to wed you. Will you have him?" she inquired of Nancy.

Nancy flushed. "He's a bit older than me, but a man should be older than his wife. And I have never heard evil said of him, mistress. We are equals within the household, though he stands just a bit higher than I do, which is proper. We would, I believe, make a good match. But I would wait until we have returned from court."

Elizabeth did not ask if her tiring woman loved Albert. Love was usually not a consideration in such a marriage. "Then you are willing?" she said.

"Aye," Nancy said. "I am willing."

"Then we will tell him together." And she sent for Albert to attend her. "Nancy has told me she is content to wed you, but no banns shall be published until she and I have returned from court, Albert. Is this your wish, Nancy?"

"Aye, mistress. I shall go out into the world one more time, and then return to marry you, Albert," Nancy said. "If this will satisfy you then we are pledged."

"I am content then too," the hall steward said.

Elizabeth took Nancy's hand and put it into Albert's. "Go along now," she told them. "Make your plans for when we return."

When she told her uncle and Baen they both teased her for being a fool for love, and, laughing, Elizabeth agreed she was. Now they waited for her royal escort to arrive, and even though they expected it, it came as a surprise when the troupe of men-at-arms with their Tudor-rose badges arrived one afternoon. It was already past mid-April.

Captain Yardley presented himself politely, and then told Elizabeth, "We must begin our journey tomorrow, madame. The queen has ordered that we proceed with all possible haste to Greenwich. She is most anxious to see you." He was a grizzled old soldier who had obviously been in the king's service for many years.

"I am ready," Elizabeth told him. "My baggage cart was sent ahead several days ago. We shall stay tomorrow night at Otterly, and after that my uncle, Lord Cambridge, has arranged for my accommodation."

"Very good, madame," Captain Yardley said. "A baggage cart would have slowed us down."

"I am going to court at the queen's invitation, sir. I cannot bring but one garment. We will meet the cart at Otterly, and after that it is up to your men to guard it. If it takes us several days longer because we are slowed by it, then the queen will forgive me for the honor I will do her by, as her friend, showing to my best advantage," Elizabeth said sharply. She looked the queen's captain directly in the eye as she spoke.

"Aye, madame," he said laconically. *Another high-spirited wench like the king's new wife*, he thought.

"Mama go?" young Tom asked in the morning as Elizabeth prepared to depart.

"Aye, but Mama will come home soon, my lad," she promised him, picking him up and kissing his rosy cheek. "Be a good boy, young Tom." She set him down, and he toddled off with Sadie, who had graduated from his cradle rocker to his nursemaid along with her mother. Elizabeth felt suddenly overwhelmed. Tears slipped down her cheeks. She didn't want to leave Friarsgate. She didn't want to leave her husband and son. Why in the name of heaven had Anne ordered her to court when she knew how much Elizabeth disliked the court? Well, she told herself, she wasn't going to learn the answer to her questions until she reached court. With a sigh she mounted her horse.

Lord Cambridge and Will were among the party returning to Otterly.

And Baen had decided to escort his wife that far. " 'Tis past time I met your sister and her husband again," he said. "We are, after all, kin."

Elizabeth had not discouraged his company. "Friarsgate will survive a day or two without us, sir," she had said.

"If you would prefer I shall remain behind," he said with utmost seriousness.

"Nay!" And then, seeing that he was teasing her, she swatted out at him. "Scots villain," she muttered.

"God's blessed bones!" Banon Meredith Neville gasped to her husband, Robert, as her youngest sister and her husband entered their hall late that afternoon. "I am still amazed by my sister's giant of a husband. And a handsome giant at that." She embraced her sibling, whispering to Elizabeth as she did so, "Is he that big all over?"

"Aye," Elizabeth murmured low. "Jealous?"

Banon giggled. "Mayhap a little," she admitted. Then she looked up at Baen. "Welcome to Otterly, brother. I am glad that we are met again. Come, Rob, and greet Elizabeth's husband."

"You are every bit as lovely, if not more so, than when I last saw you, mistress Banon," Baen told her, and he kissed both of her cheeks. Then he turned to shake his brother-in-law's hand.

Banon flushed with pleasure at the compliment. He might be a Scot, and a Highlander at that, but his manners were perfect. His mother had taught him well, she thought. "Can you and Will join us for supper, Uncle?" she asked Lord Cambridge.

"Indeed we can," he replied. "Your sister and her escort must leave at first light, dear girl, and so I shall make my farewells tonight. How odd. I had thought to be envious of your visit to court, Elizabeth, but I find now that as the moment approaches I am most relieved not to be going."

"Uncle, I cannot believe that," Banon teased him, and they all laughed.

When the meal had been finished Lord Cambridge took Elizabeth aside to wish her Godspeed. "Be kind to Philippa," he said quietly. "Use your own goodwill to help her. You know her devotion to the princess of Aragon, and if Anne Boleyn died tomorrow the king would not have Katherine back. It is a son he wants, and she could not, cannot, supply that. And store up what goodwill you can for yourself and your family, dear girl. Your absence will not be forever."

"I still do not understand why she wants to see me," Elizabeth said.

"You are, dear girl, most likely the only true friend Anne Boleyn has ever had. How sad that is, but it is, I suspect, the truth. She is not an easy creature. Treat her with kindness, but come home to us as soon as you can." Thomas Bolton embraced his youngest niece, kissing both her cheeks, hugging her to his heart. "God and his blessed Mother go with you, dear girl."

Once again Elizabeth felt tears pricking at the backs of her eyelids. "Thank you, Uncle," she managed to say, and she kissed him back. Then Will came and wished her a safe journey. Finally he and Lord Cambridge departed the hall.

The two young couples sat for a time before the fire in the hall, talking. Banon and Robert Neville had decided they liked Baen Mac-Coll Hay. He was a country man, and there was no pretension about him. They were country folk too. Philippa and her husband intimidated them. Baen was the perfect mate for the lady of Friarsgate.

Elizabeth could not argue their conclusion. Together in the guest chamber given them she sat quietly on the settle by the fire as her husband stood behind her brushing her long blond hair. It was his habit each night to do so, and she loved the quiet time they shared together. "I shall miss this," she told him softly.

"I shall miss it," he agreed, pushing aside the thick tresses and kissing the nape of her neck. "Do not linger longer than you must, sweetheart. I am lost without you, I fear, and not ashamed to admit my weakness to you." He lay the brush down and, coming around to face her, drew her up into his arms. "You are the most beautiful woman I have ever known," he told her passionately. "I cannot believe some courtier did not snatch you up when you last danced attendance on the king."

"My blood is not blue enough. My estates are in the far north. I had no great name or useful connections," she explained to him. "That is their way, and I was not unhappy, Baen." She reached up to caress his face. "I will come back to you," she told him. "The court holds no fascination for me."

"Yet you go," he responded.

"Aye. You know why. I am commanded by the queen, and for no other reason. Do you not understand that Anne commanded because she knew that if she had simply asked I would have cried off, Baen? 'I will not beg,' she wrote. Instead she commanded."

He sighed. But then she reached up and drew his head down to hers. They began to kiss slowly, deeply at first, and then as the heat of their passion began to increase in intensity, more fervidly. Two tongues, wet and hot, danced together with each other. He held her face between his hands, covering it with kisses. She returned those kisses eagerly. Her chemise and his long-tailed shirt fell to the floor. He was hard with his need for her, and she hot with her need for him. He bent her over the settle, her palms flat against its seat. His hands gripped her hips as he entered her in a single smooth motion, driving himself deep into the hot maw of her sex.

Elizabeth arched her back. His eagerness had but matched her own. She closed her eyes, relishing the ardent motion of his lust for her. Small mewling sounds escaped her as the pleasure he was offering them began to spread at a leisurely pace throughout her body. "Don't stop!" She gasped. *Dear God!* How could she do without his passion in the next few months? She wouldn't think about it. She would simply enjoy the here and now with him. Her thoughts melted away. Only the sweet sensations of their pleasure remained. And then he cried out sharply, and she felt his juices flooding her.

For several long moments his fingers continued to grip her tender flesh. She was going to be bruised there, Elizabeth knew, but she didn't care. Finally he straightened himself up, which allowed her to stand as well. He said not a single word to her, but led her towards the bed that they would share tonight. Falling into it together they began to kiss and caress once again. The night was yet young.

# Chapter 17

❦lizabeth Hay reached Bolton House in London to find her eldest sister, Philippa, there. Both were surprised to see each other.

"What are you doing here?" Philippa wanted to know. She looked
tired.

"The queen commanded me to court," Elizabeth answered her
sibling.

"The queen is not at court," Philippa said, and then the realization
of her sister's words hit her. "Oh." She made a face. "That woman who
attempts to usurp the queen's place called you. I cursed her recently in
Queen Katherine's presence, for it is forbidden to say a bad word about
the king around her. Do you know what that sainted woman said to
me, sister? 'Do not curse her, Philippa. Feel sorry for her. Feel sorry for
that wretched wanton creature who has taken another woman's husband, and now proudly displays her belly to all.' I hate her! I shall
never feel pity for her! I hope she miscarries!"

"Philippa! Philippa!" Elizabeth put comforting arms about her eldest sister, who now began to sob. "The king needs a son, and your pa-
tron cannot bear him that son. He is not the first king to put aside an
infertile queen for a more fecund and younger queen. Your loyalty to
Queen Katherine is admirable, but do not let it blind you to the reality of what has happened. Continue to love and serve your mistress,
but do not hold Anne responsible for Katherine's inadequacies," Elizabeth advised.

Philippa shrugged off her youngest sister's arms and comfort. She
pulled a handkerchief from her sleeve and wiped her tears away.
"Anne Boleyn will never be my queen, Bessie. Never!"

"But she is Henry Tudor's queen, sister, and please, please do not call me Bessie," Elizabeth said quietly.

"How long are you going to be here?" Philippa asked. "The court is at Greenwich, as you know."

"I wanted to rest a day before I must fling myself into that maelstrom you so enjoy," Elizabeth said with a small smile. "The queen sent me an escort. I have ordered them on to Greenwich to tell her I will be with her in two days. I will go downriver by barge, and have already sent my baggage and my horse with my royal guards. Now tell me what you know." She drew Philippa into a window seat overlooking the river.

"Very little," Philippa said. "There were rumors all winter. Then at Easter the marriage was revealed. I am not certain when it was celebrated. After Christmas, I have heard. You will know more when you reach Greenwich. They waited for Cranmer to be approved archbishop of Canterbury by the pope. Once that was done Cranmer declared the king's marriage to Queen Katherine null and void, and his marriage to Lady Anne a true one. Now she parades her belly, the little whore!" Philippa's lips were set in a bitter line, and her eyes were hard.

"How are my nephews?" Elizabeth asked quietly. There could be no reasoning with Philippa over this situation, and she felt sorry for her eldest sibling. Yet she admired her too. Philippa had never known when to give up.

"Henry is still with the king, but he is getting too big to be a page. Owein remains in the Duke of Norfolk's household. He tells me Norfolk is surprised that the king finally married his niece. He does not entirely approve, but he will use the Lady Anne to his own advantage, for that is the way he is. They are an ambitious family, the Howards. Hugh lost the place he was to have in the princess Mary's household. The king has pared her staff to the bone, as he has my mistress's. But Crispin cajoled the king to take Hugh into his service, as Henry will soon have to leave it. Actually 'tis a better position for my son. I am grateful he was given it."

"And your daughter?" Elizabeth asked. As long as they spoke on the family Philippa could not become so agitated.

"She turned three in December." Philippa's face was now relaxed and glowing. "No mother could have a sweeter daughter, Bess . . . Elizabeth. And Mary Rose is intelligent too. Why, she can already recite her ABCs and count to twenty. I have high hopes for her, sister. Crispin adores her, and she quite has him wrapped about her little finger. I should be very jealous of her but that my husband loves me."

"I am happy for you, sister. You seem to have everything you always wanted." Elizabeth's gaze went to the river. "I do not really like the city, but looking downriver I can see the beauty in it. And is it my imagination or is the town creeping closer to Bolton House, Philippa?"

"London grows," Philippa admitted. "Now tell me of your family."

"Young Tom is almost two, and Baen is the perfect husband for me," Elizabeth said with little sentimentality, but she smiled as she spoke.

"A Scot," Philippa murmured. "How like our mother you are. But I am glad you are content. Have you seen Banon?"

"Briefly on my way south. She thrives as always. Her bairns are as noisy as ever, and her Neville as devoted to her as he ever was, if not more." Elizabeth chuckled.

"And you are happy with Friarsgate?"

"Oh, yes!" Elizabeth exclaimed. "I hope you do not regret your decision."

"Never! Brierewode is my home. My life should be perfect if it were not for poor Queen Katherine's lot. She is so noble, and so brave. And none can say a word against the king in her hearing. She is still devoted to him despite his unkindness and that of his wretched whore."

"Anne is not an unkind person, Philippa," Elizabeth defended her friend.

"She is an arrogant and vindictive bitch!" Philippa cried. "She has even threatened to make the princess her servant!"

"Indeed," Elizabeth murmured. "And do you really think the king, who adores his child, would tolerate a woman who threatened such a thing? You are listening to unfounded gossip, sister. Your devotion to Queen Katherine has blinded you. You must learn to control your feelings lest you endanger your sons' careers."

"Why should I take advice from you?" Philippa demanded to know.

"You are a country woman, and you have no idea what life in the court is like."

"Because I am your little sister, and despite the fact you have turned into a pompous prig, I love you. And Uncle Thomas said I must help you, for he knew you would feel this way, Philippa. Be reasonable, and be sensible. You can do nothing to change what has happened to Queen Katherine. As I have previously said to you, the problem is the king's lack of a male heir. If it had not been Anne it would have been someone else. You must think of your sons. Disapprove if you will. You are surely not the only one who does. But keep your anger to yourself. It does you no good, and it does poor Queen Katherine no good. While Anne is not cruel, she will remember a slight done her, and eventually find a way to repay the person in kind," Elizabeth warned her companion. "Your irrational behavior could reflect upon us all, and we have held royal favor now for many years. That favor comes as much from the king as from Queen Katherine. If you cause us to lose it, Mama will certainly not think kindly of you." Elizabeth reached out and took her sister's hand in hers. "Remember that the family is everything. Nothing is more important."

Philippa sighed. "I know you are right," she said, "yet I cannot help but be angry at everything that has happened."

"You are a consummate courtier, sister. Mask your anger. Do not tell me you haven't done it before, for I am certain you have," Elizabeth said. She arose. "I have been traveling for what seems forever. I want a hot bath, a good supper, and a bed that is not home to a family of voracious fleas. Will you be here when I wake up tomorrow?"

Philippa nodded. "I'll go down to Greenwich with you," she said. "Crispin is already there. We are asked to the coronation. While some, like the Duke of Norfolk's wife, will not come, my husband says we must."

"The Duchess of Norfolk is Anne's aunt," Elizabeth said, surprised.

"By marriage, not blood," Philippa answered her. "And like me she is devoted to Queen Katherine. Ohh, that I dared be as brave as she, and refuse to go!"

"You have not the name," Elizabeth answered dryly. "Nor are you family. Anne does not like either her uncle or her aunt. She will not be sorry they are not there. And she will sooner than later discover a way to repay the duchess for her contempt." Elizabeth kissed her sister's cheek and departed the hall where they had been sitting. Reaching her old bedchamber she found Nancy awaiting her.

" 'Tis good to be back in a respectable house," Nancy said. "They're filling your tub now, and the water is so hot it would peel the skin off a peach."

"When I'm through you bathe," Elizabeth said. "It may have rained most of our way to London, and while that kept the dust down, the road was still dirty." Waiting for the serving men to leave, she then loosened the tabs holding her skirt up, and unlaced the petticoats beneath. They fell to the floor, and Elizabeth stepped from them. Unfastening her bodice, she handed it to Nancy, who had gathered up the dusty skirts. Next came her stockings and chemise. Climbing into the tall oak tub, Elizabeth sighed gratefully. "Have I anything to wear to court, or must you refurbish my traveling garments, Nancy?"

"It will have to be these," Nancy said. "Your trunks are by now at Bolton House in Greenwich, mistress. We have a day, and I'll have your skirt and bodice respectable by then. I'm going to take them off right now and into the gardens to shake. Then I'll hang them out by the kitchen to air. You just enjoy your soak." She hurried out.

*Well,* Elizabeth thought, *here I am again in the one place I vowed never to be. London. And the court lies ahead of me. The journey was tedious. I hated every step I took away from Baen, young Tom, and Friarsgate. I hope the queen will not keep me away from them for too long. What can Anne Boleyn want of me? I have nothing to offer her. She has attained her goal. She is the king's wife, and shortly to be crowned queen. She is carrying the king's child. What can she want?*

Elizabeth had asked herself this question over and over again as she had traveled south from Friarsgate. But she had not come up with an answer. She prayed she would not get to Greenwich to learn that Anne had merely called her on a whim. Yet when Elizabeth had requested an escort from Anne, one had been forthcoming. She would know soon enough. Emptying her mind of its confusion, Elizabeth washed her long blond hair, pinned it atop her head, and washed herself before sitting back in the water for a few minutes to relax. She needed food, and she need a good night's rest. She did not need to be asking herself questions that only Anne Boleyn could answer.

The next day she and Philippa spent together. Sitting in the gardens of Bolton House they watched the river traffic and talked of their childhoods, of their mother, and of Friarsgate. Philippa was surprised—and yet she asked herself why she would be—at her youngest sister's maturity and great sense of responsibility. She realized how much like Rosamund the youngest of her daughters was. Elizabeth was fascinated by her sophisticated elder, who had so skillfully negotiated her way amid the high and mighty all these years. It took a rare talent to survive within the royal world. The sisters realized that they were gaining a deeper understanding of and respect for each other. The two young women felt closer to each other than they had ever felt in their lives.

The next morning, they prepared to depart for Greenwich. The house barge bobbed at the quay at the foot of the gardens. The bargemen wore the Earl of Witton's livery. Philippa was dressed in a silk gown so deep a green it seemed almost black. The square neckline was embroidered with pearls, and the fitted sleeves were trimmed with creamy lace. About her waist was an embroidered girdle of gold and tiny seed pearls. The long rope of large pearls about her neck was pale gold. Upon her auburn head the Countess of Witton had set a gable hood with a veil that covered her hair. It was very much in the style of Katherine of Aragon.

"An English hood would be more flattering," Elizabeth said quietly.

"It's old-fashioned," Philippa said.

"No more so than the gable," Elizabeth murmured.

"I will not wear a French hood!" Philippa declared.

"Then either wear the English, or wear just a veil over your hair," Elizabeth said. "Anne notices things like that. She is very conscious of fashion."

Philippa made a derisive noise, but she pulled the gabled hood from her head, calling to her tiring woman as she did. "Lucy! Fetch the English hood. I've decided to wear it instead of this gabled one." She looked at her sister. "Are you satisfied now?"

Elizabeth grinned and nodded.

"Is that the gown you arrived in?" Philippa demanded to know.

" 'Tis all I have. My trunks are at Greenwich. Nancy refurbished it," Elizabeth told her sister.

"Aye, and did a fine job of it too," Philippa said. "Tell me you didn't ride astride with your legs showing," she begged.

Elizabeth just laughed. "You would have been more shocked if I arrived in woolen breeks of Friarsgate blue," she said.

Philippa shook her head. "Aye, I would have," she admitted, smiling. "The color suits you. 'Tis like doeskin. I have always liked that light creamy brown, but alas, I am too sallow for it. With your blond hair and fair skin it is quite lovely. There is no decoration on the bodice, though, and those marten cuffs are a bit plain. So is your hood."

"But it was perfect for traveling," Elizabeth said. "And once I have paid my respects to the king and his new wife I will return to Uncle's Greenwich house to change into something more appropriate. But Anne will appreciate that I have come directly to her from London, not even bothering to change, so anxious am I to see her."

"I would not have thought you so devious," Philippa remarked, as her servant, Lucy, set the English hood on her head and settled the veil that went with it.

Elizabeth grinned. "I go the sheep and cattle markets, sister, and bargain better than most men. I may not be the courtier you are, but I still know how to dissemble in order to gain what I want. You do not have to live at court to learn such things. 'Tis the way of the world."

Philippa thought a moment, and then she chuckled. "I suppose it is," she agreed.

Together the two sisters exited the house, their serving women behind them, making their way down to the barge. It was the time between the two tides on the river, and their bargemen were able to row swiftly through the city, beneath the London bridge, and down to Greenwich Palace. When they arrived at the stone quay with its steps leading up to the lawns they were met by servants who helped them from their barge.

"Row back to the Greenwich house quay," the Countess of Witton said. "We will be staying there, and will not need you again today."

"Yes, m'lady," the head bargeman said politely.

Their tiring women in their wake, Philippa, Countess of Witton, and Elizabeth, the lady of Friarsgate, moved across the lawns. To Elizabeth's relief she spotted the king and the soon-to-be-crowned queen walking with a group of courtiers. Nudging Philippa, she whispered softly and set their direction towards Henry and Anne. Reaching them, Elizabeth made a deep curtsey, and then waited for Anne to acknowledge her.

"Why, look here, sweetheart," the king's voice boomed jovially. " 'Tis the Countess of Witton and her sister, both come to do you honor."

Anne looked not at Elizabeth, but rather to Philippa. "Do you come to do me honor, my lady?" she demanded to know.

Elizabeth held her breath.

"First honors must go to the king, your highness," Philippa answered. "And then to the queen."

"Well said! Well said!" The king chuckled before his prickly bride could demand to know which queen. He could see how difficult it was for Philippa, and he appreciated her loyalty. His gaze swung to Elizabeth. "You have answered my wife's request to join us, Mistress Elizabeth," he said. "I am both flattered and surprised."

Request? Elizabeth almost laughed aloud. "I was honored, majesty, to be asked to join the court at such an auspicious time," she murmured. "My mother sends her kind regards to your majesty, and to your highness."

"Still wed to her Scot?" he demanded to know.

"Aye, your majesty."

"And am I to understand that you have followed in her footsteps?" Henry Tudor said, his small blue eyes narrowing.

"I fear so, your majesty," Elizabeth admitted. "I seem to have a weakness for Scots gentlemen, as your majesty may recall from my last visit."

Philippa poked her sister nervously.

The king chortled knowingly. "The gentleman still resides with us. I am sure you will renew that old acquaintance, Mistress Meredith."

"Mistress Hay, your majesty," Elizabeth gently corrected him. "My husband's name is Baen Hay."

"Baen? 'Tis an odd name," the king remarked.

"It means fair-skinned, and he is a most fair man," Elizabeth said, "and every bit as big as your majesty."

"Indeed," the king said. "He did not come to court with you?"

"Nay, your majesty. He is the steward of my manor, and of necessity needed to remain home," Elizabeth told the king. "He is no courtier, but a man of the land."

"But he let you come?" Again the blue eyes narrowed.

"He would never disobey the king's command," she replied.

"Then you have tamed this Scot of yours, Mistress Hay," the king responded.

"I have indeed, your majesty," Elizabeth said.

The king laughed loudly. "You may both walk with us," he said.

The sisters slipped in amid the favored courtiers. Philippa knew some of the women, and spoke to them as they strolled along. Finally, however, the king's wife made plain her desire to sit, and a comfortable chair was sent for and hurriedly brought.

"Continue on, my lord husband," she told the king. "I know how you love your exercise. But allow me a companion to keep me company."

"Who would you choose?" the king asked.

"Why, Elizabeth Hay, of course," Anne said. "Come, Elizabeth, and sit by me here in the sweet grass," the young queen invited.

Elizabeth obeyed as the king and his party moved off. "It is good to see your highness again," Elizabeth said.

"Anne, now that we are alone, Anne, for mercy's sake," the queen told her companion. "Thank God you came!"

"You gave me no choice," Elizabeth said with a small smile. " 'You are commanded to court,' " she repeated Anne's message. "And in the spring, when there is so much to do at Friarsgate," she scolded her friend.

"I feared if I just asked you would not come," Anne admitted.

"I know," Elizabeth said. "What is the matter, Anne? You are married to the king. You carry his child. You are to be crowned queen in June. Is this not all you desired? What more is there for any woman?"

Anne Boleyn's fine eyes filled with tears that she quickly blinked back. She bit her lip nervously. "Aye, it is everything I wanted, and more. But they all hate me for it. They thought I would become the king's mistress, and that they would reap the rewards of my sacrifice; and when the king tired of me they would wed me to some wealthy old man who would pay them handsomely for the privilege of having King Henry's former mistress for his wife. But that was not good enough for me! And I did not give in until last September. I held him at bay for ten years, Elizabeth. You know I was not wanton, though everyone believes it of me. My father will not speak to me any longer. By replacing old Queen Katherine he says I have disgraced the family. In his eyes a mistress was a more honorable position. My mother will treat with me only in secret, for my father has forbidden her to speak with me. My uncle of Norfolk has shared his displeasure with me as well, although he will use my newly exalted state to whatever advantage is best for him. My sister is jealous of me, for I have done what she could not. As for my brother, George, he cares for nothing but himself, not even his wife, though I do not blame him there. Jane is a silly, pretentious creature lacking in both charm and wit. And she is ambitious, but for what I cannot fathom. I am alone, Elizabeth. I have no one."

"You have your husband who loves you," Elizabeth began.

"Loves me? Nay. No longer. Perhaps in the beginning. Perhaps even during the chase I led him. But now? No. He wants nothing of me but a son. If I give him a son I am safe, Elizabeth. If I do not I do not know what will happen to me," Anne said desperately. "What was my dream is becoming a nightmare."

"Moods such as yours are common when carrying a child," Elizabeth soothed the queen quietly. "I am here now, and I will do whatever you need me to do so that you will not be afraid, Anne." She took the older girl's icy hand in hers, and rubbed it to try to bring warmth back into it.

"Did you have moods of despair?" Anne wanted to know.

Elizabeth chuckled. "I was enceinte without the blessing of the church. You see, I seduced my husband that summer I returned home," she explained. "We handfasted ourselves to each other. Then the autumn came, and he returned to Scotland. I was furious, for I foolishly believed he would remain with me. I loved him, and he loved me, but he was gone. I threw myself into my work. And after Twelfth Night I realized that I was with child. Our committal would make the child legitimate, I told myself. I did not send to Baen, but I sent for my mother and told her proudly that I was with child. There would be a new heir or heiress for Friarsgate."

"You seduced a man?" Anne's dark eyes were suddenly sparkling. "Oh, Elizabeth, how daring of you! As always, you do not disappoint me. Tell me more!"

"My stepfather and my uncle, Lord Cambridge, went up into Scotland in the midst of the winter snows. They spoke with Baen's father and arranged the marriage properly. Baen is his father's eldest son, but his bastard, you see, so the master of Grayhaven was content to have him leave his house to come to me. They brought him back to Friarsgate, and we were wed in the church. But I was angry at Baen for having left me in the first place."

"I would have been too," Anne agreed.

"Nay, I see now that I was wrong," Elizabeth told her friend. "Without realizing it, or perhaps I did, I tried to force my husband's loyalties. They could not be forced. No one's can. But I let my anger continue to control me. Then in the midst of my labor Baen apologized for leaving me. How could I not forgive him? But the anger I felt could not have been good for my child. Fortunately by the time he was born we were reconciled," Elizabeth explained. "You can no longer think of anything else but this child, Anne."

"I know," came the reply. "England needs a prince. How many times have I heard that said, Elizabeth? They do not care if I live or die. England will have its prince. That is all that matters to my husband, to the court, to the country. They will revile me, but England must have its prince." Her tone was becoming agitated.

"Anne, Anne," Elizabeth cautioned her. "That was not what I meant. The child within you is fragile and helpless. You are the only one who can protect it. It is Anne's child. Not England's. Put your hands on either side of your belly and cradle it. The bairn will be comforted by your touch."

The queen did as Elizabeth had bidden her. Suddenly a smile lit her face. "I feel it!" she said excitedly, her voice filled with wonder. "I can feel my child!" She looked down at Elizabeth, seated in the grass next to her chair. "You see! I need you, Elizabeth! You are the only person who cares for me. I am not so afraid when you are with me."

"I should not remain away long," Elizabeth began, but the queen waved an impatient hand.

"You cannot leave me!" she cried low.

"Anne, I have a husband, a child, lands. My responsibility is at Friarsgate. I came not just because you commanded it, but because of my friendship for you, but I cannot remain with you forever."

"Until my child is born," the queen said. "You must stay by my side until I have given England its prince. Promise me, Elizabeth! Swear it!"

Elizabeth sighed. This was not what she had anticipated or wished, but this girl who had been so kind to her once needed her. "I will stay until your bairn is born," she promised the young queen. And then she patted the hand in hers.

Anne smiled her little cat's smile. "I knew you would not desert me," she said. "The others all have, but I knew you would not." She laughed softly. "We shall share all sorts of secrets, you and I. And all the fine ladies who serve me will be jealous."

"And so will my sister." Elizabeth chuckled. "She prides herself on being in the midst of things important here at court."

"Your sister does not like me," Anne said, her look dark.

"Nay, do not be angry at Philippa. She met the princess of Aragon when she was but ten years of age, just about the same age you were when you went to France," Elizabeth explained. "She was invited as a maid of honor when she was twelve. Our mother was raised with the three princesses, which is why as unimportant a family as ours was given such an honor. And after our mother left court she remained friends with both the princess of Aragon and Queen Margaret. Philippa emulates our mother's loyalty. She is not a woman for whom change comes easy, I fear, but she respects the king, and will never show you any disrespect, like so many others."

"Can she lay aside her loyalty so easily?" Anne asked.

Elizabeth chuckled again. "It has nothing to do with loyalty. Philippa will be loyal to the princess of Aragon until death. But she is also ambitious for her sons. The eldest serves the king as page, but he will soon go home, for he is becoming too old for such a position, and as his father's heir needs to take his place by Crispin's side at Brierewode. His youngest brother, Hugh St. Clair, will take his place. The second of my sister's sons serves your uncle as a page. He was to go to Wolsey, but Wolsey's star dimmed and went out, did it not? And Philippa made certain her son's career was not blocked before it began. Nay, Philippa will be respectful of you, Anne. She is prickly, but her heart is a good one, and she loves her family."

The queen laughed. "You always tell me the truth, and you rarely couch it in diplomatic terms, Elizabeth. That is why I both like and trust you."

"I will never betray you, Anne," Elizabeth said quietly.

"Here you are all alone, your highness!" A sharp-faced young woman was suddenly by their side. She did not bother even to look at Elizabeth. "How is it you have been left so?" She waved at a passing page. "A stool, boy, for my lady Rochford. Quickly! Oh, poor, dear sister! Are you filled with the ennui of your condition?"

Elizabeth's eyes met the queen's and she swallowed back her amusement.

"Lady Jane Rochford, this is my friend Elizabeth Hay, the lady of Friarsgate," Anne said. "Elizabeth, this is George's wife. George always thought Elizabeth amusing when they last met," the queen said wickedly, for she knew her sister-in-law to be a jealous woman. "I sent for Elizabeth to share in the joy of our coronation."

Jane Rochford stared at Elizabeth, assessing whether she was to be bothered with, but noting her garment decided she was not. She nodded a bare greeting, which Elizabeth returned in the same insulting fashion. Lady Rochford was annoyed, but she could say nothing under the circumstances.

"Are you staying at your uncle's house?" the queen asked Elizabeth sweetly.

"Indeed, your highness, I am. I shall not need accommodation at court for myself and my tiring woman. If I might now be excused, as you have other companionship. I came directly from my journey, and have not yet had time to change from my travel garments into proper clothing." Elizabeth arose from her grassy seat.

"Of course, Elizabeth," the queen said graciously. "And tell your sister, the Countess of Witton, that I am pleased to see her with us."

"I will, your highness, and thank you," Elizabeth said, curtseying gracefully, and then she backed the proper distance away before turning and moving across the lawns.

"The Countess of Witton?" Jane Rochford said. "That rather countrified girl is the Countess of Witton's sister?" She was surprised. This would take a reassessment.

"Why, yes," Anne said. "And Lord Cambridge is their uncle. Elizabeth is a very wealthy northern landholder, Jane. We became friends when she last visited court. Her mother grew up at the court of King Henry VII. She is not nobility, of course, but she is very, very well connected. I sent for her, for she amuses me with her honest speech. It is something I rarely hear. She left her responsibilities, her husband, and her child to come to me. She is a true friend."

Lady Jane Rochford heard the rebuke in the queen's voice. She stared hard at the retreating form of the lady of Friarsgate. How was this young woman going to fit into the scheme of things? And just how amusing had George Boleyn found her? And would he seek her company out again?

Elizabeth could feel Lady Rochford's eyes burning into her back as she hurried across the grass. She was going to go to Bolton House so she might change her garments. Not watching where she was going, she suddenly found herself stumbling into a gentleman. Surprised, she offered her apology. "I beg your pardon, sir."

"Elizabeth? Elizabeth Meredith?" She heard the soft burr in his voice, and as she looked up, her eyes met those of Flynn Stewart.

"Flynn! I was told you were still at court. Did you not follow my advice and ask your brother, King James, for a rich wife?" Elizabeth asked him.

"I did, and he said he would consider it, but while I remained his eyes and ears here at court a wife in Scotland was of little use to me," Flynn told her with a grin. "I am afraid I agree. But tell me, did you find a husband worthy of you?"

"I did," she told him. "Like you, he is a Scot, but let me go now. I am just arrived, have paid my respects to the king and the queen, and would now hurry to my uncle's house to change clothing." She made a motion with her hands. "As you can see I am not dressed for court. I shall see you again." And she moved quickly by him onto the woodland path which led to Bolton House Greenwich.

Why was her heart racing? she wondered as she hurried along. She was a happily married woman. Yet still, she had been half in love with him once, and she suspected he might have loved her had his duty not interfered. What was it with men and their duty? It was the excitement of the court and her surprise at meeting him so precipitously, she decided as she reached the garden wall. Seeking the key, she opened the little door and stepped through. The scent of roses reached her nose. Nothing had changed here, and then she laughed at herself. Of course nothing had changed. It was May again, and the last time she had been here it was May. Entering the house, she called for Nancy.

While the court watched in amazement, newly confirmed Archbishop of Canterbury Thomas Cranmer had convened an ecclesiastical court at Dunstable on the tenth day of May. Katherine of Aragon might have attended it, for it was near where she was currently staying. However, she ignored it, as she had most of the king's proceedings in this matter. In Katherine's mind she was Henry's true wife and queen. The mother of his heiress. There was nothing further to discuss. The session was a short one. On the thirteenth of the month a decision was reached. The marriage of Henry Tudor to Katherine, the princess of Aragon, was declared to have never been, never existed. It was null and void. The king had been a bachelor on January twenty-fifth when he had married Anne Boleyn. She was his legal wife and England's true queen. The child she carried now would be legitimate. Many in England had wept when that verdict was pronounced. Katherine, of course, did not accept such a decision, and fretted for her daughter, Mary. If Mary was bastardized then the kind of marriage she needed to contract would not be at all that to which she was entitled. Katherine would fight on for her daughter.

It had been decided that Anne would go by river up to London on the twenty-ninth day of May. Her first destination was to be the Tower of London, where all kings and queens awaiting their coronation stayed until a crown was placed upon their heads. And nothing would do but that the royal apartments be refurbished beforehand. For days craftsmen had been busily working to make everything perfect. The ancient walls were replastered, and then repainted with several fresh coats of paint. Windows were freshly glazed, with new leading separating the glass panes. New carpets were brought in, and new tapestries hung. Furniture was regilded. And now the royal apartments awaited the monarch and his soon-to-be queen.

The lord mayor of London had had fifty barges from his own guild of haberdashers gathered to sail downriver to Greenwich. Beautifully decorated and flying multicolored flags, banners, and streamers, they would meet Anne's barge and escort it to the Tower. Preceding the lord mayor's own vessel was an open flat barge called a foist. Upon it was the great red Pendragon of Wales to honor the king's house of Tudor. There were savages in skins and particolored silks dancing with fanciful and colorful monsters who roared and belched clouds of fire. To the lord mayor's right was a barge known as the bachelors' barge, upon which were a dozen trumpeters and other musicians all playing merrily. To the lord mayor's left another foist floated, this one containing a great display of red and white Tudor roses, and rising from amid the roses was Anne's own personal device, a white falcon, beautifully carved, painted, and gilded. Around the roses a bevy of virgins garbed in white silk robes sang sweetly and danced together.

Reaching Greenwich this grand procession anchored and waited. At three o'clock in the afternoon Anne appeared dressed in cloth of gold, her long black hair streaming down her back. She was attended by a great crowd of ladies, but only she would ride in the royal barge. Her ladies would be crammed into several barges that would join the procession. Several noblemen had brought their barges downriver to join the procession. They included the Duke of Suffolk, the king's brother-in-law, the Marquess of Dorset, and even the queen's estranged father, Thomas Boleyn, the Earl of Wiltshire and Ormonde, who did not want to be viewed publicly as being at odds with his daughter now that she was about to be crowned.

The Bolton House barge carried the Countess of Witton, her sister, the lady of Friarsgate, and three other court ladies of Philippa's acquaintance. They were most grateful for the transportation, and for not having to be jammed into the other barges containing the queen's ladies. Anne had wanted Elizabeth to travel with her, but Elizabeth's wisdom had prevailed in the matter.

"I can be companionable to you only if you do not offend my betters," she explained to the queen. "There will be enough jealousy over your favoring me as it is. It would be dreadfully insulting to everyone if I were in your barge. You know they would find ways of keeping us apart, and perhaps even appeal to the king to send me home."

"He would not do it!" Anne cried. "Not now!"

"But your behavior would embarrass him, Anne. Do you truly wish to embarrass the king? He has been very good to you, and stands by you against all," Elizabeth said. "Philippa and I will travel in our own barge." And so they had. It was hung all over with tiny bells that tinkled in the light wind and bobbing waves. Anne remarked afterwards that she had thought the decor on the Bolton House barge most unique and charming.

The procession made its way back upriver. Many merchant and military vessels lined the banks of the Thames. Each offered a gunnery salute to the new queen as she passed by. The air was filled with smoke and noise. The loudest boom, however, sounded as Anne's barge, flying its white falcon pendant, reached the Tower. Here the Lord Chamberlain and officer of arms greeted her and helped her from her vessel. For a brief moment Anne savored the day, which was a perfect one. Then she allowed the Lord Chamberlain to escort her to the king, who awaited her atop the quay. He greeted her with a kiss, murmuring in her ear, "Welcome, sweetheart!"

Anne relaxed, and for the first time in months she felt safe. Everything was going to be all right. Henry loved her. The child within her was healthy. She had her friend to keep her company and raise her spirits. Turning, she smiled more broadly than anyone had ever seen Anne Boleyn smile. "My good liege, my lord mayor, members of the haberdashers' company, my lords, and ladies, good citizens, I thank you from the bottom of my heart for this most gracious welcome. God bless you all!" And, raising her hand, she waved. A small cheer arose from the crowds watching. Anne, however, did not notice the paucity of the cheer, for she had already taken the king's arm and was being escorted inside.

Behind her the great barge in which Anne had ridden bobbed at anchor, its twenty-four oarsmen having disembarked. The vessel had previously belonged to Katherine of Aragon. It was probably the finest barge in England. Katherine would have no further use for it, Anne reasoned, and ordered her chamberlain to confiscate it and have it refurbished for her.

Chapuys, the ambassador from Katherine's nephew who was both king of Spain and the holy Roman emperor, complained to Cromwell. Cromwell soothed the ambassador's ire by assuring him that the king would be distressed by this knowledge. Chapuys then brought his complaint to Anne's uncle, the wily Duke of Norfolk. Thomas Howard smiled his cold smile, and agreed that his niece was the cause of everyone's distress and responsible for all the misery now afflicting the court. A rebuke was issued to Anne's chamberlain, but Katherine's arms were removed from the barge, and Anne's were added despite the king's alleged unhappiness over the matter.

But the real distress over Anne's now-public union with Henry was among the people. They had loved the princess of Aragon, and did not wish to accept this wanton witch who had cast her spell over their beloved king. In the churches of London, when the time came to pray for King Henry and Queen Anne, many in the congregations walked out. Furious, the king called for the lord mayor of London, and told him in the strongest terms possible that such a thing was not to happen ever again. The guild heads were to be told this, and they were to tell their workers and their apprentices. And they were to admonish their wives as well. Criticism of any sort against Queen Anne would from this moment on be considered a punishable offense.

The streets of London were cleaned and freshly graveled, with special places barricaded off so spectators might watch the procession in safety. And pageants were to be prepared for Anne's coronation by the various guilds. The lord mayor did as he had been bidden, even ordering the foreign merchants to take part in the festivities and prepare tributes to King Henry's wife. Most did so reluctantly, but now all was in readiness.

At the Tower the king and the queen and a few chosen guests had gone to the newly redone royal apartments. There had even been a new door made for the entrance into the garden. A feast was to be served. There was the freshest fish brought up from the sea this morning into London. Fat prawns broiled in white wine. Icy oysters. Creamed cod. There were venison and boar. A swan stuffed with a goose stuffed with a duck, stuffed with a small capon that was stuffed with tiny songbirds, roasted and set amid a sauce of dried cherries. There was bread, butter, several kinds of cheeses, and a great charger of the king's favorite, artichokes. Finally there were cakes soaked in marsala wine, jellies, candied violets, spun-sugar subtleties, and the first strawberries of the season, with freshly clotted Devon cream.

Elizabeth had not been asked to the banquet. She was not important enough, but she waited in the queen's apartments as she had been asked for Anne to return. When she did Elizabeth found Anne in a foul mood. She pushed away her serving women and shouted at her ladies to leave her be. "Elizabeth will attend me. Go find your beds, you group of gossips. Bride, you are to wait outside," she instructed her tiring woman. Then she slammed the door behind them. "Bitches!"

"What has distressed you, Anne?" Elizabeth asked her.

"Mistress Seymour," Anne replied. "Meek, mild, mealymouthed Mistress Jane Seymour! If you had seen her making eyes at my husband, Elizabeth. The little virgin was just asking to be breached by the king. He's getting restless, Elizabeth. My belly is not a pretty thing, I fear, and his lusts must be satisfied. Why can he not leave me be now, and restrain himself?" Anne flung herself onto her bed.

"Sit up," Elizabeth said, "and let me loosen your laces and get your shoes off." She helped Anne to sit, and removed her bodice. Then she undid the tabs of the queen's skirts, unlaced them, and drew them off. Rolling Anne's stockings from her slender legs, she shook her head. The queen's ankles and feet were swollen. She slipped her shoes off.

"You are so good to me," the queen murmured as Elizabeth laid her slippers and garments aside. "Your very presence soothes me." Then she brightened. "Was not today a triumph? The weather is so wondrously fair. It is as if God is smiling down on me. How clever of you to put those darling little bells all over your barge."

" 'Twas Philippa's idea," Elizabeth said. "She knows how much you appreciate originality and novelty."

"Indeed," Anne said. "Are you certain she was not trying to steal my thunder?"

Elizabeth laughed. "Do not be foolish, Anne. No matter her love for the princess of Aragon she would not dare such behavior. Philippa is far too correct in her manner to do so."

"Do you like your sister?" Anne wanted to know. "I don't like mine. When we were in France her reputation was vile. She looks like an angel, with that halo of blond hair and her blue eyes, but she was the biggest whore at the court. King Francis called her his English mare, he rode her so often," Anne said. "Now she is married, and so prim and proper, as if I or anyone else would forget her previous behavior."

"Family is everything, Anne," Elizabeth said. "You should try to make peace with the lady Mary now." She propped several pillows behind the queen, and several more beneath her feet. "Would you like some wine?"

"Water it," Anne instructed her. "I am very thirsty now."

The door to the queen's bedchamber opened, and the king strode in, an eyebrow lifting as he saw Elizabeth. "Good evening, Mistress Hay," he greeted her.

Elizabeth curtseyed. Then she handed Anne her goblet. "Good evening, sire. Would your majesty like to be alone with the queen?" she queried him.

"Aye," he said.

"I don't want Elizabeth to go," Anne said petulantly.

"Your highness, you place me in a difficult dilemma," Elizabeth gently chided her friend. "It has been a very long day for you, and you need your rest. If I am to remain by your side tomorrow, so do I. And the king, your husband, would speak with you privily." She curtseyed politely to the royal couple. "I was taught that it is a wife's duty to obey her husband. Forgive me, but I must accommodate his majesty wishes." She curtseyed again, and backed from the bedchamber.

"A wise young woman," Henry Tudor said, "and one who knows her place."

"Why do you always scold me these days?" Anne began to sob.

"Now, sweetheart." The king sat down on the edge of the queen's bed. "I do not mean to chastise you. Did I not give you a perfect day?"

"Aye." Anne sniffled. "But the people don't like me."

"They will once our son is born. How can they not love the queen who gives them a prince?" the king wanted to know. He laid his hand on Anne's belly and felt the child stir strongly beneath his touch. He smiled broadly. "Our child will be one of England's greatest monarchs," he told her. "I just know it." Then, leaning over, he kissed her gently. "Elizabeth Hay is right. You need your rest." He stood up.

"Where are you going?" Anne wanted to know. She was suspicious of him.

"To join my companions and play cards," he told her.

"Send Mistress Seymour to me," Anne said. "I shall have her read to me until I fall asleep. And she will sleep on the trundle, so that should I need something in the night she will be here to fetch it for me." She smiled her little cat's smile at him.

The king chuckled. "You have sharp eyes, Annie," he told her. "But rest assured that I love you best, and will love you even more when you birth our son." Then, with a bow, Henry Tudor left his wife.

# Chapter 18

O n the day following the queen's entry into London there was lit- tle official activity. The queen, in her sixth month of preg- nancy, spent her time resting and playing cards. There was to be a banquet given for the eighteen noblemen being created Knights of the Bath the following day. The queen, however, did not attend this men- only function. Sixty other gentlemen would also be knighted, but in the usual way. Later in the evening the eighteen were bathed and shriven according to ancient custom. They would have honored places when Anne formally entered the city, and then later at the coronation itself. The king wanted to make the occasion of his wife's coronation one that would always be remembered.

The next day, Saturday, the traditional coronation procession to Westminster was to take place. Although little time had been allowed for London to prepare, the streets were as decorated as they had been when Henry had been crowned over twenty years earlier. The queen's litter would be carried along Fenchurch and Gracechurch to Leden- hall to Ludgate to Fleet Street and down the Strand to Westminster. Every house along the route was ordered to be hung with flags and buntings.

Philippa and Elizabeth were to ride among the queen's ladies. Spe- cial cloth-of-gold gowns had been provided for them. Philippa was as- tounded when she was told she might keep her gown as a remembrance of this day. "Such generosity!" she bubbled, her elegant hands smoothing across the fabric of her skirts.

"You can have mine," Elizabeth said with a smile. "I will have no use for it at Friarsgate. It is beautiful, though."

"You will have to ride like a lady, and not astride," Philippa warned her sister.

Elizabeth laughed. "I believe I can manage it," she said. "I can hardly gallop through the streets in such finery."

"Why do you think I was asked to ride in the procession?" Philippa wondered.

"I told Anne, the queen," Elizabeth amended, "that while you would always love the princess of Aragon, you were a loyal subject of the king and queen." Elizabeth chuckled. "I did not, however, name the queen, Philippa, so 'twas not really a lie."

"I should not be here," Philippa fretted.

"Your husband and your sons are here," Elizabeth said. "Besides, you love spectacles such as this will be."

"The Duchess of Norfolk will report to my lady Katherine everyone of any note who has attended. She will be so hurt and disappointed in me," Philippa said softly.

"Blame Crispin," Elizabeth said airily. "The princess of Aragon believes a woman should obey her husband. Your husband insisted you attend. He said you must put your own feelings aside and think of your sons."

"That's exactly what he said!" Philippa exclaimed. "How did you know it?"

"Because Crispin is a man of eminent good sense," Elizabeth responded.

"The Duchess of Norfolk is not obeying her husband," Philippa said.

Elizabeth snorted derisively. "In my brief stay at court I have learned that the Howard family are a lofty lot. They consider themselves better than those who sit on the throne. I will wager the duke did not order his wife to the coronation. He is in France on the king's business and is excused. She does not go because she chooses not to go. A foot in both camps, sister. One day they will outsmart themselves and fall. And his old dowager mother will be in a fine litter following after the queen. Nay. The Howards will not be considered disloyal, and neither should you."

"You have become so wise," Philippa said. "Yet when we last saw each other you were a foolish girl who showed neither respect nor manners."

"I am just a country woman, sister," Elizabeth said. "And I miss my home, and I want to be there. I am so lonely for Baen. For our little son. But I have promised the queen I will stay by her side until her son is safely delivered."

They had been walking in the tower gardens, but even so Philippa lowered her voice to almost a whisper. "What if it is not a son?" she said.

Elizabeth shuddered. "Do not even think it," she murmured low.

"They say he is dallying with a lady," Philippa confided. "But it is so discreet that no one knows who, or if it is even so."

"The queen does not like the little Seymour girl," Elizabeth noted.

"Jane Seymour of Wolf Hall?" the Countess of Witton said. "The family is of no importance, and the girl is foolish if she encourages the king. She'll end up like Mary Boleyn or Bessie Blount. A big belly married off to a nonentity, and back in the country. She is not his type. I think her rather plain, and she is beyond meek, if such a thing is possible. Nay, Jane Seymour wouldn't be to the king's taste at all."

"The princess of Aragon was a biddable wife," Elizabeth said.

"But she was intelligent, and a good companion," Philippa remarked. "Not at all like . . . this one."

"Anne is intelligent and witty, but I will agree she is hot tempered. The king, however, seems to enjoy a bit of pepper," Elizabeth remarked.

"Ladies! Ladies!" A serving woman was beckoning them frantically. "The procession is forming, and you are wanted."

Picking up their beautiful delicate skirts, the two sisters ran to join the others. They were to ride their own horses, although mounts had been provided for those who didn't have them. Philippa's mare was black, and her sister's gelding was a dappled gray. Their cloth-of-gold skirts against the dark hides was most striking. Philippa's bridle was decorated with tiny silver bells, for she had grown to love the sounds the bells made.

The queen came out from her apartments. She was garbed in a mantle and gown of white silk tissue trimmed lavishly with ermine.

Her waist-length ebony hair was loose, and atop her head was a coronet of multicolored stones that sparkled in the bright sunlight of the spring day. Her litter was lined with cloth of white gold. Four knights garbed in scarlet robes, representing the Cinque Ports, had been delegated to carry the cloth-of-gold canopy over the royal litter. The staves holding the canopy were carved and gilded, and each was decorated with a silver bell. Sixteen knights wearing suits of Tudor-green silk decorated with the king's badge carried the litter, which was led by two white palfreys draped with cloth of silver.

The queen's procession was led by twelve noble gentlemen from the French ambassador's retinue clothed in yellow and blue. The Knights of the Bath wore violet. Among the procession were many noblemen, ambassadors, and other gentlemen. There was the lord chancellor, the archbishop of Canterbury, abbots from the important religious houses, scholars, the archbishop of York, and other bishops from other dioceses. The lord mayor of London was decked out in magnificent finery, with his heavy gold chain of office across his chest. This pleased the king when he later saw him. Lord William Howard acted as earl marshall for the duke, who was in France. The lord high constable that day was Mary Tudor's husband, the Duke of Suffolk.

Preceding the queen was her chancellor, bare-headed. Behind her came her chamberlain and master of horse. Next came a group of ladies in their cloth-of-gold gowns, two gaily decorated chariots carrying the old Duchess of Norfolk and the old Marchioness of Dorset. Two chariots following them transported elderly, but not as distinguished, noblewomen too ancient to ride. The chariots were followed by another larger group of ladies in their cloth-of-gold and velvet gowns, and the queen's guard in their gold-embroidered coats. Henry had spared no expense to crown this woman he had so desperately sought to make his wife for so long. And despite the short notice given to Londoners, they had done their best to respond in kind to the grand procession.

There were pageants and other entertainments at several places along the royal route. At Fenchurch the queen was greeted by children garbed as merchants, who welcomed her in both English and French. At Gracechurch the queen stopped to enjoy a pageant presented to her by the merchants of the steelyard. It was quite elaborate, and had been designed by the artist Hans Holbein, a favorite of the king. Mount Parnassus had been replicated, along with the fountain of Helicon, which was made of marble. From the fountain four streams of wine shot up to fall into a graceful cup above before pouring over the cup into the fountain below. Atop the mountain beneath an arch topped by an eagle Apollo sat, with the goddess Calliope near him. On the sides of the mountain the Muses were seated, each playing an instrument. Verses written in gold lay at their feet in praise of the new queen. As Anne and her entourage gazed in delight and wonder at Holbein's creation, the Muse Clio arose and sang.

"*Beflower the way, citizens; offer your thanks offerings; burn your incense. Wreath your brows with laurel, and with roses. Sport ye in this day's honor. Go to meet your lady mistress, poor man and rich man. Anna comes, bright image of chastity, she whom Henry has chosen to his partner. Worthy husband, worthy wife! May heaven bless these nuptials, and make her a fruitful mother of men-children.*"

The queen clapped and smiled when the pageant had concluded, and then her procession moved on to Ledenhall, whose pageant contained the queen's own device, the white falcon wearing a golden crown. Its singers extolled the fruitful vine Saint Anne. There were several more entertainments along the way with wines flowing from various receptacles, and songs and poetry in the queen's honor.

The procession moved on through the narrow dark streets of London, swept clean of garbage for this auspicious occasion. But all the cleaning in the world could not take away the stink of the city. The ladies all carried pomander balls of oranges stuck around with cloves. And although the streets were crowded and people hung from the open windows of the houses lining the way so that they might see all, there was little cheering, and the faces were somber and unfriendly. Elizabeth only heard two "God save the queens" along the whole way. There were even cries of "Whore!" and "Witch" from some among the spectators. And several times anonymous voices called out, "God save Queen Katherine!" How hurtful it must be for Anne, she thought. But they would sing a different tune when her son was born. They all would!

Close to the abbey Anne was presented with a gold purse containing a thousand gold marks. She made a gracious speech of thanks. And then at last they reached Westminster Hall. The queen was helped from her litter, and entered the building. Refreshments were offered to her, and to all the women in her train. And afterwards the queen slipped quietly from Westminster Hall, returned without fanfare to her barge, and went to meet the king at York Place.

The ladies who were in the queen's immediate train followed her, but Philippa and Elizabeth had no one to take their horses. They were forced to ride back through the city to London Bridge, cross the river, and then return to Bolton House. When they arrived they found a message from the queen bidding Elizabeth to join her at York Place.

"Oh, bother!" Philippa exclaimed. "I had thought we would have tonight together. Crispin will soon be here, and we haven't had enough time together."

Elizabeth stared at the hastily written note in Anne's hand. The queen had been agitated when she had written it but, knowing Anne, by now was calmed and placated. "I'm taking a bath," she announced to her sister. "Then I am going to change my clothes. And then I will take the barge to York Place."

"But the queen—" Philippa began.

Elizabeth raised a hand to silence her elder. "The queen will not know the time that has elapsed, for she will be kept amused by those around her. She is undoubtedly unhappy at the reception given her by the people in the streets. What did she expect?" Elizabeth sighed. "I cannot comfort her if I am dirty and irritable." Then she left her sister in the great hall of the house and hurried upstairs.

The Earl of Witton arrived with his youngest son, Hugh. "Well, here's a good thing or not," he greeted his wife, kissing her. "Tell your mam, Hughie."

"I am to be the queen's page," Hugh St. Clair told his mother. "She saw me with Henry at York Place this afternoon, and asked the king if I was his page. The king said I was to be. Then the queen said to the king that I was a pretty lad, and she wanted me for her own." Hugh St.

Clair, age eight, looked very pleased with himself. "The king told her that on this day whatever she wanted within reason was hers. She gave me this!" He held out a length of silver ribbon. "I will carry it with me always," he told his mother. "I think the queen very beautiful, Mama. Don't you?"

"Of course I do, my darling," Philippa said. She reached out and ruffled his dark hair. "Are you hungry, Hughie? Run to the kitchens and Cook will feed you."

"I must return to the queen tonight," the boy told her.

"So must your aunt Elizabeth," Philippa said. "You will travel with her." She watched as her son ran off, the silver ribbon now tied to his sleeve.

"She has done it to spite me!" Philippa burst out. "She knows my devotion to Queen Katherine, and would take our son from me!"

"There is no Queen Katherine, little one," Crispin St. Clair said, enfolding his weeping wife into an embrace. "You are ambitious for our lads, and that is good. One son has served the king for many years. Henry is to come home with us after the coronation festivities. Another son serves in the Duke of Norfolk's household. Now our youngest will serve Queen Anne. I know you wanted him to take Henry's place, but the king has said otherwise, and you cannot change it."

"We are but pieces on a chessboard," Philippa said despairingly.

The Earl of Witton laughed. "Aye. That is exactly what we are, which is why you and I prefer the woods and fields of Oxfordshire, little one. Their service at the court will gain our lads wives, and perhaps careers in the diplomatic service if they desire it, but no more. Our glory days are over, Philippa. We will be happier accepting it."

"Do you two never do anything but cuddle?" Elizabeth asked, returning to the hall. "Hello, Crispin!" She kissed her brother-in-law's cheek.

"The king's woman has chosen Hughie for one of her pages!" Philippa cried.

"Queen Anne must really be distressed by her reception today," Elizabeth said. "Well, Philippa, 'tis not the end of the world, and you are eager to advance your sons at court. 'Tis actually quite an honor for

Hugh. I'll be back here after all the festivities tomorrow. You aren't leaving right away, are you?"

Philippa bit back a sharp retort. As much as she hated admitting it, both her husband and her sister were right. "What about your gown for the coronation?" she asked. "And no, I will not leave immediately."

"It's already in the barge. I'm taking the big one, not Mama's little one. Do you and Crispin mind?" Elizabeth asked them.

"No," Philippa said. "Hughie is here. You have to take him back with you. That woman wants him immediately."

"If your son is going to be in the queen's household, sister, you are going to have to address her in some way that does not bring disgrace upon the St. Clairs," Elizabeth said with a humorous lilt to her voice.

"I cannot bring myself to call her the queen, or the king's wife," Philippa murmured low.

"But that is exactly what she is," Elizabeth said with perfect logic. "Well, you and Crispin will decide between you what your consciences will allow. Where is Hugh?"

"In the kitchens," Philippa said. "I'll send a servant for him."

"Don't bother," Elizabeth told her. "I'll fetch him on my way." And, turning, she was gone from the hall. Finding her nephew, she told him they were leaving immediately.

"But I've not finished eating," he complained.

"You'll be fortunate to find time to eat at court," Elizabeth told him. "Come along now, or I will leave you behind. Take what you can carry, Hugh!" She hurried off as the cook stuffed several scones into the boy's hand with a wink. Once inside their barge she questioned him. "What brought you to the queen's attention?"

He shrugged. "I don't know. I was with Henry, for I was to take his place. He is going home after the coronation. He has gotten way too tall to be a page, and he is eleven now. If he weren't so tall he probably could have remained until he was twelve." Hugh St. Clair gobbled the scones in his possession.

"Give me one of those," Elizabeth said, snatching a scone from his hand. "I'll not be offered a meal when we arrive, but expected to attend the queen. God knows when we'll get to eat again. What was her mood when you left her earlier?"

"Sometimes I thought she was angry, but then she would cry," he said.

Elizabeth sighed, and considered her next words carefully. "Listen to me, Hugh. If you serve Queen Anne you must be completely loyal to her. If you overhear anything that might be of help to her you must share it. This does not mean you are to be a telltale. People will say things about the queen they should not, for many are still loyal to the princess of Aragon. Do not repeat harmful gossip, for it will hurt her feelings. In time this will pass. Anne's heart is a good one, nephew. She will have her moods, and some are very dark, but if you can you must lighten those moods." She stroked his smooth cheek. "Do you understand me at all, Hugh? You are still such a little boy to have so great a responsibility placed upon your shoulders."

"My mother does not like the queen," Hugh said.

"It is not that she doesn't like the queen, Hugh. It is that she is very loyal to the princess of Aragon. You know your mother came to court as a young girl in that lady's service. You know that your grandmother Rosamund was her friend when the two were raised in the court of King Henry VII. Change is difficult for your mother. Be patient with her, Hugh."

"Change is not difficult for you, Aunt," the boy observed wisely.

"I live with nature, Hugh, and nature is always changing, usually when you least expect it to change," Elizabeth told him. Then she laughed and ruffled his hair. "You are actually a very wise little man."

"I like the queen," he told her.

"Good!" Elizabeth responded. "I will be with her until she births her bairn. We will conspire together, you and I, eh?" And she gave him a tickle.

Hugh St. Clair giggled. "Aye," he agreed with her. And then he took her hand in his, and they were rowed down the river to York Place.

"Where have you been?" the queen cried as Elizabeth entered her apartments. "I am lost without you, Elizabeth! Ah, here is my adorable new page. I do not even know his name, but he is so pretty I could not resist stealing him from the king."

"His name is Hugh St. Clair, your highness, and he is my nephew," Elizabeth informed the queen. So Anne had not known. Good!

"Your nephew?" The queen looked genuinely surprised.

"He is the youngest son of my sister and her husband, the Earl and Countess of Witton," Elizabeth elucidated further. "And he is delighted to serve you."

"I am, your highness!" Hugh declared fervently with an elegant bow.

The queen giggled girlishly. "Do you love me, Hugh St. Clair?" she teased him.

The boy blushed. "Aye, your highness. I will serve you forever!"

The queen's usually sharp features softened. "How sweet you are," she said. "Can you play and sing, Hugh?"

"Yes, your highness," he told her. "I have brought my lute with me. Shall I fetch it and play for you now?" He looked quite eager.

Anne smiled. "Aye, I need to sleep tonight so I am prepared for my crowning. Music would soothe me. Do not be long, lad." She waved him off.

Hugh St. Clair ran from the room.

"There is a wee bit of a closet with a pallet off my privy chamber," the queen said to Elizabeth. "See the boy's possessions are brought to it. He will sleep there. I want him near me. He is untainted by the court, being fresh from the country. How old is he?"

"Eight," Elizabeth answered. "He is really quite taken with you, your highness."

Several of the nearby ladies snickered at this remark. They were, as Elizabeth well knew, quite offended that the queen showed her such favor. Elizabeth spoke softly to them, however, and pretended not to notice their pique. Driven by their own and their families' ambitions, none of them understood the meaning of the word *friendship*. A place in the queen's household was greatly to be desired. Spanish Kate was gone. Anne was queen, and to be near her was a great honor for them. It also permitted them to be near the king, and the center of everything important at the court. They cared not for their mistress. Only the prestige that being in her household brought them.

At the queen's request her women prepared her for bed. Elizabeth never involved herself in the duties of the others. She was there for the single purpose of being Anne's friend. When the queen was settled in her big bed, Elizabeth sat down by her side in a high-backed chair with a tapestried seat, and began to read to the queen from an illuminated book of folktales. Hugh returned with his lute and was permitted into the bedchamber. He seated himself on a stool by the warm fire, and softly began to play "Greensleeves," a tune written by the king for Anne in the early days of their courtship.

The queen smiled happily, her eyes closed as she began to relax. "Do you know the words, Hugh?" she asked him.

The boy began to sing them in a low voice just loud enough for Anne and her companion to hear.

Elizabeth looked at her nephew. He was so young, and yet he seemed to sense just what the queen needed. His dark auburn curls, his large blue eyes, his sweet face proclaimed the innocence of his years. *Now*, she thought sadly, *he will grow up quickly. This is not a place for the innocent.* Anne had not protested that she had ceased to read. She had fallen asleep. She had to be exhausted, Elizabeth thought, for the day had been long and hard for her. But she had carried it off with the sophisticated elegance for which she was both admired and envied. Hugh played on, one song melding into another. Eventually they both fell asleep, Elizabeth in her chair and Hugh on his stool. And, comforted by their presence, Queen Anne slumbered on until her tiring woman entered the chamber to awaken her.

It was June the first. The sun was already long up, but it was barely five o'clock of the morning. Elizabeth and Hugh withdrew immediately so the queen might be prepared for her coronation. Elizabeth quickly showed Hugh the tiny cubicle that was to be his, and sent him off to fetch his belongings from the chamber where the king's pages slept. Then she hurried to find Nancy so she might dress in her fine gown. She had hardly thought of him since her arrival in London, but now, as Nancy dressed her in the blue brocade with its silver-and-gold-embroidered neckline, she thought of Thomas Bolton. How he would have adored the pomp of this royal event. She must remember every detail in order to share it with him when she returned home. Nancy fastened the thin gold chain with its little bejeweled mirror about her waist, and Elizabeth was ready. She put her hand up to tuck an errant strand of her hair beneath her French hood.

"Here." Nancy handed her a pair of creamy kid gloves decorated with seed pearls and crystals.

"Stay by the windows and you can see the queen's procession leave," Elizabeth told her tiring woman.

"You tell me all about it when you can," Nancy said. "Don't forget a thing. His lordship will want to know every last detail."

Elizabeth nodded with a smile, and hurried from the room where all the queen's women had been dressing. She had seen the looks of envy regarding her gown. She had been absolutely right to chose blue rather than Tudor green. There were a plethora of gowns in that color, and none as nicely embellished as was her blue gown. Finding the queen, who was now dressed in royal purple and being fitted with her long ermine-trimmed cape, she asked, "Is there anything I can do for you, your highness?"

"Keep my favorite page by your side," Anne told her. Then she handed Elizabeth a clay chit. "This will get you both into the cathedral, and wear these." She gave her friend two of her household badges.

"Thank you, your highness," Elizabeth said, and she curtseyed low.

Anne gave her a quick grin and a wink. "This cape weighs as much as the king himself," she muttered.

"I will carry the train of it, your highness," the old dowager Duchess of Norfolk said in her reedy voice. "And might I beg a boon of you on this glorious day?"

"What is it?" the queen asked. The dowager had been passing kind to her.

"Would you allow your cousin, little Catherine Howard, to see your coronation? Perhaps the lady of Friarsgate would take her with her to the church." The old woman looked hopeful. "It would be such a thrilling event for the child. She has little in life."

Anne nodded graciously. "Of course," she said. Then she called, "Jane Seymour, give the lady of Friarsgate another of my badges for my cousin Catherine Howard."

"At once, your highness," Jane Seymour said, her eyes not meeting those of her mistress. She hurried off.

"I do not like that girl," Anne murmured to Elizabeth. "And I do not know this cousin, Catherine Howard, but if the dowager seeks to help her, I must too. I hope she will not be too much trouble, Elizabeth."

Elizabeth chuckled. "A proper little Howard girl? I doubt it." She curtseyed again as the queen moved off from her apartments to her royal barge, which would take her back to Westminster.

"Mistress Hay, here is the other badge," Jane Seymour said, handing it to Elizabeth. Then she asked boldly, "How is it you are here, and always by the queen's side, Mistress Hay?" Then the curious eyes lowered as quickly as they had looked directly at Elizabeth. It was a sly movement.

"I am the queen's friend," Elizabeth said shortly, and then she moved off. She had no wish to engage in conversation with Mistress Seymour. There was something about the girl that she could not quite put her finger upon, but Elizabeth knew that she didn't like her. The prim and proper attitude was a false one. She sensed that the girl was filled with guile. Then, looking about, she called for her nephew, and for Mistress Catherine Howard.

The young girl came forward, and Elizabeth was stunned by the child's beauty. She had a heart-shaped face with a pale complexion and cheeks that seemed to have been brushed by a rose. It was a sweet face. Her eyes were a wonderful cerulean blue, and the hair showing beneath her cap was a rich light auburn. "I am Catherine Howard, my lady." She curtseyed politely to Elizabeth.

"Just Mistress Hay," Elizabeth told her. "The dowager Duchess of Norfolk requested of your cousin, the queen, that you be allowed to see the coronation. I am to take you with me and her highness's page, Hugh St. Clair. Come along now. My barge is waiting to take us to Westminster."

"You have your own barge? You must be very rich," Catherine Howard said ingenuously. "I don't know anyone except my uncle, the duke, who has their own barge."

Elizabeth laughed. "I am just the lady of a northern estate. The barge belongs to my uncle, Lord Cambridge, and he is indeed very rich."

"My father is the Earl of Witton," Hugh announced to the young girl.

"Are you his heir?" Catherine Howard wanted to know.

"Nay, I am the youngest son," he told her.

"Then you are of little importance," Catherine Howard said, and she looked straight ahead.

Elizabeth laughed again. "You have been bested, Hughie," she told the boy, whose cheeks were now a bright red.

Reaching Westminster, they were just in time to see the procession that had formed, the queen as its centerpiece, and ready to proceed first into Westminster Hall, and from there into the great cathedral. It was between eight and nine o'clock in the morning. When the queen had entered the hall Elizabeth took the two children by the hand and said, "Quickly! If we do not get into the church we shall not have places despite these chits. We'll watch the procession as it comes down the aisle."

Reaching the cathedral, she offered the yeoman of the guard the clay tickets that the queen had given her. The guardsman took them and grinned at Elizabeth. "You've yer hands full with these two fine youngsters. Who be you, and who be they?"

"I am Mistress Hay, in the queen's service," Elizabeth said. "The lad is the Earl of Witton's son, her favorite page, and the lass her cousin, Mistress Howard."

"Ye're a lady from the north, unless my ears fail me," the guardsman said.

"Cumbria," Elizabeth told him.

"I be from Carlisle," he told her. "Come along, Mistress Hay, and I'll find you a place where these two young folk can see the whole ceremony." Then he led them into the cathedral's royal chapel, settling them in the far left corner of a front bench. "Just be quiet, and none will notice you here," he told them, and then he was gone.

There was a great flourish of trumpets, and the royal procession entered the cathedral. They stood upon the bench so they might see, Elizabeth in the back that Hugh and Catherine might get a better view as they stood before her. Knights and aldermen, gentlemen and noblemen, clergymen and judges came into the great chapel. There were abbots and bishops, the lord chancellor, and the lord mayor of London carrying his mace. The Marquess of Dorset carried the scepter of gold, the Earl of Arundel the rod of ivory decorated with a dove. The Earl of Oxford, who was the lord chamberlain, carried the crown. They did not approve this coronation of Anne Boleyn, but none of them would have given up his hereditary part in the pageantry. The high nobles were followed by the lord high steward, the Knights of the Garter, and the acting earl marshall.

Finally came the queen, escorted by her reluctant father, the Earl of Wiltshire and Ormonde. His titles had been won courtesy of Anne, and yet he had opposed her marriage. Seeing her with the extra panel in her gown used to mask her pregnancy, Thomas Boleyn had told his daughter she ought to take it away, and thank God to find herself in such condition. Anne had snapped back, "I am in better condition than you would have desired, sir!"

The queen walked beneath a canopy carried by knights from the four Cinque Ports. The ends of her robe were carried by the bishops of London and Winchester. The old dowager Duchess of Norfolk carried the robe's long train. The end of the procession was brought up by a bevy of noblewomen and the queen's personal attendants. Anne, despite it all, looked magnificent in her royal purple robes trimmed with ermine, a circlet upon her black hair which hung down her back to her waist.

Led to a throne between the high altar and the choir, the queen rested for a few minutes while the voices of the choirboys sang, their song rising into the high reaches of the chapel. The queen then nodded almost imperceptibly to the archbishop of Canterbury, and the service began. Anne rose from her throne and prostrated herself before the altar. When she arose the archbishop anointed her head and heart. There was more triumphal song, and the archbishop next crowned the queen with the crown of St. Edward, placing the scepter in her right hand and the ivory rod in her left. A Te Deum was sung, and the light crown made just for Anne replaced the heavy St. Edward's crown.

The queen then descended to sit back in her chair. The mass was sung, and at the appropriate moment, she took communion. As the service finally came to its long close Anne made an offering at the shrine of St. Edward, and then withdrew to the side of the choir. The procession re-formed to return to Westminster Hall. Once again the trumpets sounded, and the playing of the recessional began. The king had had no part in his wife's coronation. But he had observed the entire ceremony from a screened gallery with the specially invited diplomats from the countries he wished to impress.

Elizabeth had been overwhelmed by the pageantry, as were the two children in her care. What a tale she would have to tell her family when she finally got back to Friarsgate. Now, as they exited the cathedral, Catherine Howard said, "Ohh, I should like to be a queen one day!"

"You haven't the pedigree for it," Hugh St. Clair pronounced, getting back at the girl for her earlier slight.

Now it was Catherine Howard who blushed.

"Hughie!" Elizabeth scolded her nephew. She put an arm about the girl. "Come along, and we shall see the queen. She will be resting until it is time for her banquet."

The banquet would also be a great staged and formal event. From his secret vantage place in St. Stephen's cloister, Henry Tudor and several foreign ambassadors watched the banquet even as they had the coronation itself. There would be three courses. The first, consisting of twenty-eight dishes, was brought in by the Knights of the Bath. They were preceded by the Duke of Suffolk and Lord William Howard on horseback, and the Earl of Sussex, who held the position of sewer. The dowager Countess of Oxford stood throughout the meal to the queen's right, and the Countess of Worcester was on her left holding the queen's napkin, wiping the monarch's lips with each bite she took. Beneath the table two gentlewomen sat at the queen's feet holding a gold vessel should Anne have the need to relieve herself at any time.

When the final course came to its end wafers and hippocras wine were served to all the guests. At last the queen stood up and walked to the middle of the hall, where she was given spices and comfits from the sewer. She drank a toast to the king from a gold cup offered her by the lord mayor. Then she presented the canopy beneath which she had walked to the barons of the Cinque Ports. This was done by tradition. At six o'clock that evening, the queen left Westminster Hall and returned to York Place. The short voyage upon the river did little to settle her belly, which was roiling with the rich foods she had been required to consume. She had eaten little, but she was still beginning to feel sick. Back in her royal apartments she vomited most of what she had eaten.

"Get me out of these garments!" she shouted at her tiring woman. "I must lie down. Where is Mistress Hay? I want her with me. Find her!"

A serving woman ran from the queen's bedchamber and, finding Elizabeth outside in the queen's waiting room, told her that the queen sought her company.

"Will you be all right, Mistress Howard? The dowager has made no provision to return you to her house, so you must remain here tonight. Nancy, my tiring woman, will look after you. Hugh, come with me, and bring your lute."

"Thank you, Mistress Hay. You have been very kind," little Catherine Howard said, and she curtseyed prettily.

Elizabeth gave her a kiss on the cheek, and hurried off to join the queen.

Anne was exhausted and impatient with her women, some of whom bore extremely grand pedigrees. But she was also excited and exhilarated by the day just past. She had, by becoming queen, become a fabulously rich woman and a great landowner. Her household was huge, and even the meanest place in the kitchens was eagerly sought. Some of those serving her had transferred their service to her from the households of other great nobles. She had six maids of honor under the care of Mrs. Marshall. A number of her female relations had sought places with her, and while many had not been supportive of her, Anne had accepted them into her household because many of their husbands were important to the king. The presence of the lady of Friarsgate was incomprehensible to them. She had no noble blood. She came from the north, and if rumor were to be believed her husband was a Scot. Why was she here?

The queen held out her two hands to Elizabeth, who took them and kissed them. "Was it not the grandest day?" Anne said. "Could you see any of it? I thought my little cousin a pretty creature. Did the old dowager take her home?"

"It was a wonderful day, your highness," Elizabeth agreed. "A yeoman, recognizing that I was from the north as he was, found us a place in a corner at the front. We stood on a bench and watched your procession and crowning. I shall have much to tell my husband and family when I return to Friarsgate. Lord Cambridge will be so envious, and that is not a state he suffers often, or well." She laughed. "Little Mistress Howard is with my Nancy. The dowager forgot her. I will arrange to send her home tomorrow, your highness."

The queen nodded, and then she sighed. "I wish you could stay with me forever, Elizabeth. I always feel calmer in your presence."

"You honor me so, and I do not deserve it," Elizabeth replied. "But I have a family, and estates that need my tending. I have promised to remain with you until the prince is born, but then, dear highness, you must let me go. I do not thrive in this great town of yours. I need to be on my own lands, to smell the fresh air of Friarsgate, to see the sky and hills surrounding me."

"Your gown is quite beautiful," the queen noted, ignoring Elizabeth's speech. "I am astounded that you can keep in style so well in your far clime."

"My uncle is a miracle, your highness. Though he is a country gentleman his garb is always the most fashionable. He says his people expect it of him," she finished with a chuckle. "And I believe he does not lie. His Otterly folk love him well."

"Your highness, you really should go to bed. You have a most busy day tomorrow," Lady Jane Rochford, jealous of the attention Elizabeth was receiving, said.

Anne's dark eyes narrowed. "Never presume to tell us what to do, Jane," the queen snapped at her sister-in-law. "You are here only because you are our brother's wife." Her gaze swept the other women. "You are all here because of your kinship to us, and you can all be replaced by other women more respectful and gracious. The lady of Friarsgate is here because we asked her to come. She is our true friend."

"I am sorry, your highness," Jane Rochford muttered, her cheeks red with the queen's rebuke. *The bitch! One day I will repay you for that*, she thought.

Elizabeth curtseyed deeply. "Will you permit me to withdraw to Bolton House for the night, your highness?" she asked the queen.

"You may go," Anne agreed, understanding that Elizabeth wished to defuse the situation Jane Rochford had created. Most of the women here with them would put her outburst down to nerves. She was pregnant. She had had several very long days. It would be forgotten in a day or two by most of them.

Elizabeth withdrew, leaving Hugh to console his mistress with his lute and sweet voice. She found Nancy with the little Howard girl. "Where is the old duchess's tiring woman? Take Mistress Howard to her, and meet me at the barge quay," she said before hurrying off again. She could scarcely wait to get out of the palace.

"Where are you hurrying to, Elizabeth Meredith?" she heard someone ask.

Turning, she came face-to-face with Flynn Stewart as she had in the gardens of Greenwich several days ago. "I am going to my barge," she said.

"Not remaining with the queen? You are quite the meat of the gossips these days, Elizabeth Meredith. None can understand the queen's reliance upon you," he told her.

"I am Elizabeth Hay, Master Stewart," she said quietly. "Friendship, I know, is a difficult concept for courtiers to comprehend. Believe me, I should as soon be home as here right now, but the queen commanded me to come. And why are you here? I would have thought you would be riding hard for Scotland to tell your king of this day's events."

"King James is more than well aware of this day's doings," Flynn Stewart said, matching his step to hers. "His half sister, Lady Margaret Douglas, is one of Queen Anne's ladies. You once called me Flynn. Where are you going?"

"To Bolton House. That weasel-faced Jane Rochford caused a scene over me in the queen's privy chamber. To ease the situation I asked to be excused. I do not know how George Boleyn can stand her. She is mean and sly."

"He can't stand her, but the marriage was arranged to the advantage of both families," Flynn explained. "You know how it is among the nobility."

"She will come to a bad end; I sense it," Elizabeth said. "God's blood! I want to go home. I hate it here!"

"Then why don't you go home?" he asked her. "The coronation is over."

"The queen begged me to remain until her child is born. I could not refuse her," Elizabeth told him. "Now there is a piece of prime gossip for your master, Flynn."

He laughed. "The queen is like all mares about to foal for the first time. She needs a steadying and gentle hand. None of those peahens around her can offer her that." He chuckled. "She needed her friend, a good country woman."

"Aye, worse luck," Elizabeth exclaimed dourly.

He laughed. "Cheer up, sweetheart," he told her. " 'Tis only a few more months until England's hope is born. Then you can flee north, and be home in time for the grouse. Ah, here we are. Which is your barge?"

"I have to wait for my tiring woman," Elizabeth said. "She was taking little Mistress Howard to the old duchess's servants. The great lady forgot to make arrangements to send the girl home. I was delegated to take her to see the queen crowned, but if I am not by the queen's side then I intend sleeping in my own bed tonight."

"A lonely bed." He leered at her.

Now it was Elizabeth who laughed. "Am I fair game then, Flynn Stewart, because I am no longer a virgin?" she teased him. "My husband is a jealous man, and he is every bit as big as the king. Even more so, if rumor is to be believed."

"You certainly know that I regretted letting you go," he said to her.

"Pah! Three years ago I should have believed such romantic twaddle, but I have since learned that you Scotsmen are passionately bound to your service first, and not to your women. I seduced my husband shortly after I returned to Friarsgate, and even that was not enough to keep him by my side. He had a duty first to his own sire," she said.

"You seduced the man?" His look was incredulous. "God's wounds, that it would have been me." But he was beginning to laugh as he spoke.

She grinned back at him. "I wanted him," she replied simply.

"Do you love him?" Flynn asked, suddenly serious.

"Aye, I do," Elizabeth admitted. "I was starting to love you, and you knew it, but you would not have been the right man for Friarsgate, Flynn. And to be the man for me, you had to be the man for Friarsgate."

He nodded, completely understanding her. "But we are friends, Elizabeth?"

"We are friends, Flynn Stewart," she told him. "And I still think your king should give you a nice rich wife to settle down with, but I think you are a happier man without a wife, eh? You enjoy the excitement of this court, and all its intrigues."

"I do," he admitted.

"Mistress, I found some of the dowager's servants, and left Mistress Howard with them," Nancy said, coming upon them.

"Then we are ready to escape to Bolton House," Elizabeth said, and Flynn helped both women down into the barge.

"I will see you again," he promised her.

"Aye, you will," Elizabeth agreed.

They reached Bolton House in good time, and Elizabeth found Philippa awake and waiting for her in the great hall. The sisters embraced, and Elizabeth kicked off her shoes, loosened her laces, and sat down before the fire.

"How is Hugh doing?" Philippa asked her sister.

"The queen adores him. Why wouldn't she, with that angelic face of his, and his sweet voice? She loves having him by her, and is very kind to him."

"Then perhaps it will be all right," Philippa said.

"She didn't know who he was, sister. When I brought him to her, she said that she had stolen him from the king for his pretty face, and did not even know his name. She was surprised when I told her," Elizabeth explained. "Hugh has great charm, and has won her over. Anne is not a woman to be fooled. Your son is very lucky."

"Crispin wants to leave tomorrow," Philippa said. "He is not one for the court these days, and neither am I, to my surprise."

"I will be fine," Elizabeth replied. "The progress is not to be a great or lengthy one this summer, given the queen's condition. The child is due in September. I will go home immediately after he is born." She arose. "I am exhausted. I slept in a chair by the queen's bed last night. And then today I was given charge over the queen's younger cousin, Catherine Howard."

"There will be jousting and dancing for the rest of the week," Philippa noted. "You are likely to be kept busy, I fear."

Elizabeth yawned. "I know. God's blood, how I long for Friarsgate, and my country ways."

"And your husband," Philippa said mischievously.

Elizabeth grinned. "Aye, I long for Baen too. It is time that young Tom had a brother or a sister." She yawned again, and stood up. "Good night, Philippa. Do not go without seeing me first, please." She kissed her sibling and went to her own bedchamber.

The Earl and Countess of Witton departed early the next morning. Elizabeth watched them go, wishing desperately that she were with them. The whole long summer stretched ahead. A summer she would not be at Friarsgate. A summer away from Baen and young Tom. Sitting down on the edge of her bed, she wept. She wanted to go home, not to the joust to be held this afternoon in the queen's honor, or to the banquets and masques that would follow. She was not a part of any of it. She was not a great lady. She was plain Elizabeth Hay, the lady of Friarsgate. She didn't belong here at court.

And when she had finished feeling sorry for herself, Elizabeth called to Nancy, and they prepared to join the queen once again.

The summer months passed. Many in the court had gone home to attend to their own estates. At first the queen accompanied her husband on the annual progress, but they did not travel far from London, only briefly to Essex and Surrey. Mostly they remained at Greenwich, the king going off with his closest friends to hunt a few days at a time.

It was customary that a queen take to her apartments a month before the birth of a child, to be served only by women. Anne had chosen to have her child at Greenwich, and it was a great relief to Elizabeth when they finally settled into that lovely palace on the river.

The queen's apartments had been completely redone in their absence. Now everything was prepared in accordance with the rules for royal childbirth that had been set down by King Henry's grandmother,

Margaret Beaufort, in the last reign. The walls and windows of the queen's rooms but for one window would be covered with rich tapestries. Only women would be allowed into the royal apartments. And Anne would be forced to remain quiet in the darkened chambers as she awaited the momentous occasion of her child's birth. She kept Elizabeth by her side most days and nights, along with young Hugh St. Clair, who had become her favorite page. He had also become a favorite with the other ladies as well, who enjoyed his sweet voice, and his pretty face and manners.

Elizabeth slipped through the woods to Bolton Greenwich as often as she could. Returning one day, she found Anne in a towering rage, and none could calm her. Of course, they were all terrified that the queen's outburst would cause her to miscarry. "What has happened?" Elizabeth asked Lady Margaret Douglas, the king's niece.

"Someone has told her that the king is dallying with a lady of the court. That his hunting trips are but ruses to be with his lady love," Lady Margaret whispered. "You know how jealous of him she can be."

"God's wounds!" Elizabeth swore. "Who told her that?" She had heard the rumor herself, but had paid it little heed. Many husbands denied their wives' company were known to find amusement elsewhere. But the king was being discreet, for if he was indeed dallying with another, no one knew who she was, or had even seen anything untoward.

"We do not know," came the reply.

"Well, it has to be one of the women here," Elizabeth said, looking around. Her gaze lit on Jane Seymour, who sat placidly through the queen's tantrum, sewing. She had no reason to dislike Mistress Seymour, but she did. There was something sly about her, Elizabeth thought. "I had best go to her," she told Lady Margaret.

"Oh, would you?" Lady Margaret sounded relieved. "She does love you, and she listens when you advise her, Mistress Hay."

Elizabeth hurried into the queen's privy chamber. Anne was sobbing violently, and her hair was loose and disarrayed. There were several pieces of broken crockery upon the floor. "You are upsetting yourself needlessly, your highness," she began, and she waved the others in the chamber out with an imperious hand.

"Do you know what he said to me?" Anne sobbed. "They sent for him, you know. I told him what I knew. I told him I would not countenance his fucking another woman, and especially now, when the child is so near to being born. He did not beg my pardon, or even console me. He said in that commanding voice of his, 'You must shut your eyes, madame, and endure, as your betters before you have endured. You must surely know that having raised you to such utopian heights I can as easily lower you back to the depths.' Oh, Elizabeth, he does not love me anymore!" And the queen sobbed harder.

The lady of Friarsgate put comforting arms about the queen. "He was angry at being found out, Anne. All summer long he has kept anything he considered distressful to you from you. Some of it quite silly, I might add. Of course he loves you. Now cease your greeting, and think of the child you are carrying."

"Ohh, Elizabeth," the queen cried, "you must never leave me!"

And Elizabeth Hay felt a chill race down her spine. Never leave? God forbid! She would go as soon as the child was safely delivered and in its mother's arms. She already had Nancy packing for their journey, and had sent for a contingent of her own Friarsgate men, too afraid to ask for a royal escort lest she be denied. She was going home! She needed to be on her lands again. She needed her husband and son.

On Sunday, the seventh day of September, Anne went into labor in the great bed of state that had been prepared for the birth. Around her, the midwives and the physicians conferred, while by her side Elizabeth Hay sat holding the queen's hand. As her labor grew in intensity Anne squeezed the hand in hers over and over again until Elizabeth thought it would never be of use to her again. The cries of the woman in labor reached the courtiers awaiting word of the birth in the queen's reception room. Among them a seventeen-year-old Mary Tudor waited to be displaced by a brother. Perhaps then they would let her see her mother. Perhaps then they would finally let her marry her cousin Phillip, as her mother wanted her to do. Phillip was very dashing.

And then between three and four o'clock that early September afternoon the wail of an infant was heard. It was a strong cry, and those in the waiting room began to smile. Perhaps it had all been worth it, after all. The child, a Virgo, would be a great king. They showed the queen her infant, and Anne began to weep. Only those standing closest to her heard her soft words. "I am ruined!"

"Nay!" Elizabeth bent to whisper to the exhausted woman. "She is a strong babe, and but the first of many that you will bear the king."

Outside, it was announced that the queen had been delivered of a fair maid, a princess she had declared would be called Elizabeth, after the king's late mother. The king came, and went in to his wife. The child was healthy, he declared jovially, and the prettiest he had ever seen, with her halo of red-gold hair so like his. There would be others, he said, but everyone knew he was disappointed. Anne Boleyn's star was fading fast, and the king's eyes were already lighting with pleasure upon one of her ladies-in-waiting: the meek and mild Mistress Jane Seymour.

"We will call the babe Mary," he told his wife.

"Nay, you have a daughter Mary," Anne said with a show of her old spirit. "I have called her Elizabeth after your sainted mother, may God assoil her good soul. You will name the lads, my dear lord, but I will name the girls."

The king chuckled, eased from his bad mood briefly. Then he nodded. "Agreed," he said. "You always did know how to bargain, Annie." Then he left her.

Elizabeth came back in to be with her friend. Anne was paler than she usually was, and there were dark circles beneath her eyes, which now had a haunted look in them. "He spoke kindly to you," Elizabeth comforted the queen as those around her prepared her for sleep.

"I have disappointed him. I said my daughter was named after his mother, but she is named after you too. May she be as strong a woman as you, Bess," Anne said.

Three days after her birth the princess to be called Elizabeth was baptized by Archbishop Cranmer, immersed in the silver font kept for royal babies. She then went off to her own royal household while her mother lay in state receiving the mighty. But it all rang hollow. Everyone knew the king was unhappy, no matter his fine words. And Anne was condemned to remain forty more days in her confinement until the ceremony of her churching took place.

And then one morning in early October, as the king came from his chapel, a man with a wealth of black hair, as tall as if not taller than Henry Tudor, came down the corridor of the palace dragging two yeoman of the guard, one clinging to each of his arms. The king and his companions were both astounded and surprised. Reaching Henry Tudor, the great man shook the guardsmen off and bowed politely to the monarch.

His gray eyes engaged the king's blue ones. His garments were soiled, but of decent quality. There was a length of red-black-and-yellow plaid over one of his shoulders. He was unarmed but for a dirk at his side. "Your majesty," he said in a deep voice that hinted of the north. "I have come, with your permission, to fetch my wife home."

"Your wife?" The king was truly puzzled.

"Elizabeth Hay, the lady of Friarsgate, your majesty," the man said. "She came in the spring at the queen's command. Now I would like her to go home at your command."

Henry Tudor began to chuckle, and the chuckle grew into a great shout of laughter. The men around him looked nervously at one another. Should they laugh too? Discretion prevailed, and they remained silent. The king's amusement eased, and, nodding, he said, "Aye, Scotsman, it is time you got your wife back, and if she is anything like her mother, which I believe she is, she longs for her beloved Friarsgate." He turned to look at the men accompanying him, and, finding who he sought, he waved him forward. "I will send for your wife to come to you in my gardens. She has our permission to go home. In the meantime I give you a fellow Scot to keep you company." Then, with another deep chuckle, Henry Tudor moved past Baen Hay, the MacColl, and on down the corridor.

The two men eyed each other, and then the king's man held out his hand. "I am Flynn Stewart," he said.

"Baen Hay, known as the MacColl," was the response. "You must be the other Scot she kissed when she was here last."

Flynn Stewart was unable to repress the grin that sprang to his lips. "A gentleman does not kiss and tell, sir," he said as they walked down the corridor and out into the gardens by the river. She had not been lying: Her husband was a big man.

Baen chuckled. "Do you think she has enjoyed her time here?" he asked.

"She came for the queen, but I know she longs to go home. The queen feels she needs Elizabeth's friendship, but she does not consider her friend's husband or child or responsibilities, her own needs overshadowing all."

"They say she is a witch," Baen said.

"They are wrong," Flynn countered. "She's just an ambitious woman who has now played her trump card, and probably lost. I doubt Elizabeth could have gotten away from her but that you came to fetch her. It is better she not be caught in what will follow, Baen Hay. Her heart is too good."

"Aye," Baen agreed, "it is."

"Baen!" Elizabeth was flying across the lawns, holding her skirts up so that she would not trip. She flung herself into his open arms. "Oh, Baen!" And, taking his head between her two hands, she kissed him hungrily.

"I will bid you both farewell and a safe journey then," Flynn Stewart said. She loved him. Oh, yes, she loved him very much, and for a brief moment he was envious.

Elizabeth turned in her husband's arms. She smiled sweetly at Flynn. "Thank you," she said softly, and then together with her husband, the lady of Friarsgate walked across the green lawns of Greenwich towards her uncle's house. She did not look back, and so she did not see the woman standing alone in an upper window. She did not hear the familiar voice whisper a farewell. She did not see the single tear slip down the queen's face. She was going home with her husband, and for the first time in months Elizabeth felt lighthearted. The day was bright with an October sun. Baen was by her side. And she was going home to Friarsgate!

# Epilogue

---

## June 1536

lynn Stewart was riding for the border separating Scotland and England. He had taken a route far out of his way, but before he saw his brother, the king, he meant to stop at Friarsgate first. He owed that to Elizabeth. Looking about him as he rode, he admired the beauty of the region, now understanding Elizabeth's passion to live here, and not at court. It had been almost three years since he had watched as Elizabeth and her husband walked away from Greenwich. He wondered if she had changed, but thought not. And then he topped a rise in the narrow road, and there before him lay Friarsgate. Its fields were filled with growing grain, and its green hillsides dotted with white sheep. He halted for a brief moment, taking it all in. Could he have been happy here? Perhaps, but he could have never denied his loyalty to his brother, King James V.

Urging his horse forward, he rode down the hill along the road that passed through those beautiful fields and a small cluster of cottages. Reaching the manor house, he pulled the beast to a halt and dismounted as a stable lad ran to take his animal. Stepping up to the door, he knocked loudly upon it, and when a servant opened the door, Flynn Stewart said, "I need to speak with your mistress."

"This way, sir," Albert said, leading him to the great hall. "Mistress, a gentleman asking for you," the hall steward said.

Elizabeth looked up. Then she stood, holding out her hands. "Flynn!" Her eyes were bright with their welcome. "What brings you to Friarsgate? I hope the queen has not sent you to bring me back to court again, for I shall not come. My responsibilities have increased greatly since my return." She smiled at him as Albert brought a goblet of wine for her guest.

He took the goblet, gulping half of it down. He had not realized he was so thirsty. "I am on my way to Edinburgh," he told her. "I thought I should stop and see how you and Friarsgate are doing," he told her.

"Edinburgh is farther north, and just above the other side of England," Elizabeth said, an amused look upon her face. "You obviously have little sense of direction, Flynn." And she chuckled.

"Then I shall admit to being curious as to this Friarsgate of yours, and thought to see it. I have important news for James, and I am finally to be relieved of my duties. My brother tells me he has a rich wife for me. I am at last following your advice, Elizabeth."

"Baen should be in from the fields soon," she told him. "It is almost time for the haying to begin. Young Thomas is with him. And we have two other children: Edmund, who was, coincidentally, born nine months after Baen and I came home. And our daughter, Anne, born the fifth day of December last year. When I saw our daughter's black hair I knew I had to name her after the queen." And Elizabeth laughed. "How is she? We get little news here in our remote northern lands."

Baen Hay came into the hall and, seeing Flynn Stewart, held out his hand in a gesture of friendship. A little boy, tall, but quite young, walked with him. The child ran to Elizabeth and hugged her. "Welcome to Friarsgate," Baen greeted their visitor. He kissed his wife upon her lips, and then, his arm about her, turned back to face Flynn Stewart. "What brings you here, sir?"

"I have told him that if the queen wants me back I cannot go," Elizabeth teased her handsome husband.

Baen laughed. "Nay, sweetheart, I'll not let you go again." He looked to Flynn. "Will you stay the night, Flynn Stewart?"

"Aye, and I thank you for the shelter," Flynn replied.

"And you will tell us the news of court over dinner?" Elizabeth said.

"I will," Flynn answered her with a heavy heart. How was he to tell her the terrible news that he carried? How much did she know of what had happened in those many months since she had last been with the court? Did her sister, a countess, he recalled, write to her?

They chatted idly as the meal was served. It was a plain country meal such as he remembered from his own childhood. There was broiled trout, a potage of vegetables, venison, a roast capon, bread, butter, and cheese. The food was fresh and well cooked. Flynn watched in amusement as Elizabeth's two sons helped themselves to cherries from a bowl on the high board, and then vied with each other to see how far they could spit the pits. He had been shown the infant Anne Hay with her black curls, who so resembled her father, and was already showing her mother's lively personality.

Now the children were all sent off to bed. He sat with Elizabeth and Baen outdoors on the early summer's night. He could delay no longer. "Does your sister, the countess, write to you often?" he asked Elizabeth casually. "I should dislike repeating that which you already know."

"Nay," Elizabeth said. "Philippa goes little to court now. She is almost as much a country wife as I am. I did receive a letter from her just before Anne was born. She and Crispin had joined the king and queen on progress into Wales last summer. She wanted to visit the place where our father was born. She said it was beautiful, but not as beautiful as Friarsgate, and bleak. And our cousins there more backward than she would have expected. And her best friend resides in Wales. She said little about anything else."

"Then I shall tell you all I know," Flynn Stewart said. "Things went from bad to worse after you departed court. The women surrounding the queen were harpies. Her mother, her sister, Jane Rochford, Mary Howard, who was married to Fitzroy, the king's son, among others. None loved her, but for one: Margaret Lee. After you left she was most sympathetic of the queen's loneliness, and they became friends."

"Oh, I am glad!" Elizabeth said. "I thought of her highness so often, but I had to come home. Say on, Flynn."

"Margaret Lee was her only comfort. The king's passion for Queen Anne had waned and burned out," he said. "They quarreled bitterly, and often publicly. The king was openly courting other women—the queen's cousin Margaret Shelton, among others. The more he dallied with others, the more shrewish the queen became."

"She was afraid," Elizabeth said wisely. "Poor Anne. She was always afraid."

"Aye," Flynn agreed. "There were two confinements the year after you left, but neither came to fruition. Then the king's proposed alliances first with France, and then with Emperor Charles, began to unravel. The pope had excommunicated him for refusing to take the princess of Aragon back and restore the lady Mary. Last summer the king was despondent that all he had so long labored for was lost. The queen's star glowed briefly once more, and they went on progress together. To all who saw them they seemed happy again but for the presence of Mistress Seymour. In late autumn it was announced that the queen was once again with child. The bairn would be born in July.

"Then the princess of Aragon died on the day after Twelfth Night. The king refused to wear mourning, and threatened any who did. Instead he gave banquets and held tournaments in celebration. In late January he was unhorsed for the first time in anyone's memory."

"He is too old to play at such games any longer," Elizabeth said.

Baen nodded in agreement.

"How badly was he injured?" she wanted to know.

"It wasn't the fall that did the injury; it was his horse falling on him," Flynn explained.

"God's wounds!" Baen exclaimed. "He was not killed?"

"Nay, but he lay unconscious for two hours, and that wicked busybody Norfolk went running to the queen to say the king was probably dead," Flynn Stewart replied.

"She lost the child," Elizabeth said fatalistically.

"Aye, and that was the beginning of her end," the Scotsman said. "After that the king visited her no more. He openly courted Mistress Seymour before all. The queen was sorrowing for her child—a son, by the way—and deserted by all but a few. The court rushed to align itself with what was to be the new regime, while the king looked for a way to divest himself of the queen, and not look the worse for doing it."

Elizabeth shook her head. "I am astounded the king would bother with Jane Seymour. Her chin recedes. Indeed, she has a double chin. She is past thirty, and her youth has long flown by. Her hair is the color of dung, and not beautiful at all. And that little prim mouth."

"She is meek and obedient," Flynn said. "She never raises her voice. She has allied herself with the lady Mary."

"She is sly and guileful," Elizabeth said bluntly.

"Aye," he agreed. "But allow me to continue my tale. Mistress Seymour, like the queen, held herself off from the king while at the same time encouraging him. He gave her many gifts, but 'tis said when he presented her with a bag of gold coins at Easter she refused, telling him that sort of gift was for another time. The king considered ways to rid himself of the queen, and he enlisted Master Cromwell in his endeavor."

Elizabeth shuddered. "The man has evil eyes," she said.

"Master Cromwell gathered an alliance together of the Seymours, those unhappy in Anne's service, her cousin Nicholas Carew, and the lady Mary's supporters. Suddenly the queen was being denounced publicly for immoral behavior. Two senior gentlemen of her privy chamber, Henry Norris and William Brereton, were arrested and brought to the Tower, along with Francis Weston, Lord Rochford, and a young musician in her household, one Mark Smeaton."

"But Norris and Weston have long been with the Tudor household. Henry Norris is hardly of an age to dally, and far too much of a gentleman to do so," Elizabeth declared.

"And he denied any misbehavior, but he was tried with Weston, Brereton, and the musician. If the queen were one for dallying—and none believed it of her, though they would say nothing aloud— Smeaton would have been the most likely candidate for her bed. He is young and beautiful. They tortured him dreadfully, and he told them what they wanted to hear: that he had committed adultery with the queen. But all know it to be a lie. Lord Rochford was tried separately for incest with her. All were condemned."

"Dear God!" Elizabeth's eyes were wide with her shock. "The queen?"

"Arrested May second and taken to the Tower. She was tried on the fifteenth of the month and found guilty of infidelity and adultery. She was also charged with having plotted the king's death by means of witchcraft, sabotage of the succession, of committing sins too vile to enumerate, of bringing dishonor on her husband, the king, and her daughter, the lady Elizabeth, not to mention the realm itself."

"The lady Elizabeth? Not the princess Elizabeth?" Baen asked. He was both fascinated and horrified by the tale Flynn Stewart was telling. He sensed there was no happy ending to it, and his wife was going to be devastated. Reaching out, he took her hand in his.

"Nay, the lady Elizabeth," Flynn continued. "A new Parliament was called to legislate changing the succession. Old Crum found corrupt witnesses only too willing to testify lies and supply false evidence against the queen that would support their charges. She was condemned, of course, and sentenced to die by burning or beheading, to be decided by the king."

Elizabeth cried out as if in pain. "Dear God, could he not simply let the church dissolve his marriage, and let her go into exile in France? Why was it necessary to condemn her to death?" She was beginning to weep. Baen's arm went about her.

Flynn Stewart looked to Baen. The look asked if he should continue on with his terrible story. Baen nodded silently, and the Scotsman spoke again. "When Lord Rochford was tried separately, it is said his own wife testified he had told her that his sister laughed, saying that the king had bouts of impotence. She also hinted that her husband and the queen had been incestuous with each other."

"Never!" Elizabeth burst out. "Anne loved the king, and was loyal to him."

"On May seventeenth the five men were beheaded on Tower Green. Smeaton and Brereton were quartered afterwards. The queen was forced to observe. On the day she had been condemned, Archbishop Cranmer had pronounced the king and queen's marriage invalid based on consanguinity because of his relationship with her sister. And the queen's daughter was therefore declared illegitimate."

"Would that Cranmer had been so scrupulous before he crowned Anne England's queen," Elizabeth said bitterly. "How will he, I wonder, answer to God for his part in this terrible travesty?" Her gaze engaged Flynn's. "She dead, isn't she?"

He nodded.

"Tell me!"

"When she was placed in the Tower they gave her four attendants, none friendly to her. Margaret Lee was allowed to lodge there, but forbidden from seeing the queen. I believe that the constable of the Tower, William Kingston, did let the queen and her friend have brief moments together. They say the queen was half-mad at this point. Sometimes she made great sense, and other times she babbled. It was her fear, of course. She feared for her child, and made an apology to the lady Mary for any unhappiness she had caused her. She begged that the lady Mary watch over the lady Elizabeth. She made a final confession and took communion, declaring she was innocent of all charges. Even the priest attending her declared privately that the queen was an innocent woman.

"On the morning of the nineteenth day of May, she dressed herself in a beautiful gray brocade gown and pinned her hair beneath a black velvet cap trimmed with pearls. Sir William escorted her to the scaffold, where she removed her cap and then mounted the block. The courtyard was filled with spectators. They poured out of the court and down the hill and surrounded the White Tower. No foreigners were allowed, at the king's command. The day was sunny and bright. The king would not allow her to be burned, and brought a swordsman from Calais for the execution. Kingston allowed Margaret Lee to be one of the four women escorting her. The queen gave her her book of devotions. They say she spoke bravely at the end. I was not there, for no foreigners were permitted. My account was given to me by one of Cromwell's secretaries, who accompanied his master to the execution. Norfolk was there also."

"Aye, he would have been, wretched man!" Elizabeth said angrily. She could not cry now. She would cry later, when she was alone.

"The king married Jane Seymour almost immediately afterwards," Flynn told them. "So now it is Queen Jane."

"Was she at least buried with some honor?" Elizabeth wanted to know.

"Not really. No coffin had been prepared. Her women took her head and wrapped it in a cloth. It was placed with her body in an old arrow box that was found. She is interred in the Church of St. Peter ad Vincula in the tower. Elizabeth, I am so sorry to have been the bearer of such awful tidings, but I knew you would want to know. Not from wicked gossip, but the truth."

Elizabeth stood up and looked at him. "Thank you," she said quietly, and then she left the hall. But still the tears would not come.

Anne Boleyn, that ambitious and frightened young woman, was dead. Anne, her friend. Her heart felt like a stone in her chest. She would never go south of Carlisle again.

The following morning she bade Flynn Stewart farewell, and wished him good fortune in his marriage. Then she sent a messenger to Otterly begging her uncle to come at once.

Thomas Bolton did not dally. There had been rumors, of course, just reaching the remote manors of the north. Elizabeth's message had mentioned a visitor from court. He and Will cantered across the hills to Friarsgate to learn what had transpired. When his niece had concluded her tale, Lord Cambridge shook his head wearily. "I have grown too old," he said, "to comprehend the ways of the mighty. God rest Queen Anne, dear girl. As your Scots friend has said, many believed her innocent, and I do too. The king's behavior was vengeful and cruel, but then the best influence upon Henry Tudor was the princess of Aragon. Have you cried yet? You must weep your heart out, my angel, or you will get sick, I fear."

"I cannot cry, Uncle. I am yet numb," Elizabeth told him.

Lord Cambridge lingered at Friarsgate for several days, and on the morning he was to return to Otterly a messenger arrived from the Countess of Witton with a letter for Elizabeth. Opening it, she read it, and suddenly Elizabeth began to weep. She shook with the great tearing sobs that came forth from her heart and soul. Astounded, Baen, Lord Cambridge, and Will could but wait until she had ceased her sorrow.

Finally Thomas Bolton ventured, "Dearest girl, what has your sister written that had sent you into such great grief?"

Elizabeth looked up from the parchment and said, "She left Hughie her lute, Uncle."

And Lord Cambridge nodded. "Let none speak evil of this unfortunate queen to any in this family," he said quietly. "For all the ill spoken of her, she was a good woman." He enfolded Elizabeth within his embrace. "Now, dear girl, you have wept for your friend, and must move on again with your life. Let me see you smile, my darling Elizabeth. It is what she would want. Anne Boleyn never lived her life in halfhearted fashion. She lived it with gusto, with style, with elegance, and you must follow her example. Well, perhaps not entirely, dear girl." And he kissed her on the forehead.

Elizabeth began to laugh as suddenly as she had wept. "Oh, Uncle," she said. "There is no one in the world who can put life in perspective quite as well as you can. Do not ever change." And she kissed him back on his ruddy cheek.

"Dear girl, at my age change becomes quite difficult, but one should always be ready to change. It is what makes life worth living. I never look behind me, Elizabeth, because I always want to know what is around the next corner. Of course, I have gotten into some difficulties over that trait of mine in years past, have I not, dear Will?"

"Indeed, my lord, you have," William Smythe agreed dryly, but he was grinning as he said it.

"Well, my angel," Thomas Bolton said, "it is time for us to begin that tedious journey back to Otterly. I shall come again, for, despite my horror of rustic living, I do absolutely adore Friarsgate. For some reason I always have." He kissed her once again. "Good-bye, good-bye, my darling girl. Keep well, and keep that Scotsman of yours happy, but I can see how he adores you totally, delicious fellow that he is."

Elizabeth and Baen moved outside to see Lord Cambridge and his Will off. They stood watching as the two men trotted off down the road on their comfortable matching bay geldings.

"He's right, you know," Baen said quietly. "We must move forward with our life. You were never comfortable with the court, Elizabeth."

"Nay, I wasn't," she agreed. Then she said, "It's almost Midsummer, husband. Do you remember that first Midsummer we spent together?"

"Aye," he said slowly, "I do. Do you wish to revisit that summer, Bessie?" he asked her, a slow smile creasing his face.

"Nay, I wish to move forward and make new Midsummer memories, Baen MacColl." And, picking up her blue skirts, Elizabeth began to run towards the lake meadow, stopping but briefly to turn and shout at the man following after her, "And do not call me Bessie!"

# About the Author

Bertrice Small is a *New York Times* bestselling author and the recipient of numerous writing awards. In keeping with her profession, she lives in the oldest English-speaking town in the state of New York, founded in 1640, and works in a light-filled studio surrounded by the paintings of her favorite cover artist, Elaine Duillo. Because she believes in happy endings, Bertrice Small has been married to the same man, her hero, George, for forty-two years. They have a son, a daughter-in-law, and three adorable grandchildren. Longtime readers will be happy to know that Nicki the Cockatiel flourishes along with his fellow housemates, Pookie, the long-haired greige and white feline, Honeybun, the petite orange lady cat with the cream-colored paws, and Finnegan, the naughty black kitty.